Cipher Number 7

By Lars Handstein

This is a work of fiction. Names, characters, places, and incidents either are the product of the author's imagination or are used fictitiously, and any resemblance to actual persons, living or dead, businesses, companies, events, or locales is entirely coincidental.

ISBN: 9781717917140

With love to my parents
Cheryl and Arne

1

Schumann said music allows us to communicate with the afterlife. Ivan Stavros didn't believe in an afterlife, but on this day, from the third floor balcony of a rented beach house, watching a man and a boy just at the water's edge through a tactical spotting scope, he hoped there might be.

"Evening, James," Ivan said, not that anyone could hear, least of all James and his child, off in the distance. "This isn't my call. I'm just a tool. Try not to think about it."

James would never understand even if he could hear Ivan. Perhaps Schumann was right. Otherwise death was too abstract and too tragic. Self-awareness made the prospect of eventual oblivion feel fatalistic. Losing sentience at the moment of death struck Ivan as nihilistically flawed, even if consciousness—human consciousness—earned too small a footprint in the universe to matter. James would call it his soul, taking the family to services at the United Methodist Church each Sunday.

"Tell your boy you love him, James. You carry that forever, whatever forever means."

Ivan poured dark wine into a highball glass, the only adequate vessel he could find in the cupboards. A little spilled on the railing and he wiped it with the cuff of his flannel shirt. The glass's heft felt good in his hand, a sense of the gravity of things. A shame it did nothing for the taste. Ivan stared into the shallow murk as if the offensive part might be distinguishably visible.

The boy scattered seagulls, their distant cries inaudible from where Ivan watched. James lured the birds with bits torn from a blueberry bagel and they swooped in circles, ever vigilant of the terror in mottled fleece pullover, outstretched arms grasping for tailfeathers. The boy left footprints in the damp sand, waves reaching in to wash them away.

Ivan remembered an analogy drawn by one of the Greek poets his father so loved, of the fuse lit at birth that advances toward a certain end. We never see the bang. Made the concept of soul sound promising, but Ivan was reluctant to go that far. Conscience would have to do, music its conduit. Yet something comprising even a teaspoon's worth of emotional sacrifice was more valuable than all the blood and muck and awkward bits left behind.

If Ivan had to punch that ticket, destination unknown, the transition deserved dignity. Not this chemical contrivance. Someone owed two coins to the ferryman, and Ivan felt they were unjustly being exacted from his fee.

The brooding weather over Puget Sound agreed, filling the intermission between existences like a Haydn overture.

No, not Haydn. Ivan emptied the glass. Not even Shumann. Something deferential, solemn.

James's expression, sitting in the sand with arms around his knees, was warm, charmed, even proud if forced to acknowledge it. James married an assistant curator for the Seattle Art Museum, himself an investment analyst for a venture capital group with offices on Union Avenue. Bank records confirmed the obvious, he was wealthy. James would have to be to live in West Seattle, a stones throw from Alki Beach where his child's fanciful pursuit now played out against unhumored birds.

Ivan's client, Hizer Pharmaceuticals, was also wealthy. Several months had passed since he'd met with their nameless emissary, but Ivan's ability to recall that tedious conversation became an occupational curse.

***

"We need someone discreet, Mr. Stavros."

Ivan nodded. "Discretion comes at a cost," he said, still not convinced his question had been adequately answered: Why me? Ivan's coarse beard did little to mask the skepticism marked by the angle of his jaw.

"Your impeccable silence is also valuable to us."

"Sure."

"It's just a glitch."

Ivan decided that might be a good name for the man, who was perhaps a decade older than Ivan. Glitch, mid-fifties corporate sycophant lighting a cigarette in a Bolivian café, where *No Fumar Por Favor* signs would be blasphemy. In Ivan's mind, the larger company's mistakes became embodied in their agent's entire constitution, a suspicious discomfort mated to inhospitable twitchiness that drove the cartilage of the man's larynx up and down violently. Ash tumbled, Glitch flicking the filtered end like spanking an insubordinate child, his frustration awkwardly absent from the dialogue.

"It's a degenerative disease. It'll start making an appearance in six to eight years. Destroys tissues at the cellular level."

"You act like they already have it."

"They do, all seven. It's in their DNA."

"So fix it."

Glitch's eyes snapped up, pupils unnaturally narrow in such a dark booth. Ivan thought of a faltering engine, wiring harness suddenly ripped out, or a record needle dragged through scratches in the man's basic functions. He possessed latent brutality, kept in check by verbal scorn that drew both Ivan's sympathy and disgust.

"Do you think we just issue recalls? Broken seatbelt tensioner?"

"It doesn't work like that?"

"No. It doesn't."

* * *

Mom brought the boy to school each morning and James picked him up in a sporty German car. Ivan approved. Family ate out over three times a week, usually in one of Alki's restaurants, but work obligations for both parents often muddled routines.

This week a special exhibit, a controversial Spanish painter who'd incited a few conservative protesters, kept the wife working late. Hard to tell what wound people up. Not much difference between Anne Geddes and Richard Avedon, in Ivan's opinion. And yet no one protested Anne.

Just James and his boy tonight, pizza by the slice and Italian sodas drunk through tall straws. An hour later came the only reliable routine, sunset near the water when weather was nice.

Tchaikovsky's requiem reached a foreboding theme just as cumulonimbus dark bulges unfurled from the south, potentially putting the whole plan in jeopardy.

"I haven't done anything yet," Ivan said, staring up at the sky. He could feel its criticism and he probably deserved it. "Go away."

He drank another glass of wine and scowled.

Tchaikovsky believed without music, more reasons would exist to go mad. Ivan rather thought there was more madness in the world than could ever be healed by music, and surely Tchaikovsky's miserable life was evidence of this.

Focus.

Kid was in the first grade. He could read at a third grade level but still liked stories read to him at bedtime. He loved dinosaurs, especially big ones, carnivorous and with a penchant for seagulls, no doubt. At school he drew dinosaurs with ambitious rows of teeth to the extinction of all green markers, brought them home to scatter over the floors, an exhibition that drew entirely different protesters.

Good kid.

James spent last Saturday getting hands dirty weeding between beds of pansies and columbine along the front walk. The boy classified weeds differently, which didn't include all the strewn dandelions dad uprooted, and he collected them in a purple cup. Throughout the week James seemed happy, whistled a tune Ivan recognized, drove a little faster, kissed a curator deeply bent over in his arms. Why not? This was a good week for him. James closed financing for a major project, something to do with what company records called *Low-Earth orbit solar infusers.*

The whole thing was a shame. Ivan really liked the man. James wore denim to the office because he believed it made him appear younger and risqué. He wasn't perfect. Medical records revealed a mild peanut allergy and a poor sperm count. He nursed unnecessary guilt about an affair for which she'd long since forgiven him, went through more energy drinks than were good for his heart, habitually lost on Emerald Downs bets, and collected too many speeding tickets. Ivan couldn't blame him with a car like that, kid cheering him on from the carseat. Boys love fast cars. James was a good father and he didn't deserve this.

Just so Hizer Pharmaceuticals could avoid some litigation?

Watching them didn't mean understanding or empathizing. The difference between amateur and professional was not one of skill but motivation. Amateurs act for the love of something, while professionals are paid.

Ivan was the latter, but he didn't feel like it.

Not today.

* * *

"You realize you're actually saving them," Glitch said.

He passed the tablet across, allowing Ivan to key through target profiles, noting they were all the same age, the narrow window of Hizer Pharmaceutical's involvement years ago.

"Why did you wait so long?"

"We just found the glitch."

"Glitch?"

"It's complicated."

Ivan smiled and shook his head, irritated by the things large corporations deemed complicated, which didn't include killing people.

He took the contract and Glitch drew from a breast pocket an envelope and slid it across the varnished surface in a motion so cliché Ivan felt a simultaneous surge of novelty and shame picking it up. The only thing worse would have been to find it stuffed with Bolivian bank notes.

Instead he found a row of tiny blue capsules, each smaller than a grain of rice, suspended in a hydrogen cell-powered thermal cooler to keep them frozen.

"It's just a precaution. They're stable at room temperature, even at temporary frictional velocity. They won't dissolve until body heat—"

"I know how they work." Ivan pocketed the unit and left the envelope on the table where it would irritate Glitch, the fraud of his efforts to be inconspicuous. "Do you want confirmation?"

Glitch shrugged. "My people would like a photo."

"Because you don't trust me or you don't trust these?"

Again Glitch sidestepped his question. "If you don't use all twenty, we want them back." Only when he drew on the cigarette did the skin of his neck lay still. Otherwise it looked like a rodent scurrying beneath a rug. "You might have to wait a while. It's not some simple toxin."

"How much is a while?"

"Five minutes?"

"Why do you sound like you don't know?"

"We haven't tested it on humans."

Ivan stared at him, brittle tolerance dwindling over a protracted minute, then said, "Do I look like an FDA approval board? If you want them dead, my .338 Lapua Magnum can do it in four minutes and fifty-nine seconds less time. From a mile away."

Glitch scoffed. "Oh, rich. That sounds inconspicuous."

"Dead's dead." Ivan raised a glass and drank to his own pithiness. "There's nothing inconspicuous about death. I prefer a clean kill. Spam guns piss me off, too many variables."

"Listen, Stavros," Glitch said with two fingers pointed, cigarette between nearly burnt to the filter, sweat seeping from his overdressed collars in a climate too humid for either of them, "we're paying you enough to do it any way we like."

So much for discretion. "What is it?"

"Fluid suspension, sophisticated proprietary inducer, triggers accelerated homocysteine production in the body. Getting hit shouldn't feel like much more than a bee sting, and the surface is coated with an enzyme that'll seal the wound."

"And then?"

"Five minutes, we're guessing. Atrial blood clotting on a massive scale, and if they're lucky, a quick and lethal ischemic stroke."

"And if they aren't?"

"Acute myocardial infarction. Pop goes the heart." Glitch mimed this with hands and a grin. "No trace of foul play. Examiners can chalk it up to bad health or bad luck. Who gives a shit, eh?"

The film in Ivan's beer glass smelled sour. He was done. A bullet may be messy, but it was swift.

"Ever had a heart attack?" he asked.

"Not that I recall," Glitch said with a nervous chuckle.

"Oh, you'd remember," Ivan said. "Rather makes a bee sting a meaningless event."

* * *

Sunlight suddenly pierced the lodgepole pines in front of the beach house, its bright fingers stretching across the floor and into dusty stucco-trimmed corners. Ivan initiated a diagnostic on his scope and then watched the boy crawl out of his rolled-up denim pants. What was their conversation?

I'm going swimming.

Isn't it too cold?

No daddy, it's not!

Okay Tiger. Don't go too deep.

Or some such drivel, Ivan imagined. A Romak 3 provided the contingency plan, and at this distance, a 7.62 by 54 round would positively take his head apart. But Ivan wasn't being paid for humane. Then again, the noise and the mess would bring cops. Passive acoustic sensors would triangulate the sound waves, identifying the beach house as source, which would require a hasty exit to which Ivan was not inclined after a bottle of shitty wine.

Using a loading assist he chambered the tiny blue seed into a Soluble Projectile Magnetic Pulse rifle, or what the black market called a spam gun. Impregnated with magnetic properties, the capsule lay suspended in a generated field in a position measured in nanometers.

Resting the rifle on the balcony railing would be convenient if death was still a spectator sport. Twenty-first century concessions called for propping the rubberized feet of the bipod indoors on a chest of drawers he'd dragged two meters back from a window facing the length of the shoreline. Around the perimeter of the reticle, digital information spilled down in columns. Distance to acquisition, wind direction, temperature fluctuation, humidity, pressure, GPS, ballistic angle. Target fixed at 292.3 meters. Crosshairs migrated to compensate for wind, vector and gravity as infrared scanners cancelled out the variables between them.

Ivan watched James help the boy struggle free of the fleece pullover and shirt. Maybe it was the last intimate act he would share with his son?

The boy waded waist deep, hands held aloft, palms just above the surface as though he could by sheer will of his small reach push the cold away. James tossed last bits of bagel out and a flock of gulls, like the streamers of a kite, swarmed after them.

Square breathing to bring his heart rate down, the evening air brought Ivan prawns cooked in too much butter, the sweet odor of a natural gas forklift, acoustic guitar played on the concrete steps descending to sand just across the boardwalk. Out in the distance ferries excreted industrial vapors. They passed through the manzanita shrubs outside, divergent smells mixing with that of fresh caulking on the sill. All of this became a composite of Ivan's situational awareness, the dull ache of treachery professionals don't feel. He'd lost the touchstone in his memory that echoed faintly while he searched remnant sounds back to sources that made these moments inevitable, the music that failed even Schumann and Tchaikovsky's sanity.

A lifetime of training said to pull between heartbeats, but all he could think was *Fuck it.*

He placed the crosshairs right below the boy's ribs where the tissues were soft and organs less vital. He squeezed the trigger, curtains in his periphery dancing in slow motion. No sound but the magnetics bringing the capsule to exit velocity, the light crack of breached sound barrier, physics of impact translating speed into a shockwave of thermal energy that brought it to an abrupt, deformed halt in the shallow wound.

The boy stumbled, scratched his side, no blood. He moved deeper into the waters of Alki, and for a moment his blonde hair, carried along by the wind, felt like the essence that was already leaving him. Waves washed away the footprints.

Ivan didn't watch.

* * *

Six down, one to go.

The mechanics, chemistry, simplicity and comprehensiveness of it all failed to make this kill any easier than the last five. No one had ever asked him to kill a child. The ripple effect was more profound with children, and no one would know that more than James. What would his own father have said?

Nothing, Ivan realized.

He crossed an area rug woven like a homemade potholder, flat and frayed over a creaking cedar floor. The room had a contaminate dampness that crept from crevices and made Ivan's skin itch. Massaging his beard, he slumped into the strung cushions of a rattan chair. Drank right from the bottle now, no advantage gained from decanting. Within minutes, still a quarter full, the bottle landed in the hollow bottom of a trash bin with the resounding impact of Ivan's opinion. Sirens passed outside the windows.

"You're too late."

Four girls and three boys, all pill-babies, all purchased from Genesis Life Solutions. GLS was one of Hizer's subsidiary cash cows.

"He would say nothing at all."

People had their needs, their vindictive or retributive impulses. Ivan's were vicarious at best. He felt like a middleman, a negotiator, a sort of actuary for the value of life. He was a veteran of death and its instruments, just like his father, whom he loved so much, in spite of memories that recently haunted him. The day he turned five, when he was still Nikos.

He'd held grain under the toothy mouth of a goat in the farmland outside Khalkis. His father crossed the distance between the field house and Nikos, long shadow now engulphing the dirt in which Nikos stood. The elder Katramados drank from a Coke bottle, a box under his arm and a cell phone to his ear. He spoke in clipped and profane Greek, and then in Albanian, which Nikos also understood. Abruptly ending the call, he bid Nikos drink from his bottle. No spirits in it today.

His father waited, hands on his hips, staring at distant crops of wheat and alfalfa. Nikos felt tension building, an event he later knew marked father's acceptance of him despite his mother. Acceptance wasn't the right word. More like indoctrination to his clandestine world.

With hazardous ceremony filled by the rough body language of excuses, his father gave Nikos the box.

It was made of fine wood with brass hinges and clasps. Bedded between recessed velvet within lay the gift of his first gun, a SIG Sauer 9 millimeter. It was beautiful and heavy and inscribed along the precision milled slide in ornate gold:

The dead know the language of flowers only
so they keep silent

Nikos could forgive his father. This was all the man knew. He would say nothing, the poetry of George Seferis filling a void. It wasn't the gift that made Nikos into Ivan. He closed his eyes, still feeling the shadow, smelling hyacinths and lupine. The faint echo. Pasts, like futures, were confusing—maybe even more so.

Pill-babies, Jesus.

Life wasn't inherently precious and he wasn't responsible for reconciling personal conscience with the judgment of business. Easier when they weren't kids, though.

It was like having no conscience at all. If there *was* an afterlife, he had nothing to send.

For a moment Ivan felt sick and he treated it with Ibuprofen and Scotch. He rinsed his face with soap and warm water. His past wasn't so much remembered as worn, unbuttoning the flannel shirt down over a litany of well-tread scars.

Genesis Life Solutions machines were familiar to Ivan, modern day ATMs for sperm banking. One could hardly miss them in public spaces, airports, hospitals and pharmacies.

"A software error," Glitch said, "affecting the genotype matrixing with the DNA of every child purchased from this Seattle vending machine between 0300 and 2100 hours."

Glitch pointed to the date and product data. Seven purchases logged.

Patrons needed a State-issued parental license. With a blood sample the machine processed DNA and narrowed down from a characteristic pool possible choices a mother could make: male or female, brown or blonde hair, blue or hazel eyes, height, build, skin tone within biological reason. Options weren't limited to physical. Mental acuity, cognitive capability, scholastic aptitude, amiability, sociability, dexterity. Some choices compromised other features. After all the steps the kiosk formulated a sort of seed. From a vast database of proprietary DNA sequences it would thread together a full double helix chain using nucleic acid substrates. Indemnity and Liability clauses acknowledged. Credit accounts billed. Out pops a soluble capsule and applicator designed to ensure ideal depth.

The irony. A soluble capsule for the creation of life and another to take it away. Easy come easy go? Hardly.

Pill-babies were designed against many threats of disease. No AIDS, mumps, diabetes, tuberculosis, multiple sclerosis, arthritis, not even chicken pox. No guarantee against heart attacks or cancer, threats DNA could only mitigate.

Humans can foul even the best-laid plans, law of entropy or something.

Is chicken pox significant enough to constitute an important childhood event? Probably not, he decided. Hizer sparing pill-babies a thousand little red lumps hardly made up for the raw deal Ivan carried out, for what now felt like a paltry sum of money. Renegotiating wouldn't help.

Ivan collapsed the bipod, packing his disassembled spam gun into polycarbonate cases. Next a tripod and tactical spotting scope, but not before giving confirmation video a perfunctory once over. In James's arms the boy weighed nothing at all, a soaking bundle of limp limbs. If this scene demanded ethical inventory, the boy wouldn't get it from Hizer, introspection and accountability not being corporate strong suits. Easier for them to outsource morals. Ivan decided it wasn't his problem.

Outside a large western facing window an overcast pall descended into amber evening hues and it was beautiful. The glass between him and the night opera reflected his dissolved ghost, also pacing back and forth just outside, empty Scotch glass in hand.

He went in search of ice cubes for a second Scotch and found the freezer trays empty. Goddammit.

Focus.

He was letting the littlest inconveniences irritate him disproportionately and the sensation was unfamiliar and exhausting.

Three Scotches later Ivan heard a party in one of the neighboring bungalows spill over with flamboyant laughter, everything still right in the world. He tossed a tablet down on the glass coffee table next to the Scotch. A blue line illuminated around the tablet on the table's surface. A pleasant surprise. No automated ice cube maker, but gesture interface projection in this rickety looking furniture.

Ivan authorized the link and flicked the last child's trait profiles out onto the glass surface. The projection sorted them into data groups.

Number 7.

Spread before him was a digital mock-up of what the target might look like now, assuming insertion of capsule within four months and a full term pregnancy. At six the subject would be 114 centimeters tall, approximately 19 kilograms, dirty blonde hair, brown eyes. Caucasian, another male. Another corporate product, which begged the question what being human really meant? Was Ivan just stamping an expiration date on the boy's packaging?

Number 7 was engineered to be of moderate intelligence and gifted with environmental adaptability. Quiet, contemplative, obsequious. All good traits for the well-behaved child. The ugly miracles of genetic engineering.

Ivan swiped the surface and the image scrolled through more characteristics. High levels of amiability, passive as opposed to aggressive. A high propensity for curiosity, a trait Ivan believed to be a poor choice. Curiosity is trouble in modern conformist America.

What about indifference to human life?

Was Ivan indifferent? No conscience?

People had their reasons. He was just the intermediary.

Lastly, in the spectrum between sciences and the arts, Number 7 was biased toward the latter. Did he draw dinosaurs with green markers? No athletic qualities, a lean build. No intricate technical acumen.

In other words, Ivan's father would never have given this boy a gun. He would never be an arms trader, a fighter, a hitman.

He would never be anything at all.

2

Small fingertips traced diamond patterns stamped in the sheet metal. He counted the bumps by feel. He was warm and sticky, the heat turned up very high. Palm pressed flat against the patterns, he could feel the cold outside the bus. They must be going north. North was cold. He couldn't see out the window, so far over his head. Just a white light, an overcast nothing.

The bus creaked and groaned, bounding through dips and potholes. After some hours it started to slow down. Around him, seats in front over the top of which he couldn't see, and behind him where he wouldn't look, other boys cheered with loud whistling noises. They too must be hot.

Bouncing motions made him wince, leg irons cutting into his ankles. The chain between the two heavy loops dragged on a long rubber mat, but his feet couldn't touch the ground. His wrists were cuffed to a chain around his waist and when he stretched his hand out the tugging squeezed his tummy.

He could see a pattern in the holes cut through the steel wall a few rows up, connecting them in his mind, into diamonds. He counted the holes.

Beside the toilet at the back of the bus was a cage with a policeman. The boy needed to pee, but the man had a tall gun, and he didn't understand all the rules, or what would happen if he moved. Would he be shooted?

He was too scared and now he sat in his own wetness. It soaked through the huge orange jumpsuit in which they'd chained him. No one said anything. It was so hot the pee eventually dried and some of the smell with it.

He marveled at the markings scratched into the plastic seat in front of him. What did it say? The bus made lots of turns now. They were closer to prison.

Latching his fingers under the belly chain, he counted the links up to twenty, then started over at his left thumb, all the way back down to one. He smiled and did it again, feet swinging with the motion of the big gray bus.

When they stopped, a policeman unbolted the cage. Everyone was quiet. Cold air rushed in through the open doors and the boy tingled all over from stillness, tiredness and fear. The policeman was angry.

"You will file off the bus in an orderly fashion and line up along the wall. You will follow all instructions immediately. If you cooperate you will be on Mainline before dinner."

A cheer went up. The boy didn't know why.

When it was his turn he slid off the seat. He'd long since lost his sandals and his bare feet touched the dirty black mat. He was shorter than everyone else. He struggled on the steps down, his ankles raw. When he ran out of railing he fell into a deep slush. A strong hand yanked him up by the collar of his coveralls, effortlessly and violently.

He cried out.

Now his feet buried into the cold slush, zigzag patterns from the bus tires leaving dirty lines in it. Looking up he found himself surrounded by walls and fences going in every direction, loops and loops of sharp wiry stuff, gray colors. He slowly shuffled to join the other boys at the wall. Behind him his leg iron chain jingled and slurped through the snow muck like an animal chewing on his heels.

"Where are your sandals?"

I don't know, he tried to say, but all that came from his dry lips was a whimper. His toes, bright red, peeked from the folds of orange jumpsuit. He stared at them, ashamed.

"I said, where are your sandals?"

There were lots of policemen now, all around the bus, in dark blue uniforms.

"What's your name?"

He lifted his head. "Dakota?"

The officer looked at the clipboard in his right hand, held it firmly by the top, his curled fingers plump like hot dogs.

"But everyone they call me Cody."

"Not here, they don't. In here you're Brenner." He pointed them through a sliding door with battleship rivets. "Enter the tank to your right. Don't get cold feet!" He laughed.

Benches lined the small room, steel toilet in one corner. The other boys made lots of noise, talking and talking, yelling. Dakota couldn't make much from their words. They were ordered to kneel on the benches and face the wall. Dakota couldn't manage, the leg irons tripping him. He fell on his back, simply rolled over and kneeled on the floor. No one cared. Policemen went around, unchaining them all. Boys rubbed their wrists and ankles and so did Dakota, wet jumpsuit itchy against his skin. He scratched and scratched but the itch sank deeper below the surface. It made his eyes water. He wiped his face on his sleeve.

Boys divided into two groups, some excited to be back. The rest, in prison for the first time, stayed quiet like Dakota, huddled in on themselves, little boats waiting to sink. One stood on the bench, fingers clawed in the cage mesh, looking out but not seeing anything. He was holding on, the rest of him drowning.

Police radios burped up little bits of noise and chirpy salutes, then faded around corners. Boy's names were called. The toilet flushed, a huge whooshing noise that made Dakota jump, louder than any toilet he'd ever seen. He could smell himself now and wanted a bath. His butt and legs itched. He hid behind his bangs, pretending to be invisible.

"Brenner!"

Barefoot, he trudged from the cage and sat in the plastic chair where he was told. A policewoman towered over her desk, tapping away at a keyboard with the longest fingernails Dakota had ever seen. Bright red, and for that moment he was fascinated. He swung his legs back and forth, distracted from scary thoughts. He didn't even hear her the first time she spoke.

"I said, I need your name!"

"Co—Dakota."

"Dakota what? With a K?"

"I dunno."

"You don't know yo name?"

"Dakota," he said. "Dakota Brenner."

"Middle?"

Dakota looked around. "Middle what?"

"Jesus!" red fingernails said. "Don't know his own goddamned name."

He listened to her fingernails click so he wouldn't hear her be angry. She'd pause, frown at the screen, and continue. A flash of light came from the next booth.

"Put yo hands on the scanner," she said.

Palms flat on the glass plate, greenish lines of light underneath traced his hands and passed several times. He held his face to a mask when told, squinting when more light poked his eyes.

"I'm cold."

"Me too," she said, but it didn't sound like she'd cared how he felt. She couldn't be cold, she was wearing a lot of uniform and a coat thing with no sleeves.

"Take your shoes off and stand on the plate, feet inside the lines." She looked at his bare feet over the top of her desk and shrugged in disgust. "Never mind. Just stand on it."

He could see kids getting their pictures taken, and this seemed like something to look forward to. He liked that and bunched his toes while he waited.

"Are you suicidal?"

"What?"

"Do you want to kill yo'self?"

"No!"

"Do you need protection?"

"From what?"

"Protective custody?" Dakota shrugged. She told him she'd put it down as a negative but to tell an officer if he changed his mind. Dakota couldn't change his mind, since someone had decided for him anyway.

"I'm assuming you know nothin about your medical history?" she asked.

The vacant look he gave her seemed like a safe answer. He felt like gum on a shoe. There was no need to make her more angry.

***

He was told not to smile for the camera but he did anyway, happy to be out of the wet jumpsuit. He'd been made to strip and dump it in a plastic bin with four wheels. He bent over and found another wheel in the middle of the bin. Five wheels.

Next was Holding 2, benches concrete now, windows instead of fence between them and the hallway. He held his knees to his face, the other boys crowding around him. He didn't know concrete had such a smell, and not just dust, other smells, people smells, sweat, dirt, pee, and they were crawling and leaping off the benches and yelling and smelling. They talked about the last time they were down. Others asked what happens next?

"Ain't nothin," the big boy said. They all listened. "You're getting Tagged and Bagged. Don't ask no stupid questions cause I ain't trying to be sitting here all day. Sooner we get on Mainline the better. They hand you your roll, you're done. So quit crying."

Some of them *were* crying. Not loudly, but Dakota knew by the way they rubbed their eyes red they were as scared as he was. He wanted to cry, but no one was coming to help. Their bodies twitched. He wondered if cows feel bad with no clothes on? He didn't think so. Pretending it was a cowbarn, he decided they were all cows waiting to be milked. His pretend was easy.

"Brenner seven-one-nine!"

Dakota leapt to his feet, stung by his own name. He followed the voice through another steel door, just like the other boys. None of them came back.

He was thrust into a narrow booth like a shower, bright lights shining on him, a drain under his cold feet. He tried to stand on scraps of mat to keep off the drain.

She bulged out of her uniform all over, like her tummy was trying to get out, bubbly and lumpy. She told him to stand, which made no sense because he was already standing. Lumpy said she was logging identifying marks. Cold spread from his feet to the rest of him, the warm lights helping only a little.

She had lots of gadgets on her belt, all in special pockets with snap-down flaps, round and tubey and square, but all black or shiny. Dakota's tool belt had lots more colors. If he ever saw it again he'd give it to her. She'd be much happier. Everyone should have more colors.

"Any tattoos?"

"What?"

"Turn around." He did a little twirl and Lumpy said he didn't have any.

Scars? Scratches? Unhealed sores? She was angry, said these were Yes or No questions and to stop shaking his head. He swallowed and said No even when he didn't understand her. Birthmarks? Warts? Moles? Abnormalities?

No.

"Are you carrying anything on your person today?"

"What?"

"Listen!" She yelled. "Do you have anything with you?"

Dakota looked down at his pale tummy, the rest of his naked body. Maybe she was just stupid. "Can I have some clothes?" he asked.

She ignored him.

"Do you have any contraband concealed in any of your body cavities?"

No. That was easy, he had no cavities. His dentist said so. He got coloring books for no cavities and wondered if he should tell her.

Run your hands through your hair. Good. Show me your right ear. Your RIGHT ear. Now the left. Hold your head up so I can see in your nose. Open your mouth and run your fingers through your teeth. Good.

Dakota heard a yell nearby and stumbled.

"Stand up!" she said. "We're not done."

He could hear crying and felt his own body shaking, heart beating against his small ribs.

Hold out your hands, palms forward and spread your fingers. Backs of your hands. Turn around. Raise your arms and show me your armpits.

It felt like a Simon Says game. His feet prickled. He wanted to scratch his toes really bad, but Simon didn't say so.

Hold up your right foot. Your RIGHT foot! So I can see the bottom. Good. Left foot. Bend over and spread your cheeks. Turn around. Move your testicles to the left and right.

He stared at her.

She threw up her hands. "I don't care which left or right, son."

"Huh?"

"Those," she pointed. "Never mind. Just lift them. Good. You're not concealing anything."

She must be stupid, Dakota decided.

He watched a boy walk towards an arch and look at it over his head. Maybe he thought it would fall on him? Worse, red lights all along its edge lit up and made a terrible noise.

"The doctor's ready for you," she told Dakota.

In the next booth a policeman tossed him on a padded table with a paper top, just like his doctor's. This doctor didn't smile like him, though. He took Dakota's temperature, and Dakota breathed deeply the way he knew he should when the doctor put the stethoscope on his chest. Then on his back.

"I'm cold."

"Yes," the doctor said, poking a light in his ears and nose. "Almost there."

"She already looked in my nose."

He told Dakota to lie on his back. He pushed fingers in tickly places, stomach, then lower, and up around his neck. Then lifted Dakota's legs by the ankles and tugged him around like a trussed animal. The alcohol smell made his heart leap, but the needle was in his arm so quickly he didn't have time to panic. At first he squeezed his eyes shut, but couldn't help his curiosity, and watched the doctor fill three glass tubes from the thing stuck in his arm. Blood the same color as the first lady's fingernails.

"DOC 620.020 requires blood samples be taken for RFLP and DNA identification as well as testing for immunodeficient diseases—AIDS, HIV and Hepatitis A through K."

He sounded smart.

Dakota thought he was getting his blood pressure taken, but the machine they buckled to his arm didn't squeeze. Instead it started stinging him and didn't stop for over a minute.

"Stand still during imprinting," said the officer.

This must be why the other boy was crying. Dakota bit down on his lip and squeezed his eyes. When they took it off, his arm was raw, and the doctor wiped away blood, two colors of it, black and red.

"Turn him over."

He was just starting to sense he'd be all right when he found himself face down on the mat, his arms behind him, pushed against his neck, the doctor holding a long metal stem with a sharp, curved tip, something cold and wet between his shoulder blades, his heart beating so fast he couldn't cry out.

"This is your ID tag, an RFID that gets scanned at all checkpoints, lets Custody know where you are, contains medical information, HSR's—Health Status Reports. You don't know what I'm talking about, I imagine. Don't worry, this won't hurt."

It was this moment Dakota remembered for a long time, the first lie that taught him people in prison didn't know it was wrong to lie, and would do it to him every day.

Piercing and burrowing under his skin, the stem instantly made his stomach sick, a pop he felt like a nail hammered onto his spine and he wanted to puke. All his muscles went stiff, then limp.

"You said it wouldn't hurt," he cried.

Trying to breathe, the policeman's hands squeezing him to the mat, he gagged so hard he was sure he'd wet himself. The paper was still dry. They let go and peeled off their gloves, pulling new ones from a box. His throat closed up, air sputtering into his lungs, and then it came out in great sobs.

"Don't remove the band aid for at least eight hours," Dakota heard, just a sound in the distance, like his ears were floating away. They dumped him on the floor. He didn't think he could move but they yelled at him.

Behind him, as he walked to the arch, Simon's voice. Birthmarks? Moles? Warts?

The scanner wailed and a towel roll was thumped against his chest, his hands jerking to take hold of it. Inside a pair of underwear with blue piping, white T-shirt, white socks. Tears rolling down his face weighed on his cheeks before falling.

He'd asked for clothes because he was cold and naked. Holding them now he felt, deep down inside, that clothes couldn't fix prison cold.

He would always be naked.

3

"The court will please rise. The Honorable Vicki Logan presiding. You may be seated."

In Pat's estimation, Judge Logan looked rather like Ruth Bader Ginsburg, a previous justice of the United States Supreme Court who'd been of some inspiration to Pat in her early years. Logan too was gaunt, almost skeletal, but carried an austere sense of import and control.

Through the double wooden doors marched a younger woman whose sharp dress gave her artificial stature. Of course her high heels helped. She tossed a voluminous pile of folders on the prosecution's table and they spread like dominoes.

"I apologize, Your Honor. I was indisposed, Judge Richter's court."

Tony Wu leaned over and whispered to Pat. "I told you she'd be late. It's legendary."

"And the defendant?" Pat asked.

"He should already be here." Tony looked at his watch and shrugged. "We're at the mercy of Pierce County Jail. Who knows."

Pat lifted her tablet and looked over probable cause documents from months ago while the judge and her clerk exchanged prefatory matters. "I've looked over this case. I'm a little concerned, Tony. Is this real? Where are the police reports?"

"I only put the preliminary file on your distribution. The rest is coming, as soon as you're officially assigned. The court sealed critical parts of the docket entirely, but I can open some of the privileged materials to you now." Tony flicked the documents off the left side of his tablet and their corresponding tabs appeared on Pat's. "Look, I can't tell you how glad I am you're willing to handle the appeal, Pat. This one's important."

"But is this accurate? He's five years old?"

Both prosecution and defense tables had been set with a stack of paper cups and decanters. Tony pulled a paper cup, leveled the decanter, and yanked back when the dispensed fluid showed no promise of coffee. The name Tony Wu was practically synonymous with Pierce County Department of Assigned Counsel, reputation growing fast in legal circles. Remaining in DAC might stymie his career unless he replaced the Department's retiring head. Tony was certainly accomplished enough to start his own private practice. Yet he still didn't know to bring his own coffee to court.

He gave Pat a helpless shrug, as if to say even these minor injustices should count. Pat pulled the lid off a Starbucks she'd picked up on the way through the lobby and poured half into his cup.

"You don't need to do that."

"Anything for a gentleman. Besides, you're running this show. I'm just here to watch."

"Thank you." The speed of Tony's sip failed to warn him it was still hot. He flinched. "We're not doing much today. We finalize the judge's Adjudication. I bring my motion to assign you as appellate counsel at state expense. You don't even need to be here, but I appreciate your support."

"Judge Logan's new to me. Sometimes it helps for me to see, to put a face to the record."

"Of course."

Pat touched each tab and scanned through documents. Tony used a pen to intermittently tap his forehead or scratch beneath his trim black hair, neither action bearing any connection to the concentration on his face. Pat wondered whether poor Tony, who like her still believed in what he did, also struggled to understand how these things happened. How did we come to this?

From what wretched details she read, an answer could hardly be found. Pat's concern grew from a sense that she must have overlooked a critical detail. Just weeks earlier Judge Logan had looked down from that bench at a child only just past his toddler years and rendered a life sentence. Pat needed to hear the voice behind this judgment to try and temper the surreal impression left in her mind.

Tony emptied the paper cup and Pat filled it again. Tony's body language filed an objection, but his silence accepted. Time to properly sleep, given his caseload, was probably irreconcilable.

Judge Logan finally addressed the court and both Pat and Tony signaled with their cups the show was rolling. Cheers.

"Coming on for hearing today is finalization of adjudication in the case of State versus DCB. May I presume all parties in this matter are prepared to go forward?"

Tony looked around as though he'd inconveniently misplaced something. "I apologize, Your Honor, but it appears as though my client is, um—"

"Do we have Mr. Brenner in custody?" the judge asked.

Checking a computer, her clerk answered, "It looks as though he's already been transferred to DOC."

Judge Logan nodded. "Perhaps the jail mistook the order of commitment as finalized. We can reschedule, file a transport order."

But already Tony waived off her proposal. "I see no reason. He's already been sentenced. He can't sign his own name anyway."

Judge Logan asked Tony about the CASA, spoken like the Spanish word for *house* rather than the initials for Court Appointed Special Advocate. Tony reminded her the court held *in loco parentis* of Dakota Brenner, that the CASA was from an unrelated civil matter, and Mr. Tony Wu himself stood now to represent the best interests of the child.

"I'm satisfied, counsel. Moving on, your motion to withdraw and substitution of appellate counsel is before me. I've only glanced over it briefly, perhaps you can—" Judge Logan flipped through the pages, "Has he or she filed assignment of error?"

"She did not, Your Honor, I took care of that. Let me introduce Ms. Helen Patricia Naughton, a private law firm."

Pat considered standing but let her age permit a dignified nod. Her legs had always betrayed her, be it varicose veins, edema, ankle pain. Switching to appellate law many years ago kept her off the feet and had been a welcome change.

"Your office is in Seattle?"

Pat cleared her throat. "Yes, Your Honor, but I work on appeals throughout the state."

Before requesting an explanation from Tony, Judge Logan fixed on Pat a disdainfully suspicious glare with which Pat had learned embodied how most Pierce County judges felt about outsiders. This courthouse entitled itself to a method of justice that invited a disproportionate number of judicial error appeals for the state, and they guarded their temple zealously. Pat instantly, as though by telepathy, knew Ms. Logan shouldered the same corrupt mantle.

Now made to feel uninvited and uncomfortable in this small courtroom, Pat turned her attention to the mundane surroundings while Tony spoke.

"The decision comes down to resources, Your Honor," by which everyone knew he meant time. New Years arrests overburdened office staff even more than normal. "This is a case of first impression for the Court of Appeals. It will require counsel with the knowledge and experience to properly frame complex legal arguments. I'd rather not ..." Tony twisted his hand in front of him, searching for the right phrase, "...I'd rather not allow the case to fall to an indifferent firm unwilling to devote time to comprehend the breadth and scope involved here. Ms. Naughton is very capable and has been handling these sensitive juvenile appeals for over twenty years. She has generously offered to pick it up in our stead."

Tony pulled along the precise edges of his suit. Pat simply nodded once again, the State's counsel taking her turn to say even less of substance than Tony.

Pat felt a sudden pervasive despondency but what brought it on was unclear to her. Surely this courthouse had a Media Courtroom, reserved for high profile cases. Those had panoramic views, loaded galleries, real granite and high-backed leather chairs, which made the defendant's doom that much more certain. An expensive machine at work. No such treatment for Dakota Brenner's case. And why not? Would public outcry have absolved him? Had the Prosecutor once again yanked the Fourth Estate's short leash? If media courtrooms were Bentleys, then justice in America was predominantly handled in Hondas.

It was in a mean wooden chair like this the boy sat following his arrest on September 17th to be arraigned on suspicion of various sex crimes. Beneath him an uneven expanse of soiled gray carpet. Out this eighth story window he would have seen the towering concrete ugliness of his jail when they amended charges to several counts of rape and molestation. Sentenced in this unremarkable room, only one among many facing the same routine, judge proceeding from one to the next like an auction block.

Judge Logan repeated herself. "I said, do you have any objections?"

"I'm sorry, Your Honor. No."

Motion granted. No one seriously expected otherwise, even if Pat was an outsider. Tony signed on behalf of his missing client while she watched the closing commotion of courtroom procedure with a feeling of anticlimactic gravitas.

State's counsel already checking her appointment calendar to fit in a restitution hearing.

Pat scooped up her tablet and Tony followed her out of the courtroom. Embrace the brevity of it all if only to salvage this case before *next* Christmas.

* * *

Pat ordered wine, a Lambrusco she thought might be reasonably dry. As the waiter moved off, Pat signaled him back, ready to order the rest. She and Tony decided to split a pizza, biased toward mushrooms for her if she conceded his preference for Canadian bacon.

The restaurant was Tony's choice, a little cave nestled in the slope of Tacoma's steep streets with a real stone oven. Deep in the back and windowless, their booth remained dark, low wooden beams charred and damaged overhead, rusted anchors protruding, ready to hang stable ropes and harnesses.

Two salads landed, fresh grated parmesan cheese, Tony pinching his eyes, tearing apart a breadstick, Pat giving the wine a taste, nod of approval—a whole ceremony preceded getting to the less palatable business of Dakota Brenner.

"If the court's his parent, why does he have a Guardian ad Litem?" she asked.

"CASA," Tony said. "I don't know. It has to do with a previous civil matter. He showed up after the arrest but can't tell us anything." Tony tossed his hands out as though helpless, equally baffled by the circumstances.

"Civil how? Is Dakota a ward of the State?"

"Not exactly."

"So he has parents?"

"Not exactly. Not anymore." His fork became as much a device of explanation as a food conveyance. "He had parents, but I never saw them. I wasn't really on this until after the arraignment. I heard there was an incident in the courtroom during arraignment, and proceedings were subsequently made closed to the public. Court seized custody, evicted the parents permanently, and for reasons still unclear to me, I can't even talk to them. It's all blacked out in the police report."

"That's very passive voice, Tony. *Who* made the proceedings closed to the public?"

"Logan. Influenced by the CASA and the State."

"And you don't know why?"

Tony shrugged. "The aforementioned incident. And don't even ask, the record's sealed. I don't know anything."

Pat set her fork down. "How is that even possible? You're Brenner's attorney. How can you be put in the dark?" Another shrug, but more scornful than apathetic. "What do the police reports say?" she asked.

"They're sort of generic, as though cribbed from a dozen others, change a name here and there. Dakota and a girl at his kindergarten ostensibly played a personal game of show and tell on the recess yard."

Pat laughed.

"It's not funny anymore. You know how zero tolerance policies work these days."

"I'm sorry. I guess it's the absurdity of the reaction I find humorous."

"Anyway, school policy, mandatory reporting. The girl shared with a friend who told someone, who told someone—it got to a counselor, all hell broke loose, a meeting's called, poor girl's in tears now, police all over the place. Dakota's male, so he's the aggressor."

"Naturally," Pat agreed. "Sexual inequality aside, I'm more concerned about the fact that Dakota and the girl are in kindergarten. Kindergarten!"

"The laws are different now." His fork took a dive. "I'm as culpable a witness to it as you, even if you do have a twenty year lead watching the decline."

It was true. Juvenile convictions skyrocketed in response to public concern about safety and it was a dragnet. Amendments to the Revised Code of Washington, RCW 9A.04.050, underwent a subtle change. Years ago the provision said children below the age of eight were presumed incapable of committing crimes, though the presumption could be removed by proof they had sufficient capacity to understand the act or neglect. When recodified, the legislature simply reversed the scales. Now children eight or younger were presumed capable of criminal intent unless this presumption was challenged. His defense would have to show he had insufficient capacity. In lay terms, whether he knew right from wrong.

Which was an untenable threshold, where common experience told Pat children *did* understand. Even young children can be little terrors and know when they're getting away with something. They know what the spanking is for. Pat knew this from her own childhood, if not for the fact she had no children of her own.

A life sentence is a hell of a spanking, though.

What does a five year old know about his sexual nature? Does he see a boundary or know when it's crossed? When does his curiosity about girl parts go from innocent to rape? Would any child know this? She put the question to Tony.

"No, Pat. Of course not," he scoffed. "When I was five my genitals relieved my bladder, and that was it. I didn't understand bonus features until much later."

Pat laughed. Nevertheless, something was missing. Show and tell isn't rape. "What's he done? I'm curious, you see, because this is a life sentence, way outside the standard range. In Washington, life means *natural* life. Did he discover his bonuses?"

"Discover what?"

"Bonuses," she said, "not the other word."

Tony turned pink. "Of course. Sorry."

"Medical examination? Broken hymen?"

"I don't think it was that deep."

"Then what are we dealing with here?"

Pizza arrived and they didn't resume conversation for several minutes. Tony eagerly took advantage of the interlude.

Pat enjoyed the cozy large charred bubbles formed in the crust that came close to the flame. So much food today was uniform in its plastic wrappings, and this imperfect anarchy seemed beautiful. Like misshapen cucumbers in a home garden or the familiar bumps in her driveway deformed by the great roots of oak trees. They pulled slices from the platter and webs of cheese thinned to sinews, Tony profiling slices for the fewest mushrooms. They took their time.

"Did she testify?"

"Who?"

"The girl."

"Oh, her. No." Four slices remained and Tony refilled both their wineglasses. "No, the court brought her testimony in through the counselor. I objected, hearsay, but it was deemed admissible under the excited utterance exception. You know, the hearsay must be believable because people don't lie if agitated by the moment?"

"I'd challenge that ruling, but it's a weak argument."

"Agreed."

Pat thought of all the court expressions which over thirty years created a new lexicon undermining every constitutional protection people thought they had: hearsay exceptions, harmless error, inevitable discovery, good cause, sneak and peek, plain view doctrine, reasonable suspicion, qualified immunity, good faith reliance—the list was endless. If not for the hard work of people like Tony Wu, pushing back against the eroding tide of police power, the

Constitution and all the Amendments might as well be printed on toilet paper. If she didn't persist in the fight, all was lost. There was nothing *harmless* about the errors committed to put Dakota in prison.

Red marinara spilled onto a napkin, which she'd only unfolded on her lap out of habit. She wasn't concerned with maintenance of the dress. Her wardrobe functioned like her shoes—practical. She had two suits reserved for oral arguments and even those might as well be comfortable.

Tony, on the other hand, dressed crisp and professional, the consummate courtroom presenter, slightly Asian, articulate, clear, onyx cufflinks and pinstripes. She'd first met Tony Wu at the University of Washington, one of the law schools where she was invited to lecture. Tony sat in the back row but asked all the right questions. She'd immediately known he was destined for defense law. He wasn't cynical, just wary of state power and police intent. He questioned everything, animated by individual rights. He could reserve his displeasure only so long, and now he unloaded the real danger in Dakota's trial.

"The State had their doctor—and I use the term loosely—evaluate the boy." He held up his hands in defense to the look on Pat's face. "It wasn't my decision. I didn't have a chance to object. The State, the police, they rushed in before he was even assigned an attorney. You know how it goes. I got the psych evaluation the same day as the affidavit of probable cause. I moved to suppress the report because at his age it isn't voluntary, but whom am I suppressing it from? Juveniles don't get juries. The judge had already seen it anyway."

"And what does it say? The report, I mean."

"SVP," Tony said. "Sexually Violent Predator. In twenty-six pages it's the doctor's opinion that Dakota is sexually deviant, a risk to the community, and should never be released." He emptied his glass. The wine bottle sat empty and he looked around for their waiter. "You see? This whole *crime* is nothing, just the means to get caught. His real crime is *being* sexually deviant."

"Do I have the report yet?"

"You have it now." Tony's hand swept the air.

She could think of so many other things she'd rather read. "How did he make this finding?"

Tony only skirted the question. "He works for the State, Pat. He's paid to say whatever is convenient for them. It's a crime, now, what goes on in our minds, and they're the authority over it. Truth has nothing to do with it. God help me if they see what I really think of state-paid bootlickers."

"I'd sentence you to eat the last slice of pizza."

"You're too lenient." He pulled it onto his plate and carved it into pieces with knife and fork, which made Pat wonder what New Yorkers might call a crime against tradition.

"Manifest injustice to give him a sentence within the standard range, they said."

"What was the standard range?"

"Considerably less than life. Does it matter?" He thought about it for a moment. "Ten to fifteen. Years that is, not months."

A waiter brought the bill and Tony signed the tablet. Pat offered to cover it, but Tony insisted. "Our office is grateful for your assistance and will gladly call this a consultation cost, I'm sure."

The word *deviant* always rubbed Pat wrong. "Who defines deviant, Tony?"

His expression held an uncertainty about how deep a question she was asking. "I don't know anymore. If I ever did."

"Deviation from what? Normal? What's normal anymore? When I was a child—or you for that matter—weren't we curious? Normal. Didn't we flaunt ourselves if ever so briefly for the taboo thing of it? Normal. Did our parents roll their eyes? Just kids being kids. Isn't that normal?"

"Of course, Pat."

"So who gets to decide?"

Tony shifted his weight, his head. "Well, one Supreme Court justice's litmus was 'I know it when I see it.'"

"That was about obscenity, pornography. But it makes my point, doesn't it? How can a legal system function when we graft onto objective criteria the much more fuzzy concept of intent, our state of mind, something we really *don't* know, and pay snake charmers to conjure for us. You either did or you didn't do something. Everything else is speculation. That's not worthy of a civilized justice system."

Tony chuckled, but not with a lot of mirth. "It's funny you should use the term snake charmer."

"Charlatan, whatever, it just came to mind."

"No, it's perfect. Because, licensed psychologist or not, he didn't use the MMPI or other pycho-social evaluation questionnaires. He used a plethysmographic examination. All very scientific."

The vulgarity of this literally made Pat's neck tingle, hairs rise. As crude as the polygraph tests prosecutors loved to fall back on, plethysmography occasionally showed up in her juvenile appeals. Once even in a boy as young as ten. So it shouldn't have shocked her, and yet it did. Dakota had been strapped to chair, a wire attached to his penis, while he was forced to watch and hear pornographic material. Purporting to graph his response to inappropriate stimuli, the machine did nothing more than plot the erectile dilation of the boy's penis.

"That's absurd," Pat said. "He's five."

"Technically six at the time."

"Big difference. They traumatized him."

"It's not as barbaric as the sentence he got. I mean, really. In ten years he might not remember that doctor, but he'll remember prison. He'll still be in it." Tony threw down his napkin.

"Not if *we* can help it." She shook her head. "All over something that isn't a crime."

"Pat, there was never a crime. This isn't about what he did. This is all preemptive. It's about what they say he *might* do."

4

What was identity? To Ivan the question seemed more important than *Who am I?* Identity was such a malleable artifice. Ivan Stavros was just another name on a forged birth certificate, licenses and accounts, mutable and worthless. Only misplaced faith in identity gave it value.

To Approach Control, Ivan was 318 Victor Foxtrot, descending from 20,000 feet on approach to McCarran International Airport in the middle of the night. It gave security people comfort, this belief in the legitimacy of 318VF, in Ivan Stavros. But the symbols didn't tell who he was, and Ivan could shed them so easily, a mere change of clothes.

Locating Number 7 renewed all these old reflections. Ivan had no name or DNA for the boy, or any of the other standard symbols of identity. Now he understood the obsession with identity, the insecurity for lack of it.

He bought a bottle of Drambuie at the duty free and ate a light breakfast in an airport restaurant before visiting the concourse branch of Citibank. Something about the croissant left a nutty taste in his mouth and made the routine task of requesting retrieval of a safe deposit box distracting.

In a private booth Ivan removed an alloy box. A chip under the skin of his palm triggered the lock and disabled a tamper switch which would otherwise incinerate the contents. He swapped his wallet for the one inside, which matched the accompanying ID clip for Mr. Stevenson, a name calculated to be forgettable. Ivan felt a little rush, like the cool fabric of a clean shirt. Who am I?

He was the product of thirty years finding peaceful refuge in anonymity, names as diverse as the colorful customs stamps in passports he stashed around the world in deposit boxes just like these. Every cell in his body felt liberated by these aliases, a sensation still as intense as the first time—when he was twelve years old and only known as Nikos, and suddenly loosened his attachment to such things as names.

* * *

Nikos and his father made their way about the busy port at Haifa. Yannis Katramados affably shook hands with officials and customs agents, many with whom he was obliged to share drinks. Yes, yes, old friend, he'd say. The family is good, thank you, send their greetings, business is terrible, always terrible, Greece wounds me, wherever I travel, and what of you?

Nikos was used to the facility with which his father could put down drink after drink, never feeling the cumulative effect. He claimed to have been drunk only once, among the crowds following Seferis's coffin through the streets of Athens.

"We were still under the militant junta then, all the oppression and censorship. But we sang the poet's banned words of resistance anyway."

Ambassador to the United Kingdom and Nobel Laureate, Seferis didn't live to see the end of Papadopoulos's regime.

"Missed it by three years," Yannis said. "Seferis was a great friend of mine. I was too young then to understand the tragedy we faced, but I knew enough of political detention and torture, all the purpose I needed. So we drank and cried, maybe more than was good for us."

Even decades later Yannis remained loyal to Greece, no matter the betrayals and fractured freedoms of the past.

Nikos enjoyed travelling. He was fascinated by local customs and, having grown up among a disparate family of revolutionary enablers whose trade demanded sacrifice, he marveled at the wealth and excess others enjoyed. It was Seferis who told Yannis *Wherever I travel Greece wounds me,* a reminder of the political treachery they'd suffered together, but also of pride felt for a country with so much rich history. Maybe it justified for Yannis this spartan gypsy lifestyle, but Nikos felt he was missing something. He secretly daydreamed of a future filled with excessive luxuries, and felt ashamed for wanting what his father happily did without.

With container KOSU 026405 3 45G1 safe aboard the transport vessel Kretos, Nikos and his father drove south to Tel Aviv to see Uncle Ellison. Even in winter the cool Mediterranean air bore no resemblance to other places Nikos had traveled. It was rich and seductive, a music swimming through the fingers he held out the rolled-down car window.

Ellison took them to the Hatikva Market, a colorful collection of concessions and bustling crowds. Yannis looked for unique gifts for friends in Greece and bought lotions made with medicinal Dead Sea salts. Ellison showed them a beloved vendor with excellent stuffed pita bread. Nikos couldn't be sure but thought it might be saffron in the falafel.

They drove slowly back through congested streets of Tel Aviv's ubiquitous Bauhaus architecture, stopping along the ritzy Dizengoff Street where everyone either had money or at least appeared to. Nikos noticed more than one store displaying intricate bridal gowns. How could there be so many? Young women inside tugged at the fitting, attentive couturiers kneeling with pins lined up between their lips.

Yannis and Ellison lingered in the Dizengoff Square so Nikos could admire the colorful rings of Yaacov Agam's fountain, flames rising from its peak.

Ellison ran an errand and met up with them again that evening under the canopy of an outdoor café on Ben Yehuda Street. Dance music escaped from one of the nearby nightclubs now so popular in Tel Aviv, but not so loud as to interfere with the lively street entertainers. Yannis gave Nikos some coins with which to tip the musicians. Even the simplest guitar tunes seemed energized by something intangible and exotic, and Nikos clapped for each.

Ellison was the second half of Yannis's K&E Import/Export business. They blessed the safe travel of container 026405 with beer. Dark and redolent, foam ran down the glasses, a film of carbonated bubbles popping and drying into tiny white freckles. Nikos helped himself to dates and nuts from a dish at the center of the glass table.

Ellison couldn't be Yannis's brother, so *uncle* was just affectation, but one Nikos never questioned. All semblance of family to him was amorphous. Apart from K&E Import/Export, Ellison's real work was for a technical division of Israeli Arms, where he did advanced design and programming of next generation weapons. It was obvious why Yannis found the business relationship practical, but how he'd met Ellison was never explained to Nikos. Ellison always left undone the top buttons of his shirt, the corners of oversized starched collars hovering as though ready to take off like a paper airplane. He was so slender a man. In Nikos's imagination, Uncle Ellison was carried off on those airborne collars. Around his neck Ellison wore a silver chain from which dangled a Star of David with Hebrew inscriptions. He told Nikos they read *Never Forget.* Ellison blamed Britain for Israel's hostile neighbors but still drove an MG with a missing ragtop. He objected to the quality of American weapons, but when they came over labeled *foreign aid,* he gladly resold them to competitors. He spread his arms over adjoining chairs, glass dangling precariously by a rim grasped only by fingertips, dark patches of hair between each knuckle. Ellison's gaze was so assured, as though viewing the future, the distance. Nikos decided his uncle suffered some macrocosmic claustrophobia, which included a fear of being too far from the broadness of ocean or oppressed by cultural uniformity. He couldn't so much as tie himself to the same woman from day to day, let alone marry her. A lot like Nikos's father in that respect and, like Yannis, when Ellison had money he travelled.

Nikos was pretty sure Ellison had money, as his gifts to Nikos were generous.

A group of high-spirited young women strolled by, arm in arm, fed by a common punch bowl sized drink. One asked Nikos if he had a girlfriend? He could tell they were American but wasn't sure what to say. He blushed and they laughed.

Uncle Ellison waited for them to pass before handing Nikos a small package wrapped in light blue paper.

"It's time you had at least one of these. Maybe another in the future, but learn this one for now."

"What is it?"

"Open it." Ellison was fond of his looks and disappointed with the monk-like bald spot growing prematurely large for a man as young as he. Unconsciously running his fingers along the scalp, he and Yannis shared a special-occasion smile.

Inside Nikos found a passport, an Israeli one with his picture and new information. Ellison must have been well-connected, for the passport already showed telltale signs of distress indicating sufficient usage to make it appear less conspicuous at border control points. In addition, several pages were pre-stamped with authentic passport control emblems, places Nikos had already travelled, like Albania, Belgium, Malta, everything around the Caucases, Switzerland and a blue seal for far away Malaysia. Nikos liked Kuala Lumpur's exotic festivity and questionable commerce. The kind of place six thousand firing mechanisms were modified on the cheap.

With accompanying birth certificate and papers, it was the first of many legends Ellison would fabricate for him. Nikos studied the details carefully, committing them to memory. He believed his uncle could singularly understand his happiness. New names felt like freedom—anonymity was freedom.

"Ellison's also arranged a safe deposit box for you in Jaffa, nearby. This is for crash use, emergencies."

"The rest is already there," Ellison said. He counted off on his fingers. "A pre-paid Nokia cellphone, change of clothes, a stash of different currencies, € 2,500 in varying denominations, maps for the soft routes through Syria, Turkey and Eastern Europe. Did I miss anything?"

Yannis's facial expression inventoried the list. "First aid?"

"Can he suture a wound?"

With a grimace Yannis lifted his sleeve, showing off a slightly uneven scar with dots on each side. "He's getting some practice."

"Not a pretty sight. How did that happen?"

"Occupational hazard," was all Yannis said, glancing a warning look at Nikos.

Nikos knew better than to elaborate. His father endured Marta's hysterical tirade. A frequent companion of Yannis's, Marta was armed with some sort of sharp kitchen implement and Yannis refused to fight back. He decided Marta's wrath was justified since she'd caught Yannis screwing her oldest daughter as well. Nikos practiced on Yannis's arm for the more sensitive wound Marta left on the buttock. Yannis didn't show that scar, on which Nikos felt he'd stitched a much straighter line. Too bad. Nikos clenched his mouth, trying not to snicker, thinking what a spectacle that would be on Ben Yehuda Street.

"He should have a spare gun in the box, too," Ellison said. "Something small and concealable."

Yannis nodded. He ordered another round in Hebrew, a tongue very different from those Nikos already knew. Nikos listened intently, because languages were also freedom.

Later Ellison made a few calls to friends and found Nikos a Glock 26 sub-compact nine-millimeter for the safe deposit box in Jaffa. Ellison objected to Glocks, but Yannis insisted on account of a light trigger pull. Nikos tried on several harnesses and picked an adjustable one that fit the weapon snugly against his ribcage, with slots for two extra eighteen-round staggered magazines and a suppressor. Ellison's prejudice against Glocks didn't jade his insistence one could never have too many bullets.

Yannis and Nikos flew from Ben Gurion Airport and within six days caught up with container 026405 in a state-owned bonded storage yard near the port of Thessaloniki's impressive old customs house.

Heavy rain dripped from the corrugated channels of enormous container stacks. It was a pleasantly cold day with a warm soak, gray and formidable, but suggesting renewal of everything that flowered. His father said, "Angelos Sikelianos, he would call this 'the earth's heavy smell.' Feel it?"

Nikos nodded.

Inside a long warehouse began another maze through wooden pallets piled high and wrapped in plastic. Forklifts pushed goods into dark corners and a stagnant smell came in humid waves, a bursting of bottles lost under the weight of burial.

The main office stood like a lighthouse in the sea of trade, a sheetrock shell with conduit running down from the rafters above, light spilling from behind venetian blinds. Yannis gave the door a perfunctory knock and pushed it open. He fell heavy in a swivel chair with worn cushions and duct tape wrapped around the support.

Ordos was on the phone and waved a hand to say he'd only be a minute.

"I have a container full of washing machines you should take off my hands," Ordos said when he hung up. From the bottom drawer of a file cabinet he drew a bottle of ouzo and the three cleanest glasses he could find. He filled each a few centimeters, thought better of it, and tipped in some more.

"What would I do with washing machines?" Yannis asked. He took his glass and with a clink said, "To your health."

"To your brand new German washing machines."

"I don't need washers."

"They're washers and dryers," Ordos said, coupling his hands one above the other, "good ones, Bosch, and there's fifty, but maybe I sell them like there's forty, eh?"

"I don't need washers."

Ordos shrugged. "Neither does the buyer or he'd have picked them up two months ago. I'm trying to get them off the pier, make room for tractors."

The management office was the embodiment of every portside container yard the world over. A disheveled river of carbonless forms spilled from patchwork desks and cabinets. Spreadsheets burned into computer screens and fax machines chewed through paper. A Bunn coffee machine made an unlikely noise, something like a cough or throat clearing, which at any rate didn't change the level in the decanter.

It occurred to Nikos the office was remarkably empty for this time of the morning. Usually it teamed with many more people, cigarette smoke pooling opposite the small vents.

"So, I have a little problem," Yannis said.

"Yes?"

Yannis handed him the bill of lading for container 026405 and Ordos stabbed away at a stained keyboard, intermittently swearing at the machine and acknowledging inventory information on screen.

"What are these?"

"What does it say?"

Ordos squinted. "'Scitex . . . Dolev.' They're made in Israel?"

Yannis shrugged.

"What are they? Probably some kind of weapon."

Nikos felt his heart stop. He was conscious of being the apprentice and tried not to assume anything, never mind speak. He wasn't even sure of sitting down, so he pressed himself against a corkboard and tried to hide his anxiety behind the glass, sipping slowly. Yannis and Ordos might be good friends, small bribes and favors, but not so close Ordos wouldn't alert customs if he thought a container deserved closer inspection.

Yannis didn't miss a beat.

"You think so? Maybe we should check them out. We pull one in here, plug it in, see if it makes coffee or peace with the Palestinians."

Ordos laughed. "You can forget about that."

"Country's a mess," Yannis agreed. "The boy and I spent a few extra days, see the sights before things go to pieces. Netanyahu's stirring up shit on the West Bank again." He drank the rest of the ouzo and held up a finger. "And Sharon? That clown . . . he's going to trigger another all-out war. I should start shipping my coffee machines from China like everyone else."

Ordos filled both their glasses and made a toast. "May his own people shoot him too."

"Benjamin or Ariel?"

"Either one. Both. Who cares? They've got a precedent."

"You're talking about Yitzhak? Rabin? He was a pacifist. The new hawks are all Likud party, trigger-happy. They're just as likely to shoot each other before the university students get around to it."

They each shared a deep laugh. Nikos smiled watching his father's finesse. Ordos asked if Customs gave Yannis any grief, and Yannis ran with the humor. Of course, always grief—the duty fees here are outrageous. Another deep laugh.

"So, I said I had a little problem," Yannis said. "Ta Nea doesn't want them anymore."

"The coffee machines?"

"Sure. But I found another buyer. I just need you to set the papers in my name and I'll have a truck here this afternoon to cart it away."

Ordos shrugged, took the bill of lading and wrote in the changes, stamping the shipyard's seal across the bottom. "Bring two trucks and take these goddamned washing machines too."

"I'll see what I can do." Yannis's tone suggested the possibility of commitment.

Nikos bounced on his toes. It was a clever and somewhat repeatable trick. Greeks were highly suspicious of cargo out of Israel—and who, apart from the United States, wasn't? Customs was unlikely to heavily inspect cargo destined for delivery to Greece's largest newspaper, Ta Nea. A Dolev was simply a machine for burning negatives to speed plates to the presses. More importantly they had lots of useful empty space within. Customs focused on containers going to unfamiliar addresses, and all Yannis had to do was claim the shipment himself before the company realized they hadn't ordered it. The process was relatively safe, for Yannis could blame Israeli companies for anything Customs found and walk away. He was just the transport facilitator.

"Far easier to share drinks with officials as our friends," Yannis said. "Should we have a fleet of lousy smuggling ships? Flit around in the shadows? Treacherous landings in the middle of the night? Police board us, we have to shoot them?"

Nikos shook his head.

Just before dark Nikos and his father unloaded the container into a large barn in Langadhas not far away. The farm belonged to a friend sympathetic to K&E

Import/Export's business. Together they pulled Uzis and Tar 21 bullpup assault rifles from the cavities of the Scitex machines, reassembling electronic equipment panels to sell to another buyer of printing equipment.

Lined up on the rolled-out canvas, they were a beautiful sight, an arsenal so large and oiled and new and precise, Nikos couldn't help tears while assembling them and slapping magazines into the receivers. He had lots of practice and worked with staggering efficiency. From the surrounding pens came the bleats and moos of curious farm animals. Even years later Nikos would smell a weapon's machine oil and, in the same breath, sense the odor of cow dung and damp grass bales, the earth's heavy smell. The warmth of the animals comforted him against the tingling excitement of such a profitable run.

Their timing couldn't have been better. A week later one of the ELA's domestic terrorist offshoots bombed the Barclays Bank branch in Piraeus. The Revolutionary Nuclé protested everything NATO, U.S., EU and any financial supporters. Nikos sympathized. Following their modus operandi they called ahead with a warning to prevent casualties. Even so, after the mess RN made of Athens' court buildings in June that same year, officials used the Barclays bombing to lock down ports, increasing inspections.

Nikos felt sorry for Ordos, who didn't need the extra hassle.

Yannis wasn't accustomed to indiscriminate spending, but this was his biggest haul in years and he started speaking of his vineyard and winery. He owned neither but it was a distant and maybe somewhat romantic dream.

"On one of the islands, Nikos. Maybe Santorini, eh?"

"You want to make wine?"

"Mmm. Perhaps not Santorini, too barren, too many vampires," Yannis said, alluding to the local folklore that volcanic Santorini served as haven for retired demons. "Maybe Náxos or Páros, where the soil is rich. You've been to Páros. Remember the smell of thyme? The flowers? Good place for a vineyard."

Nikos nodded. Better than the smell of manure. His father's fantasies were good ones.

That night they stayed with the farmer and his wife. She laid a table of warm soutzoukakia and mashed potatoes with melted cheeses. Nikos felt fortunate. He enjoyed the strong cumin she'd put in the meat cakes, cinnamon in the tomato sauce. She kept insisting he have more—more for a growing boy. Nikos had so many mothers, scattered as haphazardly as Greece itself.

Yannis judiciously drank their tsikoudia, the strong distillation of wine press pomace summoning creases in his face the wine itself never would.

Later the woman went upstairs to fix them a place to sleep and his father asked Nikos, "How many H&K MP5s do you think we can fit in a washing machine?"

* * *

From a terminal of McCarren International Airport Ivan watched sunrise subsume the awesome glow of the Las Vegas Strip.

Yannis was right about Ariel Sharon. Less than two years later he and a thousand of Israel's green uniformed IDF pranced through the sacred Temple Mount, Sharon unable to restrain his typical inflammatory rhetoric. It didn't matter if Arafat *did* officially approve the visit, nor that Palestinian violence was already planned. Sharon got credit for inciting the Second Intifada and Israelis still elected him Prime Minister the following year.

Old history now. Ivan let out a long breath.

He still remembered the name on the passport in the safe deposit box in Jaffa. It was still there, updated over the years. Today he was Stevenson, a special section government contract, authorized through what remained of Operation Stellarwind, D634-L8 clearance enabled. Today he would share drinks with officials as friends.

When the flight took off he was surrounded by forty other top-secret government workers as diverse and plain as the complement of a Detroit city bus. Their ordinary appearance reflected the ironic search for Number 7, which should have presented no problem. Yet here Ivan was, chasing down a far more intriguing mystery that had quickly gone beyond unassuming Seattle. So much for appearances. Ivan looked at the disinterested passengers around him, eating or listening to music or working on tablets, and wondered how secret projects could be embodied by a scene so profoundly banal? He thought of sitting with his father and uncle in a Tel Aviv café, sharing drinks and enjoying the festivity. Identity is only as good as faith in it.

The pilot signed off with the tower and switched to unknown encrypted radio and transponder frequencies. They flew south for ten minutes, then abruptly broke right and made directly for the Nellis Range military airspace, disappearing into the black abyss of America's secret realms.

5

Dakota pulled with his arms and legs. He couldn't move. What he could see was pale and milky, and it occurred to him that he might still be dizzy. He tugged harder, but then his head hurt. The way a scabby wound would itch and burn, somewhere above his right eye. But he couldn't feel it with his hand.

He blinked his eyes to clear the fuzziness and tried to remember what happened.

He'd been dressed. He remembered that. Sitting on the floor and pulling on the rest of the clothes they gave him, over his arms and legs. Somewhere on the floor, after walking through that noisy arch and after a long, wide, huge hall with green steel doors. They gave him tan-colored clothes and a tan jacket that didn't really make him feel any warmer. Not when they pushed him through the doors at the end of the big hallway into a white and gray world of fences and wires and metal and concrete. A great maze of walls and metal pressing in on him.

He remembered this now because it scared him very much. The sight was now etched in his head.

There was snow? There was still snow, on both sides, when he went into the building and when he came out on the other side.

He had shoes now, with velcro straps so his feet wouldn't be cold. His feet were okay.

C-105. The policeman pointed and he followed. He craned his neck to see above the high fence. Walked to the middle of a large building with two fat ends, lots of chunks sticking out from the middle, and he thought of the way a dandelion grows, and you can blow away its white fuzzy stems, leaving just the middle. Each chunk had windows and he counted them. Three floors of windows.

Orientation is at the PAB tomorrow at eight hundred hours following mainline. Failure to appear will result in an infraction. Do you understand?

No.

He dragged the bedroll behind him by the corner of a sheet. Through a plexiglass slider then another one. Into a large room with metal tables and metal stools, all bolted to the floor in patterns and surrounded by huge steel doors with large rivets, three floors high. He could see all the way up to skylights so way far up it made him dizzy. Green doors, with black numbers. They were already counted. The huge open room smelled like cleaners, the green kind. He could smell animals too. Zoo animals that liked to play in mud. He thought of zebras and for a short moment he was happy.

Upper bunk! Do you understand?

Cody dragged the sheet into the cell at the end of the policeman's finger. There was a ladder bolted to the end of the bunk. He remembered that. Into his cell he dragged his sheets and blankets. Behind him he heard cheers and taunts and bad words and angry noise. He jumped when that big riveted sliding door slammed behind him.

Nothing.

The room had nothing but white everywhere. The metal desk, the bunks, the ladder, shelves. All metal, all white. On the desk sat a brown paper bag. Inside it he found sheets of white paper with lines on them, envelopes, a three-inch long rubbery pen, paper cup, shaver. He knew it was a shaver, a plastic one, and he dropped it because he knew the blade would be sharp, it would be dangerous. Soap in a clear plastic wrap like cellophane, a little toothbrush and a clear tube of toothpaste with clear gel in it. He didn't open it.

On the top bunk lay a gray plastic mattress and that's where he struggled to go. It looked softer than the floor if only a bit more.

He remembered that.

What happened next?

He couldn't keep his body from shaking. It shuddered, panicking. His whole body wanted to cry. What now? What do I do? Does the door open? Ever?

Laying out his blankets on the top bunk he found scratches in the paint. Colored scratches through the sick white paint, and he ran his fingertips through them looking for meaning or maybe desperately feeling for the feel of whoever scratched them, as if feeling the scratches could help him understand who else had been here. He noticed his fingernails had become very long. He felt the scratches with his fingernails, and it comforted him. There were deeper scratches, three of them, and the color of the paint underneath was green. Not dark green, not forest green. Crayola lime green. He picked the color out of he big yellow box in his mind and saw a person drawing. He smiled.

He remembered smiling.

And falling.

Down off the bunk where they'd forgotten to put in a safety rail and landing on his stomach and bumping his head. Hard.

That's why he hurt so much now. His head must have hit the stool, he decided, because when he fell, face first, he thought he could see that stool coming at him.

Everything was fuzzy.

Alarms somewhere, radios chirping. They cuffed his hands and feet again and dragged him. He couldn't see their faces, just the blue legs of their uniforms, face down. He was always pressed against something. If they stopped moving they thrust him stomach first against a wall, legs dangling beneath him. He couldn't see.

The air was cold, then wet. Dank and nasty, warm again, unnaturally, like the bus, not like the sun. He blacked out.

* * *

There was still nothing to see. He knew he was on his back now looking up. There were many long lights tucked in the ceiling corners, great big bright tube lights. He closed his eyes and the backs of his eyelids were bright red.

Breathing hurt and drool built up at the back of his mouth. He wanted to spit it out, even with no way to wipe it from his face, but the trying hurt and when he breathed that dirty air, a strap across the chest dug into his ribs. So his face stayed wet. There were zebras, he believed, where he'd come from. And here a smell like slimy mushrooms. The smell was worse than zebras in zebra cages and worse than monkeys, even monkeys that threw their poop, because monkeys do that, he knew. Hyenas smelled like this.

He could see the straps on each wrist and leg. They'd taken his clothes away but he couldn't remember being stripped. His hands and feet felt numb. He couldn't take the deep breaths he wanted. The straps pulled so tight.

Whatever he was strapped to must be metal. He decided it had to be because it smelled like metal. Metal had a smell, and a feel. The surface stole warmth from his shoulder blades and from his thighs and from his legs and from his butt. All of these felt numb. How long had he been here? Was it hours? It felt like hours. He cried.

* * *

"I have to pee."

"I can't move you."

"But I have to pee."

"I'm sorry. I can't move you until Mental Health approves it. They could be here tomorrow. If you're lucky, you won't have to wait until Monday. Here, try some Jello. It's red."

Beneath Dakota's head the officer had placed some sort of vinyl wedge. With the cushion, Dakota could swallow from a white plastic spoon small chunks of Jello the officer spooned into him. The officer was patient. Dakota could hear it in the man's soft voice, an older voice, like a grandfather's voice. He could see it in the man's green eyes. They were wrinkled behind bushy silver eyebrows. Anderson was his name.

Anderson was nice, but he wouldn't undo the straps. Anderson brought food. He sat in a tall chair that he wheeled through the plexiglass slider beyond Dakota's feet.

Jello was pretty good, but his stomach hurt now, his insides pressing with some urgency on his bladder. For a time he faithfully chewed what Anderson spooned into his mouth. All of it was soft and gooey and not always as good as red Jello.

"Why I got to be tied up?"

"For your safety. You're classified as a threat to yourself."

"They watch me?"

"They watch you, yes."

"With a camera?"

Anderson tilted his head to follow Dakota's eyes to a video surveillance camera just over the slider door, like an eyeball looking down at Dakota, a microscope and he a sample in a tray.

"Yes. They watch you with a camera."

"Why?"

Dakota tried to blow a lock of his dirty blonde bangs off his eyelashes. He struggled with his breath, the breath he couldn't get enough of to blow away things that tickled him. Anderson reached over and took care of it.

"Why do they watch?"

"They just do, kid. It doesn't mean anything. Try to ignore it." His voice wasn't angry, just tired.

An intercom blared. "Are you almost done, Anderson?"

Anderson looked at the camera as though it were a person's face. "Gimme a couple minutes, Shafer. He's almost finished with this meal."

The intercom came back. "Control's been asking why Suicide 2's slider has been open for twenty minutes."

Anderson waved away the camera and muttered under his breath. "Fuck Control."

"I gotta pee so bad," Dakota said.

Anderson sighed. "Yes, I know this. I'm sorry, it isn't me. They're watching me too. Only Mental Health can let you out. MHP. They'll be here tomorrow. Judy will visit soon, Brenner. I'll be here until two if you need anything. Not that I'm allowed to bring you anything."

Dakota started to cry again, quietly. Only large tears, no sound, a slow trickle across his cheeks.

"Do you want me to leave?" Anderson asked.

"No!" Dakota yelped, biting back his sodden voice. "Don't go, don't go, don't please don't go," he cried. He imagined a room without Anderson, without anyone, just the darkness of the plexiglass slider between the two large toes of his cold spread-apart feet. His body sent him angry news, itchy here and then deep chills. He clenched against the restraints, toes curling. He counted to ten, counted down and said, Please, please don't go. Warm and terrible, he felt it trickle over this legs and plink onto the concrete floor, into a drain. He went limp and let out a whimpering sigh because he'd lost.

"Feel better? Ready for more Jello?"

* * *

"How are you feeling today?"

She was in Anderson's chair. Judy was sitting in Anderson's padded chair. Judy, from Mental Health.

"Where's Anderson?"

"He's not here today."

Oh.

Judy was round, he decided. All sorts of round, roundy shapes pieced together. Even her dark hair was roundy. She had a tablet and it beeped as she checked things off.

Mr. Brenner, are you suicidal?

What?

Do you want to hurt yourself today? No. Do you want to hurt anyone else? No. Do you know what day it is? No. Do you know what date it is? No. Do you know what time it is? No. Do you know why you're here?

"Why I'm in jail?"

"No, I'm asking if you know why you're on Suicide Watch."

"Because I bumped my head? Can I go now?"

No. People who want to commit suicide don't usually want to kill themselves. But you didn't look for help—to change your mind. The officers wrote in the log that you were alone in your cell. This makes you a particular concern. You're classified as the highest risk level to yourself. If I feel your condition improves, I'll move you next door. You'll get one blanket, a smock, shower sandals and your own toilet.

Dakota didn't understand her. She babbled on and on about diagnosis. Suicidal ideation. Risk assessment. Unit team meetings. Classification reviews. That perhaps a cell to himself was a bad idea. That Brenner would be safer with another inmate while in population. She talked about reviewing this with the Facility Risk Management Team. Today? Probably not today.

Oh no no, no, he cried.

Probably Monday, two days from now.

Oh no. Please don't go don't go it hurts it hurts it hurts please don't go Don't Go! I'm sorry I fall down and I'm sorry please please don't leave me!

He squirmed and yanked at the straps.

"If you don't stop banging your head they'll strap your head down as well."

"Please don't go."

She was gone.

* * *

The lights never went out. All day. It was always day. Dakota slept in spurts but woke up because of the lights. Police banged their metal flashlights on his door. He was scared to sleep because he was even more afraid of waking up again and still being here. He pleaded for sleep. Begged the camera, the walls, the white walls, the angry lights, the corners of his concrete cube, and finally, he begged his body to sleep. He lifted his head and sank again, escaping sobs bubbling like a squashed jelly packet. Whimpered and begged to sleep and never wake up. He was tired and dirty. Tired and weak and the straps cut into his skin. At moments they felt so tight, against his wrists, his ankles, his stomach, that he thought he might be upside down and hanging and he couldn't be sure and it made him dizzy and sick. He vomited but it went nowhere, just dribbled down his neck. He wanted to cover his face with his hands and hide. Hide in a corner. Under a blue blanket. Blue because blue would be soft. Blue would be comfy and would protect him and he'd hold it, hold this blanket over his head, his face and hide and never wake up and he would dream and in this dream he would see Mom and he would be clean inside and outside and would never lie on his back again and never feel pain. Under a blue blanket.

* * *

Officer Russell's eyes were tiny dots in the middle of his whites. Russell's teeth ground together, tongue packing chew into a swelling under the lower lip. Russell held out a pair of handcuffs and sawed the teeth through the catch again and again as he paced around Dakota's table with a smirk on his face.

"You shoulda killed yourself, you shit."

Oh no.

"Shoulda just killed yourself. We oughta just leave you here til you die. Look at you. Shit all over yourself like a baby. Like a baby shits on itself. You're disgusting. Shoulda killed yourself."

Dakota whimpered in fear of Russell's voice. Russell banged the fat end of his metal flashlight on the edges of the steel table as he made slow laps around the small cube. When he banged it hard Dakota bucked against the straps, spit up through his nose, his mouth, and cried out, with his eyes shut tight so he couldn't see Russell.

Russell laughed.

Russell spoke to another officer on his radio. Really? he said. The surveillance camera feed is down? Well, that's just too bad. He said it with a sticky voice.

Dakota held his eyes shut very tight. He could hear Russell's laugh roaming around him. He could feel Russell's spitty words drizzle down on his body. He believed Russell would hit him with the flashlight. He pushed his hands and feet into the table out of fear that the flashlight would hurt. But Russell didn't hit him. Russell spit on the flashlight. He didn't hit him. That's not what Russell did with the flashlight.

Dakota screamed.

***

"He won't eat," the doctor said. Judy was nearby. "He hasn't said anything all morning."

"He looks like he's in shock," Judy said.

"How long has he been on strapdown?"

Judy checked her tablet. "Forty-two hours."

Doctor pulled at the boy's eyelids. Felt his chest, his arms his forehead near the bruise. He moved around with gloved fingers looking for something.

"He's breaking out, an acute rash," Doctor said. "Look at his arm. The barcode's probably causing it. I'll give him a non-steroidal anti-inflammatory."

Dakota lay still when the needle entered his arm. He believed a huge colony of fire ants had begun to crawl all over his skin and if he moved they would eat him.

"He can't stay on suicide watch," Doctor said. "He's in shock. He's going to suffer mental degradation. Physiopsychological effects. His heart rate's fallen dramatically. His blood/sugar content's too low, body temperature too low. Amazing considering how bloody hot it is in here."

Judy touched Dakota where his skin was breaking out the worst and also where his urine stung, itched and burned so badly that his eyes watered. His skin was bumpy, dry patches that stretched and peeled, sweaty lemony salty rotting smells, and a terrible tingling swept from his middle, burning and flaring up again and again. Burning so badly that he lay in terror of having to pee. It would run like a fire down his legs.

"Admin says I can move him on Monday."

"Where to?" Doctor asked.

"In with McCarty."

"Okay," Doctor said. He prodded Dakota's stomach. "I'll give him a sedative for now." Another needle. Dakota's eyelids felt stiff and then wet, pushing over his glassy red eyes like waves washing over sand before he lost consciousness.

* * *

When Dakota woke again, all of it was gone. Several minutes passed before he realized he could move, and that when he did, his surroundings were soft and comfy. He focused his eyes and pulled a blanket that was laid over him. A cotton blanket, woven with pale purplish threads.

He saw that this room had all sorts of things, and he was stimulated by all the color. His head hurt. He tried to sit up and his body also hurt and he made a sound. Not a loud sound, a soft chirp of distress. Being tied down for so long made moving again a novel and curious sensation, and not at all easy because he was stiff and numb.

Suddenly a huge boy loomed over him. His face was pockmarked, body covered in drawing, hair a curly black mess.

"You all right?"

"Uhh . . ." was all Dakota could manage.

"Don't worry. You'll feel better. It's just a tranque. Tranquilizer. Mood stabilizer, same crap. A gumball. Do you remember what they gave you? Klonopin? Seroquel? Remeron? Trazodone? Doxepin? Or the *really* good stuff?"

Dakota was suddenly aware of the boy's large hands seizing his wrist where a swollen red stripe encircled it. He was squeezing his fingers around it. Then the hands were on his neck, and Dakota panicked.

"Nope. It's not Simitrex. Heart rate's normal. You look pretty doped, though. Probably want some clothes, eh?"

Dakota pushed up on his elbows and found himself in his underwear. The big boy was going through a pile of laundry on the floor. He tossed Dakota a huge pair of gray sweatpants his little legs would be lost in. The big boy helped him into the sweats, one leg at a time.

"I'm Teagan. I heard the Code they called in C-Unit on Friday. By the way, it's Tuesday, squa, which means you were on strapdown for three days. Ain't it a bitch when shit like that happens on a weekend? But that's DOC for you. Gotta wait til Monday, cause nothing happens on a weekend. You've been out for like a grip. Maybe since noon yesterday. You were sweating really bad but tranques will do that to you. It's all right though cause you probably won't get PTSD. Hey, I made up your bed for you."

Dakota nodded. He tried to look thankful because he couldn't say anything yet.

"No sweat. Let me tie that off for you," Teagan said, and he pulled the drawstring tight around his waist. "They said your name's Dakota. The pigs, that is. Wondered if you were Indian with a name like that, but you're kind of pale, wasichu. For an Indian. You're in my teepee now, so I'm calling you Cody. That okay with you, Pocahontas?"

Cody took a deep breath. "Everyone they call me Cody."

Cody smiled. He held out his arms.

"Whoa. No huggin, Tonto. Let's just go one step at a time, okay? Save the huggin for your pillow. And the waterworks too. You gonna be all right?"

Cody nodded. He sputtered something unintelligible. Teagan, clearly a little uncomfortable, as if a strange and foreign animal had been foisted upon him, tried to size up his new cellie.

"You're gonna be alright, spud."

6

Out of the plane's window Ivan saw the angle of the morning sun pluck the Pintwater Range off the valley's surface. No alarms sounded, no turbulence, no electrostatic tingle to accompany his trespass into secured military airspace.

With Kinetic Avionics SBS-1, amateur plane spotters within fifty miles could track this flight as it dropped altitude over Groom Lake. Maybe they'd be excited, the caffeine of government conspiracy. The bird touched down smoothly and somewhat distantly from Desert Rock Airstrip where she was supposed to land.

Ivan thought it was a bigger conspiracy that a dried up pit was called a lake.

His fellow passengers boarded other transports to secluded black-bag offices scattered from Yucca Flat to Mud Lake, another colossal dry misnomer. Ivan's connecting flight promised a more exotic destination. He needed help, the search for Number 7 having hit a dead end in Seattle.

* * *

Maria Bonholler owned the Parenting License ID used to purchase Number 7 from the Genesis Life Solutions machine. She lived with her husband of nine years in a University District apartment. She had no registered children, which didn't mean anything. Kids are a big decision. Maybe she changed her mind, it didn't work, she forgot to register the kid. Or she hadn't used it yet.

After nearly seven years? What was the shelf life on GLS pill babies?

Maria Bonholler didn't exist.

This wasn't immediately apparent, but took little time to confirm. Very few false identities were perfect, something Ivan discovered years ago chasing CIA agents, who were more careless than one might suspect. Maria's was no different. A false identity demanded many disparate documents not only exist but correspond: birth certificate, social security numbers, education records, medical and immunization files, DNA profiles, credit and banking history, employment, and DOC numbers. Department of Corrections numbers in the U.S., for many years now, were simply assigned at birth or naturalization as a matter of course, probability of convictions as high as they were in a police state. Maria's DOC number was her downfall, belonging to someone who died after the PLID was issued, but before the GLS purchases.

Rather a bad oversight.

Ivan slogged through the rain on North Seattle's steep streets checking what he already suspected. The address didn't exist either. Not enough internet returns on her name, nor database entries, to be real. The weather soaked through his trenchcoat. He disliked Maria Nobody for living nowhere.

Using 4096 bit double key-pair encryption he sent this update to Glitch, along with his opinion that she would hardly be a lawsuit liability if her existence was a forgery. Maybe this was some black market thing, though Ivan couldn't fathom the motivation. He even offered to pro-rate Hizer Pharmaceuticals for one less corpse.

He shortly received Glitch's response: Stand by.

Waiting didn't irritate Ivan. Patience was not a virtue. Patience is contingent upon expectation and Ivan expected nothing. Patience became irrelevant, especially where he billed for downtime. He imagined Hizer was deciding how much they wanted to trust him when such a valuable commodity could hardly be bought or sold. All their money didn't buy his. Was that expected?

Even so, a month seemed excessive. Seattle was a pleasant city in which to spend leisure time, however, and when Glitch finally met with Ivan again, the Starbucks coffee shop booth seemed appropriate.

"We ran the name across GLS's database and found a couple more hits."

"Hits?"

"Transactions," Glitch said. "What's so funny?"

"You," Ivan said. "You and this language you've adopted to refer to people, procreation, babies, as though merely corporate stock points."

"You're killing them. What gives you the right to criticize?"

"Who said I was being critical? I just think the obfuscation says a lot about you. Maybe you think you're selling fertilizer for a lawn instead of a uterus." Glitch's right eyelid started twitching and Ivan wondered what he was losing—patience, dignity, or just sleep. "Get to the point."

Glitch drank plain coffee, an order so baffling in a place like this the confused girl asked him if he meant with *water*? Yes. Water.

"GLS says she purchased three products from their vending machines in Seattle."

"Products means pill-babies in your jargon, I'm assuming?"

"Are you fucking with me?"

Ivan ignored the challenge. "She purchased them at the same time?"

He shook his head. "A couple years apart."

"Busy woman," Ivan said, picturing a *No Vacancy* sign over the poor woman's womb.

"Quite." Glitch seemed about to say something else, but hesitated for over a minute with his mouth open. Finally he managed, "And one in New Hampshire."

"Pardon me?"

As before, Glitch's mannerisms were detached from his verbals in such a way that he maintained a line of sight over Ivan's shoulder, a blind spot, which made Ivan uneasy. He wished Glitch would snap out of it.

"Ms. Bonholler's maternal rapacity struck while visiting New Hampshire. A remote town in the boonies called North Conway."

"Must not be remote if GLS put a machine there," Ivan said. Glitch just shrugged. "Was the New Hampshire purchase around the same time as the others?"

He nodded.

Glitch wore the same suit as last time and Ivan wondered if it were reserved precisely for clandestine business. Did it make him look underhanded? No more than the disgusted smirk he adopted for contact with a blue-collar world. Or for that matter his voice, a blackened blunt instrument of rhetorical inflections that forced others on the defensive. Every word interlaced by multiple levels of half-truths. Had he and Hizer already run Bonholler to ground? If so, why did they still need Ivan? Did she keep buying pills despite failed pregnancy? Was she wealthy and desperate or just selling them? Who would *buy* them? It was true there was no guarantee a tailored trait would come up dominant instead of recessive, but this became almost a complete statistical improbability if the pill user wasn't the one whose DNA had been sampled.

Why New Hampshire, of all places? And don't think about sending me there and putting me on hold, he wanted to say.

Then it struck him. "The GLS machines, they take a blood sample, yes? The seed gets built from a DNA composite. Do you have the DNA on file? Can't we use that to track the actual identity of the purchaser?"

"Bingo. We thought of that. GLS doesn't keep the whole chain, just enough to assemble the product at point of sale. Which means we can't match it against NDID," he said, referring to the National DNA Identity Database. "Our lawyers say it's a privacy issue. Ridiculous, really."

"What are you not telling me?" Ivan said.

Glitch loosed an uncharacteristic laugh. "There's a whole lot we're not telling you. But I'll give you this much. The computer stores a hash-code return on the DNA build to verify customer. She's a different woman."

"Different in Seattle than New Hampshire?"

"Not the same any of the four times."

Which meant what? This could seriously complicate his search. He tried to conceal his frustration. Four different women used the same forged PLID—assuming it's not one woman with four DNA samples. The ID belongs to a third party, and its use is subject to loan or purchase. This was an unlikely scheme. He couldn't see any profit motive, and the card's systematic use was careless, sloppy. A local hustler who sells the card to someone in New Hampshire after realizing how stupid he's been? Designer babies for unlicensed parents? Was that even a hustle?

Number 7 would be hell to locate.

"So what?" Ivan abruptly said. "I don't see the point in going through all the trouble. Six are already dead, there's no class action, to use terms your bean-counters comprehend. Let's wrap this up. I have other things to do."

"Yes you do."

* * *

Help lay 380 kilometers southeast of Groom Lake. The connecting flight dumped Ivan in Bluffdale Valley on a dirt strip loosely connected with Camp Williams. The Uinta National Forest, visible from above like green moss on warped pine, was proof Utah had a rich ecosystem. Bluffdale was not part of it.

The shadow of the Wasatch Range covered isolated polygamist groups who apprehensively shared obscurity with an entirely different religious sect. The Utah Data Center could not be a more insipid name for the National Security Agency's most powerful supercomputer and decryption analysis facility. Four 7000 square meter cathedrals housed wall-to-wall Cray processor cabinets. A dedicated 65-megawatt power plant within the security perimeter fed its hunger and cooled its fever. Layers of stout fence and biometrically secured visitor center stood between Ivan and the contact who'd generated the ID dangling from his jacket.

Mr. Stevenson suffered from nerve damage and Crohn's Disease, which involved implants. Ivan's digestive tract misadventures were all triggered by more personally culpable means—sour sushi, drinking binges, disagreeable jobs involving dead children. But Mr. Stevenson needed a Client File Record excuse for all the wiring skeletal topography scanners found throughout Ivan's body. He refused to answer any of their questions.

To agency members who believed NSA stood for Never Say Anything, this had the ironic effect of corroborating his highly classified status.

Retinal pattern scans opened doors through conduit-strung hallways smelling of hot metal filings and kiwi peels. He found a small office with one sexy executive chair and a sad, plastic pot tree. Ivan's past turned from various screens to face him.

"Good morning. It's been a long time, Little Nikos."

"Ivan now. And not so little anymore, Uncle."

Ellison had gone completely bald now. He wanted to age like Sean Connery (and who didn't?), but had to settle for something remarkably close to Patrick Stewart. He'd been woken from a somnolent boredom akin to channel surfing. The immediacy of circumstance had always irritated Ellison, but this didn't dampen his instincts.

"Have you brought me something?" Ellison asked.

"Why can't this be a social call?"

Ellison gestured to his surroundings. "Not here, it can't be. Is that Drambuie I smell?"

Ivan pulled a bottle from a mostly empty briefcase. "I might have started in on it a little early. Long flight. Well, not so much long as tedious." He inspected the level through the brown glass. "Plenty left for you."

Ellison thanked him and poured into two coffee mugs. He then led Ivan on a circuitous route to a rooftop balcony. Ellison hated his office, the windows didn't open.

"I'm surprised you were allowed to bring it in."

"I told them it was your wedding anniversary."

"Did I get married? No one tells me anything around here."

"That's because here doesn't exist," Ivan said.

"I wish that were true."

The air's transition to a stifling heat was all too swift and entirely without humidity. If there was a horizon between amber desert and the sweltering sky it was gone, as though Vaseline were smeared across the panorama's lens. Luke Skywalker lost his foster parents in a place more hospitable than this.

"Let's call it a drink to retirement," Ellison said.

Sound of clinking mugs lost in the ether. "Mazeltov."

"Don't be an ass."

"You're not retiring, are you? Don't you have to wait until you're sixty-five like everyone else? I still need you."

"No one needs this." Ellison spread his hands along the railing and gusts rippled the shirt about his loose frame. "I can't retire, not from here. I'll never get out of here, will I?"

"No." It wasn't a threat, just the sad truth. At least not if he were left to his own devices. His masters changed, but Ellison's servitude remained the same. He was well past sixty-five.

"What happened, Nikos?" He held the mug by the rim, Drambuie one finger slip from staining the barren soil four stories down.

"What happened? Is this a big picture question?"

Ivan got no answer.

The UDC was an insidious masterpiece of oligarchy a long time in the making. To say no one needed it was to forget that very few people decided what everyone else needed, Constitution be damned. Here doesn't exist. Government agents never entered AT&T's San Francisco SBC building at 611 Folsom Street back in 2003. They never secured room 641A next to the communications switches and installed a Narus 6400 Semantic Traffic Analyzer. When ends justify means, Bush II denied he was responsible for the immunity given to corporations who sold every U.S. citizen's phone and Internet privacy. It never happened.

The sheer scope of investigation was staggering. Where the crime is unknown and everyone's a suspect, it's not the same as sweeping bullet casings into evidence bags. There simply weren't enough bags—not until the UDC, a facility capable of storing and sifting literally yottabytes of eavesdropped conversations and national security camera footage. Operation Stellarwind started with AT&T complicity, but it ended here with something called Deep Packet Inspection. Ivan wasn't sure how big a yottabyte was, but if it was measured in denuded cacti and evicted desert squirrels, too big by far.

That's how it happened, Uncle.

They'd each been sucked into it in different ways, Ivan believing he'd managed to escape. He wanted to agree with Ellison, that no one needed such a wholesale probe. Yet here he was, standing atop the government equivalent of spray and pray. This kind of indiscriminate targeting was anathema to everything he knew.

Ellison kept his focus distant, but Ivan knew he was deep in thought.

After a few minutes Ivan asked, "Remember Melina?"

"Who?"

"She had one of the barns, in Khalkis, you remember. When we sold the G3's? To the Mataj clan from Shkodër? They had some blood feud and came down to Khalkis, and we sold them the guns."

Ellison nodded. "Melina. She made the pastries, the phyllo dough filled with custard. Sort of lemon flavored?"

"Galaktoboureko. Yes, that was her."

"You know she died. Someone told me a stroke."

"I heard," Ivan said. "She was very faithful to us, to the business. I'd like to believe the food didn't do it, but she *was* a good cook."

They shared a somber chuckle.

"Didn't your father and her often . . . they were close, I mean—apart from business?"

"You mean did Yannis plow the field? That goes without saying. Many fields. No woman he couldn't seduce."

"You sound jealous."

"No." Ivan thought about it. "Maybe a little. Yannis was always good with women. He had that mischievous expression, like Roger Moore. Or Benny Hill. Melina liked that." Ivan pressed back on the railing, stretching so hard he yawned. "Right up until I shot her tomatoes."

It was Yannis's fault. They'd taken one of the G3 rifles, screwed on a muzzle brake, scope, and made adjustments so Nikos could learn how to be a good sniper. The gun was heavy, ground too damp, soaking through his shirt where he lay, chest going numb, summer bugs crawling beneath and swarming above. He was miserable. Yannis said these were distractions. He needed to be comfortable with what can't be altered, to focus. Focus on Melina's tomatoes, only 150 meters off. A good sniper, he said, feels the presence of time, the movement. Death's not just a matter of accuracy, but ultimately the order of things and finality in terms both clean and humane. Yannis told him, "In the field there are many bullets labeled *To Whom It May Concern*; a sniper's round has written on it a name and time of death." Ivan still clung to this sense of responsibility.

He told the story to Ellison, who nodded and asked, "Any tomatoes get hurt?"

"Eventually. I should have stopped after just one but, discomforts aside, it was too much fun. These were big rounds, temporary velocity cavity bigger than the tomatoes themselves. They just vaporized. Turned out every single tomato for two rows was named in that gun's magazine."

They toasted dead tomatoes and laughed.

"Melina was furious, withheld anything remotely intimate for months. Yannis said they were the most expensive tomatoes he'd ever seen."

"Your fault," Ellison said.

"Of course."

Ellison hadn't missed the point Ivan's story implied about indiscriminate targeting. "You think this place is a shotgun."

"Nearly a blunderbuss."

A klaxon sounded and something like a turbine spooling up rumbled the structure beneath them. "Cooling pumps," Ellison said. "The racks are getting some exercise." Before Ivan parsed the lingo, Ellison asked, "What are you working on?"

"The usual."

Ellison shook his head. "Which means I'll read about it in an obituary."

"You don't approve." It was the second time in a week Ivan fielded the vibrations of disapproval and though Glitch's were amusing, his uncle's were not.

"I could care less." Ellison again gestured to his surroundings. "We've already established this crypto prison is no moral high ground."

"Don't act as though you have no scruples. You didn't invent this machine, you were dragged here. What's keeping you from leaving? Go back to Israel."

"There's nothing for me there."

"Jesus!" Ivan loved Ellison, but his uncle's stubbornness worsened with age. "There's nothing anywhere. You *make* it."

"No, *you've* made it," Ellison said. "You've been chasing these people, looking for your father, for so long now, you don't even think about the cost or how you pay for it. This isn't like some hobby you indulge, work at the office and race cars on the weekend. You've lost respect for life, least of all your own. You play this dangerous game with gray area consequences."

"Uncle, you've said this before."

"And I'll say it again, as many times as it takes for you to—"

"To what?" Ivan realized, old as the argument was, he loved Ellison too much not to understand what this was really about. "You didn't care about bloodshed when you took payment for helping smuggle guns to the Osetias, or Bengasi, or Yemen, or Algeria. You didn't protest when those guns fueled riots against Berisha's government. I was there, I killed people! We—"

"Because Albania was a mess, Nikos! Because it was the right thing to do. Did you even know what the cause was? Maybe you did, but you were ten years old. You did it because your father's war had to be your war."

"I love my father, and that's enough reason."

"I loved him too. But this isn't Greece. You're not fighting for Greece, you're fighting to get him back. I gave up that fight, Nikos, and so should you."

Ivan felt energy surge from his feet up. "He's not dead."

"I didn't say he was."

"Yes you did. It's what you meant."

"Dammit." Ellison struggled with what to say and his frustration haunted Ivan with an eerie emptiness as vast as the silence that followed. The ticks and hums and damp emanations of the NSA's machine talked to the desert, hearing only the screach of raptors waiting for things to die. "All I'm saying is I lost him, and he hasn't come back. I believed I'd lost both of you. I emptied the barn, checked the drops, called everyone I could think of. Two years! Do you know what that was like for me? Two years before I heard your voice again. Why do you think I'm here? Because if they seize you again, I'm on the inside. I'll know what to do. But Yannis? I've looked. The CIA doesn't have him, not anymore. How long should I wait? For me the good old days are over."

For a moment he seemed ready to add more, but said nothing.

Ivan felt selfishness ringing somewhere in his head.

Ellison had all the resources but Yannis was his catalyst and suddenly Ivan wished he knew more about their friendship, but the wooden taste in his throat was the realization he never would. Ellison couldn't part with it. That ounce of his uncle's lifeblood dried up, and with it any excitement about the future. In his heart Ivan knew it wasn't about tyranny or inequality or political or social injustice. Were it that simple, Ellison wouldn't be employed by the NSA. He needed a purpose, and Yannis gave it to him.

Ellison finished his mug, stared at the bottom, and in a sudden burst of anger flung it as far as he could. Sunlight flashed off the orbiting ceramic like a heliograph. Sentry's weapons turned on the sound of its shattered landing.

He turned and leaned back on the rust, evidence that nature still exercised some authority here. "I'm sorry, Nikos. I'm sorry I don't have your faith. Maybe they didn't kill him. Maybe he's somewhere."

"What does it matter?" Ivan said it despite knowing it mattered deeply to him. He embraced Ellison. "I've got a plane refueling and waiting on a municipal airfield in Nevada. I came just for information, but it's clear you need to get away from here for a while. Think of it like an adventure, the ones we used to have. Bring a passport, any except the real one." Anonymity is freedom.

Ellison's smile seemed resigned, but the smallest spark of interest showed, the mere temptation. What was Ivan dragging him into? But that was part of the intrigue, right? In the end it didn't matter. Ivan needed his help, and Ellison had the hardware, experience and instincts to narrow the search.

Ellison glanced skyward, unmistakably asking forgiveness of the heavens, then at Ivan. "What can the world's largest blunderbuss do for you?"

* * *

Their destination would be Florida and Ivan was pretty confident about what Ellison found.

The algorithms pressed into service an army of silicon and fiberoptic nerves. A palpable hum coursed through the hive of artificial intelligence and perhaps Ivan understood the NSA's reverence for technical hardware. From exabytes of cumulative camera footage stored by the NSA the computer identified a common link using the dates and locations of the four purchases. The best image angle came from a surveillance camera over the entrance to a Walgreens drugstore. That she was also in North Conway made the shotgun search fairly reliable.

And it wasn't Maria Bonholler.

Ellison ran it through image filters and facial recognition, then cross-referenced with Homeland Security's massive database of drivers licenses, passports, mugs, student IDs and visas.

Sharon Paley. Slightly reddish hair, resident of Miami.

A processor in Ivan's right temple received the file transfer and software update, progress bars and diagnostics in his field of vision. He was surgically mated to what Israeli Arms' subsidiary simply called a Neural Rig. It was Ellison's project. Micro electrodes grafted into the skull bone received signals from Ivan's brain and controlled the processor. Power came from chains of thermocouples nested among his intestines.

Many years ago, when the U.S. learned what this top secret system might do for war-theatre weapons guidance, the Defense Advanced Research Projects Agency pressured their good friend Israel and bought out the entire project.

Ellison reluctantly went with the purchase, but not before outfitting Ivan with a mixed gift—state of the art Enhanced Environment technology and status as a guinea pig needing occasional updates. Advancing from DARPA to the NSA's dark infrastructure, Ellison continued to provide those updates to Ivan's Rig, as well as any incremental improvements he made.

Years of dependence on the symbiant system made Ivan feel naked on the rare occasions when it failed or crashed. When he received operational data it was no abstract scrutiny; the Rig pulled associated internet information and other stored image data, organizing it so the mere flicker of his thoughts could shuffle it though his peripheral or central field of vision.

Now Sharon Paley occupied his virtual desktop.

Demographic: thirty-two year old grade school teacher, married once, divorced once. Ex husband indicated he was the wealthier of the two by far.

Destitute teacher Paley has forged PLIDs and she buys designer pill-babies. For others. Using someone else's DNA. And brings the capsules back to Florida? Why go to Washington in the first place? New Hampshire? Does she get paid? How much? By whom? And what's the motive?

Is there a Number 7, and if so, where is he now?

Sharon Paley would know.

Ivan had upgraded the engines of his Bombardier Challenger 300, a pair of Honeywell HTFs, 6800 pounds of thrust each. Flipping the Master preceded the stir of hydraulic pumps and booting of auxiliary navigation computers. His system acquired telemetry data from satellites and synced it with onboard laser ring gyros. Ivan activated his flight plan with Ground Control and ignited both turbofan engines. The plane taxied out onto runway 12R.

Liftoff was uneventful, the throttle in Ivan's right hand belying the sheer thrust at his disposal. Droplets of water against the windshields shook and shimmied, sucked off the surface by forces outside.

"Challenger 318 Victor Foxtrot, twenty-four hundred feet checking in," Ivan radioed to Departure Control.

The Controller's response came back immediately. "Challenger 318 Victor Foxtrot, climb and maintain ten thousand, contact center 132.82. Have a good flight."

Ivan ignored him, setting his altitude selector for 45,000 feet to steer clear of commercial traffic. He turned navigation over to the autopilot.

He couldn't help feeling atypical fascination and attributed it to his destination. Miami was like a second home to Ivan. So much corruption, sin and retribution. And exercised so freely. They were his kind of people. His business card could say Hitman and they wouldn't blink an eye, a lucrative industry worthy of respect and approval.

Ellison cradled the dwindling Drambuie bottle in his lap. Uneventful or not, this flight was everything the man needed, a catalyst, and he closed his eyes as though on a Harley in the wide open.

Ivan wasn't certain he could reconcile the path of the last twenty years, but Ellison was wrong. Ivan did respect life, including a humane and final end. He sincerely hoped there was no Number 7.

At 490 knots he'd touch down in four hours and twelve minutes. Then he'd know.

7

New sunlight passing through the rain-drenched windowpane lent the Tackroom an aquarium atmosphere. Pat found Chris slumped in a reclining chair, one hairy foot propped on a filing cabinet steadying the whole affair, ziplock bag of ice pressed to his forehead.

"Good morning," Pat said. "You're in early."

"Uh-huh."

Pat shook the wet folds of her umbrella and slipped it into a stand by the sink. "Are you okay?"

"Sure. Back hurts."

In the sink lay a pile of coffee mugs the size of cereal bowls. Chris believed every cup of coffee deserved its own clean mug. An army of mismatched ceramic vessels dragged him through the long nights. Pat realized her only paralegal wasn't in early—he'd never left. She wouldn't bother asking why his back hurt, or what it had to do with the forehead. Christopher Gammon would ignore her. He wasn't rude, just selectively oblivious, his mental shifter in neutral, with sudden spurts of intensity that made him appear out of phase with surroundings.

Pat could have employed someone with more social sense, but paired with these inconvenient qualities was the sharpest unlicensed mind in Seattle. Chris's singular focus mirrored her own passion for helping those facing legal perils. Chris was worth every penny of whatever she paid him, despite appearances.

"Brenner file came over last night," he said.

"Dakota Brenner?"

"He gets the north wall." Chris's less-than-specific gesture found a space of sheetrock abused by numerous colored push-pins. "I made space, assigned a project number."

"Thank you." Pat checked the time and started cleaning a mug Chris named Bertha, the ample mistress with handles on both sides for when his insomnia required a two-fisted grip. Though Pat was head of the firm, she didn't mind mundane tasks that gave her time to inventory the work ahead. "If Mr. Bowers calls, I—"

"Reschedule. Put him on Friday."

"Yes, good. I'll have the Gilchrest draft—"

"It's done. I was bored."

"Done? Not filed, I trust?"

"Jesus. No, it's on your . . . your . . ." another indecipherable gesture. The ice bag landed on the office carpeting with a sloshy thump. Chris's thought processes outpaced any need to signal where he'd gone. He continued to talk while digging through an inbox tray filled with two inches of beach sand. "He's got a jurisdiction problem, but I can't find details explaining what happened."

"Gilchrest?"

"Brenner." Chewed pens planted in the sand parted and Chris exhumed and opened a foil packet of blue pills he swallowed dry. Pat hoped they weren't Demerols, which would render him useless the rest of the day. Chris seemed to read her mind, rolling his eyes. "It's just Percocet."

"Is Percocet worse than the other pills?"

"Only with whiskey, which you've hidden in the conference room."

"Should I get it?"

Chris seemed to consider the offer seriously, then shook his head. "See, at first I thought some of the clerk's papers were missing. All the police reports are Seattle PD, but it's a Pierce County case? Something's fishy."

"Are we still on Brenner?"

"Yes. Keep up."

Perhaps not every penny.

"It's scandalous. There's no request for change of venue by either side, no findings of fact, no whatever." Chris looked around, unspecific confusion written on his face, as though eluded by his own train of thought. "I need coffee."

"I doubt that." Preparing coffee was a time-consuming process for the thirty-five year old.

Chris pushed both palms into his eye sockets and groaned through the gap. "Give me fifteen minutes. I'll send the file to Gibson and we can go through it, get a game plan together."

Pat tossed him a green REI mug.

* * *

The Law Offices of Helen P. Naughton were a modest affair. Leased on the tenth floor at 4th and Union in Seattle's business district, the suite was a quad of rooms, utility indirectly proportional to size.

Tall shelves surrounded reception, lined with legal case volumes, their aging tan and green spines numbered along bands of dark ochre. A lawyer's wallpaper, true, but unlike her younger colleagues, Pat collected the books from the time she started practicing law forty years ago, not a surplus sale.

Two adjoining walls of glass looking over Puget Sound provided a stunning view from her conference room. The room had presumably been built around the huge mahogany table at its center. Made cozy by plush leather chairs, the wood exuded a rich aroma of the cigar smoke of previous tenants' negotiations. Pat felt badly for having mitered its surface to inlay glass electronics—the standard for modern conferencing—but she simply couldn't replace it. The table wouldn't budge.

The Tackroom was where the real work of Pat's firm was done. Part utility corner, Chris commandeered it and over a period of ten years filled the space with accoutrements designed to pacify his obsessive-compulsive traits. The cappuccino machine, for instance, a brass antique monstrosity of plumbing rescued from a bistro and dragged up nine flights of stairs on a day the elevators were down for repair. Its operation baffled Pat, but Chris rolled valves with familiarity. There were worse drugs, she decided, and the benefits of having an in-house barista outweighed Chris's annoying idiosyncrasies.

His habits included a pedantic need to visualize each case. Chris printed off core documents, tacking them to the walls—hence the room's name—lacing colored strings between tacks according to timing, sequence, relationship or by some other criteria he never bothered to explain. When a case progressed poorly, Chris would add the defendant's photo to the mess to galvanize his efforts, hinting at an empathetic connection to humans his behavior seldom demonstrated.

When juggling a number of appeals simultaneously the Tackroom's paper-cluttered walls resembled the movie script stereotype of a psychopathic stalker's shrine.

Chris reluctantly ceded space for a Gesture Interface Projection wall so Pat, who didn't mind visualization but wouldn't squint to read the papered walls, could more easily consult with him. Despite his preference for the tactile, Gibson grew on Chris, the name he assigned to the wall in honor of a computer in a cult-favorite-movie from before his time. The system could interpret a number of human gestures with eerie accuracy using field scanning. To Chris it became another novelty, like the unsolved Rubik's cube sitting in the sandy inbox.

* * *

Four hundred milligrams of Brazilian roasted caffeine did much to counteract whatever restless stupor the night inflicted on Chris. He'd even combed his brown hair back from the half-mohawk of desk napping. On the wall Gibson sorted document tabs chronicling a small boy's odyssey through the criminal justice system.

"I hate to dampen your efforts, Chris, but unless defense counsel made objections, jurisdiction is presumed waved."

Jurisdiction meant which county court had authority to oversee prosecution of Dakota Brenner, generally the county in which the crime occurred unless a change of venue request was granted due to media attention or other reasons. Of course any court could assume jurisdiction, particularly in child sex cases where location of the crime was seldom recalled with certainty by underage victims. Attorneys often didn't contest jurisdiction because it wouldn't matter—forest for the trees, in the long run. Pat was accustomed to appellate records with no objections.

Standing five feet from the GIP wall, Chris flicked a finger at the first tab, initial police report expanding to center. "Seattle PD files this, King County prosecutors pick up the case, Brenner's charged by information, numerous counts for allegedly sexually assaulting a fellow classmate, the case is assigned to the Honorable Judge Schraeder, who's a crooked crony shit, but at least it's not Pierce County, right?"

"I'm listening." Pat crossed her arms and tried to scan for whatever Chris was leading up to.

"Before he's even assigned an attorney," Chris yanked a second tab, "Schraeder recuses himself. No explanation. So does the next judge," third tab, "and judge number three changes the venue to Pierce County. Brenner's facing trial in Tacoma."

"Reason?"

"Gibson, page two."

Pat read the Findings of Fact and Conclusions of Law memorandum. Chris sped through the next page, back and forth looking for more details.

"Seems he played a little fast and loose with the facts, eh Pat?"

"What's paragraph six? 'Action is necessary in consideration of *In re the Matter of the Welfare of CKL.*' That's the only justification? Who's CKL?" When courts want to protect the identity of minors in civil or criminal cases, names are reduced to initials.

"Gibson, pull court file on *Welfare of CKL.*"

A progress wheel appeared, computer accessing King County's network. Then a warning popped up.

"CKL's been sealed, Pat. We need a court order to view it. I've got a template I can fire off today, if you want."

Pat held up a hand while she thought for a minute. Jurisdiction issues were good lines of attack when possible. King County Superior Court was no paragon of legal fairness, but it wasn't Pierce County, a court whose rulings formed the basis of entire law school courses on unethical legal interpretation.

If Pierce County obtained jurisdiction unlawfully due to inadequate cause, Brenner could get a new trial in King County where he had a higher chance for successful defense. Appeals, like everything else in law, weren't about right or wrong, just which argument had the best chance for success. Any other errors committed by the court would become moot. Chris was right on track.

Pat's first concern still prevailed, though, that this speculation was worthless if jurisdiction had been waived.

"You're in luck, Pat. Gibson, court docket for *State v. DB*, Pierce County number zero three one—" Gibson already dropped a new set of tabs down the right side of the projection and Chris swept the third file into view. "First thing Tony Wu did for Brenner after DAC assignment,"

Chris said, referring to Dakota Brenner's attorney from the Department of Assigned Counsel. "Not only did he object to jurisdiction, he filed motions to return venue."

Pat read the motion. "And Tony also asked to unseal CKL. Which the court denied."

Chris's profanities worsened as he paced. "CKL is an old matter. How does anyone's welfare, six years ago, have anything to do with Brenner? How could they deny the motion without looking at the file?"

"Oh, I'm sure the judge did look at it. That doesn't mean he let counsel see much."

"Isn't that unusual?

Pat shrugged, not from indifference, but recalling Tony's warning that this case needed her firm's attention. This isn't something Tony would have dropped, and Pat wondered if he'd learned anything further, perhaps even from Brenner?

"Let's find out. Gibson, call Tony Wu," Chris said, thinking ahead to the next obvious step.

When Tony answered he seemed pleased to hear from Pat, until she explained the call, and they both heard Tony's long exhale. Gibson authenticated Tony's request for audio encryption security.

"Obviously this would come up. I did find something but it makes no sense, so I am sure it's an error."

"What kind of error? What does CKL have to do with Brenner?"

Tony waited before answering. "I'm almost sure I'd be breaking the judicial order by even sharing this with you. I don't think I was supposed to find it." Another long silence ensued.

"Spit it out," Chris said. "The suspense is killing me," he added, sarcasm none too subtle.

"So, okay. Look, I drove up to Seattle and had a chat with my friend in the clerk's office. He found an affidavit dated two months after the order to seal CKL. It just certifies the transcription of proceedings as correct, and maybe the clerk thought it was inconsequential. Here's the thing, the document lists two DOC numbers associated with deliberation of CKL."

"Excellent," Chris said. "So who's CKL? Because I can't find any directory matches for those initials. Assuming you traced the DOC number through—"

"Dead end," Tony said. "Belongs to a girl born four years ago, doesn't even have a criminal record yet. If you saw the file date, you know the welfare matter is from six years ago."

"Which means what?" asked Chris.

"The number was retired," Tony said, "assigned to someone else, which I didn't think happened to old DOC numbers."

"It's rare," said Pat. "When DOC is trying to conceal something, a suspicious incident or embezzlement fraud, they use retired numbers to mask guilty parties. Perhaps this isn't so sinister, though. You said there were two numbers, which means CKL could have been reassigned."

Tony chuckled. "That's what I figured, but it can't be. The other number is Dakota Brenner's. And if this *is* sinister, a child's a bad scapegoat."

"And Dakota?" Pat asked. "Does he know anything?"

"Nothing."

* * *

Before hanging up Tony affirmed he'd tried to reach the boy's parents, but with strong vehemence the father had said neither would speak to him. Tony had never heard the word *lawyers* pronounced so pejoratively. Since the court assumed *in loco parentis* of Dakota, there was nothing Tony felt he could do.

Chris put milk back in the mini-fridge and tipped hazelnut flavor into a fresh cup of coffee. He offered to make Pat some, but she declined, saying there might not be time before leaving.

"Where are you going?" Chris asked, flicking her appointment calendar up onto Gibson.

"We. Where are *we* going. We need to meet with the parents. Since you aren't technically a lawyer, maybe he'll talk to you." Chris's posture crusted over. Pat rolled her eyes. "Yes, I know how much you love field trips. Find out if they can see us this morning or later on today."

Chris sat down with a crash and pulled all Brenners out of the directory, isolating address and number for a Charles and Lily Brenner, parents of Dakota. Chris yet again demonstrated oblivious insensitivity to Pat when Charles's picture came up.

"He looks like a pretty old bastard. Maybe he's the grandfather?"

Sigh. "How old?"

Chris waved a hand left, sending the demographic to Gibson. "Sixty-seven, according to this." He asked Gibson to search profile and sort by relevance within the Brenner project number.

Pat watched background data drop into sorted groups. "Here it is. They're licensed foster parents. Dakota's adopted," Pat said.

"Shit."

"Stop swearing, Chris. It doesn't mean the man won't know anything. If the adoption date lines up, Dakota came to them practically the day he was born."

"It's not that." Chris made a hand grab at his console and threw it at Gibson, transfer showing Lily's death certificate. "Little over six months ago. And here's a standard press release from Pierce County deputy spokesperson Fred Royer assuring us no foul play was discovered surrounding her death."

Which meant Lily was in county jail when she died, and that there was almost certainly foul play, if you asked Chris, Mr. Royer's impeccable record of obfuscation notwithstanding. Held on contempt of court, she'd died of natural causes in an overnight segregation cell.

When Chris tried to leave a message on Charles's answering machine, the line interrupted, followed by dial tone. Pat thought she heard a receiver and brief domestic noise.

"He's there," Pat said. "Shirt and tie, Chris, and nice shoes."

"Shit."

* * *

Twenty minutes after exiting Interstate 5 onto Marginal Way, they emerged from industrial shipping container wasteland into a run-down neighborhood, as many trash bags lining windows as glass. They took Chris's old Volvo station wagon thinking Pat's Audi might be too conspicuous in this outskirt of Seattle.

Chris despised formal wear on account of a childhood phobia to buttons. "They betrayed me," was all he would say. In the Tackroom's closet he kept an assortment of dresswear to satisfy various requirements, velcro or zippers stitched under dummy buttons, ties ready to cinch, the majority of knot glued in place, just like the shoelaces. Emptying the unfinished coffee into a travel mug, Chris drove in the brazen way one might expect of a prodigy who couldn't be bothered to pass University of Washington legal exams. If not for his participation at seminars where Pat lectured at the university, she would never have discovered him. Chris joked he'd eventually graduate *malis cum laude.*

A brownish, scrawny dog dashed across the road and Chris leaned into the brakes. The animal disappeared under the rotting porch of yet another house with no visible number, no mailbox, and no apparent occupants.

A few houses gave evidence of odd and even numbering on opposite sides of the street, though the even side was nothing more than tall grass abutting a compound fence, burned kitchen appliance rusting into a patch of weeds. By process of elimination they found a two-story with a tarp down half the roof, bicycles and a riding toy leaning against an aluminum boat and trailer with no tires. Wild deer brush separated the driveway from an overgrown front lawn with assorted stone flower beds in need of care. They could smell something burning in the distance, synthetic as opposed to wood, unpleasant like charred plastic. A scaly mess of paint pulled away from the warped boards of the porch. Despite this, a swing bench hanging by two chains had brightly embroidered cushions. A dirty welcome mat with sunshine smiley face invited them to have a bright day.

The doorbell didn't work, but a knock brought an elderly man to the door. Large glasses propped against the thinning wrinkles below his eyes, he told them he wasn't converting to Jehovah's Witness.

* * *

Had Pat understood the rock-bottom state of Charles's emotions, what he would do only hours after they left, she wouldn't have insisted the man consider civil action for what the jail did to Lily—money couldn't fix what Charles lost.

He did not receive Dakota's appellate team well, indicating in no uncertain terms his disgust with the entire system that took away his family. Perhaps it was only deference to Pat's age that prompted him to give them a chance. He later said only someone from his generation could understand how crazy the world had become.

"Are you a lawyer too?"

"Hell no," Chris said. "I drive the green taxi."

And it was to Chris that Charles unloaded his grievances.

Charles and Lily drove down to the Pierce County Courthouse for Dakota's arraignment. Charles tried to calm her, even though he shared his wife's outrage. The stenographer failed to transcribe the verbiage Lily hurled at the prosecutor and judge, and it got her a contempt ruling and jail overnight. Lily took medications for what Charles called a *dicky-heart*, a heart already enduring too much strain seeing Dakota in chains. The Pierce County Jail refused to provide the medication to her, even though Charles showed them medical records and prescriptions. Lily didn't make the night.

Pat worried Chris would respond poorly to Charles's offer of coffee but her paralegal's enthusiasm over the potential lawsuit Lily's death established gave Chris enough fortitude to be gracious and swallow even the most naked instant brand. Charles mistook Chris's behavior for sympathy, which it may or may not have been. With Chris it was hard to tell.

Later on Charles even let Pat look through numerous photo albums Lily made during the many years of their foster care. Pictures revealed a world very different from the derailed existence Charles now lived. Camping, fishing, smiles, colorful Christmases, even if frugal. Foster parents in Washington State were not paid well. People like Lily and Charles did it out of love.

The philodendron in the pictures now lay dead in its clay pot, yet crayons and Lego still collected dust in abandoned play areas of a living room filled with safe furniture, soft rounded edges, children's books along bottom shelves.

Only Dakota had baby pictures. The oldest children had graduation photos, but Dakota didn't appear with any of the other children. Charles explained that Lily and he had largely retired. Jessica and Ariel were their last foster children.

He said Dakota was Jessica's son.

"Her son?" Chris asked, surprised.

"Our grandson. He was so sweet, so smart."

Sensing Charles was breaking down, Pat said, "I'm sure he still is. He's at a modern facility just east of the Cascades. You could even visit him."

But all Charles did was shake his head.

In fact he couldn't visit Dakota. The Department of Social and Health Services stripped his parental license, and now DSHS had Charles under investigation, claiming Dakota's sexually assaultive behavior was learned.

"Why doesn't Jessica care for Dakota?" Pat asked.

"She's dead, from a drug overdose. It happened a while ago now. She was a good girl, but she had many problems. She was involved in something, I don't know what. The police know. Some knacker knocked her up, and then she died, lost the baby. Poor girl."

When asked who Dakota's father was, Charles just shook his head and looked away. At length Chris explained his concerns about the change of venue and asked, "Do you know who these initials belong to?"

It was as if Chris had a thrown a switch on Charles's hospitality, the old man's demeanor instantly changing. He told them to leave. Chris retrieved a business card and asked Charles to call if he had more to offer, but they were both hustled out the door, all the more confused.

* * *

'Jessica' was Jessica Lapinsky, and Chris had difficulty tracking her path through foster care homes. She'd been with the Brenners the longest, almost a decade. Before that, a home in Renton, from which she'd been abruptly moved with no indication why.

"I've got it," Chris said an hour later. He flicked an old *Seattle Times* article up onto Gibson.

"Give me the digest version."

"Seattle police chief ten years ago is accused of sexually abusing a foster child in Renton. Everyone denies it, yada yada yada, investigation yields nothing, no surprise," Chris doing scene-montage in scornful fast-forward, "attributed to the child's drug use, problems at home, child is moved from the foster home."

Pat digested this for a moment. "We don't know that it's Jessica. We don't even know if the child in the article is female. I admit it bears some indicia of coincidence, but—"

"The judge who handled the inquest," Chris said, cutting her off, "is Douglas Schraeder, who everyone suspects is still on the police chief's payroll, even if no one can prove it."

Now it was her turn to swear. This was more than coincidence. More still that Schraeder also sealed the docket for *In the Matter of the Welfare of CKL.* It was no secret that Schraeder and the Chief's political friendship went back many years, with no small amount of favoritism.

"Do you suppose Dakota Brenner's the chief's son?" Chris asked.

"No. Jessica would have been too young to conceive. The timing doesn't line up, even if her allegations were true."

"And if he was? He could still have been abusing her years after the allegations were dismissed. He probably threatened her."

Pat sighed. "It seems far-fetched, even with the police chief's impunity for the law. Exceedingly careless and unlikely."

"Among their chiefs, impunity and carelessness has a precedent. Remember Brame?"

David Brame, 2003. Killed his wife in a parking lot in front of their young kids, then shot himself. Subsequent investigation revealed shocking police corruption, including concealed and buried unstable psych profile reports on Brame.

"I don't think it lines up," Pat said. "Something feels wrong. Besides, Brame was the Tacoma police chief, not Seattle."

"Ah yes. I see the distinction."

Pat was sure he didn't. "Charles was certain Jessica had drug problems."

"Thanks for reminding me." Chris spun around and sent Gibson another document. "Jessica's certificate of death. Brought to an emergency room in Seattle having polluted herself intravenously, claimed she was saving her unborn baby, but they both died. This coding here," he pointed, "means a police report was filed in conjunction."

"Let's see the report."

"No such luck. It's sealed with the CKL docket. Probably says the fetus shared the chief's DNA, and that he gave Jessica the drugs," Chris joked.

Pat had trouble finding humor in this. At some point they needed to catch a break so they could pursue the strongest appeal for Brenner.

"Charles probably knows what's in the police report," Chris said. "And he's been threatened to silence. That's why we can't get the truth from him."

Hand to her temple, Pat accepted the offer of coffee this time, and even considered something stronger from the conference room. She didn't relish the idea of contacting Charles again, but he was likely the only source of information. He had every right to be jaded after losing his adopted son—his grandson, actually—and wife to a justice system that to a layperson could appear cold and ineffectual.

Pat needed to convince Charles that whatever he was withholding might help free Dakota.

But whatever Charles knew, he took with him.

Three days later police retrieved Charles's body after a DSHS investigator reported a stench coming from inside the Brenner home. Self inflicted gunshot from a .38 caliber revolver properly registered in Charles's name, not hours after Pat and Chris had left.

Pat couldn't help feeling responsible in some way, and attended the modest burial on a cold day with rain that dampened the ground without seeming to fall. She felt burdened as the last person to see Charles alive, and that she should have been more sensitive. No one should die bereft and miserable. Solzhenitsyn wrote that the suffering of a prison sentence is felt by the family of inmates as much as by the inmate. A sister of Charles's at the sparse vigil assured her Charles died long before this, that his spirit went with Lily. Small comfort.

"How do you cope," Pat asked Chris, "even when the wrongs are indirect or unintentional, when the suffering isn't caused by malice so much as apathy, and chalked up to the natural process of law. Then someone tells you there's no foul play."

Chris tossed chrysanthemums into the grave. "Apathy *is* foul play."

8

"Swallow this." Teagan dropped a pink and white capsule into Cody's outstretched hand.

"What is it?" Cody said.

"Benadryl." Teagan reached over and grabbed a package off the desk. Cody could see little bubbles with more pills in them on the front and foil releases on the back of the cardboard sheet. He tried to count the bubbles, but Teagan kept shifting them. "Pigs left them for you. You're supposed to take one every six hours. I was kind of hoping they'd be something with more bang in them. Benadryl's just candy. You need something to drink it down with?"

Cody was still inspecting the tiny capsule in his hand. He nodded. "What's it for?"

Teagan stood up and reached across his top bunk. His hand returned with a clear plastic mug. A rather big one, half full of brown water. Teagan took a sip from it. Scowled. Definitely not too hot for the boy, he muttered. "Benadryl's a histamine blocker. For allergies. Itches, rashes, decongestant, sleep aid, or just because. I'm guessing they put you on them for your barcode. You've been scratching it on and off for a day now." Teagan pointed to a space on Cody's left arm just below his shoulder. There he saw a raw, red area a couple of inches square, and in it, a hazy bunch of black lines.

Cody took hold of Teagan's cup by the handle. Then gravity kicked in and Teagan's hands shot out to grab it before the cup emptied out over the bed. Cody needed both hands.

"Give me the damn pill."

"I'm sorry." Cody dropped the pill on the bed and shrank away. "I'm sorry."

Teagan saw Cody's sudden fear, and his face softened. "I'm not angry."

"You said a bad word?"

Teagan was bewildered. "What bad word?" But Cody didn't answer. "You mean 'damn'? Damn's not a bad word. Fuck's a bad word."

Cody suddenly looked like he'd cry.

"Open your mouth." Teagan tossed the pink pill in there. "Now drink."

Within moments both the drink and the pill were running down Cody's chin. Teagan leaped up and grabbed a white towel before the mess reached his blankets, then started swearing again. Really bad words this time, and now Cody did cry.

"Aw Jesus Christ, squirt. It's just coffee! You don't drink coffee?" Cody shook his head. "Everyone drinks coffee."

Teagan rubbed the back of his neck. Cody looked up at him like a puppy being scolded for peeing on the rug. He wanted Teagan to take back his cup and the awful stuff inside it. Teagan paced the cell and said things like holy crap and I don't believe this.

Cody waited.

He swallowed the pill with water. Plain water. It made his arm itchy, he thought.

"It doesn't come off?"

"What squirt?"

"The stuff it doesn't come off?" Cody pointed to his arm.

"No, it doesn't come off. Not while you're in here."

"Why it doesn't?"

"It just doesn't, but it won't always itch. Quit scratchin' it. You'll fuck it up."

* * *

Cody's first hours with Teagan were much like his first bicycle ride. The idea excited him, but the process scared him silly. Cody's head hurt from Teagan's many bad words. He still wasn't certain when Teagan was angry or if he just said those words because no one told him he shouldn't. When Cody asked about this, Teagan just laughed. His laugh made Cody smile, but it was a rough laugh, a noisy laugh, and Cody thought of a weed-whacker when he heard it.

Teagan must be a happy person. Magazine clippings taped all over the walls, mostly of cars, the fast kind. On his desk were pencils, colored pens, scraps of paper, and bits of food both inside and outside of tupperware dishes in front of a television that, Cody soon learned, never turned off unless Teagan was sleeping. Sometimes not even then. Coffee stains, lots of them, and laundry everywhere. It must be laundry because it wasn't folded, any of it. Cody couldn't even see any of the tan prison clothing in Teagan's cell. His eyes were drawn to Teagan's faded blue jeans, his light green and yellow shirts and plaid shirts in blue and black and white and checkered boxers and little red spots with black streaks and so many other colors. Cody could feel his excitement build and build. Tossed everywhere, anywhere, and if they hung, it was only because that's how they landed. Teagan's explanation for this was simple.

"Shit happens."

It does? Yes, it does. And Teagan explained to Cody what that meant. It meant that this was their cell, their home, if Cody kept what happened in here in here. Cody nodded, not really understanding. Including Cody's business, Teagan said, which was complicated. Teagan said he already knew Cody was a chimo, but that he didn't care.

"A what?"

"A child molester. But if anyone else asks, just say you don't want to talk about it."

Cody's eyes fell to his lap. He played with his fingers as if he'd just discovered they could overlap. He felt sick. I don't want to talk about it, he said.

"I'll bet you don't."

Cody had to think of him, Teagan said. If his friends thought he had a chimo in his cell, they'd make life rough for him, and Cody would be the first to go. Go where? Just go. Not my problem. So keep your mouth shut. Cody felt his stomach shift and bubble, insides gurgling around. Teagan glanced at Cody. Don't start crying squirt. You'll be all right.

Teagan made Cody cocoa. He left the cell and came back with crayons for him. He threw Cody a pair of guillotine nail clippers, and when Cody couldn't manage them, patiently clipped each of the boy's fingernails and toenails. He made Cody some cinnamon and apple oatmeal. Cody believed it might be the best kind of oatmeal. He found Cody a coloring book with cartoon characters in it. Cody scribbled away happily, inside and outside the lines, and if he left his crayons on the bed or on the floor, Teagan never noticed. Near the cell door lay a solid steel contraption mostly attached to the wall and from it came a lidless steel toilet bowl, and above that a small sink. Cody was sure it would swallow and eat him alive, but when he couldn't hold his pee any longer, he climbed onto it, discovering how cold the metal was on his bottom. He struggled with the machine's flush button, but like the whole hulk, it wouldn't budge. Teagan flushed it for him. Effortlessly. He called Cody a wuss. Teagan tied together the legs of Cody's huge gray sweatpants while his legs were in them and watched him stumble and plunk down on the mattress. Teagan laughed. He made funny noises and Cody giggled uncontrollably because he couldn't figure out where they came from, and he was enchanted by these things Teagan presented for his entertainment. Then suddenly Teagan stopped and backed away. He asked Cody when he'd last showered. Showered? Yeah, showered, Short Spork. But Cody didn't say anything, not sure why Teagan didn't understand that little boys didn't use showers. Never used anything but a bathtub? Not even in county jail?

"I used a wet cloth."

"Well, not in here. You stink."

Cody sniffed himself, somewhat unsure whether to believe Teagan. Looking somewhat mortified, Teagan helped Cody learn how to use a shower for the first time. Their tier took a wide loop around in a circle, and behind the stairs, were three showers. Between him and the dayroom was a railing, three rails high, and a huge drop. Cody looked down and felt his knees wiggle with weakness. He could see other children's faces far below. The other kids watched Cody trudge to one of the shower stalls. Teagan glared back at them and Cody couldn't make out what it was Teagan was trying to tell them with this look. The big boy turned on the shower. It gushed forth from a narrow head with a great blast. Cody just stood there.

"Get in."

"I can't."

"It ain't too hot. Get your butt in there and wash the guck out of your ears." He handed Cody a bar of soap, a blue one with swirls, and Cody traced them with his fingers.

He stepped out of his rubber shower sandals and was suddenly yanked back from the torrent of water.

"What the hell are you doing? Keep your shower shoes on, squirt! Do you know what kind of shit breeds on the floor of this thing?"

Teagan pulled the curtain on him, and Cody squealed as the water tried to drown him. His first minutes were terrifying, scared to stay under the flood, but sure that Teagan would be angry if he didn't. He rubbed his eyes with both balled up hands and felt the trickle and drip of water from his nose, his ears, down between clenched shoulder blades, and finally from the fine threads of hair clumping like a mask over his face. And suddenly it was okay. He took shallow breaths so water didn't go up his nose and he picked up the soap.

It was nice being clean. He smelled himself back in the cell. Lavender, just like the soap. He liked this smell and sniffed his arms, hands, the soft wrinkly flats of each foot and smiled. Teagan laughed and called him stupid. Which seemed okay. Teagan's voice meant good stupid, not bad stupid. Cody looked out a narrow window at the back of the cell just above the desk and saw that it was snowing, and his brown eyes shone bigger, features animated by this discovery.

"It's snowing! Teagan, it's snowing! Snow!"

His excitement was lost on the older boy. Teagan shrugged and told Cody to get his finger out of his nose. "Convicts don't pick their noses, squirt."

* * *

Cody didn't leave the cell for several days. He could see a large open space beyond their window surrounded by fences and razor wire and perfectly flat with the softness of freshly fallen snow. He wanted to track his feet through that perfectly unmarred blanket of white, and trace patterns through it with his fingers. Teagan told him the yard would be closed until the snow was cleared. Inmates were not allowed to make snow angels, snowmen, snowballs—not even piss in the snow. The last suggestion had not occurred to Cody. Teagan left every morning for work. He didn't say what kind, just disappeared through the huge sliding cell door and miraculously reappeared each afternoon through the same door. Cody would jump off his bunk and clap each time as if some incredible magic had brought Teagan back again. Teagan's eyes rolled, fingers running through his scruffy mop, still unsure how to take this absurd fanfare. Teagan didn't appreciate the depth of fear Cody held each morning that one day the big boy wouldn't find his way back. And how would Cody manage if he didn't?

One day, Teagan came through the door kicking a large brown paper sack. Cody lay on his bunk in Teagan's sweats and a white shirt, busy coloring on a page of a drawing book. Mickey Mouse was getting a green nose, and Teagan was swearing again. Cody stopped coloring, laying flat on his chest, his little feet kicking back and forth in the air above his bunk, fingers in both ears waiting for Teagan to stop cussing.

"I almost went to the goddamned hole today!" he yelled. The slider slammed shut behind him.

"What's that?"

"Get your finger out of your nose. What's what?"

"Whatsa hole?"

"You know, the hole? Seg. Ad-Seg. Administrative Segregation, IMU, Intensive Management Unit, solitary confinement, all that. Because some stupid pig wants to take my address book."

Cody had suspected there were animals in this prison, and Teagan had apparently seen the pigpen. Cody was jealous. Teagan held out a red-covered booklet with worn and dog-eared edges, curved suspiciously like his rear.

"I'm coming out of Property," Teagan continued venting, "and this pig, whatshisname Russell, wants to pat me down, you know, get his grope on, and next thing I know he's going through my address book one page at a time and reading my private shit." Teagan looked at Cody who had gone a little stiff. "Are you okay?"

"Imokay."

"So he's runnin his gums like he's going to take it because, well, just because, and I gave him a piece of my mind."

Teagan was busy stripping off his wet clothes now. A rainstorm, maybe snow, but mostly wet. The cold nights would turn the snow to ice and then new snow would fall on top, and everything would be even more beautiful, Cody thought.

"But I was ready to bomb on this dude, for real." Teagan made punching gestures in the air, then stopped because Cody still looked pale. "Are you okay, squirt?" Cody nodded. Teagan looked away and rummaged around in his desktop debris. "So I'm all wound up now. Need some coffee and a Seroquel."

"Was he angry?"

"Who gives a shit? I'm a convict. I don't waste my time worrying about some punk-ass cop's feelings."

Teagan's hotpot was always on. The dial was set to off, but steam formed under the lid. Teagan had jerry-rigged it so now the thing would boil on the High setting. For Teagan, breaking DOC rules was like a second language he spoke fluently. He poured water into his cup. Even before scooping two spoonfuls of Keefe instant coffee into the water, a filmy brown residue already staining the cup brought the drink halfway to color. He took his time. Sipped it. Scrunched up his face. Then chugged it.

"See, it's like this squirt. There's three types of prisoners." Teagan counted them off on his fingers. "Residents, inmates and convicts. You just have to decide which one you want to be. Me? I'm a convict. Take after my brother."

"You have a brother?"

"He's my half brother."

"Is he my age?" Cody asked.

Teagan grunted. "He's oldern'n me, squirt. He's doing time at Walla Walla. Life. Armed robbery is a one strike, and he had some other strikes besides. But he's cool. Adam's my role model, except I'm a nine-millimeter man, and Adam likes those forty-four magnum hand cannons. But Adam's a savage, believe that."

"Am I a convict?"

Teagan flipped some channels on his TV with the extended toe of his left foot. Chugged from his cup and belched. "You, squirt, don't even rank."

Cody took hold of his left foot and tugged the heel into his back for no apparent reason. But it felt good and he decided he didn't need to know what Teagan meant. "What's in the bag?"

"Clothing package," Teagan said, jumping to his feet. "My mom sent you something, too. I was supposed to get a meat and cheese package, but this is more important. I can jack meat and cheese from the kitchen. We had to fight hard to get personal clothing back in prison."

"You fight?"

Teagan balled up a carbonless paper from the bag and tossed it in the toilet. "Nah. Not me personally. Inmates pulled a work-stoppage over at the Reformatory, the one in Monroe. Pigs always cave when they're losing money."

One of the fingers of Cody's free hand became his chew toy. Teagan was relating details about a riot, lots of sentences ending in bloody. Cody didn't like the sound of it. He thought about flowers, blue flowers, and it calmed him down. Teagan pulled a new pair of jeans out of his bag, and when he tried them on, Cody could see that the material was laced with silver threads that formed quilted patterns and all the diamonds fit together evenly. Cody smiled to himself, and his bangs slid off his face as he turned his head sideways to change the direction of the diamonds. He wondered why cheese couldn't be wrapped up in the clothes to keep it safe and come in the same box? Cody's favorite cheese was yellow.

"Did you know cheese comes from cows?"

"Yes," Teagan said. He didn't seem interested.

"It doesn't come out like cheese; they have to make the cheese. Cows make grass into cheese . . . I mean milk, which they keep in their . . . is like a bag maybe but it's part of the cow and it comes down into four, um . . . they look like kinda like . . . "

"Udders. You're talking about udders. I know what they look like. Hand me that belt."

"We got to go and see a big cow farm with so many cows so they can't all fit sometimes, I think." Cody spread his hands to illustrate this astonishing number. "They eat the grass that's green and make it into milk for cheese that's white—the milk is white. I don't know how they do it. It's so cool!"

"I doubt the cows make it for cheese, spud. I'm guessing they had other plans and got robbed."

Cody rolled closer and sat up, his hands playing entertaining shapes in the air as he described the process by which these many cows were robbed. "They take turns and line up and the men they put these things on the utters, it looks like an upside down spider with four legs because cows they have four utters. They suck all the milk out, very hard so it all comes out."

"No shit?" Teagan adjusted himself.

"If the cow he only has four utters and I think he likes, he likes to get out all the milk because it's so heavy if he has to carry it everywhere."

"She. Cows are 'shes,' not 'hes.' The udder hanging off a male cow has white stuff in it too which surprisingly turns to cheese all on its own." Teagan had a nasty grin on his face when he looked up from tying his new basketball shoes. "Don't eat that cheese."

"I like cheese." Cody suddenly sat up straight, his eyes wide. "You know what I see?"

Teagan looked around the room expectantly, then realized he was chasing the idiosyncrasies of Cody's toddler-like speech patterns again.

"I see a cow, he pees all over this man because he's in this ditch, the man he is, and so he's under, I mean, the cow utters are, they're there, at the same height as his, the man's height, his eyes, I mean . . . " Cody paused, realizing the last sentence had hardly made sense to himself, never mind Teagan, who was looking at him with a raised dark eyebrow, the eyebrow that made Cody feel stupid. He decided that fixing the sentence would be too much work. "Cows, they pee so much."

"Can we not talk about cow piss?" Teagan threw a pink shirt at Cody that he'd drawn from inside his brown paper sack. "Here, put this on."

"Teagan?"

"Uh-huh?"

"What happens if all the utters they don't work? Does a cow still make milk? Where does the grass go?"

Cody had peeled his white T-shirt halfway off when Teagan said, "They shoot it in the head and make it into hamburgers."

Cody stopped moving.

Teagan reached over and tugged Cody's shirt off of him. Out popped the small boy's face looking very distressed.

"They kill it?"

"Yeah, they kill it. Where do you think steak comes from? Roosters?"

"But does it got to be dead?"

Teagan tried to figure out a suitable answer. There really was none. "Cows aren't like a bank, squirt. You don't take out a hamburger loan and mortgage it back to the cow to keep her alive. It's a cow's life, dude—ground beef or milk. Take your pick."

After thinking it over for a couple of moments and more chewing on his finger, Cody said, "It's so sad. I like cows."

"Me too, squirt. Medium-well with steak sauce. Now put this shirt on."

Cody was soon lost in the folds of the huge pink canopy, a small animal in a net. He gave up and submitted to Teagan's help. A moment later Teagan managed to coax Cody's head and arms from the sleeves and neck.

"It's a little big."

"You think?"

But despite his sarcasm, Teagan was excited. He pressed his hand flat on Cody's chest, and moments later, said it worked. What worked? When Cody looked down, he found a purple handprint on the shirt, and he couldn't help but clap in excitement and fascination. Teagan told Cody that his mother had bought it because she remembered having such a shirt as a child and that she'd never thought they'd remake them, shirts that changed color.

"But she's full of shit. They didn't have technology like this when she was a kid. Anyway, the shirt's yours."

Cody fingered a small logo print near the bottom of the shirt, and Teagan told him that it read Hypercolor. "It's mine?" he asked.

"Yeah. It works on body heat. You're a little toaster, so it'll work good on you. Like a mood ring. Purple means Pocahontas is happy. Something like that."

"Why you're giving it to me?"

"Because pink is not a convict color."

"You don't like pink?"

"No. Pink is for queers. It's all yours. Speaking of which, guess what else convicts do?" Cody just looked blankly at Teagan, who scratched the length of his taught ribs. "They don't sit around hiding in their cells like house mouses. They go to chow and sit together. You gotta start coming to chow. My friends think you're some kind of weirdo, which probably isn't too far from the truth. But I'm tired of bringing back food for you in my pants every night. Your probation period is over. You like spaghetti?"

Cody nodded.

"Well, this spaghetti is the most tasteless, watery shit you will ever eat, but it beats starving cause I am not putting that down my pants for you. You're going to show your face on mainline and keep your mouth shut unless you're stuffing bread, Jello or noodles in it."

Cody could feel prickly things erupting all over his skin and on the soles of his bare feet. He grabbed his toes and rocked back and forth on his bottom. His tummy got sick. "What if they ask a lot of stuff so I don't know what I want to talk about anything because I don't know who they are?"

"Jeez, was that a question?" Teagan looked dumbfounded. He reached across the island of blankets Cody lay ensconced in and bonked the side of the boy's head playfully. "Run that shit through the confabulator again, Einstein."

Cody rubbed his temple. "I don't want to talk."

"I'm telling you not to, stupid. I'll do the talking. Beats saying, 'Who? My new cellie? The pre-schooler? Nah, he's hiding under the bunk again.' Catch my drift?"

* * *

Cody held onto Teagan's pocket, his fingers inside and latched tightly. The ground beneath his black shoes slushed and squirted. Around him moved a great throng of children, all taller than he, staring at him in a way that made him want to melt into the snow. They were so noisy. One of them pinched Cody on the cheek, another swatting him on the bottom. He grabbed around Teagan's leg and pressed his face against him looking for help.

"Aw Christ, squirt. No humpin my leg in public. And get your thumb outta your mouth, we'll be eating in less than five minutes."

In the chowhall Cody took his tray, which popped through a slit in the wall. He wanted to say thank you, but there was no one to thank. He counted the lights on the ceiling. He counted the policemen. His legs swung back and forth, just off the floor, and Teagan did all the socializing with his many friends.

Later Teagan would ask him how he'd gotten so much of the sauce on his shirt when he'd hardly eaten any?

* * *

Back in their cell, Teagan unzipped Cody's jacket for him. Shook his head looking at the marinara painted canvas of Cody's white shirt. Off it came. Cody pulled on Teagan's pink shirt. He sat on his bunk and bunched the fabric in his little hands, marveled as it turned a light violet, then a dark purple. He pulled it flat on his tummy and watched the surface slowly fade and shift hues. All but one tiny spot. Where his belly button was. He couldn't imagine why Teagan didn't like this shirt? Pink was a pretty color. So was purple. This shirt had both which made it twice as good. Maybe they weren't his favorite colors.

Everyone should have a favorite color. How else would you know which shoes you like or which M&M's tasted the best or which shirt to wear to the zoo or what cars to count on road trips? These were very important things.

Cody kept his eye out for colors Teagan might like. Colors that might be his favorite. It wasn't easy. Everything in prison was white—dark white, light white, off-white, enamel white, bright white, moldy white, dirty white, old white, plain white, new white—and metal. Lots of metal. Bare, shiny, exposed, rusted. If metal was a color, Cody was skeptical. Metal was only pretty if it was shiny and it could reflect other pretty colors. Like his purple shirt.

His other clothes were all a dull khaki. White. Even the chow hall trays were simply beige. It left Cody with a pervasive sense of sadness. There should be more color. Everywhere. Even fish wore pretty colors. Like rainbow trout.

On a sheet of paper, a white one, he drew some blocks. Big squares. He used different colored crayons for each one and then drew rainbows, using each of the colored crayons in the right order. The rainbows went from box to box, like tethers holding them together, rainbow ropes anchoring his boxy-boats. He drew circles. And circles in circles. He took his time and soon filled the page with many-sided shapes. He drew flowers, blue ones with green stems and red ones with blue stems and green grass all around. Orange grass, too, so all the grass wouldn't be the same color. More rainbows. He drew a frog, a blue frog because he liked blue. Ocean blue for fishes. Then colored circles around the frog, red and yellow and purple and pink and orange and green. Lots of roundy shapes.

Teagan rolled over in bed. "Cody. It's Saturday. Don't you sleep in?"

"Look what I drew!" Cody held up his drawing proudly with both hands so Teagan could see.

Teagan sat up in bed and rubbed his eyes. He leaned down from his bunk and squinted at the page Cody held up for him. "Jesus Christ, it's a fagot parade."

"It's a rainbow world! I drew it for you." Cody was beaming. "Is so if you can pick your favorite color."

"Goddammit." Teagan flopped over and pulled the blankets above his head. His voice was muffled by the pillow, but Cody heard him say, "I'll pick a color later. Leave it on the desk. Go to bed. It's Saturday."

"I can watch cartoons?"

"Huh?"

"Saturday morning cartoons?"

"Sure. Whatever, squirt. Use the headphones. I'll be up in six hours."

"How much is that?"

"I'll be up at noon. When both hands point straight up. On the clock. Noon. Good night." Just when it seemed Teagan had checked out, he rolled back over, the lines of his pillow-embossed face visible over the side of his bunk. "And Cody?"

"Uh-huh?"

"Convicts do not draw rainbows."

9

Ivan flew low over South Florida with the sprawling Everglades ecosystem stretching for hundreds of miles below. Its peaceful beauty belied the difficult struggle between preserving South Florida's natural ecology and its erosion by a rapidly expanding population.

How Florida became a tourist paradise mystified Ivan the same way the idea might have humored the first Spanish ships who made settlements here. An early pioneer, Julia Tuttle talked railroad magnet Henry Flagler into laying track south along the Atlantic coast of Florida. He liked the idea of rich farmland. Speculators raced to drain vast tracts of the Everglade's marsh and carve it into property investments that would later go bust.

The naïve human desire to conquer nature still hadn't overcome tropical perils, but inroads, such as Walter Reed's discovery in the early twentieth century that mosquitoes carried yellow fever, made migration more feasible. A profusion of hotels soon sprung up which would later be commandeered for barracks during World War II. Domestic industries serving military training centers also sustained the influx of residents who years later marveled at the sight of Apollo missions pushing the next frontier from Cape Canaveral into space. Disney World and the Port of Miami cruise lines galvanized Florida as a vacation hotspot. A new species evolved, the Snowbird, retired elderly getting sunbaked and pickled in flip-flops and highballs beneath pink and blue neon art deco lights. Miami Beach was a thing. An eclectic mix of Cubans, Haitians and Jamaicans gave cultural contrast to a unique locale infamous for

Gatsbyesque decadence practiced by jetsetters and locals alike on the boardwalks and in the Bayside promenades.

Barely a block away, beneath the 395 overpass, a cardboard box shantytown of poverty reminded tourists that under Miami's colorful skirts lived the same miserables whose misfortune seemed inevitable to balance the grotesque wealth prancing around South Beach in bikinis and Ferraris.

Ivan's first Florida exposure was far less exotic and came just a few years after Yannis first initiated young Nikos with the nine-millimeter gift. A category five hurricane had plowed across the peninsular state, intense wind speeds in excess of 300 kilometers per hour devastating everything south of Miami.

Yannis found a 4Runner with a lift kit along A1A he was sure the dealership wouldn't miss. Half of the lot's new cars were scraped into the frontage of a Service Merchandise store. Strangely, the storm had declined to damage some of the rounded glass showrooms, an odd anomaly Nikos couldn't help noticing.

They drove through Perrine neighborhoods where uprooted tree and palm frond shreds obscured the point of having roads.

Nikos was shocked. Vegetative shrapnel splattered the cinderblock walls of homes with roofs peeled off, trusses dominoed across the top like the desiccated bones of dinosaurs. No fences remained standing. A mess of colored ceramic roof tiles pocked the muddied grass. Without the dense palm and tree canopy to shade them, the exposed coral hued homes stood like damns against a tide of debris including ride mowers, and even boats blown kilometers from any dock, all crumpled against front doors. In-ground pools under tattered screens overflowed with dirty water in which wheelbarrows and plastic riding toys floated. Large central air conditioning units torn from the sides of homes had been blown like bramble down roads, coming to rest in obnoxious places and causing Yannis to swerve the truck.

Clinging to denuded bushes everywhere were wet shreds of pink attic insulation. The din of a thousand home generators filled the air.

Nikos was still learning English. Yannis translated the messages spray painted on some of the houses, even though the meanings were unclear to both of them. *You loot, we shoot* and *I have a piece of the rock.* How could wind alone so completely devastate the area? What were they doing here? he asked.

Homestead Air Force Base was compromised by the storm and Yannis received information that a ridiculous stockpile of military grade weaponry was flooding into the black market. Yannis wanted a piece of the action. They were meeting a guy known only as *Carlos* to see what could be shipped out of the U.S. while police remained distracted by the chaos.

It was all in Ivan's memory now. Below his plane was no sign of the landfall menace benignly dubbed Andrew so many decades ago. Nature had proved it wouldn't be conquered, and life went on.

He intercepted the localizer seven nautical miles west of Ft. Lauderdale Executive Airport where Carlos kept a private hangar. Sunshine glinted off his fuselage even while ominous thunderclouds to the west drew moisture off the Everglades grasses, building in turbulence toward the coast. Brilliant red flame Poinciana trees dotted the urban landscape.

The Sunshine State was home to more Carloses than Colombia, but to say he knew Carlos of Florida implied only one man to those whose loyalty Carlos owned.

I'm looking for Carlos.

Quien es Carlos?

No, not Carlos. Carlos.

Oh, *Car*los! Si, señor.

A friend in the trade, Carlos asked Ivan if he needed anything else? A car perhaps? Sure. Nothing too ostentatious, something to cruise around Miami with, if possible.

Carlos would understand this. *Underworld* didn't really describe Carlos's affairs, for that implied a conflict between organized crime and society where police fought for the latter's safety. In Miami, police worked for Carlos. In exchange for complicity they received protection from drug lords, the least of Carlos's enterprises. Law enforcement was an integral component of the smooth flowing profit mechanism shaking hands with the tourist economy. Everyone was happy. Ivan couldn't help but respect the scale of Carlos's influence, which made the covert operation Ivan's father once ran through Greece seem trivial.

Inside the hangar waited a classic E-Type Jaguar. The car was likely older than Ivan but in impeccable condition.

Ellison rolled up his sleeves in the suffocating humidity. "Your friend has good taste."

"Yes he does."

***

"She's not a federal agent?"

"If she worked for any part of the government," Ellison said, "I'd know about it. Why does she have to be FBI?"

Ivan drove with the top down so he could hear the V-12 engine reverberate off the canopy of banyan trees over Old Cutler Road. Soft speckles of sunlight pierced through and rolled along the silver paint. Hand-laid walls of coral lined the road, over time becoming entwined in the aerial prop roots of the trees. Behind the exotic landscaping hid the estate homes of Coral Gables's wealthy.

Perhaps Sharon Paley wasn't a federal agent. Still, it was a lot of air travel for a schoolteacher. He reminded Ellison of this.

"So what? She likes to travel."

"Atlanta, Los Angeles, St. Louis, Chicago, New York, Boston, DC, Sacramento, Houston—and that's just this year. She never stays long, in and out. Is she sightseeing? Relatives? I think not. Besides, she can't afford it."

"Gulliver Academy is a private school," Ellison countered.

"Which means they pay her even *less*. Someone's affording it for her even if the credit card is in her name. The only expenses placed on that credit line are mileage and the considerable cost of designer babies purchased using forged Parent License IDs."

"Not entirely kosher," Ellison conceded.

"I figured she might be investigating Genesis Life Solutions for some government arm."

"She's not a U.S. government agent."

"Foreign service for the Brits?"

"I checked with them as well. Nothing."

"What about the Israelis?"

"Really Nikos? They don't give a damn about pharmaceutical kiosks."

The recent rainstorm had drawn out the smell of jasmine and ylang ylang. For Ivan, Miami's surroundings always possessed a fairytale exhortation. Like the masquerade ball where every woman was a mystery attended by soft smells, inviting gestures, and arcane etiquette. Behind the mask lay calculating schemes, debauchery and unscrupulous conduct taken to its zenith. Miami behaved like so many rich petticoats which, when lifted, revealed the undercarriage of poverty exploited by industry kings. During World War II, Philip Wylie wrote criticisms of the idle rich, *The men who have sacrificed most meet in Miami those who have sacrificed the least.* There was a time when Miami was the drug and murder capital of the nation. Not much appeared to change.

Was Ms. Paley a player in that game? "If she is a government agent, she won't need a physical office or classroom for cover. We'll know soon enough." Even at this leisurely pace they'd reach the school in ten minutes.

"And then what?"

"We talk to her."

"You know what I meant. Is she a target?"

"I'm not killing her, Uncle. My work's more diversified these days."

Ellison watched the Fairchild Tropical Botanical Garden go by. He didn't say anything but it was clear he wasn't convinced, a very stoic expression reflected in the side view mirror.

"All right," Ivan said, "Ms. Paley's part of the search, but there is a target in the end."

"There always is."

* * *

Gulliver Academy catered to children of the elite, its façade an architectural cross between Ivy League crests and southern plantation house. Kids in uniform polo shirts made their way about gardened outdoor courtyards. Sandstone pathways traveled through nearly uninhibited growth of palms and birds of paradise. Sharon Paley did have an office. They found it along a two-story stretch of classrooms extending to the campus pool.

"Shit," Ivan said, staring not at an electronic lock, but an old knob requiring an actual key milled from brass.

"Are you kidding me?" Ellison said.

"I haven't picked a lock in years." Ivan hadn't meant to sound so defensive. "How should I have known they'd be so antiquated?"

"It's an old school." Tumblers surrendered to a couple deft maneuvers of a torsion bar and rake. "You know what they say about riding a bicycle."

"Wear a helmet?"

"Don't patronize me, Nikos."

By the time Ms. Paley's class periods ended and she returned to her office, Ivan and Ellison unearthed from the woman's desk drawers a great deal of information. She was no federal agent, that was certain.

Ms. Paley taught Intermediate Biology, which could be ironic if the class covered reproductive science. When Ivan pictured the term *test tube baby*, though, it did not include the clumsy hands of middle schoolers siphoning expensive GLS sperm into petri dishes. The idea stretched credulity. Did the school fund research for Ms. Paley in addition to her teaching? This seemed unlikely, more a university level endeavor. And she didn't have the background suggesting a liberty to dabble in tenured research. The remaining accoutrements left Ivan with the impression Sharon Paley was not particularly erudite.

Her purse was the sack style of a sensible woman who knew life didn't fit in anything Prada. Ibuprofen, two prescription drugs, depression and allergies, neither made by Hizer Pharmaceuticals. A diverse array of cosmetics, everything from eyelash volumizer to an eggplant colored nail polish. Marlboros and butane lighter inscribed with love to the most beautiful wife—her ex had picked a circumspect attribute. Who divorced who? Ivan helped himself to a cigarette while he continued to rifle through Ms. Paley's file cabinets and desk. Nineteen numbers in a phone. Ivan ran down each through his rig looking for patterns, but her contact list was an ordinary mix of coworkers, friends and restaurants. Standard apps, no travel plans or flight ticket codes. No unusual recent calls, not entirely certain what usual would be. Chapstick, sanitary napkins, toothbrush, electric keys to a Honda, though not necessarily an Accord. She struck Ivan as more of an extrovert.

Three ring binders with old lesson plans more aligned with chemistry than biology. She must have filled a flexible slot teaching whatever was needed from year to year. Coffee stained Code of Conduct book from fourteen years ago propped up by a labeling machine. Pens, whiteout tape, two RFID entry tags to clubs in downtown Miami, one he recognized, the Spider Web. In the next drawer, resting on some dogeared books, was what looked like a largish eyeglass case, but when he popped it open discovered Ms. Paley's prescription was a chrome vibrator, model name Home Alone 9. Definitely an extrovert. Flipping through an Oxford Biology Dictionary beneath, out popped three Parenting License IDs, none in either her name or Maria Bonholler.

Hello, bottom drawer, bottle of cognac.

Ivan filled two cups when Sharon Paley walked in. No mistaking her amber red hair. Ivan instantly liked the looseness with which she fit herself into casual summer fabrics that still achieved something richly feminine. Open toed shoes, the nails carefully manicured and painted like a row of blueberries peeking from the modest pumps.

"Excuse me? Who the hell are you?"

"Please have a seat," Ivan said, Ellison closing the door behind her. "I understand you teach biology to eighth graders, which explains the Ibuprofen. I sympathize. But I'm not here for a biology lesson." Ivan laid the three PLIDs on the table slowly, like dealing Texas Hold'em. "I'm studying economics. Yours specifically."

* * *

Four hours later, inside the Spider Web, a narcotizing rhythm of music filled the dark spaces between stage performances. The club had the advantage of accommodating quite a few people while absorbing them into secluded enclaves that made it feel considerably more exclusive. No tacky attempt made to promote a theme consistent with name, although the drink couriers' black leather apparel gave them a sinewy arachnid silhouette against the laser lighting. Just such a one ascended into Ivan's booth to pour Pinot Blanc for Sharon, bourbon for Ellison and Ivan. She introduced herself as Katya and drew from the table's surface a holographic menu. Ivan couldn't tell from the names if the items were food, drink, drugs or prostitutes, and waved it away. Sharon, however, asked Katya to bring a bottle of Jim Beam. She seemed to act on impulses too spontaneous for regret, completely unfazed by Ivan's efforts to intimidate. Cornering her felt like throwing change in a pinball machine, which conversely got Ivan's bells and whistles pumping.

He'd expected an interesting explanation for why a divorced biology teacher jetted around the country weekly with borrowed DNA and forged PLIDs to buy pill-babies. The real story was even better than he imagined, the conversation in Sharon's office still fresh in his mind.

"Bioconnect?" Ivan had asked.

Sharon explained she acted as a chaperone to women all over, ensuring specific predetermined traits were properly programmed for each child and fertilization took place. For this she was paid under the table by a local infertility clinic, BioConnect Industries.

Ellison brought information up on a tablet. "They're located in the north part of Dade County, about a thirty minute trip from here. An hour if Ivan drives."

"I had the top down," Ivan said to Sharon, as though an excuse.

"Are you two cops?"

"Do we look like cops?" Ivan said.

"Would you tell me if you were?"

"Probably not."

"Figures."

Let her believe whatever she wanted. Sharon was by no means stupid. Ivan told her helping them might not even interrupt the disreputable business in which was engaged.

"There's nothing illegal about it," she said.

"Nothing illegal about carrying fake parenting licenses? Receiving illicit income to sheltered bank accounts?" Ellison went on. "And why are women all over the country paying for help operating a pictographic kiosk? Are they that stupid? In which case, why are you helping them breed?"

"They're not paying for anything. BioConnect pays them. They're just surrogates."

"They're what?" Ellison looked from Sharon to Ivan, the term meaning nothing to him in this context.

Ivan stretched into Sharon's office chair, placing both hands behind his head. "A surrogate carries babies to term for someone else. Sort of like rent-a-womb. And Ms. Paley returns to retrieve the babies."

"No, someone else does that. I just handle the first part."

"So you're a cutout. And what does BioConnect do with the babies?"

Sharon shrugged. "I don't know."

"And you figured this was legal?"

"I'm paid enough not to give a shit," she said.

Later on, at the club, Ellison would tell Ivan he and Sharon had a lot in common. Ivan felt the comparison meritless, mumbling something about Sharon's perplexing lack of maternal instincts for a teacher.

Sharon reluctantly disclosed Peter was her contact at BioConnect, but the company directory listed no Peter, which Ivan expected. Peter provided the entry RFID for the Spider Web where he owned a private salon, Sharon receiving instructions while under the pretext of clubbing. All his business was conducted from the Spider Web. What kind of business? Another disinterested shrug.

"He's probably not even affiliated with BioConnect," Ellison suggested.

"Let's find out."

On the drive to Miami Ivan hacked the Spider Web's evening list, registering Ellison and two guests to a booth the club's floor plan suggested would give them a good observation point.

While the club smelled of synthetics and the occasional odor of steaming appetizers floating by on serving trays, the subtle sensations were of imminent sex. Ivan wasn't immune. He found himself behaving awkwardly suave, seduced by Sharon's efforts to get him on one of the dance floors, then drinking considerably more than he'd intended before nine in the evening when Peter walked in with an entourage of well-dressed businessmen.

"The fourth and fifth are bodyguards," Ellison said.

"How can you tell?" Sharon asked.

Elbow on the table, Ellison's palm gestured his response. "The way they walk, who they look at. They're not paying attention to the conversation between Peter and the other two. The suit cut and shoulder posture suggest weapons under their jackets."

"Kimber 1911 semiautomatics, right-handed blokes, both of them," Ivan said. "The short-haired one has a knife, eighteen centimeter blade, under the opposite arm."

"Jesus." Sharon seemed impressed.

Less so, Ellison rolled his eyes. Enhanced Environment implants overlaid weapon scans on Ivan's field of vision, sophisticated enough to inventory all the rounds in each magazine.

"Who's Peter?" Ivan asked.

Ellison complained about the lighting, but managed to secure a reasonably good image for the CIA network to chew on. It didn't take long for the process to send back a profile.

"You're not going to believe this. A little truth in every lie. His name is Samuel Coletti and he *is* listed as affiliated with BioConnect Industries. As the CEO."

Sharon looked smug, but this revelation hardly lent credibility to the enterprise. "The other two?"

"Also business owners, both French nationals. One's a digital media distributor, and the other," Ellison shook his head. "It doesn't matter. Neither company is remotely related to infertility, unless they're just fronts."

Ellison swiped through several more screens of information, but Ivan decided they'd got what they came for.

Sharon and Jim were well-acquainted friends, and she drained the bottle on the way out with a tolerance bearing no relationship to her physique.

10

Suddenly the count light came on and Cody yelped, burrowing into the blankets. That light always scared him even after a month of this routine. Their room was almost always dimly lit by Teagan's lamp, or moonlight and perimeter lights, leaving streaks and bands through their slit window.

The count light came on and everything went blindingly bright. Two officers made their way around the tiers and checked in each cell door window.

Why do they have to count us? To make sure we're all here. Four times every day? Teagan had just shrugged.

Cody yelped when he heard the officer bang a flashlight on their steel door. "Bottom bunk! Show your face for count!"

Cody turtled his head out from under the blankets but kept his eyes bunched tightly shut. Tonight was worse than other nights. Tonight Teagan had plans. The way Teagan used that word implied all sorts of things, and none of them, circling around inside Cody's troubled head, felt right or remotely safe. The tension made him jiggle and shiver. He felt a cool tickly restlessness nibbling at him in his knees, toes, tummy, ears. Every part of him charged with fear and anticipation.

The count light went out.

Teagan rolled out of bed and his lithe body slipped to the concrete floor. He landed on all fours, not making a sound. Cody thought of the way a ferret, long and bendy, swings and jumps around, never making a sound. Teagan worked his hands under Cody's bunk, along the edge where the steel frame boxed in the space. In one swift motion, he'd placed his right foot on the edge of Cody's mattress, his other leveraged against the opposite wall, high up. He looked like he was leaping but standing still, and Cody focused on the veins in Teagan's foot, the moonlight from the window picking them out. Cody counted them, wanted to touch them. Teagan was busy ramming the tool he'd retrieved from under the bunk into the screw holes of the box that contained their cell lights, fishing out with determined twisting each oddly shaped screw.

"Cody, get the light so I can see what I'm doing."

"Is it gonna hurt?"

"What?" Teagan said.

"I said is it going to hurt?" Cody asked again.

"Jesus Christ. Just shine the light up here, squirt."

Cody pushed the blankets off and stood, his head nearly touching the bunk above him. He unclipped a plastic light and clicked it on, his small hands fumbling it, light bouncing everywhere. When he managed to shine it towards the ceiling, Teagan's long shadow pounced against the wall, and light sprayed over that dark corner where the steel toilet sulked. Cody tried not to have to pee after the lights were off because he was scared of the metal monster. Maybe something dangerous hid under the water? In the pipe? It doesn't, squirt. But how do you know? Can you see when it's dark?

"Teagan, if we get caught, so like if they see us, are we going to be in big trouble?"

"Uh-huh," Teagan said. So casually in fact that Cody's anxiety level spiked.

Cody pulled his knees up with his free hand and rocked, bunching and unbunching his toes. "Is it going to hurt?"

Teagan opened the box that held the cell lights and was digging in its gutter. Down to Cody's bunk he threw his tool, a blue plastic toothbrush that had been melted at one end to fit the screw heads. Next Teagan tossed down a funny looking chunk of parts with wire leads. Cody's tummy clenched, danced as if infested with crawly things. He knew there was a reason Teagan wasn't answering his questions.

"Is it going to hurt?"

Teagan leaped down and crawled under Cody's bunk. "Not as much as the spanking they're going to give you if they catch us."

Cody swallowed. "Wh-what?" Teagan's head was banging under the bunk, and he was swearing again. Bad words. Cody put his fingers in his ears and waited. Suddenly, he heard Teagan clearly.

"Take your shirt off, squirt."

"Now?" Cody peeled his shirt off. The cool air of their cell raced up his skin, and he felt sick. "I don't feel so good, Teagan."

Still under the bunk, Teagan just mumbled. "Dumbass."

"Teagan, I gotta pee."

Teagan's stirring beneath the bunk halted. Teagan said, "What are you waiting for, squirt? Permission? Go handle your business."

Soon they both sat Indian style on Cody's bunk, a pool of Teagan's collected items between them.

"Got the heebie-jeebies out of your tank, squirt? Cause we're about to get started here, and if you piss the bed, gettin nabbed by the fuzz will be small beans next to what I'm going to do to you."

Getting nabbed by the fuzz must be like getting pulled by the hair. Cody was glad he didn't have any fuzz. Just in case, he covered his crotch with his hands. "Is it gonna hurt?"

"No."

"Are you lying to me?"

"Have I ever lied to you, squirt?"

Cody thought about this for a second. "Yeah."

"So what have you learned?"

Cody's stomach heaved and he dropped his head. "It's gonna hurt."

"Lie down and keep your hands out of my way."

Teagan straddled Cody, legs tucked back on either side of him. If Cody had any thought about escaping this event, Teagan's considerable weight pinning his body cemented his surrender. Teagan set things on his chest. Their weight seemed to tunnel beneath the surface of his skin, and Cody tried to work his mind into a resolute state. Teagan looked positively eager, plans and ideas erupting all over and causing him to glow. Teagan was not really blessed with good looks. His pock-marked face took a beating from the beginning of puberty, from pimples, from drugs, and from just plain ordinary beatings. They left scars and crooked shapes in his nose. His hair was an unruly bird's nest. Teagan combed it, but this didn't really make a difference. He had, however, a sturdy chin, and this seemed to hold the rest together in spite of the damage.

"Hey, squirt, you can breathe, you know."

"I can't feel my . . . my . . . because you're sitting on it."

"Good."

With a black magic marker, Teagan drew a circle on the left side of Cody's chest and Cody giggled because the felt tip on his skin tickled. "Prolly put it here," Teagan said. "It's good and flat. It won't hurt as much there either." Teagan watched Cody's brows knit together. "Look squirt, it's kinda supposed to hurt. Otherwise it wouldn't be worth it, right?"

"I dunno," Cody said.

"This is important, spud. You're supposed to remember this forever. In ten years, you ain't going to remember being in diapers, tying your shoes for the first time, learning to ride a bike, your first hit of dope—well, you might remember that if the dope is good. The rest of that crap your brain doesn't care about. It'll be gone. But you'll remember your first tattoo, bro. Believe that. Why? Because it's going to hurt."

* * *

Cody was lost in a really wonderful dream a few weeks before this. A warm and sunshiny dream. He was with his dad in a little metal boat with metal benches, out on the water. He couldn't tell where the water was in his dream. Just water, maybe a lake. Dad cast his line into the lake and drew it in. Cody loved water, loved it more than nearly anything else. His toes were getting wet, over the side of the boat. He could feel the water rise and fall over the length of his feet as the boat rocked. He could hear the buzzing of dad's fishing line, buzzing and buzzing and buzzing.

Then suddenly the water faded, the whole wide lake before him crept into a shadow, a dark mud in his mind, and when he opened his eyes and realized it had just been a dream, he cried.

He discovered the buzzing was Teagan. Sitting at the foot of Cody's bunk, Teagan drew on his own arm with a very funny looking pen, and it buzzed. He thought it strange that Teagan was awake and wondered if maybe it was time for mainline already?

"Nah, squirt. It's two in the morning. Go back to sleep."

"What are you doing?"

"Wouldn't you like to know?" Teagan crawled over Cody, pushing the boy's head into the bed sheets like an animal, a big jungle cat subduing its prey. Cody wasn't scared, but the image of Teagan eating him briefly flitted across his mind. "Sit still and I'll ink you some psychedelic freckles."

Cody pushed Teagan off and the big boy explained that he was shading a tattoo, a Celtic cross and Celtic knots around his arm.

"Does it not fall off then?" Cody asked.

"Nah, squirt. It never falls off. It's permanent. Never washes off neither."

Cody traced his fingers along the swollen flesh at the spot where Teagan's Celtic cross stood blue-black against the angry red skin. "Do you like it?" Teagan asked.

"Uh-huh. You do this one too?"

"I did all of these," Teagan said, holding out his chest and arms proudly.

Teagan took Cody through each tattoo on his body one by one. The evil joker on his chest. Like on the deck of cards, but mean looking. Over his belly button he read off the word Peckerwood, and Cody laughed. Not that kind of pecker, dumbass. It means Woodpile. White Power. He showed Cody his twisted cross, and Cody thought it looked pretty. Teagan chuckled. There were scary skulls and lots of snakes and fire and terrible things scribbled all over Teagan. It was not as if Cody hadn't known these things were there. Cody pretended they were other things like frogs because frogs weren't scary. Green frogs.

Now he watched Teagan draw and curiosity overcame his fear. But Teagan flexed his muscles and grabbed Cody, who couldn't help screaming. Teagan laughed, howled, and Cody moaned, all panic and tears. Teagan looked subdued. Cody instinctively stuck his thumb in his mouth to calm down.

Teagan continued working on the Celtic knots. At some point Cody wiped his thumb on the blanket and said, "I like your teddy bear."

"Huh?"

Cody pointed to Teagan's shoulder, high on the right side.

"You want a tattoo, squirt?"

"I got one," Cody said, holding out his shoulder, pulling up his sleeve so Teagan could see the barcode.

"That's not a tattoo. That's a brand. To make you feel like shit. Because, Brenner seven-one-nine, you are a meat popsicle, a big chunk of sirloin—well, not too big a chunk—a lump of meat, FDA approved, throw the package across the scanner, discount on aisle six. That's not a real tattoo. I'll give you a real tattoo. Someday."

* * *

That word someday was one Cody imagined as being a long way off, yet here he was only a couple weeks later being straddled by Teagan and trembling at the idea of a real tattoo. Teagan laid little trays on Cody's chest, plastic ones left over from the grape jelly. Into these trays he poured ink. His homemade tattoo gun was a bent chow hall spork with a pen strapped to it, motor from an electric shaver, a guitar string sharpened at one end down the length of the pen, protruding where the ball of the ballpoint tip would be. Wires. Batteries. Scary.

Teagan wiped something wet on Cody's chest and Cody felt all his warmth wash away instantly.

"It's just alcohol, squirt."

"Oh."

"Would you quit squirming?"

"It tickles."

"Pussy," Teagan said. He dropped his tat-gun in the ink and the buzzing started. Ink drew into the shaft of the pen. It sounded like a bee and smelled worse, like rubber and nail polish. Stinking and buzzing, just like a bee when it flies close to your ear. Cody didn't like bees. Especially ones that stung.

Teagan's tat-gun was the stinging kind.

"Owww!"

"Jesus Christ. It's like drawing on mush. Think you could flex your chest muscles or something?"

"It hurts—what muscle? Where is it?"

Teagan stood up and showed Cody his own, flexing repeatedly. Cody couldn't copy the action.

"Pussy." Teagan kept tattooing.

"I don't like this, Teagan. Can we stop?"

"Awe, shut up, squirt. You ain't got much to cry about. I done some of mine with a knife. Granted I was drunk as a skunk or blasted out of my gourd on dope."

Cody whimpered. "I'm not crying."

"It's your story, dude. You could have fooled me. Here, grab my legs and squeeze."

"Huh?"

"Yeah, squeeze my legs. Just like that. It makes your chest tighter so I can do this right."

After a while it simply felt like Teagan was rolling a pinecone across his chest. Teagan concentrated very hard. He leaned over and his neck chain with the funny curled dragon on it touched down on Cody's stomach and danced around on his skin as Teagan shifted. This made Cody feel queasy, this tickly metal object. Teagan would bite his tongue while his stern eyes focused on his drawing. He'd pause, wipe Cody's chest with a rag, then continue. Cody tried to see what it was he was drawing, but when he pulled his head up, it pinched his skin and this hurt even more. He dropped his head back.

"Feels like maybe it's going to bleed."

"It is bleeding," Teagan said rather matter-of-factly. He saw Cody's face wrinkle. "It's okay. It's not bleeding much. You bruise like a fuckin grape, though." Teagan inspected his work, then looked at the time. "Let's take a break."

* * *

"Where'd you cut yourself?" Cody said.

"Huh, squirt?"

"Where you make a tattoo you said you do it you said with a knife?"

"Oh." Teagan rolled his left wrist over and Cody saw white, damaged streaks on his arm. "Jody. It says Jody."

"Jody made it?"

"Nah, Jody's my bitch."

Cody blinked. "I think it's a bad word."

Teagan shrugged. "Probably." He threw two butterscotch candies at the floor and peeled the wrappers open, adding the pieces to cocoa powder. Then he poured hot water into the clear cup, stirred till everything was dissolved, and then added some cold water to bring the temperature down so Cody could drink it. "But it's the truth. She's a slut, and I loved her—thought I loved her."

"What's a slut?" Cody sipped from the cup, and a fuzzy caterpillar of foam stuck to his pink upper lip.

"You don't know what a slut is, squirt?"

"Is it like a puddle?"

"What the hell are you talking about?"

Cody set his cup down carefully with both hands and played his fingers in the air to show the way snow falls. "Like snow. Like when snow gets old and mushy and slutty."

Teagan rolled his eyes. "Slush. You mean slush. Slushy."

"Uh-huh."

"No. A slut is different." Then to himself Teagan said, "but not by much."

Cody traced his fingers across the swollen part of his chest. He couldn't believe it was his own skin! Like an island floating on his body. The process was pretty scary, but he trusted Teagan very much, and so when he touched himself and it didn't feel like himself, he only worried a little.

"A slut is a chick. A girl. She sells herself. That means sex, squirt. She sells herself for money or drugs or for free just because. Got it?"

"So is Jody for free or for drugs?"

"Jody's for drugs, spud. Which is too bad."

"Why's it too bad?"

Teagan took a long time to answer. "Cause Jody's dead."

* * *

Cody chewed his lower lip as Teagan continued tattooing. He thought about mom's sewing machine. How it drew lines of thread into curtains, or around the holes of his ripped overalls. Different colored strings, he'd watched the head of the machine and marveled as the bobbin spun and the color on the bobbin made a line on the clothes. Now he was the clothes. He was just a pair of corduroy overalls and Teagan was the sewing machine. Teagan's needle put lines on him. Just like the sewing machine. He pretended when Teagan touched him that the big boy was pushing him around like that pair of overalls on mom's sewing machine. He wondered if the overalls could hurt the way he did now? They must, he decided. Teagan said he was switching colors soon. What color? Does color hurt?

"Quit trying to puss out on me. I mean, you've had it good. Just look at you. You're a soft lump of cream. When I was your age, I had a six-pack," Teagan said. "You grew up on cloud nine. Well-fed, soft grass and a playpen, eh? I can tell. Happy as a clam."

"Clams they live in the ocean," Cody said.

Before color, Cody used the toilet. When he stood on the concrete it froze the soft pads of his feet and sent blood rushing through his body, pounding just underneath the chest. It was traumatizing. Cody's tattoo was so tender he believed Teagan really had used a knife, like when he was with the slush Jody.

Color was no easier, and Teagan didn't show much sympathy for the way Cody hurt.

"Yeah, yeah. I've been listening to this song all night. Truth is, I could have popped you a savage ding-biscuit, and you'd have slept through all this. But what kind of hair would that have put on your balls? This'll toughen you up. I mean, don't get me wrong, I'm glad you've had a Mister Rogers life. You'da never gotten that tummy at my place. Do you know how many dinners I've eaten out of a can? Cans we bought at Petco, squirt, mixed with pancake batter, Alpo-Bisquick calzones, watching reruns of Judge Judy. When I was five, I knew exactly what transvestites and sluts were, and that if Jerry Springer ever invited you to play 'Who's the Daddy,' do not pass go, do not submit DNA. Just go straight to jail. The first time I was in the County lockup, I was only a few years older than you. Maybe I was eight. What the hell was I busted for?" Teagan stopped talking and looked upward while thinking. "Indecent exposure. That was badass. I took a leak in a Home Depot toilet, the display model. Indecent exposure, my ass. I told the judge I thought my tool was pretty decent for my age."

"What kind of tool?" Cody said.

"It was nothing, really, because see, what the judge didn't know is that while I was pissing and everyone was watching me all distracted and stuff, my old man walked out of there with ten thousand dollars in air-powered socket wrenches."

"Air powered? With windmills?"

Teagan said he got his first tattoo while in jail. He held out his left hand and showed Cody the stretch of skin between his finger and thumb. In the shape of a triangle there were three tiny, blue dots. Cody counted. Teagan told them what they meant.

"My Crazy Life."

* * *

I can't see it, Cody said. Teagan was busy washing the pieces of his tat-gun in alcohol and ignored Cody the first few times he asked. Cody twisted his head around, trying to see the tattoo, but no matter how much he struggled, he couldn't get a clear view of it.

"Teagan, I can't see it."

"I heard you the first time. Be patient and quit tweakin. You'll give your neck a complex."

Teagan boosted himself up on the edge of the bunk so he could put his tools back inside the light housing. Cody could see the patterns of his blanket impressed onto the skin of Teagan's foot. Like goose bumps. Millions of little mosquito bites, all lined up in rows. Cody started to count one of the rows. He wondered if they had a feel or if it was just like coloring?

"Goddammit, squirt—Don't touch my feet while I'm working."

Teagan got down and slid his fingers inside the elastic of his waistband. Looked out the cell door for pigs. Their cell was wonderfully silent and beautiful with moonlight picking out a half empty bottle of Mountain Dew, making it glow. Cody felt content, as if all things were in patterns, like the moon and the sounds and lines of time itself, and all the patterns travelled in circles, circles that made them complete, in every way whole. He felt himself part of this, and when Teagan drew, there was a start and a finish and now he was whole and the pain would go away. Go in a circle and move from joy to fear to hurt to healing in one continuous smooth path that made sense and made all his sorrows and heartbreaks worth it if he could sleep in soft blankets and drink cocoa. All patterns and circles.

Teagan lifted Cody so he could stand on the sink and look in the mirror. Cody's face lit up.

"It's green! You made a green, a green teddy bear!"

"Yeah, squirt. It'll look better, greener, when the mutiny dies down in a couple of days. Then it'll be as green as . . ."

"Boogles?" Cody said.

"What the hell is Boggles?

"Boogles is green," Cody said.

"Yes, I figured that. Where's your shirt?" They both looked at the floor. Typical.

Back on his bunk, Cody gestured grandly with his outstretched hands. "Boogles is green and he's got big white circly eyes that they go boing all over and really big ears so big he falls over and makes somersaults with his ears and his friend is pink—he's maybe a cat?—because he's pink and he has a tail and he lives in a tree." Cody went quiet and stuck his finger in his nose. "It's so funny."

Teagan let another six seconds go by to absorb this puntuationless monologue. "This is a cartoon?"

Cody nodded. "And in books and in cards and on my school bag and on my pillow, not this pillow, the other pillow at home."

"Jesus Christ," was all Teagan said. He plunked down at the foot of Cody's bed, and with his arm, cleared some space on the desk. A pair of nail clippers, two pens and a jar of Vaseline hit the floor. "Well, your tattoo is not a cartoon adventure. That's a serious piece of artwork. Please don't tell anyone it looks like Boogles. My old man has a string of these bears on his gut, which hangs so far over his belt these days he can't jerk off without pulling his arm out of socket."

Cody yawned and asked, "Will mom will she be angry if it doesn't wash off?"

"You got a life sentence, spud. What your mom thinks doesn't matter anymore."

"Okay," Cody said

Teagan pulled a small Bible from behind his TV and ripped a page from Leviticus. He unstitched the ends of a Lipton Teabag, dumped the hidden tobacco into the Bible paper, and sealed it into a roll with gum tongued off an envelope. From two golf pencils, he pulled rubber bands and the wood halves fell apart, exposing the pencil leads. Teagan took each lead, one at a time, and carefully inserted them into the two holes of the electrical socket. He took great care to not touch both prongs at the same time. He twisted a wad of toilet paper around a third piece of graphite and arced it across the socket. A burst of sparks lit the wad on fire and at the same time the lamp that lit their cell went out. Teagan had tripped the GFI switch. He didn't bother to reset it. In the darkness he brought the flame to his cigarette, embers burning on inhale. Cody lay in bed, yawned so deep his fingers tingled. The smell of Teagan's cigarette felt like part of the circle of this day, and Cody smiled.

The last sound Cody heard before he fell asleep was the low moan of a distant Burlington Northern.

11

Sharon lost her garments on the way through the kitchen by pulling as many ties, not making it to the bedroom of Carlos's spare multi-level condo on Collins Avenue. Ivan felt like an F-150, dragging her across the domestic appliances on his hitch. The woman was insatiable.

In the morning she left without any verbal formalities. Ivan found a note in the bathroom instructing him to call any time he was in Miami. He couldn't help smiling, even as he applied ointment to the wounds she'd inflicted.

Ellison met him on the condo's first floor where he'd set out a breakfast brought up from his early morning stroll past a bagel deli.

"Fish anything out of her? Other than her IUD, of course."

"I know why she got a divorce," Ivan said.

"That requires no imagination." Ellison looked disgusted. "What happened? You're supposed to be getting information from her, and she ends up feeding you the biology lesson after all."

Ivan shrugged. "She doesn't remember the Maria Bonholler ID. She remembers being in Seattle, but none of the particulars from seven years ago. She doesn't keep records of transactions. Doesn't know anything."

"Which is the definition of a cutout. Your focus will have to turn on Samuel Coletti."

Ivan helped himself to guava-filled pastries that were amazing. Most of the day would be committed to reconnaissance work, a word that implied something more exciting than the reality. Surveillance was a boring test of patience waiting for people who often never appeared. He pocketed some of the pastries for later.

"Why do you suppose she does this?" Ivan asked.

"Ms. Paley?"

He nodded. "She's not supporting a family, no unusual expenses. She's not being blackmailed."

"I imagine it has nothing to do with money. Why didn't you ask her?"

"I was busy." An excuse cheaper than confession. "I just assumed that, on a teacher's salary . . ."

"You do it for the money?" Ellison cut in. "Of course not. Sharon's probably seduced by the intrigue of it all. Chemistry, hormones, wiring, humans are complicated. It's not always about money. Teaching gives a lot of people's lives meaning. Maybe Sharon needed more."

"Thank god."

"Don't be so crude. There's no such thing as recreational sex."

"No?"

"No. Your father learned that when you were born."

Worse than a slap. Ivan didn't care for the direction this conversation was going. It was his own fault. Forced to admit why, he discovered resentment towards Ellison for knowing more about Ivan's father than he did. They shared secrets Ivan didn't belong to, going back who knew how far? Ivan imagined an extensive camaraderie and adventure solidifying bonds he could only struggle to compete with. He realized Ellison might miss Yannis as acutely if not more so than Ivan, like a brother, and did he deserve it? For what reason? The whole emotion was so childish Ivan felt a quivering inside, the mutiny of pragmatism against selfish needs. Yet there it was, smarting resentment. Surely Ellison could sense this but was too decent to aggravate Ivan further. Which only caused Ivan more shame.

"Do you know who your mother was?"

"I had a lot of mothers." It was a stock answer.

"No, just one. A simple girl infatuated with Yannis because he didn't tend a field. Ms. Paley knows that feeling. Yannis disappeared for weeks, returning from Hungary, Israel, Algiers, with odd gifts for her. He was exotic for a farm girl. And twice her age."

Ellison described the girl's peasant superstitions, bringing the neighbor's boy to sit on the bed sheets before Yannis returned, hoping for a son of her own. Throwing gold coins, rice and sugared almonds on the linen like her own mother had, evidence enough of the folly of Greek rituals. Yannis didn't understand her desires, overwhelmed when Nikos was born, and not married, infuriating her Orthodox family.

"We were a mess. And nothing's changed, has it?"

Ivan nodded, not sure what he was agreeing to. He never tried to give flesh or ethos to a woman called mother. The idea felt alien. In the vaguest recesses of his memory he saw a priest holding the hand of a dark-haired woman, a prayer more like scolding, a scratchy opera record moaning away from the open door across the room. She held Nikos's head on her shoulder, the warmth of her neck, reproachful tones of the departing clergy. Nikos was too young to understand the words. Just as quickly the memory slipped his grasp with the faintest echo of her touch.

Ivan paced in front of the large glass window that overlooked the beach. From so high up, all the brightly striped canopies and umbrellas looked like pieces of candy sitting on the white sand. "When did my father recruit you? Was he expanding business, looking for an insider?"

"Who says I didn't recruit Yannis?"

"Did you?"

It was a while before Ellison said anything, and it didn't feel like an answer. There was no reason he could fathom for Ellison's reticence, Ivan's history a blind spot, the smallest amount of dirt washed away.

"We fought so hard, always in the wrong war. Your father, his father, they're heroes, Nikos. Even your grandmother was a hero." A wretched exhale through Ellison's teeth. "It's not even fair to call her a grandmother. They hanged her on the side of the road before Yannis's first birthday."

"Who hanged her?"

"She was just twenty something. Greek Security Battalions, the German Army's bootlickers. Aris was a fanatic but it wasn't enough to overcome the wave of the Nazi war machine. I think they killed Aris and Seraphis. She was another tragic casualty in the wrong war."

Ellison's monologue degraded to pronouns, clearly not meant for Ivan's consumption. He tried to make sense of it. The heads-up optic of Ivan's rig found a possible match for the names. Colonel Stephanos Seraphis helped lead ELAS, an occupational resistance group in Greece waging guerilla warfare against German troops. *Aris* returned as the possible nickname of Athanasios Klavas, the less moderate friend of the colonel.

"She was part of the resistance?"

Ellison nodded. "The communist wing. You come from a whole family of dissidents and agitators."

"*Communist*?"

"What? Why would that be so hard to believe? *Communism* wasn't a pejorative during the war. Moscow Centre helped finance, train and arm most of Greece's resistance groups, except for Zervas's EDES. It was okay to be communist so long as you fought fascism."

"Was my grandfather a communist?"

"Try not to think of it like that. It's one thing to fight with communists, another to *be* communist. Picking sides during the war wasn't a simple matter of Axis or Allies. Churchill struck a deal with Stalin to keep Greece in the British influential sphere, giving the Soviets Romania and Bulgaria, even while his troops helped EDES crush communist-backed resistance fighters like your grandmother. The infighting and power grabs were unbelievable, many summary executions and torture. It's no wonder Greece fell into civil war."

"Yannis's war," Ivan said.

"Are you sure? Subversive blood drives both the best and worst parts of you, but these weren't any of our wars. Of all the things you inherit, don't become a pawn in someone else's war, trading one prison for another, fascism for communism. Better to be small hero in your own life than a casualty on the wrong side."

"I don't take sides."

"Sure you do. You can't escape sides."

* * *

The words hung over Ivan, even as Ellison began work digging through corporate records of the elusive Coletti. He struggled to recall fragments of history that pieced together what Ellison meant about trading prisons. Did he mean the prison camps? Of course he must. German concentration camps loomed large in the history of the Israeli people. The Red Army liberated Auschwitz on January 27, 1945, rescued by Soviets. Had Ellison implied fighting Nazis for Stalin replaced those camps with the Gulag? The world's next oppressive prison system? Or was Ellison being less literal?

Miami brought Ivan one step closer to Number 7, but he suddenly felt farther away, from something larger than a defective pill-baby.

Samuel Coletti owned the majority shares in Atlas Holdings. The corporate registry was ambiguous, but from its many subsidiaries Ellison guessed it was a shell company, consolidating the liquidity of multiple corporate entities.

BioConnect was one of these and just as Sharon said, they billed themselves as a fertility consultation service and surrogacy locator. Drop-off in fertility rates made this big business. People blamed diets, GMO foods, synthetics and plastics, radiation, and a long list of other things for human reproductive failures. Ivan didn't exactly have a Jon Franzien view of overpopulation, but believed nature had the right to tell people to stop breeding.

BioConnect had plenty of competition, operating on a profit margin that didn't sustain Coletti's net worth.

A second billing was Brickell Consulting, though what the consultations involved was anyone's guess. Advice was expensive, millions of dollars running through a firm with no offices apart from a registered business address at BioConnect Industries.

The third holding on license registries was the Coletti Group LLC. Beneath this moniker were two distinct arms, an investment and securities consultancy, called CG Investments, and a travel agency. At least it sounded like a travel agency. Offshore Adventures had no net presence, no offices, and no discernible marketing strategy.

What the company *did* have was a substantial lease on a huge toy. Offshore Adventures, using the considerable income of Brickell Consulting, funneled down through the Coletti Group LLC, maintained a 70-meter Heesen motor yacht.

Ellison contacted Lloyds of London for vessel classification and spread specifications out on a gesture interface projection coffee table for Ivan to see.

"She has every luxury imaginable. Zero Speed stabilizers, massive Caterpillar engines, fuel for 6000 nautical miles at 18 knots."

"Five decks," Ivan said, rotating the image.

"Lots of space for its pools, suites, hot-tubs, game rooms, bars, multiple indoor alfresco dining options, side and rear water level launches for sea toys . . ."

"I get the idea. Imagine what it must take just to air condition all that space in the Caribbean."

"Massive supplemental generators. Take a look at deck three." Ellison pulled the image over.

"A helipad. Does he have a helicopter to go with it?"

"Sikorsky 4-passenger," Ellison said, expanding more information to the table's center.

On a trip over the MacArthur Causeway Ivan got a look at her anchored two kilometers out on Biscayne Bay. He zoomed in the scope and found a black and green flag with yellow X on her stern, homeport of operation in Jamaica. At least three security men conspicuously walked the decks but never entered the interior of the ship. A tender made regular trips back and forth with well-dressed businessmen aboard, never Coletti. Ivan tracked and identified several faces but saw no common pattern. Most weren't from Florida and only a few had substantial luggage. Pretty brazen if the bags held narcotics, even for Miami.

"Coletti maintains a fairly routine schedule," Ivan told Ellison. "Nights he's ashore, early in the morning he flies out to the yacht. Trek data shows the vessel makes regular voyages through the Cayman Islands, among other places, but docks in Jamaica for fuel. Never registers any cargo, duty import, export, or files any customs documents."

"Corporate?"

"Plays a seminal role, at least from appearances. He has degrees in biochemistry and genetic engineering. Atlas Holdings is centrally his money, but he has global accounts. He can operate anywhere but leaves few records. Dual citizenship, U.S. and Uruguay—don't ask, I have no idea. Passport data is practically static. The yacht keeps him off radar, figuratively speaking. That boat probably lights up radars in Murmansk." Ivan caught Ellison's grin. "What is it?"

"The degrees he holds. Reminded me of something I thought when we discovered he wasn't Peter, but Samuel."

"Okay." Ivan thought for a moment. "Samuel and Peter are both biblical. Does it mean something?"

"But you don't know what parts of the Bible," Ellison said.

Ivan felt a twinge of annoyance. "Peter's one of the apostles. I'm pretty sure."

"Forget Peter, he's New Testament. Samuel is the better story. He's accepted as one of the prophets. Samuel's mother was Hannah, a barren woman who made a vow to God—if he would give her a son, she would return Samuel to the Lord in his service. And she did."

Ivan laughed. "If Hannah had BioConnect, God would have no hustle."

Ellison put his forehead to hand and sighed. "It's one of God's greatest miracles you've never been struck by lightning. I just thought you'd appreciate the irony."

"What else is our prophet Samuel hiding?"

Ellison flicked another file onto the table and engineering schematics spread out, zooming in to a wireframe inset between structural joins in the hull. Shortly after securing the lease, Ellison explained, Coletti hired a Dutch company to drydock and fit the vessel with a submersible deployment hatch just forward of the engine room. What Ellison didn't have was any record that Coletti purchased the submersible to go with it, though it might be masked as something innocuous.

"That's how he brings drugs ashore," Ivan said with satisfaction, his earlier hunch pretty much confirmed.

"Lots of vessels have submarine toys. Maybe not requiring a hatch this big, but they're fun."

"Be serious, Uncle. He brings coke onboard in Jamaica, ships it to Miami—a port *legendary* for drug smuggling—never making landfall. Operates distribution through his private salon at the Spider Web. Lots of money, no obvious sources, flushed around a complex hierarchy of shell companies. And the bodyguards?"

Ellison nodded. "What's the point? Are you interested in buying his coke?"

"Leverage," Ivan said. "His other business with Ms. Paley is clearly illegal, but he'll tell us where Number 7 is if we stand to jeopardize where his *real* money comes from. And we'll need proof. We can't just accuse him of drug smuggling without something tangible."

Which reminded Ivan that, before lobbing a smoke bomb into what was surely one of Carlos's associate operations, he'd better let the man know. He couldn't expect Carlos to confirm or deny Coletti's business, but his friend seemed unnecessarily cryptic.

"A man named Samuel Coletti," Ivan said over the line. "Do you know him? Operates a 220-foot yacht named *Estrella de Mar Rosa*?"

To a man like Carlos, direct questions were the epitome of bad taste, and he took his time responding. "I wouldn't have thought you were into that sort of thing."

"I'm not. I'm using his narcotics operation as leverage to get information from him. Nothing that involves you. If Coletti sounds any alarms, I need your people to ignore them."

Carlos assured Ivan that Coletti's business was entirely independent, that there would be no call for help. Carlos recommended Ivan pay Samuel a personal visit on the yacht, and with a wry laugh, suggested Sam's inferior product lacked maturity in the growing season. He wished Ivan luck and hung up.

"If he's doing good business in narcotics," Ellison said, "how does Sharon and that scam figure in? Where are the babies going?"

"You and I smuggled guns, not drugs. If there's a trade secret or something, I'm not aware of it."

Ivan picked up his glass, residual condensation on the table forming a ring around a surveillance image of Samuel Coletti. Ice cubes had long since diluted the Scotch, which went down with all the heady confusion of history. Yannis never did it for the money. Was it intrigue, the same as Sharon? Ivan expected Hizer to pay him, but what was he really chasing?

He stood at the floor to ceiling glass and watched the restless energy of Miami off in the distance. Hard to believe John Collins dredged this pernicious paradise from salt marsh and mangrove swamp more than a century ago. Or that a couple thousand years earlier all this was the inhospitable hunting ground for the Tequesta Indians. The only thing left of them was a ceremonial circle of postholes in the limestone at Brickell Point just across the Miami River.

Yannis would hate these people. If his father stood here now and witnessed the sea of luxury yachts dotting Biscayne Bay, the writing of George Sefaris would spill out of him all over again.

Souls shriveled by public sins,
each holding office like a bird in its cage.
. . . nemesis, fate . . . bad habits, fraud and deceit,
or even the selfish urge to reap reward from the blood of others,
. . . lips and fingers that hunger for a white breast
eyes that half-close in the radiance of day
and feet that would run, no matter how tired,
at the slightest call of profit.

Very soon Ivan would be face-to-face with Samuel Coletti, and while the goal was Number 7, Ivan genuinely hoped there was more substance to Samuel's exploits than profit.

12

Teagan yelled across the warehouse for Diana. Extractor 3 was loaded and ready to go. The supervisor took her sweet time, listening to Teagan yell.

"I love hearing you scream my name," she'd say. Cody sat Indian style on a huge, heavy wooden table folding one pair of underwear after another. He liked this job. Teagan helped him get work in the WRCC laundry warehouse right alongside him. Finally, Cody knew where Teagan disappeared to each time he left the cell in the morning. DOC referred to this work as a Class II Industry job, which paid more money than a tier porter job or kitchen work, if only a little bit more. Cody didn't really understand the money part anyway. He folded things—shirts, pants, socks and underwear. Teagan was responsible for contract laundry. That meant, while Scooter and the other inmates did only the institution's laundry, Teagan and Cody ran Extractor 3, dedicated to the laundry trucked in every morning from a state-run retirement facility, Cashmere Elderly Care.

"Diana! Quit screwing around!" Teagan yelled. He looked over at Cody. "Hey, you're folding them backwards. What did I tell you? They're all color-coded: yellow in the front, brown in the back." Then to Diana, "Come on, woman! Put your shit in gear!"

When Diana finally swung her head around, a blonde ponytail tripped over her shoulder, the rest of her pack a day school bus driver fortyish body following, hands on her hips. She strutted through the warehouse, running a gauntlet of tables with an annoyed look on her thin features. Teagan was enchanted by the way she swung her hips. Restless.

"I swear to God, Cody. If there was a pencil up her ass she'd draw a string of figure eights behind her."

"Eww. Gross," Cody said. His new favorite word.

"See how she's trying to look angry? But she's not. She's faking it."

"Is because she likes you?" Cody asked.

"That's putting it mildly, Squirt. Even old women need lovin."

The pair of underwear flat on the table in front of Cody seemed big enough to fit a hippo. He leaned over in each direction to pull the corners into neat folds. He wondered what size woman they could possibly fit? He wondered if his butt would ever get that big? "Why would she have a pencil in her butt?" he asked Teagan.

"A pencil is not what I want to put in her."

"Gross." Cody watched her move in on Teagan and ask, with some exasperation, what it was that he needed? She hovered over Teagan as she spoke, her white button-up shirt like a billboard in Teagan's face. Cody watched the way Teagan pivoted around his outstretched leg to keep her at a safe distance.

She eventually laughed, disengaged herself from Teagan's air space and pushed her keys into a padlock that kept a plexiglass case shut over Extractor 3's controls. She pushed several switches and levers and then invited Cody over to hit the big green button. Cody hopped off the wooden table. He loved the big green button.

With a rusty hiss, the machine roared into motion, smells of decaying grease, worn out bearings, water, steam and pressure churning. Cody felt a surge of delight every time his finger pressed into that big green button.

Diana slapped the case shut as she came about, the back of her palm grazed across her forehead like the distressed heroine. "I slave for you."

"Whatever, woman," Teagan said.

"So how are my two favorite boys doing today?"

"Quit staring at her butt, squirt."

"There's no pencil," Cody said. He climbed back onto the table and pulled from a plastic bin another pair of underwear to fold.

Diana looked sternly at Teagan. "You dirty boy. What did you tell him?"

"Nuthin'."

Cody listened to them argue, confused that Diana could sound angry but not be angry. She was playing at being angry, which must be more fun because she was so bad at it, smiling and trying to hide it. Diana told Teagan his behavior merited an infraction.

"Which one?" Teagan said.

"I'm not sure," Diana said. She drew a small green booklet from her top pocket, leafing dramatically through the pages.

"How about a WAC 702?" Teagan suggested.

Diana, her fake eyelashes twisting, thumbed to the correct page. "Unauthorized manufacture or possession of a tool?"

"Yeah," Teagan said. He adjusted himself. "It's a pretty big infraction. I'll let you decide what's a tool and what ain't."

Diana rolled her eyes and boosted herself up onto the table, sitting with her legs swinging over the side. She ran her fingers through Cody's long hair. He liked it very much when she did that. "So how come you got to miss two hours of work today, sweetheart?"

Teagan answered for him. "He had a call-out. To go see his Mental Health provider. What's her name, spud? Judy?"

"It wasn't Judy today it was somebody else."

"Really?" Diana said. "And who was it?" She talked like her words drew big loops in the air. Cody thought it was funny, and he knew she talked like that because he was little.

"Another doctor," Cody said.

"Which one?" Teagan asked. "Dude or a lady? The fat one? Well, they're all fat. I mean the really fat one?"

But it wasn't one of DOC's doctors or nurses. This one was smaller and had a big ball of black hair tied in a bun on the back of her head. She looked different. More like a real doctor. She had a white lab coat with an orange diamond on the pocket. Cody held out his arm and pointed to the band-aid on his inner elbow. "She came to visit me, and she took maybe a lot of blood, my blood, which hurt, the needle it hurts a little but I didn't cry, and she asked so many questions."

"She probably wants to know if you're as smart as I know you are," Diana said, her hands ruffling his hair again.

Cody shook his head. "No, she wants to know how big I am and how heavy I am and what I like to watch when I watch TV and what I think about when I sleep and my dreams when I sleep and so much other stuff. I told her my favorite color is green."

"You did?" Diana winked at Teagan who now lolled his head up at the ceiling and muttered something profane under his breath.

"Uh-huh. But it's not true I lied to her because my favorite color it's blue."

"It is?"

Cody thought about this for a moment, resting his chin on his palm, his elbow on his knee. "Maybe I like blue and green. What do blue and green make?"

"A mess," Teagan said. "Blue and yellow make green."

"She has a yellow tape with numbers on it, and she uses it for sizes so she can measure me."

"She make you strip?" Teagan asked.

"No, just in my underwear," Cody said.

"Score. Was she hot?"

"Huh? Like sweaty?"

"Nah, squirt. Like, would you shag her? Well, not you. Would I shag her?"

Diana translated for him. "Your unfaithful cellmate wants to know if she was better looking than I am?"

Cody sensed a trap. "Idunno."

Diana gave Teagan a smirk and said Cody was indeed smart, tugging at the tip of Cody's nose. She said when they were done, come up to the office. "Gerald won't eat raisins."

As she strutted off, Teagan said, "Is it okay if I use an empty detergent box to send back the incidentals?"

Diana's wrist swept the air, not even looking back, "You can have any box you want, dear."

Teagan's jaw hung open. To Cody he mumbled, "One of these days, spud, I'm telling you, I'm going to pack her monkey."

Cody struggled with this image. Was Diana going somewhere? On a trip? Did she take a monkey with her? Did she put it in a cage or was Teagan talking about a suitcase? How cool it would be to have a monkey! "I like monkeys."

"Me too."

* * *

Cody had never met Gerald. But he loved Gerald very much. Gerald was Diana's third husband, his food habits pickier than those of the kids he never gave her. Diana made wonderful cookies, cakes, pistachio puddings, raspberry preserves. Gerald didn't like any of them—too sweet, too sour, too soft, too crunchy, too bitter, too many nuts. Diana brought the things he rejected into work, even though she was breaking DOC rules in doing so, and Teagan and Cody got to eat it. So Cody loved Gerald for being so picky.

Today she'd brought a whole tupperware tub of solid chocolate fudge with raisins and Cody was ecstatic. He put one chunk after another into his mouth while Teagan and Diana shared a long bout of laughter about something Teagan had said. Cody heard the word fudgepacker. He had chocolate smeared practically from ear to ear and he carefully sucked his fingers in an effort to clean them. It was no use. Brown saliva traveled in strings from his mouth to his fingers and made the mess worse.

"What the hell's wrong with your hubby, woman?"

"Who knows," Diana said. She pulled her black sneakers up onto a crowded desk with rusted corners, abraded down through its linoleum surface. "You'd think I'd know how to pick 'em after Alvin, eh?"

Teagan glared at Cody and the mess he was making. "Slow down, Cookie Monster. You're gonna be sick."

Cody's brown eyes peeked up at Diana and searched for some kind of blessing to eat the whole tub. Instead he asked, "Are you going to stay marry to Gerald?"

"Unless he dies," she said.

"Good," Cody said.

They heard Bruce's keys bounding up the stairs outside the office door. In one swift motion Diana ran a rag across Cody's face and swept the tupperware bucket into the top desk drawer. Teagan played it cool but Cody's fidgeting kept the site manager looking back and forth between the boys' faces. "Did I miss something?" he said.

"Performance reviews," Diana quickly said. "McCarty, Brenner, good work on the, um, inventory. Get started on the biobags."

She was on the team, Teagan told Cody, dragging him out of the office and down the stairs, two at a time. Screw Bruce, he said. Poor Cody's heart was still pounding, Bruce's sudden entrance having scared him silly. He felt his stomach heave, and in front of Extractor 3, he spit up some of the fudge. Teagan watched, disgusted by the sick brown drool that hung from Cody's chin down to the mess on the floor.

"Goddamnit, spud. You're supposed to chew the raisins before you swallow."

* * *

Teagan decided they should leave work early. "It would be a Class A felony to be indoors on a day like this." They rushed through work, folding Cashmere Elderly Care bedsheets two at a time, emptying out Extractor 3 to make room for biobags.

Biobags were the worst. Diana called them incontinence bags, but that was too big a word for Cody. Bright yellow with red biohazard logo, they were filled with clothes that smelled like poop or worse. Sometimes there was vomit and it made Cody want to puke.

Elderly people pooped themselves pretty often, Cody noticed. He didn't remember being embarrassed pooping in his diapers when he was a baby. He didn't remember wearing diapers much at all. He potty-trained easily, mom said, and he never forgot how to go in the toilet. He thought how sad it was to forget how to hold it in. How embarrassing it must be for the poor old people. Teagan made so many dirty jokes about them, but Cody felt terrible for them and sometimes he cried. It was so sad.

They were just finishing up when Scooter shuffled over with a unique walk that fascinated Cody, feet dragging then snapping forward and yanking the rest of him along. Teagan said Scooter couldn't help it, that it was an inbred Vietnam mine-dodging technique. Sometimes Teagan said things like that, languages Cody didn't understand.

"I saw that, Teagan, how the boss lady be humpin your leg. You gonna break bread? Can a Charlie get some grub?"

"Make it quick, Scooter. We're on our way out."

"Word from the hommies." Scooter tossed Teagan an orange jumpsuit that came over from the segregation unit. A penciled message was written on the pant leg. "Filthy's out of the hole today. Wants you to meet him on the yard."

"Thanks."

"When you getting another clothing package?" Scooter asked. "Maybe another pink shirt? You give it to me, I'll bang it baggy. Don't bother me none."

"How did you find out about the pink shirt?" Teagan, still reading the orange pant leg, gave Scooter a raised eyebrow.

"Man, the Scooter hears everything. What she send you this time? Lace panties?"

"Don't get beat up."

"Nylon stockings? You need a pimp?"

Teagan looked around for spectators before he grabbed Scooter and pinned him on the table. "I'll pimp your ass, short stuff."

He let Scooter go, and the darker boy made to fix the creases of his tuxedo and shoot his imaginary cuffs.

Teagan pointed Scooter towards a cart on the back dock. "Go grab us the biobags cart."

Scooter looked at his naked wrist for a watch. "Well, I'll be damned, Watson, it's break time."

"You don't have a hair on your balls if you don't grab that cart, Scooter," Teagan said.

Scooter shuffled off saying, "You won't say that when they're caught in your teeth."

"Asshole," Teagan mumbled.

* * *

Summer sunshine made the yard feel bigger than it really was, wind tossing Cody's hair in a way that tickled his ears.

He kept up with Teagan, running on about how Filthy was in the hole for four months. What did Filthy do?

"Probably assaulted an officer with his smell. You don't know Filthy like I do."

He didn't know Filthy at all. "If he smells so bad why he doesn't take a shower?"

"Filthy's a special case. Short bus. Real short. Remember that old movie we watched on TV about the monkeys with the Hantavirus?"

"No."

"If there was another outbreak, Filthy would be suspect. Do yourself a favor and don't get too close to him. Filthy's great, but you're on notice."

It was the second time today Teagan had mentioned monkeys, and so Cody looked forward to meeting Filthy. He peeled his shirt off, inside out, just before Teagan yelled and gave a great bear hug to a scrawny boy with bright red hair. Cody couldn't stop looking at it. Imagine! Having hair so red, so much bright color on one's own head. Out of the tufts of the boy's hair sprouted huge ears that grew sideways instead of flush with his head.

"Here's the little squirt. Cody? Meet Filthy."

"Name ain't Filthy," he told Teagan.

"His real name's Conner, spud. But I'll let you decide."

"Hello Connor." Cody shook the boy's hand but quickly let go when Teagan glared at him.

"Eh's kind of a runt, ain't he?" Filthy said.

"Filthy, you're a twig. He can't weigh much less than you." Teagan grabbed Filthy's scrawny arms and made some comment about the boy's muscles. That there weren't any.

"Yer a sheit," Filthy said.

Cody listened to them argue in a friendly way, Filthy's voice special like his hair, an earthy blabber like the way Cody imagined trees and flowers talked to each other. Special like his carroty hair, Cody thought. Cody couldn't smell him over the sun and the fir and pines. Both older boys went shirtless, wadded up and stuffed hanging out of their pockets, and Cody tried to count all the bright brown freckles that stood out against Filthy's pale back. More freckles than stars in the sky, Cody believed, some the same color as his hair. Filthy had a freckle constellation. Cody looked for patterns and then noticed Filthy's feet jostling over the sharp rocks of the gravel track they walked.

"You're barefoot!" Cody said.

"Yeah," Teagan said. "Filthy's a savage."

"But the rocks they don't poke you so much so they make your feet hurt?"

Filthy shot Teagan a confused look, one that made his matching red eyebrows twist steeply like waterslides.

"He's asking if your feet don't hurt from walking on the rocks." Teagan turned to look down to Cody. "He doesn't feel anything, spud. Where he's from they can't afford shoes so he grows his own. He's got calluses harder than DOC waffles."

Filthy appeared to approve of this compliment. A grin formed on his face that separated the bottom and top halves. His head was as wide as his bony shoulders, and so Cody imagined those shoulders holding up his smile like tent poles forking up a stretch of canvas.

"Yeah, Filthy's a savage. But it wouldn't hurt you to do a pushup now and then, bro," Teagan told him.

Cody kept watching Filthy's feet. The boy walked the way Shaggy walked from one of Cody's favorite cartoons, Scooby-Doo. They were flat and long, and they slapped the gravel as he walked. Cody thought of a frog and how a frog's feet would flop around like this if frogs could walk. But frogs hopped. Filthy had feet just like a frog! Cody peered intently at Filthy's toes looking for webbing.

"You going to stare at his feet all day, squirt?"

"Filthy he should have webs so like a frog his feet are so flat like a frog so he can hop?" Cody said.

Teagan only grinned and shook his head when Filthy asked for translation.

Filthy dug in his ear, inspected it down the length of his nose and smeared it on his pants. He told Teagan about something he nabbed from the clinic while he was still doing his program in the hole.

"Fingered me a whole mess 'em little buggers. The kind yeh like sums knocks yeh out for hours."

"No shit?" Teagan said. "What was you doing in the clinic? They prescribe you some soap?"

"I got me sprayed," Filthy said.

Teagan's eyes widened. "I'm sorry, did you just say spayed? Like a cat gets spayed?"

"Sprayed. For criblets."

"Criblets? What the hell are you talking about? Start speaking English, foreigner. What are criblets?"

Filthy looked around first, as if he were ashamed. "Yeh know," with both hands he mimed the scissors from Rock-Paper-Scissors. "Criblets," he whispered.

"Jesus Christ, Filthy! They had to spray you for crabs?"

The poor kid ducked from the embarrassment as Teagan's voice carried across the yard. Teagan was right. Cody liked Filthy a lot, but mostly because Cody's head was bursting with ideas for how Filthy was put together. Part of him must be giraffe, his neck was so long. Ears like an elephant. The monkey parts of him were obvious, and then his frog feet. Where did the crabs go? His hair was red like a crab was red.

"Hey, spud. Me and the Irish Infection gotta talk pills for a minute. Secret Squirrel shit. Go take off for a while, kay?"

* * *

Cody found an open spot at the far end of the yard, away from the games other inmates were playing. He heard their voices as if only through a bathtub drain. He lay down and long blades of grass tickled his neck and back. He took off both shoes and socks. Wiggled his toes and watched the breeze carry off the sock lint caught between them. He hoped the grass wouldn't make his back break out and itch like it sometimes did. Especially when the grass had just been cut. Why do people cut grass?

Around the yard were two layers of razor wire fencing, and when Cody looked through both layers, the mesh mixed and appeared to move like water. A neat illusion. He swept his hair and turned his head, and now he could see Tower 4. Up very high a policeman walked around the railing surrounding a glass-enclosed watchtower. Cody could see the butt of his huge gun and then the tip protruding near his shoulder. Teagan had told him that the signs attached to the fences were warnings. Warnings that anyone who tried to escape would be shot. To Cody these signs were just angry red capital letters. Cody wondered if the guard ever got bored? There was no one to shoot because there was no way to climb over so much fence. And besides, shooting people was bad. They might die, and that would be sad. Cody decided that it was a good thing no one tried to escape. That way the policeman wouldn't have to feel so bad from having to shoot someone.

Cody could smell fruit, but he couldn't see it. Apples or pears. Not when they're ripe but when they've fallen off the tree and sit on the ground and get soft. That smell. Sometimes it was strong, and sometimes he couldn't smell them at all. A flock of black birds suddenly took flight from a stock of floodlights that loomed outside the fence. Other birds, blue ones and gray ones and sometimes blue and gray ones, zoomed in and out of the holes in the fence's mesh and chased each other endlessly. Only the birds would come inside the fence, almost like a game, as if there was no fence, so that it didn't mean anything to them because they could come and go whenever they liked. Squirrels ran in and out of the forest just beyond the fences, but they never came inside to see Cody. He wiggled his toes and pretended to talk to the squirrels. He told the squirrels he wasn't scared even though he really was. He was always tense because he didn't know how he would be treated from day to day, which officer would try to hurt him and for reasons he would never understand. But he didn't say this to the squirrels. He just listened to the music of the birds and smelled the wet pine trees and the soft apples and pears he couldn't see and listened to the river in the distance which he also couldn't see. But he knew it was a river. Teagan said it was the Wenatchee River. Why would they name a river after a prison?

Cody burrowed in his pocket and fished out a package of saltine crackers he'd snuck out of the chow hall. He wasn't supposed to take any food from his tray outside the chow hall but Teagan didn't follow this rule and so neither did Cody. He took one cracker out and ate it. The other one he crumbled in his hand and tossed near the fence. Several birds swooped down and ate every crumb. Cody smiled. He wished he'd brought an apple. Teagan brought apples to the yard, and when he thought the guard wasn't looking, he tossed them over the fence. Deer would come out of the forest and eat them. Cody loved deer. Sometimes he could see animals in the clouds too.

Cody rolled on his chest and felt the grass brush against his tummy. Folded his arms. His ear close to the ground, he believed he could hear the earthworms and the beetles and the ladybugs talking to each other and the sounds their many feet made burrowing through the earth. Earthworms had no feet. They just wiggled to move around. Cody could hear them wiggling. He watched the big puffy clouds, looking for dinosaurs and turtles and hippopotamuses and, now that he met Filthy, crabs as well. After a while he closed his eyes.

Dad walked with him and held his hand. Dad told him how people breathe air and when they let out the air it becomes carbodyoside. Plants breathe the carbodyoside and make it back to air. Do plants have noses? Dad laughed. Maybe. Do plants die if they don't breathe? Everything breathes. Everything dies when it can't breathe. Even the ocean breathes. Al-gee lives in the ocean and al-gee likes carbodyside too. It turns the al-gee green just like the plants and the grass. But the ocean is blue? Look closely, sweetheart. The ocean is green.

Cody's feet trekked out into the water, and he watched his toes squish and disappear in the mud. On the beach, he could see great piles of wood that many trees had let fall into the ocean. The limbs were bright browns and reds and yellows and smooth from living in the water before washing ashore. Cody moved further into the water. He looked back over his shoulder, and dad waved from what seemed like very far off. Mom sat in her beach chair under an overcast sky and read her book and drank from a thermos. Cody could smell a campfire burning somewhere, and he looked for smoke.

He was so deep now the cold water touched the bottom of his blue bathing suit, and as the ocean soaked into the cloth, he watched the blue turn almost black and decided that the blue and green must make black. He moved slowly now because he couldn't see his feet and wasn't sure where the mud would end and the deep water begin. Slowly, slowly. The water climbed higher, higher, and his swim trunks tugged in the weak waves. Colder as well. Very cold water. He put his hands in the water and stirred it in circles, and it was so cold he couldn't feel his legs any more. He stepped out and pushed his feet deep in the rocky mud and held his hands in the air as if to hold the sky. Deeper.

Suddenly water covered his shorts and he squealed and fell in, happy.

He ran ashore, splashing into his dad's arms. You're so cold, silly, he said. Blue like the water. But isn't the ocean green? It's both. Sometimes it's blue and sometimes it's green.

Cody's favorite colors.

"Get up, sleepy head," Teagan said. "It's Yard-In."

Cody opened his eyes. The ocean was gone. He sighed and cast his eyes down to the squashed bed of grass left behind. So sad.

"How long you been lying there? You better not get a sunburn. That's a major infraction. Destruction of state property. Or self-mutilation, I forget which one."

Cody sat down and pulled his socks and shoes on. Teagan was still muttering to himself.

"Nah, self-mutilation's what they give you when they catch you yankin your crank. Must be the other one." He threw Cody a shirt. "Not like I've got to check the number. No one else out here would fit in this little rag."

Cody pulled his arms and head through the various holes and Teagan took his hand and led him towards the Field House. The sun had moved towards the western sky and made the fence shadows leap out into the yard. Cody avoided the shadows. Even that razor wire could hurt, he believed. For a moment he felt insignificant. Very small and close to the ground. Like a dandelion. Small like standing at the edge of the ocean and being carried away in the waves.

"I like the ocean," Cody said.

"Yeah, spud. Me too."

* * *

Cody waited by the cell door for Control to rack it. He'd been called down to the unit slider to get medications. Pill Line medications. Any pills that did more than Tylenol,

DOC wouldn't let inmates keep in their cells. So nurses wheeled a cart around from unit to unit and dispensed what Teagan called The Good Stuff. Cody didn't think it was so good. He'd had trouble swallowing bigger pills.

No sooner had Cody entered the cell, Teagan asked, "So what were they?" Cody shrugged. "You don't know what it was? Didn't Judy tell you this morning?"

"It wasn't Judy it was another doctor I saw in the morning," Cody said.

"She didn't tell you anything? What color were they?"

Cody held out his fingers. "Is just like this big, not round, but it's like sort of shaped like . . . "

"A capsule?" Teagan interrupted. "A gel capsule with different colored sides. What color were they?"

"I think it's red and maybe black?"

"What?" Teagan sat on the bed and thought for a minute, his chin in his hand. "I have no idea what it is. Beats me. You're definitely getting the good stuff if I haven't heard of it."

Teagan seemed to be frustrated. He was pretty proud of his knowledge of pills. He loved pills. His face lit up talking about them, counting them, thinking about them. Cody thought many of Teagan's pills had pretty colors and sometimes pretty shapes too. The pill Cody took made his throat feel icky. He asked Teagan if he knew what was for dinner? Teagan frowned and said tuna casserole.

"Gross," Cody said.

"Yeah, it's not real casserole, and you know it ain't real tuna. Probably made from sea monkeys."

This was the third time today Teagan had mentioned monkeys, and to Cody this felt like a prophesy. What was a sea monkey? His imagination played with the words. Wouldn't a monkey run out of breath under water? Or maybe they were like sea lions? Sea lions could breathe under water. Were sea monkeys tiny like sea lions? He was about to ask Teagan when the bigger boy made a suggestion.

"Let's skip mainline. Go check the fridge and tell me what we've got."

Crawling under the bunk Cody pulled out a pitcher full of ice wrapped in towels, containing various foodstuff stolen from the kitchen. "Half a sausage, some slice ham, maybe some onion and some green stuff."

"Peppers."

"Peppers," Cody said. "And six cheeses but they have white stuff on them."

"A little mold," Teagan said. He threw two chili Ramen soups against the concrete floor to break up the noodles within. "You won't taste it when it's melted. Smell the sausage. Is it still okay? I care more about whether the sausage is rotting."

Cody unwrapped the plastic and gave it a sniff. "Smells like sausage."

"Always a good sign."

Twenty minutes later Cody had a tortilla wrapped burrito lying on the bed in front of him, Teagan already on his second and verbally reliving a drug story involving a woman he kept referring to as *crafty whore.*

"You gonna chow down, squirt?"

"I wait for it to cool."

"It's cool enough already. Eat it. Anyway, I didn't wake up for eight hours. You ever fell out and not known where you was when you woke up?"

"When the police they tied me down?"

"Suicide Watch? Nah, that's not the same."

Teagan thought about for a moment and said maybe it was. "Crafty whore is gone with all my dope. Even scraped the rez out of my pipe. Ain't that a bitch?"

Cody was coughing. Part of his burrito was now mush in his lap.

"What's the matter? Send a green pepper down the wrong pipe?"

Cody tilted his head up, and Teagan saw tears running down his ruddy cheeks. "I'm not hungry, Teagan. It hurts."

"It hurts? What hurts?"

"It's too hot, it's got too much hot stuff, chili stuff," Cody whimpered.

Teagan laughed, came unhinged from the spectacle before him. Great noodles of clear snot trickled from Cody's nose. The small boy drooled and chugged Teagan's soda. It didn't help. Teagan kept laughing, but when Cody wiped his nose, great strings of mucous tethered to each of his fingers. He sneezed, puckered eyes, great spasms of head movement, hair leaping into the fluids, and with the sneezing, a huge wad of yellow snot plummeted from his nostril.

Teagan stopped laughing.

Cody shook his head, trying to release himself from the webs of his own goop.

"Stop. Stop! Okay, okay, that's enough. Quit moving, spud. Goddamn you're making a mess. Stop!"

Teagan grabbed a roll of toilet paper and unwound a heap from the roll, working fast to rescue Cody before his leakage threatened surfaces beyond his miserable-looking face and hands.

"You look like you got hit with pepper spray, dude. Really, it wasn't that bad. I just added a few extra scoops of chili garlic to beef it up a bit."

"It hurts. I'm sorry."

"Don't be sorry, spud. Jeez, you look like shit."

Teagan was still trying to clean Cody up when a flashlight shone from the door. Teagan was relieved it was only Officer Anderson, who had sense enough to know Teagan wasn't beating up on poor Cody. They shared a couple jokes at Cody's expense, but Anderson returned later with two cartons of milk he asked them not to mention to anyone.

They both agreed that, if a busload of pigs went over the side of a cliff, Anderson should be spared. Screw the rest of them. There should be more CO's like Anderson.

Before bed that night Teagan put lotion on Cody's sunburned back and asked how he'd let himself fall asleep on the yard like that? Cody wasn't used to good dreams. So many of his were sad and in prison. But his dream on the yard had been wonderful, and he told Teagan about his trip to the ocean with mom and dad. He told him about the color of the water and about algae and carbodyoside.

"Carbon dioxide. I think you mean carbon dioxide."

"Uh-huh." Cody rubbed his tired eyes. All the sun had made him very sleepy. He looked at Teagan who was camped out in the shadows at the foot of Cody's bed. "Teagan? I miss my mom and dad. I want to go home now."

"Spud, you got life. You're not going home. This is your home now." Teagan pulled Cody's blankets up for him. "You're going to be all right, spud."

13

Pat hung up the phone. "That was Percy."

"Tell me he's not coming down."

"He's coming down."

Chris drained a mammoth urn of coffee and disappeared into the Tackroom where Pat heard the sink receive his mug with a bang. "Shit."

Said without vehemence, more like fortified resignation, incoming storm, batten down the hatches. Pat's sympathy was thin. His own worst enemy, Chris refused to bridge any gap he'd created with Percy Underwood, senior partner in the penthouse firm above. Grudges tended to last longer than the stories creating them, yet Pat still recalled the slight. Chris snuck into one of the firm's parties years ago and had an orgy across Percy's desk with two of the paralegals, one of them not female. Pat could explain to Percy that Chris wasn't gay—more indifferent and maybe a little opportunistic—but Percy considered himself traditional, for whom fuzzy distinctions have no merit.

Pat suspected Percy's ire stemmed from not getting first dibs on the attractive young secretary hired for himself. He was rather shallow around women.

"I'll hide in here," Chris said.

"No you won't. He's going to expect coffee, or something warm until maintenance gets the heat back on. In fact, move your heater into the conference room."

"He can't have my space heater."

"He's bringing a client, so wear a tie."

"Shit." Chris's head popped through the door. "His client or ours?"

"He didn't say. Tie. Coffee. Move. I can hear them out front already."

Expecting to usher them into the conference room, Pat found Percy already there and rummaging in the credenza.

"Patricia, dear, I sent you down a bottle of something nice at Christmas. Do you still have it?"

Pat introduced herself to a younger man already seated, embarrassed Percy hadn't bothered. Chris and Percy were sabotaging her sanity, moreover, the practice of law, what little repute was left.

Percy looked up from his search with a bit of sheepishness in the facial creases. Roughly 280 pounds of successful gluttony grunted upright and landed in one of Pat's leather chairs, leaning back as far as the ungrateful springs would carry him.

"I'll get right to the point," Percy said, signaling the point was a long way off. "James Addleman here works for Diamondstone Investments upstairs. We're practically the in-house counsel. He evaluates applications to determine whether they . . . if the return . . . the money . . . " Percy turned to Mr. Addleman. "What is it you do?"

"Venture capital. I'm just the small guy analyzing investment appropriations."

"Don't be modest, James. The little guys don't solicit Underwood, Sachs and Ketner."

Percy dodged a glance at Pat, buffer failing him in a setting where he couldn't just ask the comment be stricken from the record. Percy spread his hands on the mahogany table as though to accentuate its vastness as a consolation.

Percy eschewed surnames whenever possible to impress listeners with his use of first name basis. That habit annoyed Pat more than the unintended scorn for firms of her size.

Chris walked in with a tray, thermal decanter coffee service and mugs, two matching and a third patterned in rainbows. Percy didn't notice on account of the icy stare fixed on Chris as he left the room. Pat's muscles tightened.

Total sabotage. Percy absentmindedly reached for a mug and jerked his hand back when he noticed the colors, a tiny squeal as though seeing an apparition.

Mr. Addleman looked exasperated, interrupting Percy's monologue of conceits.

"A few months ago my son tragically died, Ms. Naughton. My wife and I were devastated. He was healthy, smart, active . . . there was no reason for it. I've since learned things that make his death sound suspicious. Mr. Underwood informs me it may take a civil inquiry to get answers."

"I'm very sorry for your loss," Pat said. James put his elbows on the table, sleeves exposing a watch with lots of moving parts. "How is it you believe I can assist?"

Percy for once said something helpful. "James came to us because we're Diamondstone's legal arm, but his issue's not strictly company business and they'd like to avoid potential conflict of interest. I recommended he engage you. Keep it in the building, as it were." Percy chuckled as though he'd said something witty.

If Percy was passing off a client, anticipating no foreseeable legal success—meaning money—Pat was insulted. She knew Percy better than that. What was the hitch?

"I'm flattered by your appraisal of me, but surely Mr. Addleman needs a legal team specializing in civil litigation?"

"And he'll have it," Percy said. He could tell Pat was smoking him out and dismissed her concern. "This is a strange case. I'm willing to have my team do all the legal legwork. I need your name on the paperwork to make the parties happy."

There was nothing technically unethical about assuming lead counsel and subcontracting Underwood, Sachs and Ketner. As long as it didn't compromise too much of her time, she could easily justify splitting a fee, owing Percy a few legal favors anyway. The man had good instincts. Pat was curious where liability played in the death of Addleman's son?

James laid a tablet on the glass surface where Pat's conference table would recognize it. Percy promised this would take no more than thirty minutes, optimistic for him. Ensuring the possibility, Mr. Addleman did the talking as initial coroner reports organized. Pat tugged them around to view.

"Coroner ruled cause of death from drowning."

"Was he in a pool?" Pat asked.

"Chase and I were at the beach. He didn't drown. I watched him from forty feet off. One minute he's splashing and smiling, then he's face down and comatose."

"Something underwater bite him? Allergic reaction to jellyfish?"

"He has no allergies." James sighed. A concerted effort to focus altered his pallor. "*Had* no allergies."

"Water in the lungs?"

James shook his head. "I mean, yes, he did, but not enough to drown from. The coroner's botched this whole thing."

Pat sensed his anger and didn't say anything. Counties frequently appointed coroners with few qualifications and then overworked them to the point where examinations amounted to a cursory scribble on the paperwork.

Percy pulled the autopsy image and pushed it across to Pat. Aligning it to the table, she zoomed it to full size. A tag at the edge indicated 3D archiving. Pat clicked the option and arrays of fan-dance emitters lifted the body up to full-scale dimensions. The effect was disarming, a sense of being at the autopsy itself.

"This was in the coroner's file?" Pat asked.

"No, I hired a private autopsy specialist," James said.

Pat was confused. "This is how your examiner received the body?"

"As far as I know."

"With no Y-incision from the county coroner?" After forty years of practicing law, even Pat possessed rudimentary knowledge of autopsy procedure.

"Well obviously the state skipped some steps," Percy said. He had a voice that sounded as if he was constantly chewing on a piece of pork gristle. "The file's time-lapsed." He pointed out for Pat a progress table tagged with event markers. "If you can stomach some gore."

Pat eyed Percy over her glasses. He should have known better. Pat was more concerned about James, whose son this was after all. Percy's social skills were as nuanced as Chris's.

James reassured Pat he'd been through the file so many times in the past few months even he was becoming immune. Still he sighed, the gravity of it all.

Chase died from suffocation, not from drowning. Inadequate oxygenation of remaining blood and tissues was evident. The examiner ruled out neurological events precipitating trauma such as stroke or seizure. Pat pulled the pharmacology tab and found nothing foreign. The speculative conclusion was respiratory paralysis.

Pat asked why the diagnosis couldn't be more specific? James opened a file tab illustrating arcane aspects of human biology. The vertebrate nervous system relied on a neurotransmitter called acetylcholine to initiate or regulate muscle movements at neuromuscular junctions throughout the body. An unnatural surge of acetylcholine induces total muscular paralysis, including lungs.

"She found excess acetylcholine?" Pat said.

"Not exactly, too transitory. An enzyme called cholinesterase quickly hydrolyzes acetylcholine into choline and acetate, both of which are abundantly prevalent in the body and therefore of no diagnostic value. However," James showed Pat the body fluids and liver biopsy analysis, "she found myosmine, a metabolite resulting from whatever triggered the cholinergic nerve endings to induce paralysis."

James might have been reading from the report but it was clear he'd thoroughly studied the tip of the spear. James pulled a double helix from the table's interface. Stretches of nucleotides blinked in and out.

"This is where it gets strange. Entire lengths of Chase's DNA are destroyed."

"Before or after he died? What do you mean by destroyed?"

"Not destroyed so much as decayed. It's hard to tell when it happened. Cellular replication's not showing signs of degradation, so presumably close to the time of death? Then again," James tossed up his hands, "the affected structures are all in the junk DNA. We compared it to partial DNA extracted from a hair sample in his baby book. Ms. Naughton, the damage is pervasive. My examiner took multiple samples. I think Chase was defective and GLS knew it."

Finally Pat heard something related to liability. "Chase was a Genesis Life Solutions pill baby?"

James didn't answer though he must have heard Pat. He took a sip and seemed to regard the cup in distraction. "This coffee is excellent, Ms. Naughton."

***

Percy stayed a while longer but Mr. Addleman apologized for having to return to the office. Perhaps feeling he'd been uncouth, a sense that always arrived too late for Percy, he asked after Pat's father in an effort to be more personable.

Unfortunately Alfred wasn't getting any better. Pat moved him into a care facility in Bellingham as early stages of Alzheimer's gave way to advancing deterioration of mental faculties. Watching the process scared Pat far more than she cared to admit. The man who taught her to fish on

Neah Bay now couldn't remember ever owning a boat. At times lucid stories emerged, Alfred watching sea turtles bury eggs, leaving marks on the sand like a spoon shapes whipped cream. He feared for the moonlight grave of abandoned white orbs whose vulnerable lives, he said, would be contingent upon their exuberant dash for the sea someday. Motherless existence, a solitude imprinted by Darwinian lengths of time, and did they make it? Parts of Alfred's memory were still beautiful and in that way precious. Time was a fire consuming his museum.

Pat hated the diminishing options, none of which a man in his nineties wanted to hear.

"Oh sweet Jesus. Hospice? You get me a hospice lady to tell me how I'm supposed to die?" Alfred coughed and held an emaciated hand to his bald pate. "Some lady in a white frock tells me I can't smoke? Can't drink? Worries when I die there goes her job security? Fills in witness forms when I keel over?"

"Never mind. X-rays only show a small fracture this time, dad."

"Or maybe she poisons me? Drugs me in my coffee, the hag? To keep me quiet? So I lie in a worthless bed like this bed and wear clothes like this worthless rag?" He grabbed for the hospital gown as he fretted and when his hand came up empty, seemed confused. "The crack of my ass hanging out all the time? Or she speaks Filipino? A Filipino broad and I say, 'No sugar! No sugar!' She says, 'Wha? Wha?' like I'm stupid. I go to bed and she steals all the china."

"Dad," Pat put her hand on his head. "You don't have any china."

Alfred turned away, lips pursed. "I'm not stupid."

"You're not stupid," Pat agreed.

Pat braced for the visit when he wouldn't recognize her. Alfred decayed as thoroughly as Chase's DNA, but slowly so grieving became protracted guilt for not making more use of time, and what could she do now?

There was no way to explain this to Percy, who on any account ruined the moment of feigned sensitivity by suggesting revenue from Addleman's case would allow her to hire a more fetching secretary for Percy to seduce at office parties. If she ever held them.

"Contain yourself."

"Do you think this table's sturdy enough?" Percy gave it a helpless jerk.

Unbelievable. Total sabotage.

"Don't be such a killjoy, Patricia dear. I'm billing three different clients for this hour. Can't waste it watching you try on mordant faces."

Percy paced in front of the rain-drenched windows, observing the urban gloom. Maintenance still not finished, condensation forming on the inside corners of each pane, small space heater struggling away behind Pat.

"Maybe I'm not as optimistic as you," Pat said. "GLS has been doing this for a while. Why suddenly a defect? And what makes you think they'll give you anything damning in discovery?"

"You're looking at this too narrowly, sweetheart. This isn't about whether GLS is responsible or not. This is bad publicity. They'll settle to keep James quiet. Think about it. Pill-babies market on the promise they're immune to defects that plagued us for years. They can't succumb to AIDS, mononucleosis, arthritis. Can't get whatever your father has."

"Careful."

"I apologize." Percy appeared eager not to have foot in mouth too long. "That *is* how pill-babies are marketed."

Pat didn't know what to think of pill-babies, a term more pejorative every day as the decade-old technology's social ramifications panned out. Envisioned as a panacea for reproductive independence, but still too expensive for most, pill-babies created a new rift in society. Privileged classes of genetically superior children endured plenty of criticism.

Most of it came from opposing social castes, but also from preachers of the century old argument about science playing God.

Genesis Life Solutions didn't like releasing demographic data but everyone learned the statistics anyway. No one purchased black or Mexican babies. Parents wanted blue eyes and blonde hair, high metabolisms, fair skin. Far more boys than girls purchased offset the normal distribution. Did this type of selective gene inhibition undermine healthy random natural selection? Chase was all of these things. And what would happen when the first generation of pill-babies reached puberty? Pat could already foresee the new Jim Crow prejudices. *No daughter of mine's going to date inferior genetic material.*

GLS and its owners weren't exactly averse to this prejudice, borrowing the strained legal position Monsanto and ConAgra took regarding genetically modified seeds sold to farmers—the enhancements are intellectual property borne from considerable research and development investment, and passing it on indiscriminately to next generations constituted indefinite free licensing. A fee should be paid for signature DNA in each new generation. Moreover, they argued uncontrolled breeding with less desirable gene pools infringed on product quality and thus corporate reputation, for which damages might be owed.

The legal complications were staggering. What if GLS terminated proprietary gene expression after one product cycle? The same way Monsanto corn only lasted one season? Was that what happened to Chase? Was the experiment failing?

Pat took a long look at the 3D autopsy replication. Particularly callous critics called them Hitler Youth. Chase was just a six-year old boy.

"What's this?" Pat asked, pointing to an injury notation on the time-lapse.

"Nothing. Hurt himself at recess or something. Totally unrelated."

Pat pulled up the detail tab. A tiny puncture sixteen centimeters below the floating ribs, terminating in the inferior fascia of the internal oblique abdominal muscle. Linear tissue damage but no foreign object or trace material removed. A zoomed microscopic frame of the epidermis clearly showed blunt force entry.

"The examiner says it's not caused by a sharp object," Pat said.

"So?"

"She also notes that strands of tissue healing rates make the injury approximately eight hours old. Where's the bruising? Even if the penetration was sharp there should be discoloration, Percy. Children bruise far easier than you or I."

Percy shrugged. "It doesn't change liability. We've got two GLS pill-babies, same age, both die of respiratory paralysis within a short period of time, DNA's deteriorated and—"

"*Two* of them?" Pat said, suddenly more alert.

Percy spun around, sensing a misstep and calculating where it happened. "Oh, I forgot all about that. James located another family who lost their daughter one month before Chase died." Percy's grin glowed fatly against Seattle's cloudy skies. "I love class-action leverage, don't you?"

14

"Shit," was all Teagan said when the officers finally exited their cell.

Teagan and Cody sat at one of the dayroom tables looking up at their tier cell door while two officers within tore the place apart. They'd announced it as a routine search but had been in there a long time. At some point they radioed for a sergeant, and Teagan had really started swearing. Three officers now.

Cody's stomach tied itself into a heap of worms, and his heart thumped away erratically. He didn't understand what was going on, and Teagan told him to shut up when he asked anything. Cody felt it was wrong for someone to go through his things without permission, and he felt sick not being able to see what they were doing. Why? What are they doing, Teagan? Just shut up. Teagan looked worried.

In prison they never ask permission.

Thirty minutes later they all came out of the cell. One held a large garbage bag full of stuff. The other carried the same set of tools he'd gone in with. The sergeant had in his hand Teagan's tattoo gun. No wonder Teagan swore so hard.

"Offender McCarty, get up, face the wall and place your hands behind your back."

Teagan did as he was told, but not with any hurry. As he walked towards the wall he looked over his shoulder and saw Cody's tears. "Easy, squirt. I'll try to be back in a few days."

"Do not talk to the offender!" the cop barked. Cody's nerves rattled like the sound made by the cuffs ratcheted on Teagan's wrists. They led him out of the unit door.

"Where you taking him?" Cody asked, but his words were smeared by his heaving throat.

"Cell in!"

He could see one of his drawings, its crayon lines, facing outwards in the trash bag. "You take our stuff?" Cody asked, pointing.

"I said, cell in, Brenner!"

The steel door to A317 slammed shut behind Cody. He felt his insides loosen and twist when he saw what the officers had done. As if a bomb had gone off inside the room, or some terrible windstorm. They'd upended everything, torn sheets off the beds, flipped and scattered papers everywhere. Even Teagan's TV was flat on its screen. Cody whimpered and swallowed his lower lip, all he could do to keep back his tears. It was so sad. He tried to think of what he'd done to be punished like this?

He walked about and tried to straighten things. Uprighted Teagan's TV. Put the clothes back on the shelf and re-hung the hangers scattered on the floor. One of them was now broken and wouldn't hold up Teagan's yellow shirt. He laid it at the bottom of the cubby and placed the shirt on his bunk. He pulled the toothbrushes and floss out of the sink bowl and placed them back on their little shelf. The officers had torn down and taken all of Teagan's car posters. All the pens and pencils Teagan kept in an empty peanut butter jar were scattered on the desk. The jar was gone. Cody picked up the pens from the floor, the gel pen with sparkles and the one with green ink that Teagan let him use on special drawings. Those were gone as well. The colored artwork that Teagan had carefully taped on the wall around Cody's bunk had been torn away. Only a fragment of one remained, a corner hung from the clear tape still stuck to the wall. The one with his beautiful rainbows. Why did they take his drawings? How could they be bad?

Cody broke down and sobbed, long and hard, when he found they'd taken his dream catcher. The pretty dream catcher Teagan gave him, the one hung over his head so that when he slept he wouldn't have sad thoughts and bad dreams. Teagan said his Indian friend had made it just for him, and that he'd promised it would bring him happy thoughts and good dreams. Now Cody wailed, deep stomach wrenching cries and asked why? Why they took his dream catcher? Why they took his happy thoughts? He lay on the floor and to his chest he clutched Teagan's sweatshirt, tears dripping into the gray fabric.

Why did they take Teagan away from him?

***

Cody didn't leave the cell for two days. Not for work, not for yard, not to get his pills, not even to eat. Teagan's friends would hammer on the door asking for him. Cody couldn't talk. He lay on his unmade bed, rolled in a sheet, and prayed for Teagan to come back.

On the third day the door opened and two officers dragged Teagan into the cell and dropped him on the floor. They said nothing, turned and left.

Cody leaped off his bed, tripping over the sheet, his feet caught, heart racing, toes prickling with happiness that Teagan was back!

But something was wrong.

Teagan didn't move. He lay face down on the concrete and didn't move.

"Teagan?" Cody said. "Teagan, wake up, Teagan, wake up!" He knelt beside Teagan and put his hands on the boy's shoulders. Shook him. "Teagan, you're scaring me. Wake up!"

Teagan didn't move.

Cody panicked. Please don't be dead. Please don't be dead. He stuffed his hand under the large boy's chest and felt warmth and movement. Maybe this meant he wasn't dead?

Cody dragged his small fingers through Teagan's coarse, curly hair and noticed that someone had cut two spots on his head, cut the hair all the way down to the skin. On the back of his head were two little white spots peeking from his dark hair. He tried to turn Teagan over, but the boy was too heavy. Cody took his pillow and lifted Teagan's head with both hands, careful not to squish his eyes, and pushed the pillow under with his knees so Teagan wouldn't hurt from his head being on the floor. He covered Teagan with a blanket. He didn't know what else to do. Teagan was sleeping. He must be just sleeping. He must be so tired he can't wake up.

* * *

A couple of hours later Teagan rolled over and moaned. His eyes were still closed. He pulled the blanket off and grabbed his stomach. His eyes snapped open, and like a cornered animal he jerked his head around and made for the toilet on his knees and puked enormously. Cody could smell the rot of Teagan's vomit and was scared.

"Teagan? You okay? You be okay?"

But Teagan didn't answer. He pulled his pants down and sat on the toilet without flushing it. Sat there half naked with his head in hands and elbows propped on his knees. For hours. Not saying a word. Cody watched Teagan drool, waiting for him to be Teagan again.

* * *

Several hours later Teagan stood up. He sucked in a great heave of air as if he'd surfaced from being drowned. His eyes were wide now, wide like they could see things for the first time. Cody was still sitting Indian style on the concrete floor, and he watched as Teagan tried to walk and grab for the edge of the shelf. He stumbled by Cody and pushed the mess on the desk around, onto the floor, until he unearthed a bottle of Ibuprofen. Throwing the cap on the floor, he swallowed a handful with no water and belched loudly all the same.

"Goddamned cocksuckers."

Teagan was back! All of him was back. Not just his body. All of him! Cody hugged him and looked up into Teagan's dumbstruck face and sobbed, this time in utter relief.

"Jesus Christ." Teagan kicked his leg. "Get off me, squirt. What time is it?"

"I dunno."

"What day is it?"

"I dunno. Teagan, you okay?"

"No. I am damn well not okay. My head's in a vice grip, my eye sockets feel like sandpaper, and my ass itches somethin' fierce. Now what the hell day is it?"

"I dunno," Cody blubbered, overjoyed to hear Teagan swearing. "Teagan, they took so much of our stuff."

"Yeah, we got robbed, spud."

"They took my dream catcher."

"I'll get you another one."

"They took your cars, Teagan, all of them," Cody said, his arms spreading wide to show the stripped bare white walls. "They took my pictures. Why they took all my pictures? Why did they take my dream catcher?"

"Contraband, squirt. With these shits, it's all the same as a tat-gun. They have so little clue what's going on these days, they'd take your empty water bottle, infract you for contraband and not even notice you had a shank in your dirty laundry bag."

Cody wondered if Teagan was talking about something he actually had or if he was just pretending? He eyed the laundry bag carefully.

"I knew this search was going to be savage. I knew when I saw them go up in here with tools." Teagan grabbed the corner of his folded mattress and laid it flat with a plastic thump. "See? They even cut open the mattresses and hot-glued them shut. They were looking hard, dude."

Teagan moped around and kicked things, sometimes to put them back where they belonged and sometimes just to kick something. He made his bed and then helped Cody make his bed as well.

"And where did you go, Teagan? What did you cut your hair for?"

Teagan fingered the two spots on the back of his head, then slumped against the wall at the foot of Cody's bed again. He stared off into nothing for several minutes before he spoke.

"Look, squirt. Tattoo gun's a major infraction. I knew I was nailed as soon as they came up out of here holding it. Do you know what a major infraction is?"

Cody shook his head. He drank some water from a cup with both hands. Teagan explained that minor infractions weren't worth the paper they were written on. Some cell confinement, extra duty, loss of privileges. Nothing big. A major is a major. Hole time or worse. He'd taken worse.

"What's worse?"

"You really don't want to know."

"They hurt you?" Cody asked.

Teagan laughed, "Like a spanking? Nah. Not like you think, squirt. I'd loved to be spanked. Just whip me and get it over with, you know?"

Cody wasn't sure Teagan was all back now. He didn't seem to be making sense.

"An asswhooping ain't nothing," Teagan continued. "In DOC it's all about fu . . . screwing with your mind. Mind games. A tat-gun is thirty days minimum in the hole. With priors like I got? I could have been there for months. I plead guilty in exchange for what they called a negotiated sanction. I took five days of TDT instead."

"Does it taste bad?" Cody asked.

"What, squirt?"

"I said does it taste bad your tea?"

Over the sound of his piss echoing in the metal bowl, Teagan explained the cops shaved his hair so they could put wires on the head. They read him the sanction, and the doctor flipped the switch on the TDT machine.

"You hear this sound like a helicopter rotor spinning up, and the light over your head gets really bright. Then you don't hear anything, and I mean *nothing*. You just see this white light."

"Is it scary?"

"Not at first. You just sit there, waiting for something to happen but nothing happens. You wait and wait and wait but all you see is that white light, like looking into a bright white empty space, and you can't feel anything or hear anything. It's crazy. Five days of that will make you crazy."

"You sleep?"

"No, you can't sleep. You're forced to stay awake. You got to understand, it only feels like five days. The whole thing is over in twenty minutes. I guess you don't have time to sleep, 'cause God knows I've tried, but you can't close your eyes for what feels like an eternity. You just go numb in the head. Worse than any detox I ever had."

Cody was confused. "How can it be five days? It hasn't been five days."

"Could have been in my head. I just went crazy and woke up here drooling on myself. See, I'm this lab rat while they try this new thing, see how it works, see what they can do with it in the real world. They're always doing shit like that in prisons. They've been giving us TDT for about a year now. It stands for Time Dilation Therapy, whatever the hell that means. Notice how they always call it therapy when it makes you crazy? But I didn't have a choice. I couldn't do sixty or more days in the hole. Really I don't care about hole time. Just a vacation from the bullshit with meals delivered to your room, you know? But I had other things to worry about this time."

"What did you worry about?"

Teagan didn't say anything, just flipped his hand. Nothing. He mumbled and chewed his lower lip and fingered his dragon necklace as if agitated. Finally, he said, "I worried about you."

* * *

Back from the library, Teagan ripped car pictures out of magazines and taped them to the walls.

"Is the red one a fast car?" Cody asked.

"Anything's fast to you, Captain Carseat."

Teagan indulged in another automotive war story, something he and his dad fixed. Teagan made cups of cocoa for both of them, a ritual when ordering store off the commissary sheets which helped gratify his anticipation. Cody filled out his name and number and handed it off to Teagan to spend his money. Cody busied himself re-wallpapering his bunk with new drawings, green crayon poised over a clean sheet of paper waiting to be filled. Teagan said they'd just tear up his artwork every search. "Draw more and piss them off. Pigs don't give a shit about art or color unless it's the color of the sprinkles on their donut."

"So what kind of wingdams and goofdoodles should we get this week?"

"Something with chocolate in it," Cody suggested.

"Duh!"

Teagan seemed to scratch himself a lot lately, Cody noticed. He must itch a lot. Maybe lotion would help.

"There was this time we was mobbin down South Tacoma Way after my partner had just messed up a Mazda he was trying to peel. Couldn't get her started and so he puts his 357 Magnum through the lock, and that son of a bitch is so loud we was already knowin the cops were coming. Stupid. Sure as hell, there's the disco lights and we ditched at Division Street." Teagan turned and showed Cody his scars. "I ran through a grip of back yards and got iced in the tail cuz the fuzz was hot on it that night. Lost 'em and I thought I was bleeding out but Spam guns aren't really lethal."

Cody thought of a piece of meat shaped like an egg firing from a canon. "What's a spam gun?"

Teagan scratched his scars, which looked like tiny moon divots to Cody, splattered all over the big boy's back and down to his boxer's waistband. "Spam, SPMP. Soluble Projectile Magnetic Pulse. Ice guns. Hurts like a bitch. My ass is covered in pits from getting iced while hopping fences, know what I mean?"

Cody lay flat on his chest, his bare feet circling in the air while he drew green lines on another blank sheet of paper. This drawing would be a crab, he decided. Probably a green crab. "If you take a fast car you don't have to run?"

Teagan laughed. "You're getting smarter. But let me tell you a secret. A fast car is nice but it draws attention like a spook at a Ku Klux Klan concert. Might as well pull over before you even done anything. You're under arrest for being stupid enough not to ride under the radar. You know my brother Adam? The one doing life at Walla Walla?"

Cody nodded. Adam had been in a lot of Teagan's stories. Either Adam or Teagan's dad.

"Adam says you get all these guys in the big joint complaining that they got caught with a pound of dope when they weren't doing anything wrong. They always get pulled over because of a burnt out tail light, and I'm thinking, you know the pigs got your number, right? So check your goddamned tail lights before you leave the hood. But it's not about the taillight. It's because they don't know how to ride low-key. You didn't get pulled over for no taillight being out. You got pulled up because you was bangin a dropped, three-wheel moving, chrome and gold nigger-mobile. Got to have a set of wheels nobody sees. You know what me and my friends moshed in?"

Cody looked up and shrugged. "A red car?"

"An old primer gray Celebrity," Teagan said proudly.

***

"Wilson's going to Green Hill," Teagan said after a tier porter gave him the message through the door. "Wilson's what? Twelve? He's a year and a half younger than me, and he gets to go to Green Hill? *I* should be going there."

Cody pictured fields with different colored hills, mostly pink and yellow ones for some reason, and in the middle a green one with dancing bears on it. The dancing bears he couldn't explain. But they were in his head. He asked Teagan what Green Hill was?

"The big boy prison. Where I'm supposed to be. Don't get me wrong, it's a juvenile joint too, but this place is all little kids. Not as little as you, maybe, but little. I'm tired of always being around children."

Cody set down his crayon and looked up at Teagan, feeling hurt.

"Not you, spud. You ain't just one of the boys. You're my cellie. That's different." Cody didn't look mollified. Teagan held out his arms and rolled his eyes while Cody crawled into his lap for a conciliatory hug. Teagan promised he wouldn't leave. It was an easy enough promise to make. WRCC clearly wasn't going to send him anywhere else. "Wilson asked me to take care of the rat," Teagan said, "and I asked him, 'Which rat? This place is full of snitches.' But he meant the other rat."

Later that night the tier porter kicked a squashed toilet paper tube under their slider, ends folded down and taped. Cody didn't sit up the first time Teagan called to him because his stomach still hurt from puking up dinner. It was no real surprise because the meatballs were likely rotten, something Teagan called TVP, and the gravy made them worse. Ever since, he'd been drinking water like a fish because Teagan said it would flush the ickies out of his gut. It didn't fix the dizziness, though. What a terrible meatball.

When Cody finally sat up, Teagan, with no fanfare, ripped open the tube and dumped it in Cody's lap. Cody jumped, his eyes wide.

"It's a mouse!"

"You get an A for identification."

"You got a mouse!"

"Correction, spud. *You've* got a mouse. I don't want the lousy rat. It's your pet. You take care of it. Or flush it."

The mouse didn't move around much. Cody was afraid it would run off, but it scampered in small circles. Over the blankets and between Cody's knees. Cody squealed, delighted, moving about to stay clear of the little gray thing's exploration. Just a tiny mouse, a baby, Cody thought.

"It's a mouse!" Cody kept saying. Teagan got him a pet! Teagan must love him so much. "What does he eat?"

"What makes you think it's a he?"

"Is it a boy mouse?" Cody asked.

Teagan picked it up by the tail and gave it a once over. The thing clawed for traction in the air. "It's a boy mouse. It's got bigger balls than you." He set it back down.

Cody touched the fur with his finger and jumped back. Teagan said it wouldn't hurt him. Wouldn't bite. It was a tame mouse. He said Cody should let the mouse sniff him a bit to learn who he was. That the mouse would have to because he couldn't see Cody.

Cody was about to ask why the mouse couldn't see him when he held the sniffing little creature close to his face and made one of his signature exclamations.

"It's got no eyes! Teagan, it has no eyes!"

"Yeah, sort of a weird story. Wilson caught it when it was a baby, and he had some kind of leash on it. Well, it got away while it had around its neck this collar Wilson made for it, and when it came back some days later it had grown, and the collar had choked the neck so bad its eyes popped out."

"That's so sad," Cody said. The mouse crawled along Cody's arm. "Now he can't see anything?"

"Spud, we're talking about a creature with a brain almost as small as a cop's. Probably does less thinking than a sherm addict. I don't think he really notices any difference."

"It's so sad," Cody again said. Perhaps because the mouse was blind or maybe because it had no brain. "What's he named?"

"It's your beast, squirt. Call it anything but Mickey or Mr. Jengles."

Flat on his back, Cody let the mouse crawl on his tummy and giggled because the mouse had tickly sharp toes. Even if he couldn't see, he stayed on Cody's chest, and his whiskers flapped up and down as one, like the wings of a butterfly. He thought about the mouse for a long time, how sad it would be not to see anything anymore, not even yourself. At length he came up with a name.

"I'll call him Booboo. One for each eye because Booboo he can't see."

* * *

On Saturday, Cody took Booboo to the big yard. Teagan had dumped out his hobbycraft bin and laid toilet paper inside so Cody's mouse would have a safe place to live. Teagan emptied a bottle of pills down the toilet, pills he said didn't have enough bang in them anyway. He cleaned out the container and poked a hole in the lid. It would be Booboo's travel pod. Booboo slipped right inside, and Teagan showed Cody how to tuck the pill container in his underwear between his legs so Booboo wouldn't be found by any but the most eager and groping cops.

Walking to the yard in the rain, Cody wore on his face a terribly guilty look and waddled like a duck. Teagan got close to his ear and chewed him out. "Walkin like that, the pigs are going to think I've been running your guts. Walk normal, dude!"

The yard was mostly empty. The grass at their feet still clung with beads of water, the rain dying down. A damp and cool afternoon, no one wanted to play ball in this weather, and so Cody sat in the middle of the yard facing away from the tower and reached in his pants.

Booboo didn't want to leave his travel pod. He sniffed at the wet earth and did several loops inside the clear plastic. Cody thought he must be scared. Scared like Cody was the first time Teagan brought him to the yard. He put his head low to the ground, hair falling on the grass, and whispered to Booboo so no one but Booboo would hear him. He told Booboo not to be scared.

It worked. The tiny mouse slowly crawled into the grass and squirmed between the stalks of drooping dandelions. He reared up on his hind legs and worked his pink nose through the flowers. He moved from flower to flower as if carrying secret messages between them. His fur turned a darker gray. Rainwater soaked into him, making him look pathetic, and he sat up and ran his paws through his whiskers and over his face and ears. He did this exercise quickly, and Cody, flat on his chest, was fascinated. He tried to imitate Booboo. Teagan, on the other side of the yard walking with Scooter, just shook his head watching Cody do this funny dance in the yard.

Booboo never crawled very far. He made friends with some ragweed and buttercups and circled as if lost. Maybe he thinks it's dark out because he's cold, Cody thought. Maybe he doesn't think at all? So sad. Cody petted Booboo with one finger, all the way from his pink nose to the tip of his soggy tail. He pulled up some grass and stuffed it into the pill container. Then the head of a dandelion. In went Booboo when movement was called. Cody stuffed the pill container into his pants. Poor Booboo was cold and wet, and he couldn't see anything, not even the sunshine or the pretty yellow flowers and he didn't know the grass was green and he could see nothing but blackness and Cody cried for Booboo because he had no color in his world. He cried because with no eyes Booboo couldn't cry and so Cody cried for both of them.

It was so sad.

* * *

That night Cody puked up his dinner again. He lay on his bunk and moaned. Teagan knew it wasn't the food. Spaghetti was Cody's favorite, and although nasty, there was really nothing in it that would make Cody sick. Then came the diarrhea. Sitting on the bowl, Cody leaned over, face in his hands, cold sweat visible on his forehead.

"Where's it hurt, spud?"

"Hurts so bad," he cried.

"Yeah, yeah. *Where* does it hurt? In your stomach?"

Cody nodded his head. The boy's hair clung to his ears in damp clumps. His sweat smelled rank, as if urine were coming out of the skin. And Cody seemed to know this. "I can't go pee," he said. "It hurts when I, when I, I push and it hurts and no pee comes out."

"It's probably a twenty-four hour bug," Teagan said. "Shit it all out, bro. Show it who's boss."

Half an hour later, Cody was still clutching his stomach. Rocking back and forth, completely empty and pleading for the pain to go away, over and over and over. He rolled himself into a blanket, sweating, nose running, clutching his stomach.

Teagan asked about everything he could remember his own mom asking—Fever? Sore throat? Stuffy? Sore muscles?

Just in his tummy, Cody said, but pointed to parts of his body even Teagan's near absence of anatomical knowledge knew wasn't the stomach.

"Are you sure it's your stomach? Cuz you're pointing at your junk." Cody pulled his waistband down. "Jesus, bro. How you gonna go and get an STD without getting laid? Ain't no topical medication going to fix *that* color."

"It hurts," Cody wailed, as if Teagan hadn't heard the first twenty times.

It dawned on Teagan that it wasn't just the last two hours Cody had puked up. He'd been sick on and off for a while now. How long had it been? Teagan froze.

"Spud? How long have you been taking those pills? The new ones, with red and black colors?"

Cody didn't answer, head limp, breathing too slowly, chest and hands clammy.

Teagan ran to the cell door and pushed the call button.

15

Underwater lights ran the perimeter of *Estrella de Mar Rosa*'s hull, one every few meters, giving her seat in the water an ethereal glow as though viewed through an old Starlight nightscope. Ivan and Ellison's zodiac floated a half-kilometer away, tethered to a channel marker buoy. Sitting low against the water made Samuel Coletti's ship appear surreal and magnificent. A full moon painted her pearlescent superstructure in the dark silence while fireworks on Miami Beach, getting a few days head start on the Fourth of July, splashed colored fragments of light off the chop.

"She's a beast."

Ivan lowered his spotting scope. "Aft guards, duel MP7's. The one in the stern's carrying an H&K 416 carbine. Couple of automatics under the jackets, same as the ones at the Spider Web."

"Sports car," Ellison said after a minute. He fumbled in the watertight pockets of his drysuit. "I always figured that's how I'd die. A day would come when all the money I never get to spend would burn up on a well-kept sports car, something old and British. Something reckless."

"Didn't you once own an MG?" Ivan checked GPS data, finding Coletti's helicopter still not airborne. "What's this all about? I mean, it's never too late for a midlife crisis, I suppose."

"I wanted to die in a sports car. Not at eight hundred rounds per minute. As usual we're fabulously outgunned."

"With any luck, the guards won't even see us aboard. Show a little optimism. After all this is your plan."

Ivan lit a cigarette and watched Ellison's disapproval. Ivan gave him a shrug as if to say, no one saw anything.

"I have faith in the plan, Nikos. We did the same job on the PLO in Libya when you were still in diapers."

"Who is *We*?"

"I was in my twenties then. Not seventy-two."

Ivan checked the movement of the vessel's guards. A sports jacket was a hell of a dress code at this time of year. Ivan seldom felt humidity rivaling Florida and, even with the ocean breeze, he didn't envy Coletti's security force. "So, you're over seventy. You're in better shape now than you ever were."

"Certainly not from bad habits."

Ivan held out his cigarette as if to say *this?* Ellison only scowled. Ivan tossed it overboard. Hypocrite. What about . . . ? But none of Ellison's bad habits came to mind. Maybe he didn't have any. Which made the rebuke more irritating. Ivan watched it float away under the red glow from a direction light atop the buoy and shrugged again. "What happened with the PLO?" The smell of cordite from the fireworks finally reached them, and just as quickly faded in the early morning air.

"Nothing too crazy. We had information about weapons smuggling, and sent in an amphibious team to bomb Abu Nidal's boat right in their harbor."

"You and the CIA?"

"The funniest part was our inside man, the Tripoli harbormaster. He thought we were a vessel underwriter out of France and kept selling us intel even after the arms shipment went under right there at his dock." Ellison checked the valve mixture settings on both rebreather units. "CIA? Why would they care about arms in a port in Libya?" Ivan wanted the cigarette even more now, tired of Ellison's evasions. This was the man who helped him recover after abrupt ejection from an Egyptian prison. He'd taught Ivan anonymity was the only true freedom, the only real safety, but Ivan hadn't taken this to mean between the two of them. There were no secrets when Yannis ran things. Were there?

Ivan's lengthy silence must have urged Ellison to offer some explanation. "Do you know what a Katsa is?"

The term sounded vaguely familiar, but he couldn't place it. "Japanese cutlery?"

Ellison squinted in thought. "Might be that as well." They heard a distant helicopter, but Ivan confirmed it wasn't Coletti's. Ellison said, "Katsa's are case officers. At The Office, as we were encouraged to call it. Ha Mossad, le Modiyn ve le Tafkidim Mayuhadim."

The long form sank in, Ivan's eyes widening. "You were a goddamned Mossad agent? When the hell was this? At Israeli Arms? Or before?"

"I didn't say *I* was."

"Don't screw with me, Uncle. Were you?"

It was Ellison's turn to shrug, and Ivan knew no more would be said. He couldn't help a sense of awe. Mossad agents were the epitome of training and ruthlessness. The Kidon, Metsada's assassination unit, was so efficient, so undetectable, even the CIA had no idea how many or what jobs they'd carried out.

The sudden sense of inadequacy felt like a revelation. Who'd planned this approach after all? If Ivan thought the idea of using manatees as decoys was amusing before, it now seemed brilliant. It would have to be. Ellison possessed the best training in the world.

Ivan was pretty sure even American SEAL teams received training from Mossad.

"Coming up on mark," Ellison said, holding up his arm, wristwatch indicating they'd soon need to be underwater.

Ivan must have still had a stunned expression on his face. He snapped out of it when Ellison cast him an inquisitive look.

Underwater travel proved slow. They needed to approach from deep under *Estrella de Mar Rosa* to avoid detection. The silence was peaceful, an isolation from gravity, light and noise very much like the sensory deprivation techniques employed by the GRU. This time Ivan would be doing the interrogating.

Samuel Coletti's vessel was not without numerous security features. A series of fixed underwater lenses sent video to the bridge. Sophisticated active sonar arrays operated like an underwater perimeter alarm. Ivan had made efforts to hack the ship's system without success. He'd thought of a number of ways to disrupt the computers, but Ellison suggested letting Coletti's security systems do what they were supposed to. Disruption is too suspicious.

In preparation Ivan spent a day at SeaWorld capturing video of Bessy and another bovinely named manatee he couldn't remember. They were called sea cows for a reason. A few video filtering tricks gave the recording the passible characteristics they required.

The underbelly of ships at night are a sinister sight and *Estrella de Mar Rosa*'s sheer size made her more so. Forward of two massive five-blade screws a pair of stabilizer fins stretched out, constantly adjusting to keep the ship level. Even with underwater lights the hull was so long Ivan couldn't see more than a glow in the murk where her bulbous bow ought to be. His enhanced environment rig stepped in, aligning to the hull a wireframe overlay, identifying port and aft thrusters, cameras, sensors, and estimates of internal compartments based on infrared heat signatures.

He fired a capsule that detonated forward of the engine compartment, releasing a mess of brownish ink to tar the water space in view of one of the cameras. Kicking into alarm range of the ship's sonar, Ivan magnetized a device to the hull that played a fifteen-minute loop of manatees swimming past. Ellison was already moving back and forth along the keel attaching an array of other devices at key points.

Coletti's ship had a large deployment hatch for the submersible, opened by internal hydraulic arms inaccessible from beneath. Lucky for them, a dive hatch lay just forward of the submersible doors, and Ellison went to work on the lock with an underwater plasma cutter.

Ivan explored the rough surfaces, flickering light from Ellison's work exaggerating the somber existence of calcified water creatures clinging to the expanse, tiny shadows bouncing with an oblivious rhythm distinct from the multitude of mechanical sounds that carried over great distances underwater. Peace wasn't a sense Ivan felt often enough, and he wasn't ready when Ellison tugged on his shoulder, letting him know it was time to board.

The pressurized chamber encompassed the entire space where the submersible parked, but the hoists dangled freely, the berth empty. If Coletti did own a submarine, it was out on mission already.

A generator coming online from the adjacent engine compartment sent mild vibrations through the room. On a nearby panel a green LED pressure indicator permitted access through the squat side door. Ivan was in no hurry. They stripped off the drysuits. A handheld sniffer reported no presence of drug residue from its full spectrum analysis.

"I was expecting more security once inside," Ellison said, shining a light around the reinforced interior structure. "At least more cameras." The light fell on a series of lockers, and finding nothing suspicious within, Ellison stowed their gear in one. Coletti's compliment of scuba diving equipment was impressive, including a 25 cubic meter airbank attached to the compressor.

"I was expecting to get high off the fumes," Ivan joked.

"Drug smuggling is a fairly clean trade. Professionals don't leave piles of powder lying around. Experience suggests we'll find storage compartments aft of the engine room."

"Wouldn't that be obvious to drug enforcement as well?"

"Perhaps, but putting it on the same ventilation circuit as the engines protects the rest of the vessel from contamination. Besides, at the point when the DEA suspects you're smuggling drugs, it doesn't matter where they're hidden."

Contamination was not the word that came to mind walking between the two massive diesel power plants. He'd rebuilt his share of engines and they were never this clean. The smell was the only clue that 9,000 kilowatts of combustion slapped several tons of reciprocating parts around in their lubricated bearings here.

All they found further aft was an equally spotless machine and tool room. No secret doorways, no response on the sniffer. Ivan checked the ventilation points, cracks, service floor plates, nothing.

Before long they were among cabins of a quality more suited to guests than crew. There is a difference between cedar and Brazilian walnut, chrome plating and polished brass, office grade carpet and plush, varnish and handcrafted surfaces—a difference they could smell all around them. Nothing suggested budget limitations, unless the absence of interior surveillance electronics implied Coletti burnt the money on surrounding artwork. Ivan pointed this out.

"Are they prints or originals?" Ellison asked, inspecting the brass plates on the frames. "Who's *Riza i-Abbasi*? They may not be valuable."

"Originals, I'm pretty sure. The photos are continuous tone resin coated and the paintings oil." The artists' names meant nothing to Ivan—Sally Mann, Adolphe William Bouguereau, Edward Weston, Jock Sturges—though he did recognize William Blake. Coletti's taste in nudes was somewhat single-minded.

A chilled wine room held a full complement of largely expensive French vintages, followed by a sauna and hot tub room, one of several the ship's plan provided.

"Hold on," Ivan warned Ellison, who was about to open the next door. "Heat signatures inside."

"What kind of heat?" Ellison said in a hushed voice.

"Body heat. My rig can't get an accurate image, but there are ten to twelve distinct heat blurs. Likely too small to be human. Could be animals."

"Moving or dormant?"

"Stationery."

"Skip it?"

"I don't think so . . . "

. . . Something Carlos had said, but now Ivan couldn't recall exactly what it was. Carlos loaned Ivan a condo, hangar, Jaguar, but let him stumble on this operation blind but for the flimsiest of hints. Carlos knew what Coletti was up to. If Ivan had simply told him about Number 7, Carlos could have saved him a lot of trouble. There were no drugs to find. He'd spoken too soon about size. There were no dogs or cats.

Beautifully joined mahogany bunks lined the cabin, and sleeping under the blankets, children of all ages, none of whom, as far as Ivan could tell, matched the characteristics of Number 7.

"We assembled a pretty extensive profile on Mr. Coletti," Ellison said, "and I don't recall it saying he had any kids of his own."

"He doesn't. Let's move on."

***

When Samuel Coletti's helicopter touched down on the aft helipad, Ivan and Ellison had completed another hour's worth of reconnaissance. They'd rendered a man unconscious in the process, but he was of little interest, almost certainly a patron. They found him in the Lido Suite ill–dressed for confrontation after two boys ran out to get the man a drink.

Ivan found a phone identifying him as a CEO for a server leasing company in California. He'd recently paid Brickell Consulting LLC, one of Coletti's front companies, a handsome sum of money for unspecified services.

"Probably the Virgin Islands tour package," Ellison suggested.

"That's not really funny. What's in the closet?" Ivan said from the joined dining salon where he found a bowl of used crayons on the shelf.

"Toy storage."

"Toys? I probably shouldn't ask, but—"

"Good call."

The rear lounges faced the helipad through a pair of automatic sliding glass doors, with a bar on one side and a Hallet Davis Mini Grand tucked in the opposing corner. Ellison sat and played part of Michael Nymen's Piano Concerto. "I'm not fond of this man you're chasing, but he has discriminating tastes."

"He knows what he likes? I'm painfully aware of that."

Ivan spent time circling the room appraising a series of paintings by Wyeth, one of which appeared to have no relationship to the title. *Cat Bates of Monhegan* featured a pale lad with an oar in an eerie firelight. Bleak but oddly sensual. Matching the frames, mahogany crown molding accented the room in stark contrast to a bright profusion of yellow hibiscus flowers reaching to the ceiling. A painting behind the bar by Duncan Gleason. He read the title aloud.

"Sea Urchins."

"Yes, they should have returned by now."

"No, it's the name of this painting," Ivan turned to pour himself a drink. "Though our meeting with Coletti might go better without them."

"Are you joking? You still want to blackmail Mr. Coletti holding a bag of his nonexistent coke when he walks in? How about this. What's the man's play when finds you detaining two of his underage prostitutes?" Ellison paced the lounge, letting the reality sink in for Ivan. "That's leverage you can't get with a titanium crowbar."

Ivan once visited the Philippines where this trade was commonplace, and everyone knew the stories from countries like Thailand. He acknowledged it with a horrified fascination he imagined many shared when forging an idea about the broken emotional behaviors they expected these kids to have. What had *Ivan* expected? Just miniature versions of every escort he'd ever screwed? Maybe somber, quiet, traumatized, some unsettling mix of precocious and prurient, not-quite-human automaton, a mere object stripped of identity? All these things were possible, but if Ivan could choose a negotiation instrument, he preferred a lifeless, tightly packed kilogram of cocaine.

Ellison was right, though. He could bring himself to settle for what now came scampering from below.

"Who are you?"

Bottle of wine in one hand, long-stemmed glass in the other, the kid appearing from the grand staircase sounded more curious than anxious. Less certain were the eyes peering from behind the older boy's ankles at the lower stair.

"Who we are isn't important," Ellison said, waving him forward. "Why don't you bring me that bottle?"

"But it's for—"

"He won't be needing it for at least six hours. Can't let it go to waste. What in God's name are you wearing?"

His name was Elias, and he smiled, pulled the cork, and spent the next thirty minutes or so demonstrating a vast knowledge of mixed drinks. He had a dexterity with the bottles too accomplished for a fourteen year old. Ellison expressed approval over each concoction. Ivan trusted his uncle wasn't sampling too much, wanting him to be reasonably alert when Coletti arrived.

Jaden took his social cues from the older one. Despite any reservations Ivan held about their behavior, Jaden was every bit the temperament of a typical seven year old, running around as though his head was a fixed gyro, body tethered haphazardly and scrambling to keep pace. He jumped off the sofas, laughing with an imbecilic melody, dragging behind a tail stitched to the seat of his animal pajamas. He'd lost the shirt part somewhere, human from the waist up, like some towheaded fawn. A satyr with ten toes.

Citrusy morning sunlight washed through the slowing rotors, casting complex shadows across the Arabic furniture patterns. All the exertion left Jaden half asleep with his head in Ivan's lap, the animal legs sprawled beside him on the couch. The tail curled between Jaden's legs where he held it with both hands.

Elias left Ellison with a reddish martini and played something classical from sheet music at the piano. Like Schubert without the finesse, fingers chopping at the keys in the dissonant fashion of Chopin. *Die Forelle* should always sound so light and frivolous, as though played to an audience of bohemian cherubs. Reality was more awkward. Hitman consorting with musically inclined . . . well, not *exactly* cherubs. Elias stopped to bring Ivan another Scotch from the bar when Samuel Coletti emerged from the cockpit. The Atlantic breeze played with the white fabric of Coletti's suit in a drifting slow motion that made his converging presence feel inevitable.

Ivan imagined all the ways Coletti would crumble, glass doors parting, the sight of Ivan gently scratching Jaden's scalp with one hand, pistol in the other, Coletti with no option but to cooperate.

But the weapon trained on Samuel's head failed to elicit the reaction Ivan anticipated.

"You're earlier than I expected, Mr. Stavros." He smiled, perfect white teeth, nodding to Ellison behind the starboard bar. "And you've brought your CIA friend in a matching suit. Should I feel flattered?" Coletti waved his hand toward the stairs. *"Jaden, Elias, vayan abajo y despierten a sus hermanos y comen algo. Papa tiene un asunto privado que hablar con los señores."*

"Los niños estan bien aquí," Ivan said. Neither boy moved. *"Sientate."*

"I see how you think this is going to go," Samuel said. All the same, he found a seat across from the glass coffee table. "Go ahead. Shoot me. Your DNA predisposes you to that kind of recklessness. It'll be the last thing you ever do."

Ivan watched Ellison draw and aim for a space behind Ivan, yanking Elias out of the way by the horse-halter of buckled leather straps passing for his garment. From behind the glass doors opposite, a red dot crawled up Ivan's body and came to rest on the third unclasped rosewood button.

* * *

Even when outgunned in a standoff Ivan knew it always weighed in his favor to be aiming at the boss. He wasn't about to trade this advantage for a futile shot at the guards. Still, how had this operation gone so wrong so fast?

Worse still, how did Samuel Coletti know they were coming? And who they were? Between Ivan's carefully concealed adrenalin-driven heartbeats he tried to recall any part of their surveillance that could have been compromised. What did Samuel mean about Ivan's predisposition? What DNA?

Then it hit him.

Samuel apparently recognized Ivan's moment of comprehension. "Yes, that DNA. Three milliliters to be exact, which you conveniently misplaced in Ms. Sharon Paley. Did you think she'd just forget who her employer is over one night of rough sex?" Samuel proceeded to make an elaborate display of trimming and lighting a cigar he subsequently took no interest in smoking, though the aroma was pleasant enough. "BioConnect Industries, my company, has computers powerful enough to sequence DNA in seconds. You think I can't peek at the government's NDI Database and find a match?" Coletti turned to Ellison. "How does it feel to work for the organization that tortured your own nephew? When he was still just a kid? And now you work together?" he said, turning back to Ivan. "I must hear this story, but not before you kindly turn over your weapons."

Ivan made no move to surrender.

The man's pedigree was indefinable. His voice was not quite English and not quite South American, but nonetheless felt organic. His muted Middle Eastern appearance matched neither accent, temples shot with a silver band of hair that imbued him with a gentle severity.

When Ellison spoke to up the ante he sounded tranquil to the point of bored.

"I could go ahead and trigger the leech mines on your hull and we could all go for a nice swim."

Samuel took little time to consider this. "*Estrella de Mar Rosa* is insured. The boys enjoy swimming. You two will have to float home."

"All we want is some information," Ivan said.

"Information?" Samuel laughed. "Information worth this foolhardy gamble must be awfully important. The kind I'd have no interest in sharing with the CIA." His confidence was unflappable. Rising to retrieve a drink at the bar, he crushed out the cigar in a deliberately casual way. If he really knew Ivan, he must be aware death was imminently possible given Ivan's aim. Yet in the face of this he only became indignant, setting the glass down as though the world moved in his wake. "No, you've already seen too much. Do you have a preference for how I dispose of your bodies, or should I just throw you overboard and let the Miami police sort it out? You get nothing. You're both exceedingly foolish, trespassing on my ship, threatening me and my family. Do you have the faintest idea what you've gotten into?"

The word *family* reminded Ivan of the leverage he held, and in fact continued to hold in his lap. How could Samuel refer to these boys as his family?

"He's not really my uncle," Ivan said. He turned the gun and placed the suppressor against the crown of Jaden's head. The boy jerked but Ivan held him down. Jaden gripped his plush tiger tail harder. "My associate's not here on behalf of the CIA. We have no interest in your business. I just need to know where one of Sharon Paley's GLS purchases went."

"Take the gun off him," Samuel said. "Don't hurt the boy."

"It won't hurt him. The bullet will shatter his brain so swiftly he won't feel a thing."

Jaden squeezed his eyes shut as tears trickled down across the bridge of his nose. Ivan recalled the attributes Ms. Paley programmed for Number 7 and now they made perfect sense. Quiet, contemplative, obsequious. Environmental adaptability, amiable, passive. And curious. No doubt amenable traits for a life of buggering. Could manipulation of their DNA be in any way construed as humane, or were the traits picked for Coletti's selfish convenience?

The man's subsequent outrage suggested the latter, but Ivan sensed a tender emotion hidden between the words.

"Do you have any idea of what you're doing?" Samuel practically fell back into the chair. "Any idea the investment I've made in him? Forget the purchase cost. That's nothing compared to all the logistical expenses. I've sunk a small fortune into research and development alone. You think all this security is cheap? Or the challenges involved rearing ideal, healthy, emotionally stable companions? I'm not breeding farm animals here. Years of work go into their education, social engineering, sensitivity training, cultural awareness—enormous investment of capital and resources, long before I can earn a return on any of them. You can't just shoot him like he's some common street urchin!"

"So he's valuable to you," Ivan said. "This massive boat's indemnified, but not the crew? Of course. How do you buy life insurance for people who aren't even supposed to exist?" The action was entirely for effect, a semi-auto being equally deadly in either position, yet everyone flinches when the hammer's pulled back. "How valuable?"

Elias yanked against Ellison's grasp, his voice taking on a surprising manly anger. "Let him go, you're scaring him—*No temas, Jaden!*"

"Si, no temas," Ivan said, rubbing Jaden's tears across his face. *"Vas estar bien."*

"No . . . no tengo miedo," Jaden choked out.

But he *was* scared. His terror was a palpable smell, the rancid innocence trembling in Ivan's expanding situational awareness. Ivan could sense the guard behind him moving in closer. So close Ivan could smell the oiled components mingling with the man's nervous sweat, waiting for a signal from his boss that never came. At this point Ivan was sure he could grab the muzzle from behind his head. Why did people always want to get the business end within reach? Are you insecure about your aim? An assault weapon works just fine from a distance, he might have said in different circumstances. The room was dense, the smell of salted sunlight, gentle sensation of being afloat, alcohol residue in half a dozen glasses and a cigar wilting at the bar. What was the endgame? The luxurious yacht, maintenance, insurance, registration, employment of security, helicopter transport, suits and amenities . . . how could a mere 23 kilograms of genetically engineered catamite afford Coletti all this? Even twenty of them?

He scratched his fingers through Jaden's hair. Comforting someone he wasn't entirely prepared to kill at any moment upset Ivan's sense of decency, but not as much as the incongruous acts distressed Samuel Coletti.

"I think we have gotten off to a bad start," Samuel said. He dismissed his guards with a wave. "Allow me to extend my hospitality to you both and we can discuss détente."

* * *

"You must pardon the inadequacy of this service, but you didn't exactly make an appointment. I was fortunate to receive a message from Elias, two strange men aboard. I instructed him to keep you entertained."

That explained the ambush. When did he have the opportunity? Little bastard's youth was deceptive.

Elias made his way around, filling glasses at an open alfresco dining table one deck above the salon. Considering the exotic continental spread of fruits and pastries before them, Ivan found Samuel's high society belittlement amusing. Miami's elite wouldn't rub shoulders with him if they thought he was just a pimp. Or would they? Perhaps Ivan underestimated South Florida's sordid tendencies at any socioeconomic level.

"Ms. Paley is sometimes Maria Bonholler, but I recall retiring that sobriquet. How many years ago was the purchase?"

"A little over seven," Ivan said, "from a kiosk in Seattle."

Lazy cumulus clouds drifted like curtains across the warm sunlight that poured over the morning sea traffic in Biscayne Bay. Vessels sounded their horns to hale each other and *Estrella de Mar Rosa* returned her own deafening salvo.

Apart from the scantily clad busboy filling Ivan's coffee, it was a lifestyle he could easily enjoy.

"And why are you looking for this child?" Samuel asked, scrolling through records on a tablet.

"I've been hired by the surrogate mother to find him."

Samuel smiled. "Deceit is not becoming of you, Mr. Stavros. Your reputation lacks the benevolence of such an enterprise." He handed the tablet to Elias and with a few instructions in Spanish tasked him to prepare the crew for inbound appointments. "You're not a terrorist. At least not in the sense our enthusiastic government believes. But you had no luck convincing the spooks of this. How long did the CIA move you around?"

"Over two years, but you already knew that. Is there a reason you're evading my question? I just want to know where the GLS pill-baby is."

"Patience," he said with a dismissive gesture. "Why should you be in a such a hurry? Enjoy. We're

being social, which is the least you can afford me after the inconveniences. What should I tell my client with the tranquilizer dart in his thigh? I'll have to recompense his whole stay. This is bad business. You've cost me no small amount of money, so you can indulge me a little patience."

Pompous ass. "You have more information than you have any right to know. Where do you get it?"

"I have my sources. Two years being extraordinarily rendered through black prisons hardly endears the CIA to you, I imagine. And losing your father in the process?"

Ivan's hackles rose. "Don't screw with me. This has no relevance. I didn't come here to talk about my father."

"Why not? I see it upsets you."

"Look, if they killed Yannis, and you're itching to piss me off, just tell me and get it over with."

"I didn't say he was dead. I'm sure I don't know."

Samuel signaled over his shoulder. Two other boys came out and cleared away the table. He sent one of them to fetch a bottle of cognac and glasses, small consolation for Coletti's relentless interest in putting Ivan at an informational disadvantage.

"What I *do* know is he told the CIA nothing. He divulged no details about your modest arms trading business. He protected you."

"Why are we talking about this?"

"*We're* not talking about it. I'm talking and you're exercising an appropriate amount of restraint. Do you know the reason?"

"Why don't you tell me."

"Right now you're trying to decide how much I know about your reasons for visiting me. You feel compromised, as you should. Does this happen frequently with you? Being blindsided by your own presumptions of others? Is it arrogance? I don't think so, more of an insecurity, but you haven't identified it for yourself. You needn't be concerned. I have no idea why you want the child."

"Then why the charade? You're the one who accused me of lying."

Samuel ignored this. "You make rash decisions. You're careless and ambivalent about consequences. Don't deny it, you've overutilized mendacity for one day. It's not entirely your fault. A person's DNA is an almanac of predictable possibilities." He ran his fingers though the hair of one of the boys and down his back. "The entirety of human code contained in microscopic chains, infinitesimally small and yet capable of accomplishing such breathtaking beauty."

Elias strode up the aft companionway and returned Samuel's tablet.

Samuel now turned to Ellison. "He acquired much of his natural survival instinct from your father, but not the injudicious impulsivity."

"Who?"

"Your nephew. Half nephew, though he doesn't know it. There's no conceivable motive for him to deceive me about such an inconsequential thing, believing that you're not really his uncle, so he must not know the truth. But you're aware of it. I can see it in your eyes."

The well of equanimity Ellison drew from dried up. Noticeably uncomfortable, he examined the glass, rolling the rim between his fingers in silence.

"I can learn so much about your history, your mother, father, their progenitors, the whole family tree, Mr. Ellison. The sources of your genes are particularly noteworthy, again most likely from your father. Difficult time to be Jewish in Eastern Europe."

Vines of purple passionflowers intertwined a canopy of white lattice overhead, delicate stamens flickering in the breeze. Ellison hesitantly nodded.

"Which makes his former partner in life more interesting. That's where the Greek DNA markers come from. Where your nephew inherited his recklessness."

"What's he saying?" Ivan said. "Is he talking about me?"

* * *

Later, driving to Fort Lauderdale to reconnoiter a courthouse, Ivan tried to cope with all the frustration, not knowing who he was anymore.

Why didn't anyone tell him he was half Jewish? That Yannis and Ellison were really brothers? Or half brothers or something?

It's complicated, Ellison said.

How? Who was his grandfather? The same as Ellison's father? Why the secrets? What would it have mattered?

It's complicated.

Damn it.

Floating in a zodiac earlier that morning, Ivan was certain his superior command of circumstances would subdue Samuel Coletti, make him vulnerable and divulge the whereabouts of Number 7 against his own best interests. In the end Ivan had been ambushed on both sides, by Coletti *and* now ex-Mossad Ellison. He was so disoriented, the reasons why Samuel so eagerly offered them accommodations with a few of the boys eluded him.

"Parading them about the deck like that, wearing practically nothing."

"It's a little like the tradecraft on honeypots," Ellison explained. "He can't be sure what you'll do after discovering his tainted love boat. He surreptitiously records you doing something lewd with one or more of them, and blackmails you. Ruin his business and he ruins your reputation. Legal and illegal being irrelevant to you, that's all you have."

"Does he just assume everyone's a pedophile?"

Ellison shrugged. "Humans have done weirder things when they think no one's looking. Curiosity isn't always genetically manipulated, you know."

"Would you? Are you curious?"

Ellison didn't get as indignant about the challenge as Ivan had hoped.

Strategy for the day having gone hopelessly wrong, they still learned where to find Number 7.

"Dead," Samuel said. "The surrogate was a drug addict. They both died in childbirth. No one should be looking for him, least of all you."

Overhead a pontoon biplane soared low across Biscayne Bay, flying past the deeper blue and landing in lighter hued waters covering the diminishing coral reefs. Jaden tried to sit on Ivan's lap but settled for Ellison, the fascinated boy's fingertips making an exploration of the man's perfectly bald head.

16

No matter how hard he swallowed, Cody couldn't move whatever was caught in his throat. Flat on his back again, he gagged, unable to sit up. What was this thing in his nose?

He was in the Operating Room of the Wenatchee River Corrections Center but couldn't remember how he arrived. Wetness trickled from both eyes, large lamp with six huge lenses overhead, smell of iodine, a beeping sound from somewhere nearby. His ankles were strapped above the table, two stubby knees framing a digital clock on the far wall that read 10:47. Morning or night? Wires and tubes hung from his arm, two in the chest, right there on the teddy bear tattoo. Lots of colored tubes stuck to him with sticky clear plastic squares that looked like they were shrink-wrapped on the skin.

Cody panicked. They weren't on him. The tubes were *in* him! The beeping got faster and faster. Cody's chest jumped and fell rapidly, panic attack like a seizure. He wrenched against the restraints and cried out, so loudly he even scared himself, then broke down sobbing, trying to pull away from the nose tube, dragging his back on the sheets, trapped, terrified, shaking and angry. Then he heard voices.

The doctor with the black hair in a big ball was back. She'd come to see him so long ago and asked so many questions. Then she was gone and he didn't see her again until the day his stomach hurt so bad. Was it yesterday?

She shined a light in Cody's eyes and mouth, put her fingers on his neck.

"He's looking a lot better today."

Another doctor came around the side of the table, one Cody had never seen before. He turned on the overhead lamp and moved the light to where its warmth fell on Cody's chest. He poked Cody the same way she had. Cody couldn't take his eyes off the man's brows. Long, white, fuzzy, just like Santa Claus's eyebrows. The man's beard wasn't big enough, but maybe Santa shaves and lets it grow out at Christmas?

"What's in my thoat?" Cody asked.

"I took him off TPN at 0120 hours and inserted the formula tube," she said to the man. "They called me near midnight. One of the samples is having a 'reaction'—their words, not mine—the nurse said he'd passed out. I spent thirty minutes going through WRCC security. He was critical by the time I started diagnosis."

Doctor Santa hung a bag of green goop next to the bag with clear liquid. Cody felt the nose tube tug as Santa attached it to the bag.

"Sample had a hundred and four degree fever, advanced heart rate and suffering from acute priapism," she said.

He wound the tube through the wheel on the machine and poked buttons. Green goop traveled into the tube, around the wheel, and up the length towards Cody's nose. He panicked and yanked away, but the stuff kept coming, eventually disappearing up his nose. He could still breath. Where did it go? He burped and it tasted like peanuts. It must be going in his brain. Would his head explode? The color and movement amazed him. He wished Teagan could be there to see it.

Where was Teagan? Teagan would be worried about him. Cody knew this because Teagan loved him. Cody tried to remember when he'd last seen Teagan. It was the night Cody hurt, and the woman with the black hair was there . . . what happened? He'd been scared and covered in blood.

Someone had cleaned him, but he couldn't remember more than bits and pieces. When did it happen? She was talking to Dr. Santa again.

"I temporarily relived pressure at the dorsal vein and checked for swollen prostate, infection, cystic or rectal trauma. The sample was in a lot of pain. We gave him a saddle block. The staff here got really crunchy about removing the restraints, but the DOC nurses eventually convinced them epidural anesthesiology kind of requires access to the spine. I mean, really, where's he going to go?"

"Hmm. Yes, well, their priorities leave much to be desired." Doctor Santa booted up a computer. The optical drives and fans sounded like a turbine. "I apologize," he said, rubbing his face, "I'm still suffering a little jet lag."

"It's only a three hour time difference, but I'll let it slide." She laughed and Santa smiled.

"It feels like ten. Go ahead and set up our conference. I only skimmed the prelim on the plane. What did you find?"

She unfolded a tripod on the other side of the bed and adjusted the angle of the tablet to face Cody. "I did an ultrasound and found an anterior abscess pressing on the bulbourethral glands, which we endoperineally aspirated. He's on full spectrum antibiotics, it shouldn't recur."

"Am I sick?" Cody asked.

A video of a group of people came up on the tablet, some in lab coats with the same logo as these doctors, and the others in regular clothes.

"The committee's ready," she said.

"Are you Santa Claus?"

They both laughed. "I wish I could be. Am I fat enough to be Santa Claus?"

Cody smiled and shook his head. "You have Santa's eyebrows."

"That's adorable," she said.

They put on sea green latex gloves. Doctor Santa pulled a steel tray near the bed. Cody strained to see, but all Santa's tools looked really scary. The beeping got faster.

"What you're going to do?" he asked, but no one answered.

"Good morning, gentlemen. Are we recording? Good. The time is eleven hundred twenty two hours. We are examining sample PG-014487-M following a pharmacogenic anomaly occurring approximately twelve hours ago. Sample has been stabilized following perineal surgery and endocrinopathic stabilization. You should find the procedure already uploaded."

He repeated a lot of what she'd already said, lots of words Cody didn't know yet. Would he ever be big enough to learn so many words? It seemed impossible. The doctor stuck a syringe in one of the couplings in Cody's arm.

"We'll be performing blood work, glandular biopsies, DNA extrapolation, hormone analysis and some neural interfacing. Can you prep the neural shunts?"

Cody felt a moment of nausea and, when it passed, a lightness took over as if gravity weakened. Cody swallowed and let out another peanut burp.

Doctor Santa sprayed something deep in Cody's nostril with a plastic cone. His nose stopped working. He couldn't understand the sensation—he could still breathe but couldn't feel the air moving through his nose. Something tasted minty. Santa inserted a long, curved metal stem into the numb nostril.

"Access to the thyroidal and pituitary complex via the cartilaginous inferior fascia of the sphenoidal sinus." His hand pressed on Cody's forehead and a crunch accompanied a sharp pain, like a bee sting somewhere between and behind his eyes. Cody cried out, but it was over. The stem removed, a colorful bundle of wires remained. Cody sneezed. She wiped blood and snot off Cody's upper lip and chest.

"Not too difficult," she said.

"Self-guiding. Check for interface."

She looked at the computer. "Confirm. Partial cerebral mapping. Real-time DNA sequencing is ready as well." She passed him another sharp instrument.

"Incision near the styloid process, up through the jugular foramen, and we should have mapping of the limbic core soon."

"Not just yet."

Cody's gut trembled, but whatever they'd shot in his arm kept him from shaking in spite of how he felt. Now his jaw hurt.

"I've got a handshake error," she said.

Doctor Santa looked at the computer. "Keep clicking 'Yes'. It'll go away."

The computer fans sped up. Cody could smell something electricky, like when Teagan arced the sockets to light cigarettes, or the smell of thunderstorm rain.

"FSH is relatively high, look at this sequence in the CG amino acid bases."

"It's a signature," she said.

"Damn. He's one of ours."

"Are you talking about the sample pool?"

"No. He's a construct. Vending machine baby, from our subsidiary, Genesis Life Solutions." He turned to the Committee on screen. "Is there a file notation anywhere? He should have been eliminated during initial blood work screening."

Committee shook their heads.

"Would it make a difference?" she asked.

"If Hizer Pharmaceuticals is the father? It might. Depends on programming. He's assembled using proprietary DNA, biologically stitched together like a quilt from genes chosen for resistance to diseases and anomalies. If we'd caught this in screening, he'd never have been placed in the sample pool."

Cody wanted to tell her he was okay. He wanted her to know his favorite colors were blue and green, that he hadn't told the truth when she'd come to see him so long ago. He didn't lie, just changed his mind, and if she only knew maybe she could make him better. He couldn't say anything and felt sorry. Teagan knew everything about pills, and even he didn't know what she'd prescribed for Cody. Was he sick? Was it getting worse? Would he need more pills? Cody's stomach gurgled, fluids emptying into the tubes.

"This section of the chain is supposed to be introns. Junk DNA, it's not supposed to code any proteins. But there's a pattern here."

"Structural?"

Doctor shrugged. "Definitely structural. It shouldn't be part of the GLS programming."

He was holding Cody by the wrist near the restraint, but Cody didn't feel any sense Santa cared much. He kept finishing or starting sentences that didn't go together, the other nodding her head. The faces on screen just stared at him. Cody felt awful. He didn't want to be stared at naked.

"Genetic single nucleotide polymorphism."

"Haploid substitutions?"

"Perhaps. Whatever the DNA coded, it's fighting the test drugs."

"Like an allergic reaction."

"Sure, but at the cellular and neurochemical level, his DNA protein coders are neutralizing the drug's interaction with the hypothalamus."

Both doctors suddenly noticed the officer standing in the room.

"Yes?"

"It's time for count," the officer said.

Doctor Santa looked at her, then back to the officer. "Well, yes. I suppose you have to count them. This is one inmate. Add that to your list."

"He's assigned to Medical 4."

"*This* is a medical room," Doctor said.

"He has to be in his assigned location so we can do count."

"Sir, I can't move him right now. We're in conference. Can't you just add up everyone in the medical wing and add this one to your count?"

There was a long pause. "I suppose we can put him on an out-count . . . I don't know if there's a procedure for that."

"I don't understand what's so complicated here?" Doctor started to look even more like Santa, his face turning a flush rosy color.

"He has to be in his assigned location so we can do count."

Doctor Santa turned and whispered something to her. Cody heard a bad word.

"Well, he can't be moved."

"I'll talk to my sergeant and see what we can do."

"Yes. Do that," Doctor snapped. The officer left the O.R. "Good thing he didn't want to be a pediatric endocrinologist."

"Who thinks they want to be a corrections officer when they grow up," she said. "Or for that matter, anything more specific than *doctor*?"

"I want to be a farmer when I grow up," Cody said. "If I could be a farmer maybe I would grow marshmallows. Can you grow marshmallows?"

She smiled. "Not in this climate. Maybe further south."

The numb feeling and minty flavor in Cody's nose was gone. The sensation of lightness too was wearing off, and he could feel the wrinkles in the sheets. Now his nose just felt stuffy—it was stuffed! He turned his head and both eyes watered from the twisting of wires and tube stuck in his nose.

"I think I need to go pee," Cody said.

Minutes later the feeling went away. He decided one tube put green stuff in and the other tube took the yellow stuff out. Teagan said blue and yellow make green. If green went in and yellow came out, where did the blue go?

"I miss Teagan. When can I go? Go home?"

Doctor Santa selected things on a touch screen. "Running program 3T07."

Cody's head jerked involuntarily and he was dizzy, eyes speckling over with black dots that spun in wobbly patterns. Hs body vibrated, feet no longer cold. He couldn't feel them at all, couldn't make his toes wiggle. A warm sensation crawled down his back like he was floating from the restraints. The doctors watched him intently. What did they see? Was he melting? Could she see the spots? Cody's mouth hung open and drool ran down his cheek. Wonderful strange sensations crept all around him, like a string of warm fuzzy beads drawn through the flesh, tickling and rippling just beneath the skin. He grunted but didn't know where the sound came from. Warmth flooded through his chest and pooled in the gut. He felt so happy.

She was looking at the yellow tube. "Is this a priapic recurrence, or should we administer a PDE?"

"No need. Direct stimulation to synapses in the limbic core is a little like cheating. We've triggered the L-arginine-nitric oxide-cyclic GMP pathway. Little jolt to the brain's pleasure center and the caudate nucleus lights up, the reward complex."

She nodded. "Smooth muscle relaxation. Did you know the cGMP PDE inhibitors in Viagra were originally tested to treat cardiovascular disease? Like hypertension?"

"I recall. And all the profit came from side-effects. Funny how some drugs are discovered."

She pointed to the screen. "Phenylethylamine surge. We're breeching the neurotransmitter's threshold. I'm stepping up saline drip rate."

"Two cc's per minute should compensate for dehydration. Lower voltage to the NANC nerves. Go ahead and end program."

The wonderful sensation was gone.

"We triggered a secretable. Take a sample."

"Anywhere?"

"Yes, it's in the sweat."

She swabbed Cody's neck and stuck it in a labeled glass tube.

Cody wanted so badly to say something, but when his mouth moved he just blubbered. Committee watched him for what felt like hours and hours. Santa ran programs on the computer, wires in Cody's nose tingling as they dragged him through a multitude of exhausting sensations, some of them wonderful, and others that jerked muscles so much his chest heaved like he'd been running fast, faster than he'd ever run, and almost couldn't breathe now. Was this what they'd done to Teagan? Was this TDT? Would he wake up on the floor of the cell hurting and crazy?

Another program tasted like maple syrup on the tongue, sweetness flowing through every artery, thinned into a watery drool trickling down in the sheets. Hours and hours. They struck huge biopsy needles in him, but he didn't feel anything. Doctor Santa talked to Committee the whole time, so many big words. Cody felt sick now but couldn't throw up. He was too tired. Eyesight got blurry. Fluids leaked out of him all over the place, running down his face.

Cody kept drifting in and out of consciousness, and after so many hours struggling with the humiliating loss of control, just wanted to sleep. He thought of Teagan holding him, could almost feel it, almost hear the word *Spud*, and cried.

17

Eliv Schreiber escaped the chimney. That was the way camp inmates said it. Most of his people did not.

Even small towns like Ayia Anna felt the struggle for food during the war. Germany treated Greece like their personal grocery, shipping provisions north while hundreds of thousands of Greeks starved to death. They came for Eliv on a warm day in May. He was in the library reading. Eliv wasn't sure what the war was about and the rumors from towns around Krakòw were absurd and unbelievable. It hadn't occurred to him that simply being Jewish was so perilous.

Maria certainly didn't think so, and on that balmy day brought him a wrapped towel of still warm bread and Kaséri cheese. Spread out on the floor between the shelves of poetry, Eliv cradled her growing belly, swearing he could feel kicking that she couldn't. Maria recited verse to show him the virtue of her country's poets. Eliv shifted the dark hair and kissed her neck just below the dangly end of an impertinent earring. He promised her more when the war was over. She was never more beautiful than in these tender moments, her sweet laughter a banquet for the soul. *I could not, as I breathed, choose among the scents, but called them all, and drank them as one drinks joy or sorrow suddenly sent by fate. I drank them all, and when I touched your waist, my blood became a nightingale, became like the running waters.*

A day crammed in a squalid boxcar, pressed so tight there was no escape from human waste, made Eliv certain no torment could follow worse than this. The treatment was such a shock no one could fathom how to cope. Why them?

Temperatures dropped in the night and a dense fog heralded the final stop where they spilled onto a platform to an onslaught of coarse German orders. Blinding spotlights shone down on them, revealing truth in the rumors, worse. The acrid odor they'd smelled on approach, when the wind failed to carry it off, became a rain of soot, those who hadn't escaped the chimney, horrific but too sacred to wash away. Their families rejoined the earth as silenced ash for which the traditional rituals of grief felt insufficient in scale.

In one unceremonious instant young children, the elderly, and those deemed inadequately healthy, were torn from loved ones and sent to their death. All who remained were systematically rendered unrecognizable. Stripped of possessions and clothing, hair shaved off, tattooed and made to wear ill-fitting camp uniforms rife with lice, they resembled a gray shell of their former existence. When Eliv cried they assumed he too lost a loved one. They didn't know his tears were a prayer of thanks his child wasn't yet born and would escape the suffering.

From the day Eliv was ordered to sew the number patches on his uniform, to the day he tore them off, he defied physical and spiritual brutality by proving useful in the surreal death camp. In the darkest hours he closed his eyes, thought of Maria, and asked God to look after his child.

"Eliv Schreiber spent two winters at Auschwitz," Ellison said. "His memory of those years was quite lucid, but everything after a little broken."

Ivan had backed the Ford Transit van into a space along the exterior of a fourth floor parking garage on SE 3rd Avenue. Logos magnetized to the sides of the van advertised Hallandale Golf Emporium. With the engine off and rear doors open, the air-conditioned interior seeped away. Sitting on overturned twenty-liter plastic buckets, Ivan and Ellison loosened collars, a 12-volt utility fan screwed to the roof liner merely stirring the humid air.

"He was among the liberated then?" Ivan asked.

"Eliv? No. Hardly anyone left behind at Auschwitz lived. Germans evacuated most of the camp when they heard the Russian front closing in. I can't imagine crossing the frost on foot."

"They didn't use the trains again?"

"The Reich was really disorganized by then, running out of resources. Consider, Eliv was moved from a highly secure, organized camp to a barn in Gleiwitz. A *barn*. The journey to Buchenwald was by rail, but open cattle cars. Eliv said he and others pitched bodies overboard as they died."

Ivan agreed with Ellison's disgust. No one should die like that. Ivan wasn't averse to death, he made a living carrying it out. Protracted suffering, however, he couldn't abide.

Ivan opened a thermos of coffee and spiked it from a bottle. He was about to offer some to Ellison when he noticed the label said *Blackberry Schnapps*. Better just to stick it back in the bag at this point.

It wasn't like his uncle to be particularly nostalgic, but ever since being aboard the *Estrella de Mar Rosa* Ellison had been acting strangely. Samueal Coletti's assertion mother and child died of a drug overdose wouldn't be enough for Hizer. When Ivan asked for the surrogate's name Colletti again became guarded. Bad business, he said. However, business was a field on which Ivan could negotiate the terms. How much would it cost? Hell, Hizer was footing the tab.

"I have a proposal suitable to both our interests," Coletti had said. He tapped a figure into the tablet and passed it to Ivan.

"If you think a lousy name's worth this many zeroes, your fantasy world's bigger than I imagined."

"No, you misunderstand my intentions. I'm remunerating you for services. You'll work for me, and when the task's done I'll give you the name."

"*Work* for you?" Ivan hazarded a look at the boy in Ellison's lap.

"Again you misunderstand my business terms." Mr. Coletti stood and walked to the starboard railing, as if speaking to the ocean was more confidential. "A certain individual has become a thorn in my side. I require him handled in a manner for which your profession is better suited."

Coletti didn't just want one or two people dead. A message had to be sent. Now Ivan and his uncle watched people file in and out of courtrooms in the Broward County Court building across the street. The setup was typically convenient. After a forty-year zeitgeist of prison industrial influences, the conviction business was booming. Cities couldn't just move courthouses out of the central downtown, so annexes and expansions sprouted to cope with prosecutorial fervor, and with them the perfect sniper platform—nearby multi-story public access parking garages with easily thwarted surveillance systems.

"Then it was barges," Ellison said. "Floating north on the River Elbe, Allied warplanes overhead, Nazi troops deserting, and everything around them's been destroyed by years of war. I can't think of more dispiriting circumstances."

"I can."

"Don't be flippant. I'm trying to explain something important here."

"Which is?"

A rhetorical interruption Ellison ignored. "They end up in another barn somewhere between Hamburg and Kiel but artillery can still be heard in the distance, and gradually the command structure crumbles. Of the remaining inmates, most were too broken or cowed, but Eliv's courage was greater. He and a few others slipped away undetected in the middle of the night. They stole a car, headed south."

"Back through Germany?"

Ellison shrugged. "The mood had changed. When the radio broadcasts revealed what was really happening, most

Germans didn't have the stomach for it. Eliv and his friends found people willing to give them food and shelter."

At some point the courthouse retrofitted its windows with two-inch thick bulletproof glass. *Bulletproof* could be very misleading. Ivan handed Ellison the Barrett M197 rifle. From a lead-lined case Ellison pulled a box magazine of five depleted uranium .50 caliber rounds. The glass wouldn't shatter, but he'd be able to punch pretty good-sized holes, maybe fifteen or more centimeters wide, large enough for Ivan, in the offset position, to cleanly hit the targets. Their respective scopes worked in tandem. Ivan's painted an infrared line of sight. Ellison's detected the extra-visible spectrum, allowing him to aim for the point where Ivan's trajectory intersected the window.

"Did Eliv find her?"

"Maria? She's the real tragedy. After what he heard, Eliv couldn't bring himself to look for your father."

"My *father*?" Ellison's story came like dust shakes from a boot until finally the irritating stone is jarred loose. As it fell Ivan realized his uncle wasn't telling his own story so much as Ivan's. "Maria? She

was . . . ?"

"Katramados," Ellison said. "Eliv found Ayia Anna burned to the ground, courtesy of the ELAS resistance fighters, who shot everyone left behind days before by the Security Battalions. They'd already burnt the library and factory, and ELAS burned the rest, which seems like a counterintuitive way to recruit men, but what do I know?" Ellison ran his finger along a dusty stretch of the van's interior. "Worked for Maria."

Ivan tried to recall what Ellison told him only weeks before, which seemed related to the present narrative. Maria was Yannis's mother, which made Eliv Schreiber Ivan's grandfather. Maria was the grandmother Ellison called a hero weeks before. Or had Ivan missed something? "You told me they hanged my grandmother. Didn't Eliv look for Yannis? Surely someone told him his son survived."

"Of course. The same scattered townsfolk who told Eliv that Maria joined with the Security Battalions to torment Jews."

"What?"

"I didn't learn the truth until I found Yannis."

"I don't understand," Ivan said. "Why would they tell him that? If it wasn't true?"

Ellison shrugged. "History wrote her down as a traitor. What do you want?" He picked through worn paperbacks inexplicably crammed in the van's interior gutters. The humidity was suddenly stifling in density. Had Ivan been on the less awkward end of the conversation he'd have joked of the need for a hydrodynamic ballistic study. There wasn't much more to tell, and Ellison completed the link their family shared.

Eliv lost his soul to war and heart to Maria, whose perceived betrayal aged him another ten years. He devolved into a roaming perpetual drunkenness, a delusional half life made more convincing by discovery he'd been recorded as a casualty of Auschwitz.

"Then we get the State of Israel," Ellison said, "his beacon of hope, respite from loss, a new start, the bosom of his people, all that, and he's not going to tell his new wife the first love was seduced by anti-Semites, is he? Or tell me I have a half sibling in Greece he's ashamed to acknowledge."

"I'm sorry," Ivan said. A meaningless refrain in the circumstances.

The night before he'd filled each brass with 78 grains, pressing in a .338 Lapua Magnum round after etching *17:23* on the tail with a laser engraver. His Surgeon sniper rifle wasn't cheap, but neither was it the most expensive one he'd fired. Going strictly by the 0.5 or better MOA, modern rifles were still more accurate. But after two decades of familiarity Ivan trusted his long shots to few other guns. The upgraded

68 cm Krieger barrel helped. Suppressor sleeve stout enough to dampen an otherwise ear-shattering detonation. Couple of personal tweaks, custom-milled scope locks, balancing, lower receiver tuning, in the end an extension of his biology so comforting, resting against the comb induced relaxation dropping twenty beats per minute off the heart rate. Ivan took a refraction reading off the bulletproof glass and dialed compensation into the scope. Civilians and government employees crossed the sky bridge connecting parking garage to the Broward County Judicial Complex. Pigeons collected on the concrete part of the ledge, unwary little eyes flicking back and forth between the van's two occupants. Stick around. It'll be a good show.

"Is it wise to drink before shooting?"

Ivan's tongue ran the inside of his lower lip, thermos jammed back in the tool net. "It's just coffee."

"Right."

"Look." Ivan gestured to the tower beyond the courthouse plaza. "It's not like we're piercing ears across a football field. You don't have to be Craig Harrison to make this shot." Even Ivan could smell the telltale odor in the coffee. The truth was, he felt frustrated, something left unsaid that might have dignified the story of Ellison's father—Ivan's grandfather. The cheap plastic floor tie-downs pressing on his ribs hurt disproportionately, but he couldn't move for sheer lack of initiative. It was like living in a house all his life and discovering a new room, an important one, where books lined up on dusty shelves beg to be read and he was too illiterate to fulfill the promise. So he said nothing. Damn Ellison and his secrets and damn Yannis for being so reticent and promiscuous and bloody Greek. Damn Number 7 for leaving it up to a drug addict to utterly fail to incubate his nonexistent life, one that unaccountably became Ivan's failure, though how he didn't understand. Perhaps it was the feckless notion death should be noble, not a struggling poisoned birth, and that Ivan could have offered a much more fitting an end.

To hell with logic.

Damn Samuel Coletti's exotic life for being more coherent even while he sold a harem of featherless boys for whoever's misguided money now funded this spectacle. Ivan could squeeze the trigger only to have the crack drowned out by the puerile whimper paying for it. A proxy more culpable than Samuel. Had he done more damage holding a gun to the boy's head, or scratching his fingers through Jaden's programmed blonde hair? All for the name of a child he was willing to kill before discovering the mother beat him to it?

"Nikos! Wake up. Snap out of it. The courtroom's convening."

Focus.

"Drink more coffee. Or less. What's wrong with you?"

"It's nothing."

Ellison adjusted his posture with the rifle, several uncomfortable grunts a reminder this was a younger man's exploit. "Coming on for hearing today, State v. BioConnect Industries Incorporated LLC, et al, so on and so forth."

"Seriously? You looked it up?"

"You *didn't?*" Ellison remarked.

"I never do. A good hitman has no emotional connection to the target. I don't ask questions."

"Bullshit."

Deep breath. "As much as I'd love to argue, can this wait? Jesus. I suppose now you're going to tell me these two don't deserve to die? This isn't the first judge I've retired. I don't lose sleep over judges and prosecutors."

"What about kids?"

Damn him. A head splitting silence cut off every prematurely conceived retort Ivan tried to utter. Horn honking in the garage and the off balance whir of the fan accompanied his grinding teeth. He watched the first target take an elevated position in the courtroom. Did Ellison find out about the other six? Did Coletti? Had he told Ellison? Or was it obvious? Damn him. Focus. Natural gas exhaust from an accelerating city bus filled the space between buildings. A minute later the deputy prosecutor entered the courtroom.

Ellison chambered the first round. "But you're wrong. I have no objection in this case. The prosecutor moonlights for Big Pharma, who want BioConnect to go under so they can exploit patents. He's bribing the judge for bootstrapped, cross-jurisdiction search warrants so police can raid BioConnect on a trumped-up criminal fishing expedition. Obviously Coletti has skeletons in many closets."

"I *try* not to think about it." To Ivan hits were little more than tomatoes in Melina's garden. After a minute he asked, "Which pharmaceutical company?"

"See? It does matter. This judge is taking bribes for so many other criminal indictments he's started wearing a vest. Better aim for the head."

"It won't matter."

"True."

Hearing protection. Steady. Signal. The first two shots were 0.368 seconds apart. The second tomato, like everyone else in the courtroom, ducked under a wooden table. Likewise, it wouldn't matter. Ivan painted an infrared bead through the surface and Ellison opened the window. There is nothing subtle about the eruption of military level weapons. Violent force pounds the shooter's environment in cataclysmic ways. The damage implied by games or movies doesn't translate to the real experience, which feels more like ripping holes in the space-time continuum. It was over in four seconds.

"Wasn't Eliv—your father—relieved?" Ivan closed the van doors and started disassembling their weapons, sliding the components into inconspicuous golf bags. "You did tell him the truth, right? Maria was a hero?"

"Relief? He didn't accept it. By then Eliv had spent thirty years aching from depression. The mind is fragile. He was a survivor, but not without damage, more than most. I think . . ." Ellison paused, looking for an explanation perhaps he'd never thought of before, "I think it's human nature to want to see the best in other people, and that's what my father lost, maybe at Auschwitz or soon after. I remember him as illogically cynical, a xenophobe who mistrusted non-Israelis. When Yannis came to see his father for the first time, Eliv experienced some sort of traumatic neurological event, and we ended up taking him to the hospital." Outside the van there was screaming and mayhem in the street below. "Not long before you and Yannis were captured, he helped me bury Eliv. Those were the only two times they met. I think Yannis was hurt very much."

Ivan circled the descending ramps and barely noticed the involuntary pause as the garage's exit boom rose.

Ellison looked back at the chaos, police and SWAT cruisers massing around pieces of the building's window lying in the street. "What a mess you've made, Nikos."

"You helped."

"Against my better judgment."

Ivan drove three blocks and made a left. "There's something I don't get. In 'forty-three, in a country like Greece, the small town of Ayia Anna, no one would be expected to have identification documents or the like. When the SS came for him, why didn't Eliv give them a different name? Tell them he wasn't Jewish?"

Ellison let out an exasperated breath. "That's your problem, Nikos. You have an amazing genealogy filled with heroes and dissidents and survivors, but it doesn't matter. You treat it with such cavalier disregard."

"That's not true."

"No? Who are you? Do you even know?"

An auto mall slid by with endless perfect lines of new cars, descending economy marked out over a half kilometer. Self loathing was an emotion that until recently Ivan found foreign and here Ellison, after dropping a bomb of history, demanded Ivan reconcile all of it and find substance to his own existence. He wasn't ready, and the stubborn instinct lashed out, words his common sense and a moment's thought would regret.

"I know I wouldn't have copped to being a Jew when they're holding a gun to my head." They'd stopped at a light. "Never mind. I'll fly you back to Utah."

"Don't bother. I'll find my own way back." Ellison got out of the van, but before closing the passenger door said, "Eliv told them he was Jewish because he believed in something. You wouldn't understand that, Nikos. You have nothing to believe in."

18

Ivan sat quietly in the waiting area of Harborview Medical Center's Emergency Room holding a vase of chrysanthemums. Everyone left him alone. He looked like he was grieving, and no one knows what to say. Music piped through the speakers, the used car dealership of radio, all songs worn out by a lot of mileage on other pop stations.

Truth was Ivan had a lot of information to pore over while waiting for Doctor Hale to make an appearance. The first was an urgent message from Glitch, who suddenly couldn't get Number 7 dead fast enough. Ivan was only too pleased to file his increased expense report, which didn't phase Glitch in the least since Ivan could assure him the job was finished. Number 7 was dead. They needed to meet, Glitch said, tie things up.

The second message was two words from Coletti: Casey Lapinski. Number 7 finally had a name. Then everything became complicated.

Casey's mother, Jessica Lapinski, died September 8th. Casey Lapinski also died September 8th. Why then did Harborview Medical Center logs show Casey in the Neonatal Intensive Care Unit for sixteen additional days? Shouldn't his death certificate read September 24th? Maybe it was a typo. Back to Seattle.

Harborview kept expired patient medical records in a secure data storage warehouse in Renton. Ivan cut some corners on the ID fabrication, anticipating less screening from the argumentative young clerk named Simmons, who wouldn't give Doctor Stavros access to the records. He was downright insolent until Ivan thumped Simmons's head on the counter, uncomfortably introducing his wrist to both his shoulder blades. Ivan used the subdued moment to light a cigarette and study the retinal scanner on the terminal.

"Depending on how the next few minutes go," Ivan said, "you, Mr. Simmons, could be a medical record in this very facility. You decide what it reads. Severed C3-C4 vertebra, spiral fracture of the femur, or maybe just sprained wrist and mild concussion?"

Ivan let go and Simmons logged in without being asked. Good boy. He pulled up sixteen days of arcane medical entries made after Lapinski's death.

"Read it. What happened?"

"I don't know." Simmons stared at the screen. "I'm not a doctor."

Ivan dropped the cigarette in Simon's coffee. "I'm gravitating from mild concussion to ruptured brachial artery."

"Wait! Hold on. I think this means he was born premature . . . these are all I-V push drugs. Asphyxiation? I think they were stabilizing him, it says something about respiratory dysfunction and RDS. I don't know what that stands for."

The treatment regimen abruptly stopped after sixteen days, followed by the notation:

Refer to KCSC 25-2-08104-6

"What's KCSC?"

"I don't know."

"Figure it out."

"I swear! I don't know. Maybe it's a department, at the hospital. Ask Doctor Hale."

"Who?"

"Hale. He's an ER surgeon, the one who made the entry."

Ivan downloaded the file and thanked Simmons before thumping his brown haired melon on the desk again. Mild concussion it is. He looked harried. Sleep would be good for him. Finding and scrubbing the surveillance record didn't take long, and on the way out he took Simmons's ID clip.

Now sitting in the ER waiting area, Ivan's rig stayed busy string-searching KCSC. He dismissed KC as shorthand for Casey, returns like Kevin C. Sellerman employed by Boeing, and the Kentucky Cub Scouts chapter. He wasn't getting anywhere. Dr. Hale eventually emerged from prep staging peeling off latex gloves.

"Dr. Hale?" The surgeon was years younger than Ivan, but the stress of life or death decisions added a decade's worth of lines. If Ivan had intended to catch him during a break, this wasn't it.

"Yes?"

"I was wondering if I could have a private word with you." Ivan held out his hand and got a noncommittal shake.

"I'm afraid I'm sort of in a—"

"Five minutes. It may be something serious. I'm from Records in Renton. We're auditing and found a few erroneous details in your charts. These are official state documents, so we're concerned."

"Please come into my office, Mr. . . .?"

"Simmons." Nothing like a hint of liability to stimulate a doctor's cooperation.

"I'm sure it's just a misunderstanding."

Hale's office was too spartan for real work, and he handled the terminal like it was someone else's when locating the NFC pad to recognize Ivan's thumb drive. K-Cup coffee brewer, no mugs, no family pictures, TV on the wall set to CNN with the volume turned down, pharmaceutical company pens, dongles and handouts splayed around a weak coleus reaching across the desk and limping into a trash can stuffed with empty vending machine bottles.

"What's the issue?" he asked, distinct apprehension after recognizing the file.

"If your patient's dead, how long do you wait before cutting off administration of drugs and treatment? Two minutes? Five? Maybe ten? Sixteen days seems rather excessive, you being so busy."

"Mother died of a drug overdose."

"That's the one."

Long pause. "Why is this coming up now?"

"Routine audit."

Hale leaned closer like the walls were bugged. "The police were involved. I mean, police get involved in a lot of hospital emergencies, but this was different." Ivan just stared at him. "Look, initial diagnosis wasn't good. He was removed nearly stillborn, bloodstream toxic, respiratory distress syndrome, but we restored his autonomic respiratory system, and after a few days were pretty certain he was out of danger."

"But he died," Ivan offered.

Hale shook his head. "No. The police seemed very concerned with the deceased mother, something about her statements on intake. I was ordered to falsify the baby's death certificate, transfer continuing treatment onto a different patient record."

Shit. "Isn't that unethical?" Ivan could picture Glitch's idiosyncratic tics magnified when he learned this. "Who ordered the transfer?"

"Unethical? I don't know. Perhaps, but it's the *police*, for Christ's sake. You do what they tell you. That's what the court file concerns." He pointed at the cryptic notation starting KCSC.

"This is a court case number?"

"King County Superior Court."

"So where is Casey now?" Ivan accessed the court records server. Hale started to look suspicious.

"Are you sure you're from Records?"

The file was sealed. Ivan's rig transferred it to a remote network and he waited while a taskbar in his field of vision indicated progress unlocking the weak security protocols.

"Records would know the file's unique. And they'd know what KCSC stood for."

Not sleepy Simmons. Whatever. Ivan held up his phone. "Have to verify your information. This could take a minute."

Hale looked put out and leaned back in his chair. A stylus summersaulted back and forth through his fingers. After an awkward silence, he gestured to the TV. "Tragic, isn't it?"

"What?"

"You haven't seen the news? It's been nonstop coverage of the courtroom murders in Florida."

Ivan watched CNN play in loops what appeared to be irrelevant, street level amateur video, which gave the talking heads lots to speculate about. Hale's monologue recapped the news, pronouns like *they* filling in for everything from police to media.

"Right in broad daylight, through bulletproof glass. At first they said it was a random act of terrorism, but no group's claimed it yet. The shots came from the parking garage across the street, but they're saying the surveillance was temporarily down or damaged? They're not being specific. The judge was a pillar of the community. They ran his bio, the prosecutor's too, there's a memorial of flowers a mile long. It didn't take them long. They found him after an anonymous tip about his white van, a plumbing truck, I believe, but as far as motive goes all they're saying is—"

"Who?" Ivan said, cutting Hale off.

"The killer. They found him in bed, van out front. Pretty coldblooded, murdering public servants and being able to sleep. The man might be schizophrenic. I'm not a psychologist, but that's what police are saying. Not that it's going to matter, he'll still get the death penalty." Hale pointed again. "That's him."

CNN showed the booking photo of a dark-skinned man with oily looking long black hair and cheeks sagging into jowls. Cuban or Native American, Ivan couldn't tell. Police grabbed a face the public would believe looked the part. "Have police mentioned what's on the bullets?"

"Excuse me?"

"What was written on the bullets," Ivan snapped off too harshly. No, Hale said, nothing like that, but *they* recovered the rifle. What kind of rifle? Some sort of Remington, a common one, a twenty-two, they said.

"He didn't even dispose of it. Criminals can be so stupid."

"Are you serious?" Ivan said with a mocking tone Hale failed to recognize as he nodded. A picture of the recovered rifle flashed on the screen. "And you think the police did a good job?"

"Oh, certainly. There's a mountain of evidence."

Ivan stared at Hale for a minute. "You're a moron."

"Excuse me?"

"No. There's no excuse. A Ruger 10-22 shoots a bullet this big." Ivan held his fingers less than three centimeters apart. "You're an ER surgeon. Removed a lot of bullets from trauma victims? Because the rounds that hit these two jokers don't get removed. They remove you."

Delayed, nervous response. "You're not from Records."

"People hunt varmint with twenty-twos. You're telling me you believe such a puny round went through bulletproof glass?"

"I . . . I'm sorry. Maybe it wasn't very bulletproof?"

"Jesus!" Ivan slammed the door on his way out. Not thinking straight, long strides for the hospital exit, deciding he'd been too intense. It wasn't Hale's fault police and media were dissimulation factories, or would railroad the first random patsy for the myth of public safety. What a cock-up.

Ivan was so angry the flashing red warning on the rig went unnoticed until halfway through the parking lot. The remote network unlocked the file during his meltdown and uploaded the documents. Semantic data analysis cross-linked the content with a whole spread of new information. Red flags, warnings, something amiss located. Slow to reign in emotional outburst, Ivan was still plenty sharp identifying Hizer's red herring. He was already on his way back into the hospital, long stride turned to a run.

Casey Lapinski was now Dakota Brenner, who already had a lawyer—several. One of them recently filed a lawsuit against Hizer Pharmaceuticals on behalf of lead plaintiff James Addleman, father of Number 6. Families for Numbers 3 and 4 joined in the caption. The particulars included professional autopsy for each child and cause of death wasn't stroke or embolism, like Glitch said the capsule's effect would be. It was respiratory paralysis. The two causes of death weren't remotely interrelated. Why would Glitch bother misleading him with the ruse about homocysteine? Not that Ivan really knew what homocysteine would do. But Hale might know.

Hale's office door was locked. Ivan could hear him inside talking urgently on the phone. Impatience throbbed to an even greater intensity than before. Spectators all around, wooden door molding, the impact of Ivan's foot sheering screws right out of the metal beneath. Hale dropped the receiver and fell out of his chair.

"I just called the police. They're on their way, so you better just—"

"I don't give a shit." Ivan set the phone back in the cradle. "Do you know what homocysteine is?" Hale looked confused and Ivan asked again, louder, until Hale nodded. "Could it kill you?"

"Please . . . I didn't mean to . . ."

"I'm not killing you! I'm asking a question."

Hale crouched in the corner with hands held up as though deflecting something. Defensive instincts could be very odd. “Sure,” Hale said. “Eventually it could. It . . . it encourages blood to clot.”

“What do you mean ‘eventually’? How long?”

“A while. It takes time, to build up, I mean.”

“Not in ten minutes?”

Hale vigorously shook his head. “Demethylation of methionine doesn’t occur on that scale. It’s metabolized too quickly in normal circumstances. The process, the effect,” he spluttered. “No. Nowhere close. Even with an aberration of the plasma cells, it just can’t generate clotting on that scale. It would be days, weeks.”

“Get out.”

“What?”

Ivan pointed to the door and Hale scrambled for it.

What the hell was wrong with Ivan? His own principles eluded him. He poked around the office while his mind raced. Watered the poor coleus. On the way out he walked by the inbound police, who drew a wide circle around the man coughing through a corrugated cotton facemask.

* * *

The beach house on Alki was again available for rent. Ivan reserved it for a month. Tried calling Ellison, got no answer. Just as well. It occurred to him too late that Ellison losing Yannis as a brother might be as painful as Ivan losing the same man as a father. Drank a bottle of Bushmills over eight hours with electronic documents scattered on the gesture interface projection coffee table.

Ivan corrected the first error. The New York Times received a tip from an unnamed source within the investigation. Calibers didn’t match, no depleted uranium scrub in the suspect’s barrel. More importantly, it didn’t take the NYT long to determine *17:23* was a warning about bribery and justice from Proverbs. Prosecutors still refused to release the man after the story broke, and they certainly weren't calling for investigation of the judge or prosecutor. Which didn't stop the media racing to see who could dig up financial records faster. None of it tarnished public opinion much. Ivan thought Americans would appreciate his kind of capitalism. The justice system swindled Samuel Coletti, so he purchased services from a competing justice system.

Good luck hunting for the leaker.

The other anomaly led Ivan to the modest law office of Helen Patricia Naughton. If Glitch told Ivan Hizer Pharmaceuticals wanted to avoid a lawsuit, now that the suit was in progress, and the other plaintiffs wouldn't take long to discover, why was Glitch so eager to have Number 7 added to the mounting liability? Something didn't make sense. Why did Glitch insist on a rationale? Ivan didn't need excuses, just payment.

"Good afternoon. May I help you?"

"Ivan Stavros," he said, shaking her hand.

"Oh yes. We spoke on the phone. Please follow me. You can hang your coat on that tree if you like. Miserable weather we're having."

Ivan nodded. She had an honest smile that made him feel comfortable. He followed her into a room with tall glass windows and a huge conference table with GIP glass surface. Perfect. She called to an assistant to bring coffee. No, not Percy, no colored mugs this time, please. Percy must have a certain notoriety. Ms. Naughton's taste in wall hangings was more subdued than Coletti's. The art photography flanking a credenza was more Henri Cartier-Bresson or Ansel Adams, patiently capturing the ephemeral moments of bucolic and candid authenticity. A sad monotony of rain ran down the expansive glass view over Seattle. Creative energy hidden beneath a gothic palette of colors.

"I'm sorry to inform you, Mr. Stavros, but my office handles mostly appellate law."

"And the occasional class action lawsuit?"

She averted her eyes. After a demur throat clearing, she nodded. "I'm assisting with one specific case of interest, but the circumstances are unique. Do you have an involvement in the matter?"

"Perhaps. How does attorney client privilege work? I pay you, and then what I tell you is confidential?"

"That is the general idea."

"Then consider yourself paid." Ivan tossed his phone on the table. "Details."

The assistant brought in a tray and Ms. Naughton dismissed him. "Is this a criminal matter?"

"It should be."

"I'm required to tell you," she stirred cream into her cup, "if you have committed a crime of some gravity, you should turn yourself in."

"Interesting choice of words. And is that your recommendation?"

"God no. My counsel costs a good deal less if you haven't been caught."

Ivan instantly liked her. "You're working on this man's appeal." He flicked files off the phone and Dakota Brenner's booking photo spilled onto Ms. Naughton's table. She dragged the image into view, but it was obvious she recognized him.

"*Man*? I would have used the word juvenile."

"Practically an infant," Ivan said.

It was pure irony Ms. Naughton filed a lawsuit for the other deceased children, while also representing Brenner's criminal appeal. She was apparently not aware of any link. Why would she be? The appeals suggested judicial misconduct involving improper venue change from King County to Pierce County predicated on a sealed court file titled *In re the Matter of the Welfare of CKL*. The initials were Casey Lapinski, but she didn't know that either. Nor could she access the sealed documents, a matter presenting no challenge to Ivan.

Among the many court orders were sworn affidavits from a foster father and police officers. Jessica Lapinski, Casey's surrogate mother, told her foster father in some agitated state the baby was paid and destined for ill purposes. Other documents referred to the buyer as a 'purveyor in human sex slave trade,' and that Casey's life was in danger, the nature of which wasn't elaborated upon. Did Jessica find out from Sharon Paley? Not likely. Sharon didn't know. Other cutouts in Coletti's employ must have slipped. Then the real reason popped up why Ms. Naughton and Tony Wu couldn't have access to the court files. On hospital intake the police were more keen on prying from Jessica where the money paid for Casey went, and when she said drugs, who she got them from? Her answer was the King County Chief of Police, who easily liberated them from evidence storage. He was her long-time supplier going back to a previous foster home placement in Renton. She was nine at the time and let him rape her in exchange. The chief was almost caught but for his good friend on the bench, Justice Douglas Schraeder, who made the inquiry go away. When details resurfaced at Casey's birth, Schraeder gave the baby quasi-judicial protection by hiding him under a different name with Jessica's foster parents, an obvious flaw in the scheme, but there was no accounting for judicial decisions, and the Brenners were pretty adamant about keeping their grandchild.

No wonder the same judge, when Dakota was arrested five years later, recused himself—to protect the police report about the Chief's drug and exploitation racket. The whole court was in on it. They weren't protecting the baby from Samuel Coletti—they were protecting themselves.

How perfect the irony in Ivan's search for Number 7. Court seals file to protect chief from allegations of child rape on the pretext of protecting boy from child rape. Court locks up boy for child rape.

Time to give Ms. Naughton's law firm a leg up.

Ivan explained the court file as each critical document moved across the conference table.

"You're right. This should be criminal," she finally said. "But I can't use any of these."

"Why not?"

"Who are you? Do you work for the court system?"

"I work for no one."

"Then how will I say I acquired them? With no chain of custody authenticating provenance, they're effectively stolen. Even deniable. I can't use them as evidence. There are rules."

"Learn how."

"Excuse me?"

Ivan leaned toward her across the table "They make the rules so when they break them you know who's in charge. Your client's not in prison because they followed the rules. Now he's in the system where he can be further exploited for profit."

"Are you suggesting the prison's exploiting him? As I understand it, Mr. Brenner's staying at the Wenatchee River Corrections Center."

"'Staying'? You make it sound like he can leave." Ms. Naughton conceded his point. "He's never leaving. So break a few damn rules."

Ms. Naughton removed her glasses. She sat quietly while considering political etiquette. "My assistant and I have worked hard on Dakota's case. I have faith the court will eventually do the right thing."

The abysmal record notwithstanding. While rummaging through DOC's logs for Brenner, Ivan stumbled on medical treatment that led right back to his odious employer. No reason why Ms. Naughton couldn't see them. Good for her faith.

"What are these?"

"The State assumed in loco parentis of Dakota. In practical terms that means they own his ass and make decisions for him. A couple months ago DOC was paid by Hizer Pharmaceuticals to 'decide' some of WRCC's inmates needed a new medication Hizer's testing. Guess who made the list?"

Phase II animal testing completed, the FDA turned a blind eye while Hizer moved on to unofficial human testing, relying on the non-consent of prison inmates. Perfect laboratory—controlled drug administration, uniform feeding habits and disease exposure, secrecy and collusion, kickback revenue flowing to the hands that mattered.

Hizer was running a multistate test of a new drug designed specifically for sex offenders. Internally codenamed IPT36, it sent chemical suppressors to parts of the brain responsible for sexual feedback functions which, during puberty, give instructions to the endocrine system to control, among other hormones, androgen production. Interfering with the thalamus, hypothalamus and destroying adrocortical brain tissue, the drug ensured a child would grow up never feeling a sexual impulse. Hizer's FDA and patent applications referred to the process as androcortical chemocectomy.

Ms. Naughton stood and walked to the window, arms folded. It wasn't clear what she stared at. The aloof traffic nine stories down? Commercial freighters docked on Puget Sound? Or the sullen crows defiling cornice stone sculptures of the older buildings?

From the credenza she drew two glasses and a bottle of bourbon. She didn't offer Ivan a drink. The act was mandatory. If Ms. Naughton was appalled, this was as close as she would come to expressing it.

"I can file an injunction. Again, where do I say these came from?"

"Don't bother. I'll handle this part."

"Then why show me?" Ivan didn't answer. Her reality was too insulated. "Mr. Stavros, the full resources of my office are committed to this, I assure you. What log do you have in this fire? You won't tell me, but understand my profession holds no guarantees. What if we're unsuccessful? Are you prepared to accept that possibility?"

"Then I take it into my own hands."

"You understand why I can't condone . . . whatever you're suggesting. My representation doesn't extend that far. Not that it's clear what I'm assisting you with anyway."

Ivan waved off her concern. "By the time you need to employ the services I provide, the solution is beyond the scope of what most humans are capable of. For now this is still within your ability." Ivan nodded to the files organized in front of her and authorized distribution.

Ms. Naughton had reservations about accepting. She rolled the bourbon glass between thumb and finger in a way that reminded Ivan of Ellison. No pushover. Maybe naïve about the secret workings of the system but he didn't confuse naiveté with weakness. The difference between her and Doctor Hale was that Hale evinced no interest in seeking the truth. Helen Patricia Naughton was more motivated.

She finished the drink and opened the office network, creating a new subdirectory. Moving the files into the archive, she opted for encryption and a single-user password.

"One last item on my agenda," Ivan said, setting the hydrogen-powered cooler case on the table. Pulling on latex gloves, he transferred one of the tiny blue seeds into a small ziplock bag.

"What is this?"

"Do not, under any circumstances, touch the contents. Keep it refrigerated if possible. I need it analyzed. Hire a lab, bill me for costs. I'm relying on your confidentiality."

"Mr. Stavros, this falls outside the gamut of what I do."

"I doubt that. It might be valuable to you."

Ms. Naughton shook her head. "I'll see what I can do. Only because I'm more than a little curious. I don't believe this information, however, is the windfall you think it is."

"And if it's not, Brenner will do more time? It's easy for neutral words on a court judgment to disguise what a life sentence really is."

"I've heard inmates tell me," she began slowly, "that it's just a slower death sentence."

Ivan nodded, pleased she understood. "There's only one way to complete a death sentence or a life sentence. Dying." Ivan retrieved his coat from the tree in the foyer.

"How do I reach you? If I get any results?"

"You don't. I'll know."

19

Watching Mr. Stavros disappear through the glass doors of her office felt like a fleeting hallucination to Pat. It was as if the dismal weather forged a chimera and then reclaimed him. All she felt was apprehension, silhouetted against the murky windows holding the ziplock bag Ivan had left with her.

She collected the cups and crossed her office to the Tackroom. Chris had all of Mr. Stavros's documents cascaded across Gibson, waving his hand to dismiss each as he digested the content.

"Mr. Gammon," Pat said. She rarely used his last name without a sternness deserving of the occasion. "Did it occur to you password protection implies an expectation of privacy?"

Chris's concentration hardly broke. "That's so cute, the way you think of data protection."

"I would have let you view them, but this is one of those boundaries we talked about respecting." These stunts were not one of the benefits of having an eccentric paralegal. "I'm not amused."

"Then you're really going to be pissed when you find out what your latest client did."

"I'm not sure I want to know." Mr. Stavros's well-mannered calmness didn't hide the nefarious aura about him. Pat placed the baggy in aluminum foil and stuck it in the fridge.

"I was right," Chris said. "The police chief *was* banging Jessica Lapinski. And providing the drugs."

"'Banging' is a crass misrepresentation of the age difference between them at the time. There are more appropriate words." Washing the glassware, she reconsidered the damage the word implied. "Maybe not. You were wrong, however, about Brenner being the chief's son."

"Sure. Dakota's a pill-baby."

An alarm went off in Pat's head. A pill-baby like Chase Addelman and the other two kids. They were all roughly the same age. Was it coincidence?

"He took your Addleman file."

"Pardon?"

"Scruffy beard? Left your office ten minutes ago?" Chris made a hard landing in the swivel chair, propping his hairy bare feet on the desk again. He worked the facets of a Rubik's cube, great speed but no apparent direction. "He stole everything on the Addleman lawsuit."

"Are you sure?"

Chris flicked it up on Gibson. "Right there," he said, pointing in a column of codes. "Our network retrieval logs. When his phone docked with the conference table he ran a subroutine that robbed the vault."

Pat was furious. She wanted to chase after Stavros, but then what? She couldn't see a confrontation, and where would he be anyway? "What did he get?"

"Everything. I just said 'everything' a minute ago, didn't I? Jesus. Client notes, communications, autopsy reports, initial discovery exchange, everything."

"Aren't the files supposed to be protected?"

"Sure. Same security you just put on Stavros's files. Absolutely impenetrable." Chris drowned the sarcasm with an arrogantly long sip of coffee.

"Thin ice, Chris. Thin ice."

"Whatever."

He was glowing more than usual. It wasn't admiration for Stavros or caffeine. The glow had a narcissistic pallor. "What did you do?"

"Took you long enough." Lists of IP addresses appeared in a new window. "I tagged the Chase autopsy file."

"Explain, please."

"You're hopeless."

"Hopeless pays your bills. I can forgive a lot of impertinence in exchange for good news. Quit holding out."

Chris soured, a look that said she was playing rough. "It's a trace. The data packet goes with the file and sends a ping back each time it's moved through a server."

"Very good. So we know where he went?"

"Well, it's more complex than that, but for luddites I'm happy to—"

"You can imply I'm old later. Where did he go?"

"This doesn't tell you where *he* went, just the files." Pat waved him on. "Basically south, literally and figuratively."

The first major hub was Houston, then Brazil where it crossed their Atlantic cable. The packet went through proxies in Bonn, Rotterdam, Manila, Ankara, Odessa, and was last seen in Israel. Did Hizer Pharmaceuticals operate in Israel?

"You think he's a Hizer spy?"

"The thought had crossed my mind," Pat said.

"I'd be surprised if Hizer didn't have a facility there, but Tel Aviv's just where the metadata got stripped, along with the trace. It could have gone anywhere from there."

He suddenly jumped up and followed the path of a string between two tacks down to Chase's purchase agreement. The suddenness of his movement alarmed Pat, for he stumbled and grabbed the wall to steady himself.

"Dakota's one of the plaintiffs. Attach him to the Addleman class action." He looked up and saw Pat's confusion. "Who cares if they cut Dakota's balls off? He's going to be dead soon anyway. Hizer doesn't know he's one of the defective pill-babies."

* * *

Greider Labs was a nondescript building sharing a block with a mattress warehouse and two gas stations. Pat waited in the front lobby for Frederick to finish in the cryo storage room. A little girl wearing shorts over a bathing suit played Legos with a boy on an area rug between two RFLP machines.

Pat might have willingly fallen in love with Lance Greider years ago if not for a plea bargain and a marriage. He was a witness in a civil case, proprietary chemistry infringement against a cosmetic company. She was stuck in the same county for a few weeks co-counseling a trial for experience points, right out of law school. Lance and Pat spent the better part of a week in the professional lounge laughing and eating from little take-out boxes of Chinese sold with sporks. She'd worn her hair neatly trimmed and short back then, insecure about being a woman in a male-dominated field. She believed it made her look more assertive in court, but with Lance she suddenly wished it were long and more feminine. Tiny shames for having felt that vain could creep up on her. Lance wrote emoticonic chemical formulas in the margins of her yellow legal pads, cute smiley mouths under C_2H_5OH. Was this really the way weird people asked to go out for a drink?

Then the client took a plea on day six. Pat went back to Seattle and Lance had a couple of kids, one of whom Pat sponsored a scholarship to study organic chemistry at NYU after watching Frederick grow up, one family gathering to another, because that's what godparents did. Now Frederick's own offspring ran over to show Pat . the multicolored Lego helicopter she'd built. Where did the time go?

While waiting for Frederick, Pat tried to work out the implications of her paralegal's discovery. Chris spotted what everyone else had missed. Three families so far had joined in the class action Addleman lawsuit against Hizer Pharmaceuticals. It was one of those small details that could have gone overlooked but for the minutia that vexed Chris's caffeine enriched synapses. Chase and the other two girls were purchased not only on the same date but also from the same Seattle kiosk. Now there was potentially a fourth. Jessica Lapinski had Casey's name picked out before he was a zygote. Was it natural to name a baby she wasn't going to keep? Casey defrosted and swam upstream the same day and from the same kiosk that manufactured the other three dead children.

When the Addleman lawsuit entered the discovery phase, Pat had all new interrogatories and production of document requests prepared: Has the kiosk been reported for malfunctions, service evaluation or errors? Provide all documents associated with either the hardware or software service of the GLS kiosk? Name all parties who purchased pill-babies from the kiosk?

What if Jessica's purchase showed up? Whose name would be on the purchase agreement? Was Casey really intended for prostitution?

Whoever it was, they abandoned Casey when the police cottoned on, and now his name was Dakota.

Could it just be coincidence Pat was working on two different cases, civil and criminal, that she now knew shared a common victim? She wasn't particularly cynical, but couldn't help feeling suspicious of the circumstances.

There no longer seemed a point to working on Dakota's appeals. If he presumably suffered the same defect as the other children, it was only a matter of time before his autopsy report would also read *respiratory paralysis*. Like the dementia suffered by her father, all the injunctions in the world wouldn't stop it.

Dakota couldn't be added to the lawsuit. Not that he shouldn't be, but there was simply no way. Only a legal guardian could sue Hizer on behalf of a child. In law the damage tort was 'loss of parental consortium.' The decedent had no standing.

The State was Dakota's parent now. As Mr. Stavros so bluntly put it, DOC owned his ass. They were hardly going to sue Hizer while simultaneously benefitting from whatever commercial agreement they shared testing the pharmaceutical's drugs on inmates. Hizer wouldn't have tested IPT36 on Dakota if they'd known he was defective, or even a pill-baby. They probably hadn't even checked his DNA for the proprietary signature. The kind of families that could afford pill-babies also enjoyed a form of immunity from the law. Police tended to focus on vulnerable economic groups less likely and without resources to pursue litigation for things like wrongful arrest. Hizer really had no reason to anticipate prisons might incarcerate a pill-baby.

Frederick emerged from cryo storage and Chelsea showed him her helicopter. "Have you been keeping Auntie Pat entertained?" He felt his side and back pockets for something not there. "Thanks for coming, Pat."

"Not at all. How is your father doing?"

"Lance is back down in Chili or . . . somewhere, helping out Doctors Without Borders." He looked apologetic for not knowing with certainty. "And Alfred? Any improvement?"

"Alzheimers doesn't tend to improve, Freddy." She tried to evince a cheerful resignation to her father's circumstances. She didn't want Frederick to feel bad, though sometimes the sympathy of friends seemed to touch subjects more puissant than social formality required.

Frederick nodded. "I'm sorry."

"I'm pleased to hear Lance is staying so busy. I rather wish I had the courage to abandon everything and go off like that."

"Mom's with him. He gets a lot of help." Freddy laughed, then looked sheepish. "I'm afraid I have some bad news or good news, depending on how you look at it."

"Are we going now?" Chelsea asked.

"Yup, in a minute."

"Bad news about the pill, Freddy?" Pat asked.

"No . . . well that too, but when I asked you to stop by, I didn't know the wife got called in to work and was already on her way to drop off the kids with me."

Pat watched the boy fidget by the door. "He's yours? When did this happen?"

"You didn't hear? I'm doing really interesting lab experiments these days. Do you want one? There's no warranty, but he comes potty trained."

"Dad!" Chelsea swatted her father.

Pat followed Freddy into his office. "He lives next door. One of their classmates turns nine, and now I'm obliged to chauffer them to the party."

She was a little put out but tried not to show it. "I can come back another time."

"What?" He muscled a folder into an overstuffed file cabinet and grabbed a tablet. "Did you get the text? You're coming with us, right?" Pat shook her head, but there was Chelsea tugging on her hand. Freddy added, "Cake and ice cream are good for lawyers. Edible happiness, and you look like you need it."

* * *

The family of Chelsea's classmate had a huge house and an even bigger backyard, now crowded with seemingly the whole classroom, happily converting sugar to noise as they ran back and forth between a pool and a large, colorful inflated bounce castle. Chris would have experienced an anxiety attack from the home's austere interior. Victorian modern suited Pat, even if the furnishings tended to be more pleasing to the eye than to sit on. Was the fluctuating fashion trend tight or loose denim, or would Freddy have cared either way? They sat across from each other in a salon, his jeans contrasting with the ostentation of both couches. There *was* something fun about drinking through a curvy straw from cheap plastic cups. Happy Birthday to . . . whoever.

Watching them play was a reminder that her kid wasn't out there. That possibility for Pat had come and gone. If Freddy hadn't been joking, would she want him to synthesize a child for her? Had she ever wanted kids of her own, or was the sense merely obligation to perpetuate her family? They'd never said so, but Pat believed she'd disappointed her parents by never giving them grandchildren. Remaining desire or needs of her own she fulfilled vicariously through other's families. Even devoting her law practice to juvenile work felt like an extension of whatever maternal impulses she'd clung to. Had she failed her father? Was ambition responsible for her neglect, or was she never particularly driven by desire for offspring? Or had the idea always been that she could wait for later? Procrastination now felt like regret. Her thoughts roamed so deeply at this moment, Freddie had to repeat his question.

"Where did it come from?" Freddy asked.

"I'm sorry. Originally? I don't know. A client gave me the capsule."

"Is that what he or she called it?"

Pat couldn't remember if Mr. Stavros used the word capsule or not. Wasn't it a capsule or pill of some sort? Freddy couldn't be sure.

"How can that be?"

"I know *what* it's made of, but the nano-chemical function is somewhat a mystery. This is way beyond biochemistry."

There was a time when it was believed nano robots would infiltrate and repair eukaryotic organisms like humans, he explained, but the supertechnology was slow to pan out, and biosynthetics made strides in its place. Now labs used enzymatic assembly to create biotechnology tasked for all sorts of purposes. The most common use was gene therapy. In a process called site-directed mutagenesis, specially designed oligonucleotides are annealed to the DNA strand, a polymerase filling in the rest of the sequence using the oligonucleotide as a primer, and the original strand segment discarded. Pat's pill showed signs of a similar organic operation, but the delivery mechanism remained a mystery.

"Isn't the pill itself the delivery?"

"To get it into the organism, yeah, but to get inside the cells?" Freddy put the tablet on the low table between them. The 3D representation looked like multicolored tapioca spheres "Site-directed mutagenesis is typically done with viruses, inert forms we call a vector, docks with the cells and injects the package."

"I've heard of vectors," Pat said, wondering if they'd come up during discussions with doctors about her father's medical treatments.

"Viruses require a living organism." Freddy stabbed his finger on the tablet. "This thing does not."

"Is that a big difference?"

"Oh, unquestionably. A very big difference." They heard someone crying and Freddy looked through the sliding glass doors. Injury in the bounce house, but it wasn't Chelsea. "From an engineering standpoint, nearly impossible. This bionanite would need its own hydromobility, like a propeller, which we've done on nanoscale biomachines, but what are we infiltrating? My guess is humans, which would take 25 micrograms of nanites to effect a search of every cell within a reasonable time. Once inside the cell, it searches the nucleotides for the correct sequence. It's sort of like, if that whole pool out there were filled with Legos, and your kid was searching for one piece?"

"So it takes a long time."

"Not as long as you'd think. We've come a long way since CRISPR, the splicing process that drastically simplified gene therapy for us. Targeted mutagenesis is just part of the operation. Pat, the protein folding on this thing is very complex. I think it's designed to reproduce itself, probably by cannibalizing cellular proteins around it. And it has a life cycle, self-destructing according to organic programming."

"Sounds like you do know what it does. What's the complicated part?"

"I don't know what it does, I'm guessing. I have a feeling it's intentionally malicious and fatal, which makes the purpose of mutagenesis even more confusing. Protein folding, the way bionanites are made, is still sophisticated science. Hydrophobic proteins link and fold in patterns even supercomputers have a hard time anticipating. Biotechnology like this? The resulting theoretical structure is too large."

Pat nodded. "Too large for the pill."

"No, too large to deliver through cellular membranes."

The birthday girl's father passed by with two pitchers "Who needs a refill?" He held the pitchers up in turn as he said, "Driving or not driving?"

They both took the Not Driving, and when he left Pat said, "I'm not sure that was entirely appropriate for this party."

"I admire your hypocrisy."

"Cheers, for what it's worth." They raised their cups. Talking to Freddy, or his father, reminded Pat there were bodies of knowledge she would never understand. As hopelessly disoriented as Freddy would feel were he to be arrested, and the reasons he might call upon Pat's knowledge, she was glad to have people like the Greider family to untangle arcane sciences. Freddy was good at explanations, never too conceited with his field to find analogies others would grasp.

"Cells are like kids," Freddy said, gesturing outside. "Picky eaters, good defense mechanisms in the face of asparagus."

"Not Chelsea."

"Sure, Chelsea's a good eater. I'm just saying in general. There's a period when the waffle's got to be cut into bite-sized pieces, you know? Getting nanotechnology like this through a cell's lipid defense layers is harder by far."

There was no way to learn what change was being made to the DNA without testing on cells, which he couldn't adequately do without synthesizing more of the bionanite. His laboratory equipment wasn't sophisticated enough.

"Who *could* synthesize it?"

"Hard to say." He massaged his forehead. "It won't be some small outfit. Start looking at large multinational molecular biology companies, the kind that finance research for the big universities or have government contracts. No one else has the resources or computing power to design and build this level of technology."

Companies like Hizer. "I think I have an idea who it might be," Pat said. "The client implied studying this would help our case against a pharmaceutical giant."

Freddie's expression turned to confusion "Why would they be designing weapons?"

"Pardon me? What makes this a weapon?"

Everything else that was in it, all easy to identify. A thin layer of protease enzymes covering a chemical analogue from the lidocaine family, followed by an inert non-thermostable compound holding roughly 450 milligrams of nicotine mixed with microferrous particles.

"Nicotine? The carcinogen in cigarettes?" Pat said, a little curious.

"Cigarettes will kill you over a couple of decades. This has more than 150 times the nicotine in a cigarette. It'll kill you in minutes, suffocation by paralyzing your lungs. But it's the microferrous

particles—iron—that give it away. This isn't a pill. It's designed to be launched from a magnetic rail gun."

20

Ivan watched them move like a swarm through the hallways. Short haircuts, dark blue uniforms, thick belts weighed down by the tools of submission. Wenatchee River Corrections Center's internal surveillance network was surprisingly easy to pirate, their software decades out of date. He took control of various cameras throughout the prison labyrinth, panned and zoomed, getting a feel for WRCC's layout.

Dakota's prison was more sterile than any of the black site prisons the CIA contracted or operated. Lighting was better, really too bright, but it shown on a thoroughly modern machine. Remote operated doors from a central control point, white surfaces, no bars. A few throwbacks to archetypical construction remained, such as Titanic grade rivets pinning together steel plates and doors.

A striking dissonance remained between the intensity of WRCC's fortress and the confined class, who were little more than middle schoolers, some even younger, moving about in smart khaki and white prison clothes.

Medical 101 was supervised by a fixed fisheye camera that gave a barely useful image feed of a surgical lamp looming over a mobile hospital bed. An indistinguishable body lay on the bed.

This was Number 7? How could something so small and insignificant be this hard to find?

Hizer Pharmaceuticals employed an endocrinologist at a facility in Boston whose appearance closely matched that of an indifferent Greek hitman. Ivan uploaded the man's retinal pattern to the security clearance database of the

Washington State Department of Corrections. The quality of security was only as good as the system verifying his identity, and DOC's was ineptly programmed. Ivan spent more time fabricating the ID this time since it needed to fall back squarely on Hizer. DOC had a lot of faith in their security system. Made Ivan's job easier. Time to get it over with.

* * *

"Sign here." Her lack of verbal enthusiasm implied these signatures were destined for nothing more than storage. The officer leaned over the visiting check-in counter with an unnerving presence. A Coke can with the tab ripped off collected spent evergreen chew, a rolled up set of papers lodged in the space between two front buttons of her uniform shirt, bottle of Visine in the top pocket, flap propped up by a quick-cuff pen. Her posture dared him to ask a question she could take pleasure in refusing to answer.

Temporarily causing what Ivan imagined people with glaucoma suffer, liquid crystal refraction lenses mounted midway between cornea and the rod and cone cells adjusted his retinal pattern to match Hizer's endocrinologist. Inhabiting the persona of a professional doctor made the dismissive responses accorded one's perceived lesser easy. Impatient eye roll while the woman dug through Ivan's large steel briefcase of medical instruments. Hard to tell what contraband she thought she was looking for.

Escorting him through a twist of hallways, she detoured through a door marked *Booking*, behind which lay a processing line of unoccupied intake cages and stations where stripping, photographing, interrogating and vaccinating left behind what Ivan imagined despondency would smell like. All the seats were small benches low to the ground. Handcuffs, belly chains, leg irons and other mechanical restraints hung from heavy gauge hooks. The devices were small like toys, the halfway point between reality and dollhouse furniture.

"In there," the officer pointed to a set of double doors following a circuitous walk through the Medical wing. "Do not remove the offender's restraints or your visit will be terminated." She left.

Dakota was sleeping. Various machine beeps recorded the typical indications of life. Ivan reached up and found a switch for the operating lamp. Bathed in filtered light Dakota's pale skin gave the effect of an alien autopsy. Velcro binders strung him to the bed frame by the wrists and ankles, a virtual nest of wires protruding from every part of the prone body as if he were remotely powered. Tubes delivered and retrieved fluids for the many machines surrounding his bed. Stitches closed two incisions, a couple centimeters each, one a little beneath his ear, the other along the swollen fatty tissue of the perineum.

Behind Ivan a computer displayed reports represented by alphanumeric groups, followed by diagnostic tests of body functions shown as discrete anatomical sections too detailed for Ivan.

The visuals were unsettling enough without the smell of something like pulped, yeasty damp cashews. Dissection in progress. Ivan took a deep breath.

Was he sleeping or sedated? Ivan poked him and both eyes slowly peeled open.

"You're not Santa. Where did Santa go?"

Must be delusional. Probably the drugs.

"He's not Santa but he looks like him and I think he is even though he says he's not. Can Santa be a doctor too?"

"Sure."

"Are you a doctor?" Kid's voice was a little hoarse. "Like the other doctor? Santa?"

"Yeah."

"I'm Cody."

"Sure." Ivan hadn't come prepared to say anything. His tension grew, indecision about what this scene meant, hands in the pockets. Don't look at him. Didn't want him looking back either, the wet eyes, the need, all alone, and now someone to talk to, last words like a confession Ivan didn't want to hear. Why had he come this far into the room when it would have been easier to shoot the kid from the door and leave? Loneliness, the worst pain. "I'm Ivan."

"Ivan. That's a funny name. Are you a good doctor?"

"I don't know."

"Why don't you know?"

"Because . . ." A good doctor tries not to kill his patients. Hale was probably a good doctor. "I don't know what you think it means to be a good doctor."

"A good doctor? He knows what to do when you're sick."

"Is Santa a good doctor?" Ivan pulled tools out of his case and spread them on a table.

Dakota looked away and spoke as if he shouldn't say it. "I don't know. I don't think so."

"Why not?"

"Santa, he doesn't," a quick intake of breath, "he doesn't say to me, talk to me, like if it's gonna hurt."

"Did it hurt?"

Dakota nodded. "Not all of the time but yeah."

"Is it hurting now?" Dakota didn't answer. "What did Santa do?"

"I don't know." Long silence. "Will you tell me if it's going to hurt?"

"What?"

"What you're going to do is it gonna hurt?"

Could have done this without ever waking him up. "No."

"Okay." A smile spread across his face.

Ivan realized what he needed to do first. Behind him all the plexiglass cabinets were locked with latches and padlocks. He looked through the glass, found what he wanted. A heavy blood centrifuge machine on the counter would do. Ivan brought it down hard on the padlock, ripping screws off the frame. Helped himself to a large plastic foot basin within.

He ran water in the sink until it was warm and added hand soap from a dispenser, setting the basin on the surgical bed next to Dakota's stomach. With a cotton towel Ivan went about cleaning the kid as best he could. Dakota didn't struggle, just watched in mild fascination, Ivan rinsing and wringing out the towel at intervals. Beneath the heart rhythm electrode was a green tattoo. He cleaned the spot and found the artwork detailed and precise.

"Are you a Grateful Dead fan?"

"Dead?"

"Grateful Dead. They're an old rock band. They had dancing bears, like yours as a . . . sort of iconography."

"I dunno."

"You have a Grateful Dead tattoo. It's why I asked. Never mind."

Dakota looked at his chest. "My bear? Teagan made it. It's green, my favorite color."

"Who's Teagan?"

"And blue. I like blue and green. Teagan? I live in Teagan's room. I mean, I lived there before I got sick."

A cellmate. "Is that why you think you're in here?"

"Why I'm in prison?"

"Why you're in Medical."

"Because I'm sick?"

"Are you?" Dakota nodded and said he thought so. "Do you know why you're in prison?"

His eyes furrowed, squeamish look on the face. "I think I was bad."

"What did you do?"

"I dunno." He wasn't looking at Ivan any more.

"Then why do you think you were bad?" Ivan pulled the cloth under each arm, then wiped elbows and armpits, lifting Dakota to clean both shoulder blades and down his back.

"The bad doctor said so. A long time ago he said stuff, I don't know, like stuff, and put a thing on my . . . my . . . Teagan he says it's my dick? But I think it's a bad word. The doctor did it, the bad one. He said I was bad."

"Santa?" Dakota shook his head. A long time ago, he repeated. Kid's world was full of good doctors and bad ones and the worst criteria by which to judge them. Or maybe the only criteria that mattered, quality of life. Dakota closed his eyes while Ivan cleaned the lids, squirming when Ivan used his fingers to pull the stubborn yellow crusts from the eyelashes. Wrapping the cloth around his smallest finger, he dug in each ear canal, then wiped around the other orifices, careful not to disturb the instruments, particularly the tubes and wires stuck up Cody's nose. If he caused any pain and the boy started crying, Ivan wasn't sure he could deal with it. "I wouldn't worry about what he said, the bad doctor." Wiping down the chest, stomach, digging any gunk out of Dakota's navel. He suddenly noticed Cody's eyes looking straight into his own with earnest intensity.

Ivan wanted to leave. Right now, before he couldn't finish the job. And leave Cody here? What a mess. Perhaps there was a way to take the boy with him? Ivan didn't have the resources, time or lifestyle for some bastard kid. He wasn't even sure it was possible. If he pulled out all these tubes and wires, would Cody die anyway? If he was defective like Glitch said, would anything be more than a temporary reprieve? Really he'd be doing Cody a favor. Life sentences weren't this rotten. Only one way to complete a life sentence or a death sentence—dying. The result was the same. Isn't that what he'd told Ms. Naughton? Ivan's task simply dispensed with the interim suffering. Death should be clean and humane, even meaningful. What did Cody's death mean? Cleaning him felt like anointing a sacrifice, a ridiculous ritual. Sacrifice to who? Corporate greed? DOC's or Hizer's? To scientific vanity? If Ivan had to kill him, Cody wasn't going to go in a pool of his own filth.

Each toe, the spaces between, balls of the feet, gently the irritated ankles. Rinse. Legs, knees, thighs, back of the knees to the sound of ticklish giggling.

"Green and blue they're right next to each other in rainbows," Cody said. "But rainbows have every other color also. Do you like rainbows?"

"Sure."

Ivan poured the basin down the sink. Gray water carried off the pus, blood, necrotic fluids, urine, sweat, bacteria, dead skin, all of it. All the rot left behind by an apathetic society. He was bad. Here is his dirt.

Ivan pulled the plunger from a broad syringe and dropped the tiny blue seed inside, replacing and depressing the plunger. Cody watched his every move, apprehension growing.

Then suddenly the boy twisted his head around, trying to see in the direction of the double doors, an adept sense felt only by one who's spent time in prison. Ivan too heard the jingle of keys. Cody's eyes came back to Ivan. They both understood the keys were coming in.

Not now, not now. Shit.

Both doors banged open at the hands of two officers, the cornfed variety.

"You need to proceed to a secure location," one said. The other listened to a radio issuing noisy commands and a beep at regular intervals.

"Why?"

"We're having an emergency."

"What kind of emergency?"

"Who the hell is this guy?" one said to the other. "Come with us. Now."

"I can't leave the patient."

"We're running a fire drill in A-B Units," the counterpart offered. "No civilians in Medical during emergencies."

"Emergency? You just said it was a drill. And I'm not a civilian, I'm a doctor." Sort of.

Both officers converged. "Look, jackass, I run this show. Safety and Security of the institution comes before whatever the hell you're doing with the goddamned offender. You go where I say you go or you're gonna get hurt. Now move!"

Panic spread over Cody's face, body shivering in the restraints, tears welling up in his eyes, expression pleading Ivan to protect him. I am not here to save you, kid.

The wires embedded along Ivan's skull picked up and executed the neural instructions instantly. Every surveillance camera in the WRCC compound went dead. Electronic transmissions abruptly ended, both officer's radios silenced.

"Fuck off," Ivan said.

That was all it took. Like a linebacker plowing towards Ivan, Cornfed's massive arms aimed for a neck grab.

Lab coat swirled as Ivan turned out of the grab, dodged a flailing fist, and brought his arm down with a powerful crack through a vulnerable angle of the cop's elbow, other arm delivering an open-handed blow to that thick trunk of exposed neck. Ivan's motions were pure instinct and training, completely fearless. He wrapped the man up in a flurry of precise moves, ignoring yells as each distinct crunch signaled a new broken bone. All about leverage.

In the same event an elbow to the back of the other's head bought Ivan time to grab a scalpel off the tool tray. A savage gash rent through the leg of the cop's uniform plowed deep enough to lacerate the femoral artery, and if that didn't take the fight out of him, a last kick embossed the cop's face on the cinderblock wall with enough blunt force to leave a Rorschach of blood splatter. It was over in moments.

Ivan used their cuffs to hogtie them, working hard to pack the meaty limbs into the child-sized restraints. Probably pointless, since at least one of them would bleed out in minutes. Room was a mess. He walked back to the bedside.

"They hurt you?"

"No."

"Where'd they go?"

"Shhh. I have to leave now. In a hurry. I'm sorry."

Ivan used his hand to wrap and cut off blood flow return from Cody's right arm, cephalic vein rising to the surface. Cody winced when the needle pierced his skin, and Ivan released the pressure.

"Don't be scared."

"I'm not."

Of course not. Same programming as Jaden, and the same lies. Ivan pulled the plunger and blood filled the syringe, engulfing the pill. He waited as the warmth dissolved the capsule, blood turning black.

"Dakota?"

"Uh-huh?"

"You're not bad. Do you understand?"

"Will you come back?"

"Sure."

"But I don't want you to leave."

"I know. I'm sorry."

He pressed down, black fluid returning to the vein. Cody squeaked, eyelids relaxing. The smile faded and his body went limp.

Ivan quickly turned and uprighted the steel briefcase. The rig signaled, triggering release of secret compartments on both outward-facing panels. The lab coat fell to the floor and Ivan peeled a weapons harness from the case lining, strapping it around his torso. His hands closed around the composite bodies of twin FN P90 close range assault PDWs, securing each in the harness, additional magazine strips with teflon-jacketed hot loads under each arm. Across the front of the harness he clipped a series of concussion, incendiary and shrapnel grenades.

The last two items required assembly from parts tucked in the compartments. A full-auto modified FN57 machine pistol and a Kel-Tek KSG shotgun. Someone wrote that the KSG was what you wanted in the event of a zombie apocalypse. Ivan figured prison guards were close enough.

His steel case was layered with aluminum oxide. The thermite charge he activated would reduce it to slag. He tossed it across the room.

Behind Ivan the heart rate monitor slowed and flatlined. The computer in front of him flashed urgent messages, an alarm sounding from its tinny speakers. Ivan knew from the smell that Cody had defecated, his small body losing the battle. He didn't look.

There was nothing he could have done.

The computer read *Running program TC42 – Vascular isolation and purge.* Ivan pulled the lab coat back over the arsenal and made for the double doors.

21

Teagan was sleeping when a fierce impact on A-317's door woke him with a start. His hand swept up a slick trail of drool. Several officers were on the tier. More than two. Four, maybe even six. A lot.

"Offender McCarty! Sit on the stool and face the wall. Do not turn around or we will use force."

"If I'm going to hole, can I get a cigarette?"

"Can it, McCarty."

"That's a no, then?"

The door rolled open and two officers dragged Cody by the armpits into the cell, dumping him in the middle of the floor. They backed out and the door banged shut.

"Ho-ly shit, dude. Where the hell have you been, squirt?"

All Cody could manage was a moan. Teagan rolled him over. Cody was entangled in the oversized pumpkin suit in which he'd been stuffed before getting dragged back from Medical. Teagan yanked the canvas to bring the zipper upright and peeled Cody out of the thing.

"What'd they *do* to you? Look like you been shot with a spam gun."

"My head hurts."

"Head? Have you seen your chest? With all these little marks? Dude . . . this one's still bleeding."

Teagan patched the sores with tape and toilet paper, hoisted Cody into the bunk and dressed him. WRCC had been on lockdown for two days now, he said, and Cody would never believe it when he heard why. It was all over the news. Teagan thumped his fist on the TV power button but grew impatient with the anchor and started summarizing.

"Pigs got their *own* house kicked in for a change!" Teagan had a triumphant smile. "Whole squad of terrorists or something. They got past the security fence and fucked up a whole bunch of cops—sorry about the F-bomb, spud, but in a situation like this I need it. President's been on and Homeland Security's crawling all over. News forgot all about that dead judge in Florida. The whole administration building's peppered with bullet holes. One of the towers is gone. Gone! Did you hear me? They blew it straight up. I could hear the explosions. You were in Medical, even closer. Did you see anything? Were you in the middle of it? Is that why you're all messed up? Man, I missed a badass show." He was hyperventilating.

Cody wanted to be as happy as Teagan but something was wrong with his feelings and all that came up from his chest was sad and lonely. Cody slipped off the bunk and tried to pee. It hurt so bad at first he pinched off the end of his penis, which only made things worse until he let go, biting on his lip until the burning stopped.

"Are you all right, spud?"

He crawled back on the bunk, sad, but not completely lonely. There was Teagan. Tightness in Cody's chest choked into great sobs as he put his arms around him.

"Damn, dude." Teagan's first instinct was to pull away but he gave in. "You're gonna be all right."

Cody cried himself out and then felt stupid. He was a big boy now. Big boys don't cry.

"Sometimes even big boys cry," Teagan said.

"Even you?"

Teagan shrugged. "You ain't gotta grow up too fast."

"I missed you so much."

***

Three days later Teagan decided Cody was suffering posttraumatic stress disorder. “I don’t really know what that is, but you’ve got it.” Cody spent a lot of time sleeping. He’d suddenly shake uncontrollably, like being tasered by the officers. “Like you’re coming off dope, the DTs,” Teagan said.

“Dinner time, spud. Wake up.”

“What is it?” Cody rubbed his eyes.

Officers opened the cuff port and two soggy sacks hit the floor, followed by a pair of apples bouncing across the concrete. The hot part was a three-compartment peel-top with pre-charred, lukewarm chicken fried steak patty in the blandest starch puddle of mashed potato. Water from the mixed veggie compartment leaked across the membrane.

“They must think we’re gods. They’re giving us burnt offerings.”

Cody giggled. “Cookies?”

“No cookies. Same crap as yesterday. Eat enough of it and I’ll split a Milky Way with you, how about that? Save a bit for Booboo. I fed your rat while you were gone. No big deal since I almost can’t eat this shit no more. If I ever see a chicken fried steak patty on the streets I’ll blow chunks. Lockdowns are hell.”

Teagan had a confession. He missed Cody too. It might have only been a couple weeks, but he’d missed the silly babble, stories about ocean plankton and cartoons in the same sentence. Missed making cocoa for him, the big stupid smiles, combing knots out of his hair to the sounds of protest. Counseling him when the pigs were mean to Cody, bedtime stories, stubby crayons laying all over the place, horseplay. Even missed those mushy, embarrassing goodnight kisses.

“Which you are still strictly forbidden to tell anyone about.”

“I know.” Cody pointed at the TV. “I think that’s the doctor I was telling you about. Doctor Ivan.”

"He's not a real doctor, but plays one on TV. That's the guy they arrested somewhere on the east coast. FBI's still trying to find the rest of his crew."

Cody moved closer to the screen. "He looks a little different. Like, not the same."

"Booking pictures never look right. You look like a serial killer in yours, you know."

"Cereal killer?" Cody tried to wrap his head around this and decided he must have heard something wrong.

"You sure that's the guy? The weirdo that wiped you down?"

"Uh-huh, I think so."

"And kicked the cops' asses?"

"I didn't see it. I just heard them get beat up."

"Sweet. I wish I could have been there."

"Me too."

"What did this dude say to you?"

"He told me I wasn't bad."

"Weird."

* * *

Lockdowns *were* hell. "Nothing to do but sleep, watch TV and jerk off," Teagan said, claiming the routine left Cody with even less to do.

"And draw."

"Draw away, Picasso. Holler at me when lunch gets here."

"Aye, Captain." Another phrase he picked up from a movie. Teagan seemed to like the idea of being captain. Didn't even say anything when Cody skipped the paper and crayoned right on the wall. Paper was too small for this project, the biggest undertaking ever, with a huge forest surrounding a large lake, animals and boats. A stack of James

Michener books checked out from the library before lockdown gave Cody the height to draw clouds and the tops of the soaring pine trees that looked like upside down arrow tails.

When Booboo wasn't sleeping he explored the cell, nose first, poking around laundry on the floor, bits of squeeze-cheese burrito, and colored paper peelings from the stubby crayons. At least once a day Cody's nose would bleed for seemingly no reason and didn't stop quickly. He lay on his back waiting, Booboo's tiny claws tickling as he crawled up and down Cody's arms and legs.

"Another chicken fried rug scrap for dinner, spud. Didn't think I'd ever miss Alpo Bisquick calzones."

"What are those?"

"French or something. Like a pizza folded over except ours had dog food in them."

"Eew. You ate dog food?"

"No, stupid. The canned stuff, not the dry kibbles. It's no worse than DOC bean ravioli."

"Gross."

"Quit sticking your tongue out. You've put worse in your mouth. I've watched you."

"I just think dog food is for dogs." Cody jumped off the books, pushed the stack over, and climbed back on. Behind him Teagan cut apples into slices, smeared peanut butter on them, and handed a few off to Cody at intervals.

"Yeah, well, the dog died and the cans were left over. Nothing but the finest fare at the Mary Joe Trailer Park. Alpo Bisquick calzones it is."

"Your dog died?"

"Yup."

"That's so sad. Is that when you cried?"

"Crying's for pansies."

Cody looked with a smirk over his shoulder at Teagan. "You *did* cry, didn't you?"

"What, are we in court?"

"Did you bury him?"

"Her. It's a she dog. No need to bury her. Guts were all over the shoulder of the road. Goddamned U-Haul truck didn't even slow down." Teagan passed Cody the last slice. "Why are *you* crying?"

"I'm not. It's just so sad, you know, a truck hit her."

"Wasn't your pet. What do you care? Someday Booboo's gonna die too. Pretty soon, he keeps porking down them chicken fried crap slabs. Getting to be a little fatty. Of course Christine wasn't in any great shape neither."

"Who's Christine?"

"My dead dog. Stand still, you've got peanut butter on your fenders."

"I can clean it myself." Cody pushed Teagan's toilet paper away.

"Slob."

Teagan said Christine wasn't a picky eater, pretty much choked down anything remotely edible, even road kill, which is what she turned into, so you really are what you eat. Teagan laughed. Cody didn't understand what was so funny.

"Christine is a dog's name?"

"Dad named her after my mom when they broke up."

"That's nice."

"If you think so. Dad said it was because they were both bitches."

"Oh. Okay." Cody was never sure what to say when Teagan's family stories turned mean. Teagan told him to wrap up the artwork for the night, go brush his teeth. Teagan did the same and ran deodorant under both armpits. "Can I have some?"

"Your pits don't stink, spud."

"I know but can I have some?"

Teagan tossed him the stick. "Knock yourself out."

***

Day seventeen. One of Teagan's friends on the other side of the pod, facing the Administration building, yelled out his door. WRCC had raised a temporary watchtower, a sort of small box on hydraulic scissor lift, right next to where the old tower had been. Construction crews still marched in and out of Administration for repairs. News said the FBI let the man arrested in Massachusetts go. He had a solid alibi. Sounded like a fruit to Cody. Or the name of a beach. Alibi Beach. That would be his next art project if there was still space on the wall.

"Are you eating the damn crayons again, spud?"

"What? . . . No!"

"I can *see* you sticking them in your mouth."

"No, just my fingers, see?"

"You hungry?"

"Not really. I got a . . ." Cody picked at his teeth. He crawled into the bed and put his head in Teagan's lap. Dayroom speakers announced the afternoon count. "It's this one, it's hurting," Cody said, holding his mouth open.

Teagan touched one of the front teeth on the bottom row and Cody yelped. "Well of course it hurts, stupid. It's loose."

"Can you make it tight again?"

"It's loose because it's about to fall out, dumbass." Panic raced across Cody's skin. Teagan must be joking. "I'm not kidding, spud. Didn't you know they're supposed to fall out?"

"But yours they didn't fall out."

"Well, new ones grow in. That's why it hurts. A bigger tooth grows in its place. You're loosing your baby teeth, same thing I did when I was your age. For real? No one gave you a heads up on this one?"

"You sure you're not messing with me?"

Teagan put on his sternest look. "Serious, spud. It's the one time in your life you loose your teeth for something other than fighting, drugs, or retirement. They didn't tell you about the Tooth Fairy?"

"Tooth Fairy? Teagan, you're silly."

"Forget it. DOC doesn't support that program anyway––nothing in it for them. Fairies don't pay kickbacks."

A flashlight clanged against the door. "McCarty zero-zero-seven! Get on your own bunk!" the officer yelled.

"Shut up, punk!"

"What did you say, McCarty?"

Teagan crawled onto his own bunk. "Nothing. Now get off my porch before I call the cops. Wait . . . never mind." Teagan rolled over laughing as the officer scowled and moved on.

"You shouldn't make them angry, Teagan."

"What are they going to do? Give me cell-confinement? Don't get scared now, squirt. You weren't scared when you did the crime." Teagan's head popped over the side of the bed. "Let's pull that tooth out."

"What?" Cody clamped his hand over his mouth.

Teagan flipped forwards over the side, landing in Cody's bunk with a semi-graceful thump. "Yeah. Yank it out. If we don't it'll fall out in your sleep and you might swallow it."

"What happens if I swallow it by mistake?"

"No worries. It'll come out eventually. Out your butt, if you're lucky. The other way hurts more."

Cody gulped. "I don't want to eat it." He slowly put his head back in Teagan's lap, not sure what he'd committed to.

"You're so gullible." Teagan's pendant dragged on Cody's forehead as he inspected the boy's mouth. Cody felt a shaking like he was cold. "Check this out, bro. I'm just going to give it one good yank and she'll come right out."

"Is it going to hurt?"

"No."

"Are you lying again?"

"*Again*? That hurts my feelings."

"Yeah but is it going to hurt me more than your feelings?" Cody asked, pretty sure Teagan's emotions were as happy as the wicked smile on his face.

"Sure. But only for a second."

Cody waited a long time, staring at Teagan's upside down looming face trying to sort out the truth. Was it always going to be like this? How many teeth would need yanking? All of them? Eventually. How long would it take? Probably years. Was this because he hadn't brushed enough? Or long enough? Why does everything break?

"It's normal, just a part of growing up. Things get better."

"When?"

Teagan scratched his messy hair. "Eleven? Twelve? Somewhere in there. And don't let anyone tell you it'll make you blind. They're lying."

"What?"

"Umm . . . you gotta figure that out on your own, spud. Just trust me, things get better."

"Okay. But you have to count to three so when you're going to pull it I know?" He held his mouth open.

"Don't make such a fuss. This ain't a rocket launch."

"Uhh! You spossa counth!"

"Here's your tooth."

22

Yannis bought two plane tickets to Kinshasa the same year Kabila's bodyguard assassinated him at the presidential palace.

To say the journey set in motion an adventure that would change Nikos's life presupposed the life was one, so far, governed by patterns. Arms smuggling, however, was a patternless enterprise fraught with exciting risk and exotic travel. This trip was something more than mere change. Revelation of Nikos's purpose in life had not yet come. Maybe it never would.

Late August found Nikos and his father driving through the tropical rainforest of the Congo. Yannis kept his foot to the floor of the struggling Toyota shitbox, eeking out a surprising top speed that proved terminal to the head gasket eight kilometers outside of Kisangani. Close enough. They abandoned the truck and hitched a ride on some passing motorbikes in exchange for a few trifling wrinkled bills.

"Who's Ngouabi?" Nikos asked.

"The man we're meeting in town."

"Does he have a last name?"

"Not when he's running from RCD rebels."

Almost three years after Rwanda and Uganda dropped six thousand high-explosive shells on Kisangani, the once modern city was still a cratered mess. Nikos tried to absorb the tragedy. Ngouabi was in charge of Kabila's elite militia and relatively wealthy. Would he notice the misery, or be like every other rich person Nikos saw here, dismissing people as collateral?

"Are we helping him escape?"

Yannis circled his palm with a grimace. “In a way.”

“What does that mean?” His father’s passions didn’t include sympathy for oppressive rulers.

A flock of birds he’d never seen the likes of took flight from a tattered billboard. The dark round face was faded and defiled, but Nikos could still make out the words: *Laurent Désiré Kabila, the People’s Choice.* Apparently not.

Yannis twisted the fat antenna upwards on a high-end global satellite phone, waving it inauspiciously around as though perhaps this would attract a signal from thousands of kilometers overhead. Nikos snickered. Father had a humiliating record with modern technology.

“Give it to me,” Nikos said. Yannis wiped sweat from his forehead with a hairy arm and threw the phone to Nikos. “What’s the number?”

“Ngouabi’s run out of cash. Or at least, now that Kabila’s gone and the son is in charge, lost access to his resources. Some sort of political purge is going on. We’re in the middle of a turf war.” Yannis indicated it was still too early to call the handlers. “Hutu rebels are also chasing Ngouabi, and if they catch him, he’s dead. He’s trying to flee the country. We have money.”

This was true. Nikos was nearly old enough to be named a partner in K&E Import/Export. Their business drew large profits as Yannis became known as one of the most accomplished mover of weapons in the illegal arms trade.

“But why are we paying him?”

“We’re not. We’re buying something.” Yannis nodded and Nikos hit Send. The phone emitted a high pitched whistle of notes. No one answered. “Remember Mobutu?”

“Sure,” Nikos said. “Led a coup against Lumumba in the sixties. He was the despot here until Kabila. Didn’t the Americans back his takeover?”

Yannis nodded. “CIA had their filthy puppet fingers up Mobutu’s ass. At least for a while. Mobutu hired Rhodesian and Cuban mercenaries to keep control, fight dissenters, the

Simba rebellion, things like that. Also bought a lot of guns for them. Ngouabi knows where a secret stockpile of unused military assault rifles has been sitting in an underground storehouse all this time."

"And we're buying them?" The nearby Congo River dispatched a haphazard commerce of overburdened barges hauling fish, fruits and wares along the lazy flow through the country's northern major artery. The risk of sinking became more measurably certain as village boats lashed to the sides of the barges to pimp everything from medicine to prostitutes. Smell of sweltering vegetation and cooked cassava root present in every breath. Nikos looked around the humid post chaos of Kisangani. This wasn't an environment conducive to guns sitting dormant for thirty years. "They're probably in pretty bad shape."

"Exactly." Yannis took a good drag on a cigarette and told Nikos to hit *Send* again. "Which is why I intend to get them dirt cheap."

* * *

Ngouabi was desperate. The guns were a mixed bag. That they were in nearly mint condition was the only reason Yannis offered $100 for each. He'd have paid $200 apiece if they were in such good condition *and* not soaked in cosmoline.

"Cosmoline's a bitch," he said.

"It is a preservative," Ngouabi countered.

"How thoughtful. Clean it off."

"I cannot clean it . . ." The romantic edges of his French profanity echoed around the dusty storeroom. "These are excellent Belgiun rifles!"

"Good thing you noticed, as we wouldn't have wasted our time on another old third-world cache of AK-47's.

Market's different now. But getting that crust off them is a pain in the ass. A hundred each. U.S. dollars." Yannis handed Ngouabi the radio. "Tell my boy how many we're buying and he'll put the money in your car." Yannis held out his arms like Abraham and made a magnanimous gesture before adding, "Better make up your mind quickly. I've got a plane waiting."

"I can get three times that. You are not the only interested buyer."

Yannis nodded and started to walk off. "*Bonne chance.*" He only made it halfway to the door.

"Un moment, s'il-vous plaît!"

"No, you better take your time," Yannis said. "Call the other interested buyers, the ones stupid enough to trek out to this fertile tourist paradise to do you a favor. Spend a couple weeks working out the details, and if your many options back out, I'll hang around indefinitely. Is that how you think this works?"

"Are you threatening me?"

Yannis conjured a full-belly laugh. "What would be the point? You need me. I don't need you." He dug out a cigarette and deliberately struck the match across one of Ngouabi's wooden crates. "Hundred a piece. Tomorrow it'll be fifty. Or you can find another way to buy your ass across borders controlled by enemies who saw your face in the papers." He blew an offensive pool of smoke into the narrowing space between them. "Even my pilot despises you. If you're looking for a ride, pack your own parachute. Good advice. And free, since I hear you and your apparatchik-white Mercedes are running on fumes. Now, do we have a deal?"

"I am not a man to be trifled with."

Said with all the unconvincing umbrage of a disavowed underling on the verge of capitulation. Yannis held out to him the gold-foiled pack. "Care for a smoke?"

***

Howling winds buffeted the twin turboprop plane. Rivets squealed when the fuselage's large cargo bay got torqued by gusts that plowed a bare few beads of rain across the murky windowpanes. Most of the Libyan inland was an unforgiving parched desert, though tree scattered hills intermittently visible below gave evidence that some moisture off the Mediterranean hit the coast. Ivan arranged the sub-radar descent on a new-moon night, hoping for a dark and surreptitious sky. Forecasting neglected to mention there would be thick cloud cover, which made the planning moot. The weather proved more generous with pressure drops than raindrops. Again the aluminum bucket lurched and dropped out from beneath their feet in the turbulence. A disconcerting smell of mechanicals permeated the cabin. Distant purple lightning flashed, and Yannis said he could make out the rural dirt landing strip, glad he didn't have to put her down.

"Smuggler pilots are the best in the business," Yannis said. He patted the back of a young British expatriate, who manhandled the bare metal yoke and said he'd dropped cargo in far worse bloody weather.

After six hours in the air crossing northern Africa, *dropped* was exactly how the last fifty meters to touchdown felt. Nikos paid close attention to each control and switch engagement, fascinated, and promising himself that one day he would pilot something so ungainly through sheer air.

Nikos and Yannis moved quickly to load all the crates aboard a truck. A wind driven humidity left them sweating profusely. Yannis swore it had to be a record-breaking midnight heat. A short time later the bush pilot was back in the air. Nikos asked where he was flying next, but only got a diffident wink. Not how the business works, chap. Good luck.

Clothes clinging to their skin and collecting a fine layer of dust kicked off the roads, Nikos drove the last hundred kilometers into Benghazi where they'd buy a pair of stolen missiles and fill a few drums of gasoline.

"We need to find a parts washer," Nikos said.

"I called around."

"You called one engine rebuilder."

"So?"

"That isn't exactly calling around."

Yannis pointed at a gas depot and told Nikos to pull in. "I don't like the satellite phone."

"Use a payphone. There's one right there." Nikos ran over a curb and came to a stop, diesel motor clattering in front of the non-diesel pump.

"He wanted to know what we're washing."

"Is that another excuse? Parts."

Yannis laughed. "Miserable suspicious people. Aren't we in Libya? Don't ask any damn questions."

"You told him that?"

"He hung up."

"Are you sure?"

It could have been the phone, satellite disappeared or something. Satellites don't just disappear, father. Well this one did.

"Fill the drums."

"Stubborn Greek."

"Hypocrite."

Yannis and Nikos felt relatively safe in Qadhafi's backyard. Like the Congo, there was little here that couldn't be bribed into possibility. They'd truck the guns parallel to the Mediterranean coast by road. If any government officials in the loose outskirts of Tripoli or Algiers demanded to see their cargo, Yannis would hand them a modest manifest of Franklins, which as far as corrupt inspectors were concerned, converted smuggled military weapons into benign farm equipment. Just across the stretch of Saharan Atlas

Mountains, on the western edge of Algeria, they'd abandon the roads at Béni Ounif to slip undetected across the contentious border into Morocco. But first the cosmoline had to come off, especially if they wanted to woo a serious buyer. Better to get it over with before the last leg of the journey.

They dipped rifles in gasoline for two hours, watching the waxy coating dissolve and ooze like snot from the barrels. Scrubbing with brushes splattered petroleum saturated dirt across the plastic tarps, gloves cracking as exposure to chemicals broke them down. Only thirty guns were finished, 2470 left to go.

There had to be a better way.

"Give Viktor a call. Viktor Moshood? He helped us the last time we were in Benghazi," Nikos said.

"He's dean of a school. He only gave us a place to sleep."

"Yes, but it's a big school. He has to be influential. Perhaps he has connections," Nikos pleaded, gesturing at the futile mess they were making. "What about women? Father, you're a philanderer worse than that American Hugh Hefner. You don't know any well connected women in this country?"

"I know Viktor's wife."

Nikos sighed. "That explains a lot."

"Why do you think I don't want to call him?" Yannis emptied his glass. With dubious contrition he quietly added, "She's a beautiful woman."

"You're incurable." Nikos found himself laughing. Yannis smiled and then chuckled. He poured them both another round and toasted married women, whom surely Nikos was equally guilty of corrupting.

"Yamas."

"Yamas. Thank you."

The gasoline-soiled odor of their clothes ruined the whiskey's flavor. Really, when Nikos thought about it, whiskey ruined the flavor of whiskey. His skin crawled from the irritants.

Yannis held up his hand. "Wait a minute. I have an idea. We need to call Viktor."

"Really?" Nikos punched the number into the satellite phone. "And if his wife answers?"

"Even better."

"Absolutely incurable," Nikos said, as much to himself as for his father's benefit.

Viktor was genuinely happy to hear from Yannis and dinner went smoothly. Within hours Nikos learned what Yannis had in mind. Truck backed up to the school's kitchen loading dock, Viktor wished them luck and told them to be gone by morning. In the scullery stretched a huge, conveyor style Hobart dishwasher with multiple phases of high power well-drawn spray systems. Nikos lowered the thermostat temperature on the machine's well-heaters and Yannis filled the wells with the gasoline drums. With the valve for the freshwater rinse cycle off, they'd converted the noisy industrial dish machine into an awesome parts washer.

The vaporous high-pressure spray behind the stainless steel panels created a cloud of noxious fumes. If Nikos and his father weren't immune from euphoria, dancing around the machine like idiots, laughing with celebratory glee, drinking one beer after another, Viktor might very well have found them passed out on the tile floor. Nikos ran back and forth from the truck, rifles by the armloads. He methodically broke them apart, pulled the bolts, yanked the pins from the charging handles, loaded them into wash trays, and dumped those onto the upright metal conveyor forks. Yannis heard his boy yelling *Hurry up, old man*, but he was hard pressed to match the pace on the reassembly end. Yannis gave the assault weapons a quick spray of oil and packed them back into the crates.

The machine was magic! Hundred dollar blood guns went in one end and €1500 black market value rifles came gleaming from the parted rubber curtains at the other end.

"I've never seen anything so beautiful."

"Father, you're a genius."

"Don't tell Viktor."

"You'd be zero for two with him."

"My track record is worse than that," Yannis said. "He's a good man. We should be ashamed of ourselves." He tugged a cigarette from a pack with his lips, just about to light it, finger poised under the open lid of a zippo. Yannis stared hard at the warm spray belching from the Hobart, mumbled a curse about how he'd hoped to die peacefully, and spit the cigarette out.

***

Nikos and his father were ambushed on a cool evening counting bank notes in the back room of a weaving souk on the Fondouk Chejra bazaar. Nikos thought they were local police, or DST, the Moroccan state security, but either way their raid was too late. All they had was Yannis, his teenage son, a pair of .45's and a hiking backpack stuffed with €6.2 million euros. They didn't want handguns. They wanted a rundown Mercedes truck loaded with 2500 FN-FAL military assault rifles, two SAM launchers with ordinance, and forty RPG 7s. €6.2 million euros worth. They were pissed.

Taking an angry beat-down from local cops was a common risk, and one that hardly ruffled Yannis or Nikos. They'd been through worse. The Moroccan police had nothing and in the end Nikos knew they'd have to be released.

They'd even laughed about it!

He remembered laughing with Yannis, sitting opposite each other on the floor of a comparatively comfy holding cell.

Moroccan police had received no independent tipoff that illegal arms crossed into the country. No idea who'd driven off with the truck. Yannis and his son quickly found out much larger security organs were at work behind the seizure, and that even the loose due process in Tangier would prove too bothersome for the orchestrators.

In contrast to the Moroccan police, whose repertoire of angry violence was the desultory measure of incompetence, the American agents in perfectly tailored suits and dark glasses exercised emotionless, methodical precision. Two days in a dingy Tangier holding cell came to an unexpected end when the suits arrived, pulled a black bag over Nikos's head and shot him up with sedative.

It was the last time he ever saw Yannis.

23

In Damascus there are three imposing concrete buildings with soldiers manning the watchtowers. Just beyond the *No Photography* sign a black metal sliding gate hides the Palestine Branch of military intelligence. In the basement is Syria's most feared interrogation center, nineteen tiny cells lined up around a narrow hallway on a T-junction just past the communal holding tanks.

Nikos moved between semiconscious states. First he was on an airplane, but the flight characteristics he could sense suggested something smaller than a commercial jet. His captors made a stop to switch planes, this one distinctly propeller driven. By the time the sedatives wore off he was in a square hole one meter by two meters, and scarcely much higher. Smelling of piss and crawling with rats, Nikos became intimately familiar with cell 11 of Syria's interrogation pit.

"Why were you in Tangier?"

"I don't know."

"You are lying. Why were you in Tangier?"

"Tourists. We're tourists."

"You are a tourist?" The man, Nikos learned, was named George Salloum, and he nodded to a military uniform whose fist tightly clenched a pair of frayed fan belts.

He whipped them across Nikos's ribs.

"Why were you in Morocco?"

"Touri—We're just tourists . . ."

Nod. Another blow. Salloum took notes.

"Who is Ahmed Al-Qahtani?"

"I don't know."

Nod.

Nikos hung by his wrists half naked, and after eight hours was numb to the pain. He didn't cry out anymore.

What did they want? Even when he told the truth they called him a liar. Nikos changed the answers and was beaten all the same. Eventually he stopped saying anything and just bled on the dirty concrete. Invisible dark recesses and hallways made a dungeon out of the room. A work lamp on the floor cast all the light across and behind him, but Nikos could make out a still, slender man in a far corner. He never moved, never spoke, and never stopped smoking. He operated a video camera trained on Nikos from atop a stack of cinder blocks. Salloum took breaks to consult with the man. Nikos could make out neither the words nor the language. Spent butts hit the ground with a burst of sparks. Salloum returned with new questions Nikos couldn't answer.

Before leaving Libya he learned the Americans recently lost several important buildings in New York. His interrogation seemed to focus on those buildings.

When did you meet with Al-Zarqawi? Who is the courier? Where does the courier meet with Khalid Sheik Mohammed? What are his aliases?

Who supplies the money? Is it always in euros?

We know you had a meeting with Al-Qahtani in April; where did the meeting take place? Who accompanied Al-Qahtani? Did he receive the message? What was the message?

When the embers glowed brightly he could make out a silhouette of the man behind the smoke. The skin stretched across his prominent Adam's apple constantly shifted. Soon enough Nikos's eyes swelled shut and he saw nothing for three days.

They threw him back in the cell.

The man in the corner was one of the American suits. Just as Salloum deferred to him for direction, everyone else appeared to follow his bidding. Not out of respect. More likely they were paid. Nikos stayed locked in the pit for nearly two years while guards moved other detainees in and out of adjoining cells. Speaking softly so guards wouldn't hear, he learned cells 2 and 3 were both Canadians, Arar and Almalki. Cell 8 called himself Omar. The man in 13 was from Hamburg. Did anyone know Yannis? Or see a man who looked Greek? Next to him in cell 12 was another teenager who said his brother was in Guantnamo. Nikos had never heard of such a place.

"They can't do it there. They have laws," he said. "So they moved me here. Here they can do whatever they want."

"Who are they?"

"Americans. Are you that stupid? American CIA, they do this."

Nikos heard screams echo through the monastic hallways when the others were tortured. Having to listen was worse, either a reminder or a warning. "Don't tell them anything," Arar said. "They don't care."

They did care. When Nikos refused to speak he suffered much worse.

"What is the courier's name?"

They raped him with glass bottles.

"What are the names of his associates?"

Strapped him to the German Chair, no seat or backrest, until his spine felt like it would snap and he couldn't breathe.

"The money is from foreign banks or Tehran?"

Strung him blindfolded by the limbs and applied electric shocks to his feet.

"What happens on August thirteenth?"

Shocked his spine.

"Does Al-Qahtani use an emissary?"

Then his genitals.

"Who will attend the October ninth conference?"

Made tiny cuts all over his body and let him bleed on the floor.

"September eleventh?"

Tried to drown him.

"Who is the courier?" Salloum always dressed in pressed pants, nice shirts, fine leather shoes.

"Just make something up," Omar would say.

If the CIA knew nothing true came from this, why did they bother?

Nikos went weeks without interrogation, even a month. Devastating loneliness grew worse than the physical hunger to the point where he looked forward to being tortured and laughed when they beat him. He learned it was possible to feel nothing on the outside while nursing excruciating hatred within.

They no longer asked him anything and shocked Nikos just to watch him vomit. Salloum turned him back over to the suits. Shackled and sedated, he was flown somewhere even more arid and miserable, another torture chamber where they didn't touch him. His father wasn't in this place either.

What happened? Where did they take Yannis? Would he have survived this?

A month later Middle Eastern soldiers gave him a T-shirt emblazoned with an American pop star, loose shorts and a pair of worn out sneakers. Bagging his head again, they drove for thirty minutes and kicked him out onto the street, driving off before he could pull the black canvas sack from his head.

Nikos lay in a busy market with a small crowd forming around him. A dark skinned, well-dressed older man made an urgent call on his cellphone. He kneeled down and spoke to Nikos.

"La hawel Allah! Enta ka'wayes? Hasas b'haga?"

Nikos didn't understand the man and shook his head. The sunlight was blinding.

"You speak English? You are American?"

Nikos shook his head. "No . . . American, no. But I speak English."

"Very good." The man lifted Nikos to his feet and called for water, others rushing to bring some. "Good. Come with me. A friend is on his way. Follow, follow, we need to get you out of the street. You are going to be good. It is over now. Come."

* * *

The brain is fickle and unappreciative of the soul's search for truth. Normally able to recall inane details and conversations decades old, Ivan's memories of those two years proved stingy. Encryption was something he associated with machines, but repression encrypted the memory, turning it to static.

It didn't stop the anger.

When they'd decided Nikos had nothing to tell them, he was shipped to al-Aqrab, the Scorpion, a prison outside of Cairo operated by Egyptian State Security, who subsequently dumped him on the outskirts of the city with no money, papers or place to go.

He owed his life to Fady, a professor of medicine at one of the universities who took him home. Fady had a beautiful wife, three sons and two daughters, in all of whom he was very proud, and his family's hospitality was immense. Nikos was washed, given a clean shave and haircut, nice clothing, and nourished with good food until he regained most of the 25 kilograms lost at the hands of the Syrian/CIA partnership. Fady was able to acquire medications and treated Nikos for sores and infections. Promising Fady he would be repaid was a useless gesture. His host tried not to look offended. "This you do not worry about. God will provide," he said.

He called the Israeli number Nikos gave him and a week later new identification and tickets arrived by mail. Ellison took it from there.

How had such human kindness failed to wash from Ivan the vengeful impulses that followed? Could he blame it on Nikos? The boy? His younger self?

He remembered years of his life committed to tracking down those responsible. He made himself believe it was a search for Yannis, but knew deep down if he never found his father, he would still leave a trail of blood. Ellison tried to talk him out of it. Ivan was a stubborn teenager, and nothing changed.

"He's your best friend, your business partner, for gods sake," Ivan had said.

Ellison behaved as though he himself had buried Yannis, and grieving was the only appropriate way to reconcile what happened. Ivan was too angry for grief. He was on a mission.

Where could he begin? He started with what was known.

He'd been flown out of Morocco on a jet that would have required more than the dirt strip onto which they'd smuggled a plane in Libya. A real airport.

He looked at flight data out of Rabat's airport two days after Moroccan police took him and his father into custody. Found a GMME-OAKB air traffic control code, Rabat to Kabul, registered by a Boeing 737 business jet with the tail number N313P. The *N* indicated an American plane. The same plane bounced from Afghanistan to Syria the next day.

Two years later a Gulfstream V with the tail number N379P hopped from Syria to Cairo.

Alone the flight codes were nothing but coincidence until he discovered both planes were owned by Premier Executive Transport Services. The company was run by Bryan Dyess, who seemed to have a penchant for female employees. He owned a fleet of planes and Colleen Bornt,

Erin Marie Cobb, and Mary Anne Phister helped him lease them to customers, even though the Delaware business license was considerably more vague.

What would Mr. Dyess say when he found out his prime clients were the CIA? That they used his planes as Torture Taxis?

Ivan tracked the planes' flights by the tail numbers to the Johnson County Airport in North Carolina where Aero Contractors maintained them. Was he ready for a straight up confrontation?

"Remember me?" he'd say. "The kid you left hanging by his wrists in a Syrian pit?"

Maybe they would plead just doing their job, as if history were not replete with that excuse. They would demand their rights. Isn't that what Americans liked to say? Entitled to everything, the right to attorneys, the right to fair treatment, the right to remain silent.

They could have the last one. Ivan was all too happy to silence them. Beat them with fan belts until they told him where they flew Yannis.

Premier's office in Dedham belonged to a Massachusetts lawyer who knew nothing about the company. Mr. Dyess and his wholesome sounding employees were born between 1942 and 1967. Yet their social security numbers were all issued in the last five years.

Beyond the anachronistic disassociation of birth dates from social security numbers was that several of the employees also worked for Aviation Specialties Incorporated out of Maryland. Aviation Specialties owned a de Havilland Twin Otter, tail number N6161Q, that just happened to be flying around Syria the same day he'd been introduced to George Salloum. The Twin Otter was the propeller plane covering the last step of his extraordinary rendition to Syria.

Three planes owned by two companies who shared employees with each other across two states. Employees with improbable demographics. All three planes synced with the dates and locations Nikos was dragged around by the CIA. The ease with which the fact pattern could be discovered reflected the carelessness of the CIA. Ivan would have thought the well-funded agency capable of creating legends much more sophisticated than Ellison's. The CIA's were sloppy, patently false, and as though designed to irritate discoverers, indicating impunity more akin to arrogance than incompetence. Their supercilious efforts made Ivan hate the CIA even more. In his heyday, Ellison had made false IDs with attention to detail because people's lives were at stake. The CIA just didn't give a damn.

Linking the fake identities to the real perpetrators proved difficult.

On the east side of Highway 28, conspicuously across from the National Reconnaissance Office in the heart of Washington DC's alphabet soup of intelligence agencies, is the white concrete building of Chantilly's local post office. Behind the glass façade, was PO Box 221943, home to over 150 sterile identities the NRO used to cover for people operating the rendition program. Premier's staff were just a small part of a large CIA fraud. The scale by which America perpetrated extraordinary rendition was galling.

Ivan was still too inexperienced. What to do next eluded him and was lost in a short-lived, pointless assassination spree.

* * *

A call came through while Ivan was riding a liter bike southbound in the middle of the night. Three intervening decades of pragmatism supplanted anger. Ellison had long ago given him a trite expression about age and wisdom, but wisdom was essentially just pragmatism dressed up in honorable sounding threads.

Glitch continued to harass Ivan after he'd finished the job for Hizer Pharmaceuticals, demanding they meet to discuss other work. Ivan ignored him, sure now the gross amount of money in no way justified holding Dakota's hand like an altruistic promise and then killing him.

So he didn't check when the call source popped up on the helmet HUD, assuming Glitch was hellbent on trying to ruin another peaceful, 200 kph evening.

"Yannis might be alive. I intercepted covert traffic in the CIA's GST department. It says they moved him to Korea."

Ellison's voice possessed an urgent tenor. Yannis was still alive. The words were morphine to a laceration left open too long. His uncle stayed on the line, Ivan's motorcycle weaving through traffic at breakneck speed. Red taillights flashed across his visor until they became the blur of a world gone still next to his racing thoughts.

"Korea? Which one?"

"The CIA runs a diplomatic station that keeps an eye on Kim Jong whoever-it-is-now. All orchestration of North Korean intelligence operations start just across the DMZ in Seoul," he said. "What's that noise?"

"I'm on my way to the airport." He waited but heard no warning about rash decisions. Ellison clearly wanted the same thing. "I'll need an entry ID to the station. Overnight it to me. I keep a postbox in Seoul."

"Ivan . . ."

"You're going to talk me out of this?" Ivan swerved across four lanes and kicked down three gears to make an exit. The traffic cop in pursuit had no hope of matching the maneuver and the sirens faded behind him.

"No, by all means, rescue Yannis. But I can't get you an ID for this place."

"You just said it was a CIA outpost."

He heard a sigh.

"There are branches even I don't have access to. This one's ultra high level classified. I'm having trouble even getting a floor plan for you."

"What *do* you have?"

"Not much. The facility's off the common network. Communication goes through satellite burst signals, completely encrypted. I have records showing detainees moved to and from the station, so presumably there are holding tanks."

"Why would they suddenly move him to Seoul? Doesn't that seem strange?" Ivan waited but got no response. "Can you find out?" He spotted the municipal field ahead.

"Do I have a choice? Have a safe flight. And slow down, dammit. You're swapping cell towers like Tarzan."

"Quit tracking me."

Ellison hung up.

Sterile identities still belonged to real people. Thirty years ago Ivan had initially enjoyed the killing. *Nikos* felt vested with the power of righteous vengeance, terrorizing innumerable rendition employees for wrongs inflicted on his beloved father. But none of them knew who ran the CIA program or where Yannis went. Blind rage turned two years to static, faces and the questions now meaningless. The prospect of finding Yannis slipped away. Resentment became detachment, and detachment turned into business. Or pragmatism. People had their reasons, their retributive impulses, and he became the tool. Professional mercenary hitman.

Ivan left the bike in the hangar he'd rented. They could keep it.

Yannis would be in his eighties now. How had he stayed alive? Would he be sane? Or just a senile crazy old man? What would he look like? Would he be recognizable?

Ivan didn't care. No matter what was left of Yannis he'd be a free man.

24

Cody changed his mind about rain. A year ago he didn't like rain, a poor substitute for color and sunshine. Now he stood with face to the sky, arms outstretched, every slow drop bouncing from his eyelids and rolling through channels around the ears to trail down his neck. They joined the soggy company of drops mopped up by a state-issue shirt with grass stains from playing frisbee. If being in prison made him dirty, rain from outside the fence felt especially clean. Rain was free.

Filthy was at the other end of the yard. Filthy was his best friend, and Cody would have talked the redhead into a frisbee game, or even basketball, but Filthy was with Teagan. Cody didn't want to talk to Teagan right now. Just thinking about what had happened made him angry.

"You look like a stupid girl," Teagan had said.

"Do not."

"Yeah you do. You ain't cut your hair ever. You want to look like my bitch the whole time you're down?"

"Stop saying that!"

"Then let me cut your hair."

"You can't make me."

"What, are we in kindergarten?" he said.

Teagan liked to horseplay, but this was different. Hair trimmers in hand, Teagan yanked Cody to the floor, face down, both arms pinned under the weight of his bony knee, and shaved Cody's head raw. He didn't use the trimmer guard. Cody screamed, head pulled back by the long hair that moments later fell in clumps around him. He said he was sorry, please stop, but Teagan roughed his way through all of it.

Cody sat on the concrete, hair swept up, clutched to his chest in two tight fists, crying, scared to feel his own scalp.

"I hate you!"

"Quit whining. You'll get over it."

Hair slowly grew back over a week. Rain felt different. It no longer dripped from bangs or scattered when Cody shook like a dog. Rain helped things grow. Maybe that's why he changed his mind about rain. He wanted to get over it, but long hair was his hiding place when nothing worked, and Teagan took it from him.

In two days he would be seven years old. Teagan promised him a surprise. Cody didn't want a party. He wanted his hair back.

Leaves on the trees just outside the fence weren't yet ready to change color and fall, but a few leaves had still blown over the razor wire. He brought an assortment indoors. He hid in the narrow crawlspace under his bunk, a blanket to lay on, with a pack of fresh crayons and paper. The space wasn't smaller than before, he'd just gotten bigger.

So had Teagan. His cellie seemed more moody and the moods were fast and hard to understand. One moment Teagan would shoot rubber bands back and forth with Cody, and the next he'd get angry and Cody's games were stupid. What had he said to piss Teagan off? It was like petting a porcupine without knowing if it was coming or going, moods unpredictably cheery or painful. Teagan was losing his happy parts.

Cody laid the paper across the ribbed structure of the leaves, crayons pulling the patterns onto the paper the same way as the art project shown on TV. He changed colors to anticipate what the leaves would soon look like.

Teagan started to smell funnier too. For someone who'd once been so picky about Cody's showering habits, Teagan wasn't paying much attention to his own odor. Not that Teagan didn't shower but the effect seemed to wear off faster.

A pounding came from the desk. He wanted to look but refused to budge. Who cared what stinky Teagan was up to. More pounding, then scraping. Cody couldn't help it and peaked from beneath the bunk.

A mess of pills were scattered across the desk. With a blue Uno card Teagan gathered a pile of powder with red bits, then worked it into two rows. He curled the card into a tube and lowered his head, tube up one nostril. The powder must have a faint smell and Teagan was trying to get a better sniff. Like on the Food Network, crushing mint leaves to make them smell better.

Teagan screwed up. He sniffed too hard and accidently sucked all the powder up his nose. He threw his head back and gagged, holding the side of his nose in pain. Teagan tried again with the other row, but the same thing happened and this time it made him cough and grunt. What a dummy. Cody was glad it hurt.

"Shouldn't breathe it so hard, stupid."

"Oh, now you want to talk to me?"

Cody crawled back under the bunk. He felt the prickly surface of his scalp and a surge of resentful anger welled up in his stomach. Eyes squeezed shut hard enough that blood throbbed in his forehead. Cody kicked the wall, harder and harder, faster, until his heels went numb. I hate you.

"Quit moping and pouting like I give a damn."

Cody rubbed his eyes. He wanted to say one of the bad words, but it got stuck on the way out, sounding more like half of *fudge*. The effort scared him. He crumpled his leaf drawing. Sunlight snuck through the clouds, a narrow shaft of light cutting across the floor and under part of the bunk. Tiny specs of dust became visible, floating ever so gently around each other. He uncrumpled the paper and in the corner wrote *6 years + 363 days*. Two more days.

"Come on spud. I'll crush one for you too. Vitamin M makes anyone feel better."

I'm not talking.

"You better make up your mind quick. This shit's starting to kick in."

He had to come out anyway. Officers got angry trying to count inmates hiding under bunks. He crawled out and checked the rain-soaked clothes hanging on a hook, since officers wouldn't be much less angry counting him in his underwear. Still too wet. He pulled a pair of shorts from the dirty laundry bag.

"What's it smell like?"

"Heaven," Teagan said, sounding a lot like mom when she soaked her feet.

"What's that like?"

"Do you want one or don't you?"

"What if it goes up my nose?"

"Duh."

Teagan stared at him, eyes glassing over, the muscly sweaty odor returning. It slowly dawned on Cody that Teagan *meant* to suck the powder up his nose. "But why?" Teagan didn't say anything. He looked very tired. Asking questions wasn't a good idea if Teagan was trying to sleep. "Pills they go in your mouth, not your nose," he said.

"Look who knows everything now he's seven."

"Two more days."

"Close enough. Want to see what I got for your party?" Teagan swept the colored assortment onto the bunk and they scattered, a little like pale, misshapen M&M's.

"Pills?"

"Vitamins. I told you already."

"Vitamin M?"

"You want one?" Teagan pulled a red from the pile.

"What about yellow?"

"It doesn't matter." Teagan nodded off and jerked upright. He pointed out the different vitamins. "Klonopin,

Remeron, Seroquel, Trazodone, Haldol, Geodon, Zyprexa, Simatrex, Diclocydone, Morphine and Lithium. Mostly mood stabilizers, but if you snort 'em, you can gack out of your gourd."

"I got to put them in my nose?"

Teagan shrugged. "Swallow if you want. Children's Chewable Morphine. Kicks in faster you snort it."

"I don't know."

"Right. I'm checking out for a minute. Do what you want." Teagan pinched a wrapped green marble between his fingers. "Leave this one alone. It's for your birthday."

He barely got the words out, slumping over, totally unresponsive.

Cody pushed the vitamins around. He remembered the tube up his nose months ago. Did the doctors know it was faster? There seemed to be a complicated procedure for edible things, a code for where to put stuff. How did Teagan know the difference? What about ears? Did they get vitamins? He stuffed one in his navel and giggled. Teagan didn't move. He tried it on Teagan but his belly button didn't eat vitamins.

Cody didn't need vitamins to sleep. He could do that all on his own. He pulled the blanket over Teagan.

At the other end of the cell he pushed books over to the window in the door and climbed up to check the dayroom. Still no officers. What was taking count so long?

Cody heated up water and made cocoa with a little bit of coffee in it. Coffee's appeal was still a mystery, but mixed with cocoa it was kind of nice.

Another twenty minutes went by before Cody heard noises from the dayroom. The cops were yelling at someone on the first tier.

"FIRTH FOUR-TWO-EIGHT! BACK UP AND PLACE YOUR HANDS THROUGH THE CUFF PORT."

"Teagan? Teagan!" Cody jumped down and shook his cellie through the blankets. "Teagan, they, the cops, they're outside of Filthy's—Teagan, wake up!"

He ran back to the window, heart pounding in his chest.

"FIRTH, THIS IS YOUR LAST CHANCE. IF YOU DECLINE THIS OPTION FORCE WILL BE APPLIED IN AN ESCALATING FASHION TO ENSURE THE SAFETY AND SECURITY OF THE INSTITUTION."

Cody heard Filthy's reply all the way up on the third tier.

"Feck you, porker!"

"You heard the offender, boys. Mace him."

One of them emptied a canister the size of a fire extinguisher into the cuff port. Filthy laughed in a noisy, unhinged way. Cody gripped the narrow sill, fingertips turning white, tears falling, scared for poor Filthy.

Two officers with riot armor and shock shields plowed through Filthy's door as it opened, followed by the rest of the pack. They dragged the boy out and dumped him on the nearest dayroom table, then chained him up, cuffs around the wrists and ankles. Filthy's clothes clung to him, soaking wet splotches of orange foam dripping away. He kept spitting, even when they pulled a bag over his head. Dragged out of the unit between two officers, Filthy continued to struggle, a wild mess of jangling protest.

Cody felt like there was something he should be doing about all this, but what? Teagan hadn't heard a thing. Cody raced back and forth, wringing his hands and checking the window for more activity. Why did they want to hurt Filthy?

He drank his cocoa faster than he'd meant to and the urge to relieve himself arrived just as count was announced. Getting counted while peeing wouldn't get in him as much trouble as hiding under the bunk, but worse trouble than being counted in underwear, so he didn't move.

"Teagan?"

No answer.

The flashlight banged on the door. "Brenner seven-one-nine: when count clears, Control's going to wrack your door. Report to Admin. MHP wants to see you."

Teagan finally made a sound. He rolled over and rubbed his eyes. "What the hell did they say?" He swore a bit about the banging, stupid pigs something-or-other.

"I have to go see Judy."

"Who the hell's Judy?"

"MHP Judy?" Cody said.

Teagan looked wide awake now, confusion creasing the contours of his pitted face. Cody finally let the cocoa out.

"You're going to see Judy on a Saturday? Spud, you bumped your head. There's no Judy on the weekends."

"Teagan, they took Filthy, I think to the hole." He pushed the flush but it was stuck. He kept trying as he described the cell extraction ordeal to Teagan, who started laughing. "Why's it funny? It's not funny he got hurt."

"Really spud? Don't get your panties in a twist. I'll bet that little Irish bugger loved every minute of it. He can't help it. It's in his genes. You know he's not even Irish? I mean, his folks sort of are, but he's from Idaho. He just likes the idea. Does everything the hard way. Wonder what trouble he's in now?"

"They didn't say."

"Duh. They never do." He walked over to flush the toilet for Cody. "God, you're weak."

But when he pushed the button nothing happened. He tried the faucets.

"What's wrong?"

"Shut up, spud. I'm thinking."

Teagan muttered to himself, how the pigs couldn't know where the pills went . . . or did they?

"Spud?"

"Uh-huh?"

"Control's turned off our water. We're about to get our shit kicked in."

Cody's chest locked up. "Why? When I go see Judy?"

"There's no Judy." Teagan ran around the cell looking for something. He tore apart the clothing shelf and found a latex glove. "Judy's just smoke. You're going to Admin and it's going to be a bunch of cops and they want to know where Mr. Green is."

"Mr. Green? I don't know Mr. Green."

"And the pills," Teagan said, screaming softly through his teeth.

"Your vitamins?"

"Keep your voice down!" He pointed at the intercom speaker. "There's no damn vitamins."

Teagan loaded his vitamins into a baggy, worked the air out and stuffed it in the glove. Filthy wouldn't tell the cops anything. It must have been the sureños who'd given the pills to Filthy that ratted. "That car's full of snitches." He tied off the glove.

Would the cops mace him and Teagan? The couple inches he'd grown this year were shrinking away, floor getting closer.

"Will they mace Booboo?"

Teagan stopped his rummaging. "I'm sorry, spud. Booboo's a goner. Don't start crying, you knew this would happen someday."

Cody opened Booboo's lid. The blind mouse knew just where to look up, Cody sure his little friend could really see. He pet him nose to tail while Teagan talked.

"You can't have pets in prison. What am I supposed to do with him?"

"I'll put him in his carrying case when I go see Judy."

"There's no damn Judy! You gonna put him in your pants and hope they don't see a pill container with a fuzzy creature poking out when they strip search you?"

"What?"

"They're going to be watching you like a hawk. You gonna just drop it off somewhere? Give it to Compton while Control's got your license plate on zoom?"

"But he's just a mouse. He didn't hurt anybody."

"They don't care, spud."

Cody rocked back and forth. He wiped his face and pet Booboo's soft gray fur, tiny nose darting around. Booboo didn't deserve to die. He was a good mouse. He told Booboo he was sorry, but couldn't find words for goodbye. His hands trembled.

"How will they kill him?"

Teagan yanked his own bushy hair around, pacing with a hard, heel-to-concrete gait. "They won't spud, because you're going to let him go."

"But he'll die."

"Push him through the door crack, let him walk the tier." But what if somebody they see him— "Listen to me!" Teagan shook Cody. "He's got a better chance on his own. If he stays, he's dead. Let him go, maybe he'll come back?"

Teagan ripped a thread from the sleeve of his shirt. Cody didn't see what Teagan was up to until he turned around and showed Cody a label with a loop to tie off on Booboo's tail. It said,

If found, keep safe – 1 yellow bag – 007

Cody recognized Teagan's code signature, the idea that he was like James Bond. "What's the yellow bag?"

"Coffee." Teagan pointed to the door. "We don't have much time, so let him go. If he crawls into the next cell or whatever, I'm promising a bag of coffee if they watch your rat for you."

Cody kissed Booboo one last time. Run away, far away where it's safe. Hide. Booboo sniffed Cody's nose. He understood. He was a smart mouse.

No sooner had Booboo cautiously threaded his way through the small gap in the bottom corner of the door, Teagan dragged Cody to the bunk.

"There, I saved your rat. Now you've got to do something for me."

Just the way Teagan said this meant Cody wasn't going to like it. For a while he'd forgotten he was angry at Teagan, but now he felt it again because Booboo wasn't going to die and he had no choice but to say, *sure.*

"The cops are looking for these," Teagan whispered, throwing the glove full of vitamins into Cody's lap. "It's the only thing I can figure out that explains why Filthy's getting bagged up. The stuff ain't in Filthy's house, and I'm the pill guy, they got my ticket. They shut the water off so I can't flush 'em." Teagan grabbed his lotion off the shelf. "But they're not going to find shit because you're going to keep your mouth shut and hide them in your suitcase."

"My what? Teagan, I don't have a suitcase." Cody looked around the cell, at laundry on the floor. Was he talking about the laundry bag?

"Yeah you do, and yours is safer than mine right now."

If it was a mystery which vitamins were supposed to go in his nose or mouth, Cody never imagined the alternative place Teagan had in mind.

Face down over Teagan's lap, Cody struggled, and the moment he realized what Teagan called a suitcase, only the same stupid question rushed to mind: Is it going to hurt?

Just like every other time, Teagan lied to him.

25

In the course of a month the shades of the trees stretching down from the Bukhan-san peaks to the north would rust, a splendid profusion of color from scarlet to gold. In rural areas Chuseok harvest festivals were just getting started. Agricultural traditions counted less here in the city, where Ivan noticed a more modern culture of tourism.

"Westerners took the name Korea from the Goryeo Dynasty," Hye Min said. "One of our relatively peaceful periods, compared to the medievalism of Europe at the time."

Ivan arranged to meet her in a park next to the Sejong Center for the Performing Arts. Choi Hye Min took him to a suljip wine house where she assured him no one would care what the two of them discussed. She also insisted the food in the Myeong-dong district was authentic. Ivan was too preoccupied to care about authenticity but found her unexpectedly beautiful in ways he didn't consider typical. So he kept opinions to himself, and let her ramble about Korea's many conflicts and kingdoms.

"We enjoyed a period of unification that fostered the spread of Buddhist temples across Korea. Confucianism still guided politics and daily life, with emphasis on education and medicine embodying an enlightenment the West wouldn't see for another six hundred years. We created cast-metal movable type two hundred years before Gutenberg, if you believe it."

"I'm not really interested in Korean history," Ivan said.

"I know. Americans are never interested in history."

"I'm not American."

"Then stop behaving like one."

Ivan shrugged. A server arrived with another bottle. He let Hye Min do the talking.

"Are you vegetarian?" Hye Min asked.

"No."

"Good. I ordered you the bulgogi and a noodle dish."

"What is it?"

"Americans like it."

"I'm not American."

"Petulance is very American. Stop squirming. You'll enjoy it." She assessed him with a long silence. Ivan's discomforts were barcodes of information she read like a store checkout. "You want highly classified information, but don't trust me to order food?"

"Don't take it personally. I don't trust anyone."

"About food?"

"Especially about food."

"And you're not American."

"Is that sarcasm?" Ivan said.

"Sarcasm isn't a particularly Korean trait."

A political science university student, Hye Min took an internship with a government liaison office responsible for the SK/U.S. alliance. She also belonged to a community concerned that factions of the U.S. government were operating with competing interests. While the U.S. military presence was legitimate, her community received intelligence indicating members of the CIA were secretly selling high-tech, long-range weapons technology to North Korea through a fictitious front-company.

"Why would they do that? Doesn't that undermine the peace treaty?"

"Treaty? We have no peace agreement with the North. Your western governments signed treaties. For us this is an armistice."

"Whatever it is, why would the CIA sabotage it?"

"We're not sure of the CIA's motivation. My people suspect there are politicians with ties to military and weapons manufacturers who worry the North Korean war machine is falling behind."

"I would have thought that was a good thing," Ivan said.

"Not if you profit from conflict."

She couldn't know Ivan well enough to realize how bluntly her statement intercepted the reality of his past. Yannis and he, like any arms traders, had thrived on war.

"We contribute heavily towards border defense," she said, "an unnecessary financial burden if North Korea poses no real threat."

"It's pretty clear they do."

"Is it?"

If the threat had long since passed, and the CIA artificially maintained the pretense by propping up the northern neighbor's aging infrastructure for political and financial gain, Hye Min's community needed to know if South Korean officials were involved, or if they were pawns in the same game America played with Russia and Europe during the Cold War. She helped by spying on the local CIA presence.

The information Hye Min had was incredibly valuable, but he had a hard time imagining her conducting espionage in that beautiful lamé dress. English was her third language, not that he could tell. Her idioms were perfect.

An elderly group closer to the door broke into drunken song. Others joined in, chairs on two legs, soju liquor sloshing onto the wooden floor, and Hye Min must have known the tune, for she sang with them. Someone in the kitchen yelled and the song got louder until a stumbling chain of laughter brought their revelry back to the table. Food arrived and Hye Min was right, Ivan very much liked it. He wasn't American and she wasn't Korean, not that anyone gave a damn.

"The Mugunghwa Hotel is 140 stories, but we discovered anomalies in the floor plans on the top levels." She showed him documents from the original construction. "A joint project, the building is classified a super deluxe hotel, but the partner is a multinational front company not too well disguised. We traced it back to U.S. government offices in Langley. No local construction companies were permitted to bid the project."

"Foreign construction?"

"Halliburton."

"Figures."

"You shouldn't disparage them. It's a nice hotel."

She was right. Ivan didn't tell her he'd already reserved a suite. The structure above the eightieth floor had a rotational staggering that gave his connected rooms a vast balcony and hot tub.

"The top floor's a restaurant," he said.

"World class. Great view."

"And no spam on the menu."

"Recipes with spam are very popular here. It's traditional."

Her tone again sounded critical.

"So what's the anomaly?"

"There are 142 floors. The top two are operated by the CIA, not that we were supposed to find out."

Hangul script was carved into the edge of their table, not by design, but graffiti. Ivan had a hard time concentrating, and the discovery was yet another distraction. What message would Koreans etch into the side of a table? Was it profane? A declaration of love? Hye Min stared at him and he was drawn back to the concern about the hotel. "How could they not find out? Any idiot can count floors from the street."

"Did you count them?"

"Should I?"

"Don't bother. They've designed the windowscape to give the illusion of the correct number of floors."

There was no resemblance, but she reminded him of Berit, another woman from his past who could fix her silent eyes on Yannis with implied censure, nonspecific but manifest. She needn't tell Yannis, as he ought to simply know what he'd done wrong. For Ivan the summer in Sweden was a fond memory, presented to him as a vacation, though he knew otherwise. Yannis was up to one of his many secret projects and the look Berit Storhund gave him said it all. She'd practiced the same look for thirty years on a feckless short husband Otta, who fidgetted around her with a dim measure of defiance plowed over by apology.

Yannis and Ivan shared the summer cabin, called a *stuga*, and Otta kept a bee farm he took great pleasure in showing Yannis's young son. Ivan learned there was a dominant way to behave around a hive, and the bees knew better than to harass him and Otta. He learned a little Swedish, all the bad words, for the downtrodden Scandinavian did a lot of swearing. Nevertheless, Otta was a good storyteller when alone, a gentle person, and Ivan didn't understand why Yannis warned him to stay away from Otta.

"If he tries anything, Nikos, you shoot him in the leg, you understand?"

"Try what?"

"Just shoot him in the leg. Berit won't care."

It also never occurred to Ivan at the time why Otta's self confidence among bees never emerged around the dour woman. Ivan's upbringing left little respect for a man who let his wife treat him like Otta's, but he liked the old guy and felt sorry for him instead.

Faced with the same critical appraisal from Hye Min, he wondered who in the restaurant might feel sorry for *him*.

The childhood memory reminded him that Yannis was up there right now, and since Ivan didn't know the purpose, he couldn't know for how long. The window of opportunity might be closing fast. All he needed was the keycard or code to force the elevators to access the otherwise invisible floors. Surely Hye Min had those, or could acquire them.

"The hotel elevators don't go past floor 140."

"Sure they do. There must be several mechanical levels."

"Indeed. All isolated from the CIA floors. There's a narrow vertical corridor of mechanical operation up through the core, but nothing accessible to the station."

"Separate elevator?" Ivan asked. Hye Min shook her head. "Private staircase? Secret tunnel? Discrete doors? What about plumbing?"

"Nothing. While the hotel supplies water, we believe they have a separate filtration plant. Waste is incinerated."

"Then how the hell does the CIA get up there?"

She smiled. "Your choice of words indicates a fundamental misunderstanding. They don't go *up*. The CIA has a private helipad. They land unmarked airships, a secured freight elevator taking staff *down* into the station."

Ivan had never heard of anything so drastic. There must be some conduit to the rest of the building. Would it even meet code? What about fire or other emergency situations? Hye Min said building code was probably irrelevant to Halliburton. Her community speculated there might be a lifeboat-like ejection pod, perhaps with parachutes. So how did one get in? Should be simple enough, he reasoned. All security was computer based. Infiltrate the computer and insert a new identification. He could schedule a landing and walk in. Hye Min's people probably hacked into the station's network long ago.

"There's no network. Not from the outside."

"Communication?"

"Encrypted burst transmissions directly to one of their aging geosynchronous MILSTAR satellite relays."

Exactly what Ellison had warned Ivan about the station. Hye Min described an electromagnetic shielding, not the generic type, but a sophisticated active array, like sound-cancelling on headphones. He felt stupid asking the obvious, but why not cut the power? While he could have guessed the answer, the details still impressed. Radiation signatures hinted the independent internal power supply might be a small nuclear plant.

"It's only speculation," she said. "The hotel neither supplies their energy, nor traditional fuels."

"But the station could easily fly in fuel rods."

Hye Min nodded. Her people knew some of the agents' names, or at least code names. They were all A-2 visa, official foreign government, but getting a passkey or codes was out of the question.

"The facility is impenetrable," Hye Min said.

Ivan fought off a sense of hopelessness. Out front, in the street, he heard the sound of a baby crying. Another distraction. Late night and getting later, and all for nothing. He could feel the steep urgency like unbreathable air, or a vacuum, anger over sheer inadequacy. What would Ellison want him to do? Why was Yannis up there? What were they planning? Were there any other options? At length the baby stopped crying. "Unacceptable. I need to get in there."

"Are you sure you're not American?"

His insulted appearance met with a look of beautiful pity and a nod. Poor idiot, she seemed to say. She poured the last of the wine and finished it with a delicacy irreconcilable in someone so forward. What vexed Ivan was no concern of hers, time being of little consequence. When she finally spoke it was slow and deliberate, as though holding out for this moment.

"There is one weakness."

***

Cover would be nice. He'd take anything to mask his assent. In spring the density of yellow dust carried by winds off the Gobi Desert could be formidable. But it wasn't spring, and the rainy season's height had long passed. Ivan lucked out, the temperature falling below twenty degrees, humidity rising slightly.

When he looked down, the conditions left a layer of fog ten stories above street level, obscuring all but the iridescent collage of glowing color from street lights, signs, cars and commerce in general.

He moved a cam higher in the recess, tested the load, then pulled himself up, locking the nylon sheathed repelling cable into the carabiners. The initial fifteen floors left him wondering if all twenty kilograms of gear strapped to his back were absolutely necessary. A sharp crack erupted into the solitude far above the energy of Seoul, another pyrotechnic piton buried in the concrete gap of the Mugunghwa Hotel. Hye Min had persuaded him to try kimchi at the suljip. The fermented smell and off-season sourness were among several untenable pieces of her advice.

"You could land a helicopter on the civilian platform of the hotel roof, but there's no access across," Hye Min had said.

Which still left him traversing the structure externally, and what was he supposed to do with the helicopter? It wasn't exactly long term parking while the pilot got a drink. Too suspicious. No, Ivan needed some cushion time built into the plan. Uncertainty about the CIA station floor plan was one of many things that could go wrong. The vagueness included his father. Yannis might not be in any shape to traverse the side of a skyscraper back to a helicopter when Ivan got him out.

Reaching a height approximately three-fourths the distance between his suite and the roof, Ivan fired redundant anchors and took a break. He played out a little line and hung perpendicular to the skyscraper by the waist harness, an illusion that made the narrow vertical concrete strip feel like a dock stretching out onto an ocean of glass. He walked to the edge, peering into a crystal sea, the varying luminance created by hotel rooms like phosphorescent creatures swimming to the surface. Looking up, his reoriented heaven split between metropolitan glitter fading to the horizon of forest, and the starlit night. Far away landing lights descended to Incheon International Airport. Faint notes of music emanated from the glass floor, like a distant vessel, and he closed his eyes, hands outstretched, powerful gusts washing currents of air through Seoul from the Yellow Sea. For a time he felt peace. Like the serenity submerged beneath *Estrella de Mar Rosa*. Back then it was just a job, a mission, money . . . maybe a little excitement. The character of this climb shared nothing in common with the South Florida adventure. Now it was personal, and Ivan worried whether his judgment was clouded. It was his basic tenet a good operator, a hitman, should have no attachment to the job. He simply didn't trust anyone to take his place. Failure over his own father would not be something purchased. This was his responsibility alone.

Ivan let gravity adjust his relationship to the hotel and pulled in the cable to pursue the last leg of ascent. He switched to decay-joint anchors.

Within half an hour he reached the tricky part, navigating around the Burj al-Arab-esque superstructure that reached away from the hotel's summit to support one of the landing pads. Traversing a precarious route to the top of the pad, Ivan climbed over the wind deflectors and found the roof orientation just as he expected from aerial reconnaissance images.

"Across from the landing pad should be two doors, one more discrete than the other," Hye Min had said. "The one on the left accesses a freight elevator that descends two floors to the station's interior. Getting on the elevator is the problem. You should assume all manner of security barriers exist, pass codes, biometrics, surveillance check points, who knows."

The entrance under the awning resembled a storage garage door. Ivan counted the cameras trained on the approach. Red Carpet at the Oscars was worse, but not by much. The door that interested him was canvassed by just one lens and protected only by an electronic lock.

The access card came from Hye Min, who managed to compromise the contract personnel responsible for the low-security maintenance closet. Still risky, but moments later Ivan closed the door behind him, internal panel swapping the green back to red LEDs. She hadn't been able to get a technical layout for the room, but what Hye Min had said he should find came as a welcome flaw in CIA security.

"A local vendor filled an order for the station, an assortment of expensive fish. That was our first clue."

"Hell of a clue," he said.

"You think it was halibut?" Hye Min said, pointing to her plate. "While you *could* eat a Mandarin, the beauty would be wasted on your stomach."

He wondered if she meant in general, or if she considered his stomach a particular waste. "Why? What is it?"

"Company for the Picasso Trigger Fish and Yellow Tangs."

A fish tank, that's what she'd discovered. This didn't seem particularly revealing. "How is that important?"

"Twenty cubic meters of saltwater aquarium? How is that *not* important?"

"It's the U.S. government. They want a fish tank, they buy SeaWorld, two if the price is high enough. Maybe the station chief's ex-Navy SEAL, done a lot of time underwater." He thought of something. "Is it a training tank?"

"Sure. With ₩60 million won worth of live coral? Decadent even by your American standards."

"I'm not American."

It was no use. She'd made up her mind. He'd had a primal misgiving that if only he'd banged her, some dominance would be reasserted. The impulse immediately disgusted him for descending beneath animal lust. Sex wasn't a crescent wrench to screw off his aggravations.

And in any case she must have sensed it, quickly shutting him down. "That's not in our contract. I'll give you a phone number if that's what you're looking for."

"No." As a belated afterthought he added, "Thank you."

The CIA didn't clean fish tanks. Managing equilibrium, servicing, food delivery, replenishment, filtration and new fish were done once a week by two local technicians vetted for the job.

Plastic bags the size of flour sacks lay stacked against the far wall of a room larger than he'd expected. Deep freezers and refrigerators contained tubs of processed krill, a powerful smell. Tubular instruments in upright cabinets helped inject it close to the live coral. A complex network of pipes ran pumped tank water through monitors and filters. They disappeared to the aquarium one level below through a hardened concrete floor fifty centimeters thick, if Hye Min's information was correct.

On the floor in the center of the room a sliding steel door covered access to the top of a tank so vast the population density was North Dakota sparse. A swim in the tank wouldn't get him access to the station. Thick glass walls of the aquarium secured the internal space from the maintenance room. However, the water *was* below the frequency-shifting barrier of signal-shielding, which indiscriminately ran across the top of the tank. Hye Min was right about this one weakness. Though minor, to someone with Ivan's skills it became a gaping hole.

Ivan uncinched the climbing pack, removed a coil of prima cord and wound a length around the steel door, packing it up under the gliding lip. A remote detonator attached to the cord received a signal from a relay hidden behind the pump machinery. Across the lock of the door through which he'd entered the room he pressed another remote detonator into a shaped charge of Semtex. He opened the tank plumbing access, a pipe large enough to feed both the lead off the relay and an endoscopic video probe with a broadband antenna. Just behind these he fed a Comp B explosive to discreetly maneuver into the crevice of one of the coral structures.

A tablet showed the camera's progress, light at the end of the downstream tunnel looming larger. The moment the antenna pierced the signal-shielding separating the station from the rest of the world's electronic clutter, Ivan's tablet lit up with network traffic from within the facility.

Despite procedures used to communicate with satellites, amazing luck revealed the station's internal workings weren't encrypted. A piezo hydrophone fed him sound waves from the rooms surrounding the aquarium, carried safely across the saltwater medium, its colorful inhabitants oblivious to the North Korean intel they alone were welcome to swim through.

The noises were banal and uninformative, consistent with a visual landscape beyond the thick glass limited to an organized office and desk on one side, and a situation room on the other. Lots of expensive teak surface but no occupants. Two American flags framed a portrait of former president Reagan.

No U.S. government office really felt complete without the benevolent gaze of Saint Gipper.

* * *

"Koreans are very spontaneous people," Hye Min had said. "They're gracious, unpretentious and like to talk."

"I've noticed."

"Go ahead and notice, but laughter often masks a level of stoicism that's hard to understand. Location has its price. Korea's been the unwilling ground for many wars, most between Japan and China."

Ivan thought of Greece, World War II, what it meant to be resilient. He thought of his grandfather, Eliv. "We want to see the best in other people."

"Perhaps. Joy in life in spite of tragic history is remarkable. In Koreans it left a small streak of something like fatalism. Very hard to see, but always there."

In the days afterwards, when Ivan thought about what went wrong, this exchange would haunt him, the recurring illusion of identity. He'd believed what he wanted.

The plan once in the service room was simple.

Phase 1: Get the identity of one of their agents off the network, someone soon scheduled for arrival. Shouldn't be too difficult, since flights came and went every couple of hours.

Phase 2: Upload the retinal pattern data to his rig, to be mimicked by the LCD refractor of his eye, retrieve a floor plan and, if possible, the location of Yannis.

Phase 3: Intercept the agent when he lands, borrow his clothes, let him sleep off the trauma in the helicopter along with the pilot. Enter the facility, get Yannis, tie him into the spare body harness secreted in the drainage gutter behind the roof's wind deflectors, and jump.

Shoot any interference. With luck the backup plan wouldn't be needed.

Give or take a few details the primary plan went down without incident.

Right up to the moment the freight elevator door opened inside the station. What hit him in the right temple might have been a fist, but for the briefest moment before he blacked out, Ivan imagined having walked into oncoming traffic.

* * *

It could have been worse. They could have chained the cuffs to the floor behind the fixed chair rather than in front. They might have left him in the jacket he borrowed from their incoming agent, who'd gone rather heavy on the cologne. That would have made the headache infinitely worse.

He tried to access his rig.

Nothing.

Blood on the shirt matched a dried trail through the right side of his beard. Probably should have shaved. The processor was just behind his temple, embedded in the skull. The blow must have embedded it even further. Assume irreparable damage. Hundreds of variables pulsed through his now unenhanced consciousness.

Crisp light routed every shadow from a small room familiar enough to Ivan, one easily cleaned after messy interrogations.

"Son of a bitch."

It was a useless thing to utter aloud, and better saved for the moment coming.

By the door a keypad blinked from red to green, a loud beep as the electronic lock disengaged.

When the bald, elderly gentleman came in, Ivan's first thought was, shit, he's never going to let me live this down, but at least Yannis should be safe, another way had been managed.

His relief quickly drained like the blood from his heart.

"I'm afraid—for you—this hasn't been the best of mornings. You probably have a lot of questions. We have only one. Care for a cup of coffee, Nikos?"

Ellison set two paper cups on the table in front of Ivan.

26

"This is the moment when you need to ask yourself how much you really want to know. Your first instinct is to demand the truth. There is no truth in the world, Nikos. Every side is a compromise. Not even I know the truth."

"Where's Yannis?"

Ellison sucked air between his teeth. "You're too predictable. And of course that's why you're here, correct?" He drank from one of the paper cups, made a face, and gestured to Ivan's. "Government joe. Same shit everywhere. You might not want to swallow."

Two guards entered and took to the corners, followed by a familiar face.

Glitch.

"What is this?" Ivan said.

"Good morning, Dean. I'd like you to meet my nephew."

"Don't be an ass. Let's get this over with."

"He wants truth. Immediate circumstances or the large existential questions, we don't know." Ellison turned back to Ivan. "He hasn't even tried the champagne."

"Ask him about the helicopter."

"Is that important, Dean? He's here."

"Or maybe a paraglider. Explains the harness. Probably got it from his terrorist friend, the one whose name sounds like the naughty bits?"

"She's not a terrorist."

"Oh that's rich. Pain in the ass, the broad's whole network. Wants to know what we *do* up here. Believes in *transparency*, and all that bull—"

"Dean, don't be a bore."

"We're going to find out."

Ellison gave the fixated man a deprecating look. Little twitches erupted along the right eyelid of Glitch's face.

Scraps of black nylon fiber still clung to Ivan's shirt, like they'd sawed through his climbing harness with a serrated Leatherman. Pacing like a predator, Glitch evinced dominance plagued by confusion. They'd known Ivan was coming—of course Ellison had told them—but Glitch was apparently looking to the sky for Ivan's infiltration. If what Glitch didn't know was the plus side, Ivan's long game meant nothing if he couldn't get out of this room. He rattled the chains reaching for the coffee cup. Only half full. Punishment or mercy?

"It's not poisoned," Ellison said. "If we wanted you dead—"

"*You'd* have done it already?"

Ellison appeared appropriately hurt.

"I'll be happy to," Glitch said.

Ivan shrugged and started to drink. Words written beneath the coffee on the bottom of the cup appeared above the meniscus of tilted liquid. Ivan tilted it further and tried to inconspicuously focus on the indelibly penned message.

Play along.
If you have Plan-B,
set cup down with
left hand. E

Was this a trick? Was Ellison's betrayal real or not? There was no other explanation for the message's elaborate disguise. Large as Glitch's guile might be, it wasn't complex. He spit the coffee back into the cup.

"You wring out Glitch's underwear to brew this?"

"Glitch? Do you mean Dean here?" Ellison smirked at the rat-faced man behind him, whose Adam's apple started its signature ratcheting. "I see what you mean, and I don't blame you for disliking him. I'd argue Glitch is the reason for half your life's misery."

"Asshole."

"Stay out of this, Dean."

Dean suppressed a physical impulsivity and took succor in a pack of cigarettes. A trail of ash formed as he paced, footprints in the cancerous snow.

"Nikos, keeping the world safe, all that specious trope, is complicated. We do things we're not proud of, but for self interests that are unique to each of us. I'm committed to the wellbeing of Israel, and so are our American partners, even if Dean's interest looks like fascism. Did you know Israel is the single largest beneficiary of U.S. foreign aid? Nice to have those kinds of resources, though I won't claim we've wielded them with the diplomatic tact that warms Washington politicians' hearts. Were you aware more than half the CIA's expenses are paid to contracted employees?"

"Should I give a damn?"

"If you care about how the system works, yes. Conspiracy theorists like to use the term *plausible deniability*, but let's be honest. Plutocrats deny the work you do for them regardless. Plausibility is merely convenient. You're one of the CIA's contracts. Both you and your father helped carry out jobs too indiscrete for State Department policy wonks. Not that Yannis knew, nor obviously you."

"Don't bullshit me."

"You said it yourself. We recruited you."

Rather like providing Israel F16s and pleading non mea culpa when they bombed targets in Middle Eastern countries allied with America, Ellison suggested. Langley supplied weapons and propaganda to whichever dissident groups carried out the bloody results deemed necessary to protect politicians, and sometimes even the country. Terrorists were palatable so long as their objectives coincided with those of the United States. Anyone who cracked the spine of a Noam Chomsky book knew this, Ellison noted with sarcasm.

"For instance, Dean supported Saddam until his favorite dictator tried to back Iraq's oil reserves in euros. So, in a way, it *was* about the oil. America's security was threatened—their *financial* security. Don't scoff. Economic collapse from a destabilized currency hurts a whole nation, the kind of damage terrorists only dream of. Israel would suffer collaterally from the fallout."

Not a new formula, but one honed with much practice, Ellison said. Safety required hard choices and ignorance is a powerful self-delusion. Isn't that how Ivan avoided the taint of unscrupulous government puppet strings? Delusion in the honor of arms trading for revolutionary underdogs? If Ivan had paid the slightest caution, he'd have seen the American agency's fingerprints on every job.

Yannis's weapons and the buyers were carefully orchestrated for him. He milked a lucrative black market reputation subsidized by people wholly indifferent about costs. The FBI, CIA, HSA, TSA, NSA and the rest, were like buckets directly under the Congressional budget showerhead. Chaos in check, completely deniable. The story's complicated, Ellison said.

"Then your father went off script. Remember Tangier?"

"Vaguely. Ask me another stupid question."

Ellison nodded. "We had a buyer picked out. Instead Yannis sells 2500 military rifles to a Harakat al-Muqawama, or one of the splinter groups. Probably offered him more money. Look, the guns weren't really a concern, but SAMs and RPGs raining on Israel from the West Bank? On paper Yannis is my business partner. You'd think he'd have more sensitivity to me. I told higher ups I'd talk to him. They were beyond furious and told me to stay out of it."

Ellison didn't know Yannis and Nikos were sent to extraordinary rendition hotspots in Syria. He would never have condoned the treatment. The CIA wanted to know which Hamas cell drove off with the hardware? Strangely they'd never asked him that, Ivan said. Ellison admitted the agency knew only Yannis, and not Nikos, had the information. Then what was the point of holding Ivan?

Ellison seemed unsure whether to answer, and when he finally spoke, affected a concessional wrist flick, like an apology pried from a bear trap.

"Collateral. Dean wanted Yannis to see you suffer. He thought Yannis would give them intel to save you."

For a brief moment Ivan was confused. What did Dean have to do with Tangier?

Then the scene came back to him. A man in the shadows at the far end of a Syrian interrogation pit, fulvous light of a burning cigarette faintly describing the features of a much younger Glitch. Ivan realized his two years in prison were meaningless, now finding out Glitch fed George Salloum empty questions as part of a psychological game against Ivan's father.

"You want to kill him," Ellison said, thumb over his shoulder. Ivan didn't notice blood surging through his hands, holding the chain as though he could rip it from the concrete. "So did I. The GST department finally let me know what they'd done when there was no lead left to follow. Yannis killed himself to protect you."

* * *

The two guards stayed, but before Ellison and Dean left the room, they asked him the one question Ellison promised at the outset. What did Ivan mean in his last message to Glitch? It lay printed on a sheet of paper in front of Ivan:

Number 7 is done. If Hizer bothered
to do comprehensive bloodwork,
you'd have found him without all the hassle.

Dean didn't work for Hizer. After savvy journalists' inquiries into extraordinary rendition forced the CIA to mothball the program, Dean was reassigned as a coordinator with corporate contracts. Hizer pharmaceuticals partnered with the CIA to develop biological detection for chemical weapons. Dean still worked for the CIA but acted like a liaison spokesperson for Hizer.

Hizer didn't know the man on surveillance records entering the Wenatchee River Corrections Center, but Dean did. Hizer sent Dean data off the machines monitoring Dakota.

Sample PG-014487-M reported stable, semi-sedated conditions, interrupted by sudden fluctuating heart rate. The computer detected a powerful parasympathomimetic alkaloid and a surge in acetylcholine, conditions presenting an unacceptable risk of fatal neuromuscular paralysis. The computer initiated an intervention beginning with electrical signals to his brain to release chemical triggers boosting immunity and to counteract the foreign bodies detected in his bloodstream. A massive flow of adrenaline pressed organs into overdrive, kidneys swelling as the vascular system, assisted by the active network of machines connected to him, isolated and purged unrecognizable bionanites. The systemic shock induced cardiac arrest. Wires embedded in Dakota's chest defibrilated his heart. The rescue operation was over in six minutes.

"You're pissed because it didn't work? How is this my fault?" Ivan had said. "I did what I was paid to do. Screw you."

No, not at all pissed, Dean said, glad that Ivan had managed to locate the elusive *product.* Dean and his people would handle it from here on. When the Washington

Department of Corrections approved re-access to the test subjects—which wouldn't be long—Hizer doctors would take care of the boy. It was the message that concerned Hizer and their CIA liaison. What kind of comprehensive bloodwork? What had Ivan discovered in Sample PG-014487-M's blood?

"Dakota's a pill-baby. Isn't that obvious? Hizer doctors testing their stupid little eunuch drug would have seen the build signature in his DNA and found your missing Genesis Life Solutions kiosk purchase."

"That's it? Nothing else?"

"Why? What else is there?"

"Nothing that concerns you," Dean had said. "Your uncle thinks we should keep you on, that your services are useful. I want no loose ends. There's a good chance you'll meet your father again soon."

They'd been gone for three hours. Maybe five. The room had no clock. One of the guards had a watch, but with Ivan's rig shot to hell, he couldn't zoom his eyesight. He didn't bother asking.

His father was dead. All of three decades searching, and Yannis was dead. In the scorched earth of Ivan's memories he'd always known. Into the dry trail of blood through his beard ran a slow march of rare tears.

***

"When I finished my training for the Mossad they issued me this gun."

Ellison returned after many hours and now threaded a suppressor on the barrel of a .22 Beretta. He looked calm. Too calm.

"My lead instructor said to keep it clean, but like other agents, I would probably choose not to carry it during operations. Better to talk your way out of trouble."

"We're done talking."

Ellison nodded. "The Mossad trainers were right. I've rarely used it." He leveled the weapon on Ivan's head. "Despite the irony, it pleases me it should be of greatest use in these final hours."

"*There is no greater power now in this dark and dreary time of ours than mud and filth, nor is there even a greater sacrifice for god and country now than treachery*," Ivan said, borrowing the satire of Kostas Varnalis.

"You have much of your father in you, Nikos. Not just his love for Greek poets. Have faith. We were a mess in those days. Nothing's changed."

Ivan closed his eyes and heard both shots like two whacks of a steel-brush drumstick across hollow tree bark. For a dead man, the smell of cordite was a relief. Ellison tossed a key at him. It skittered across the steel table and landed in Ivan's lap. Both guards lay slumped in the corners while Ellison liberated them of their weapons.

"Don't just sit there."

Ivan scrambled to get out of the cuffs. "What the hell is going on here?"

"I'm sorry, Nikos." Ellison threw Ivan both guns. "I've suspected for a while Dean and Hizer were using me. I can't find what they're covering up, and trust me, I've searched."

"What's in the boy's blood?"

"I don't know. Dean said we needed this meeting to set the record straight. He had no intention of telling the truth. I learned too late he's afraid you know something important, and thinks burying you solves the problem." Ellison threw Ivan a thumb drive. "Whatever they're hiding it has something to do with *quadrinary encoding*. Don't lose this. You need it to figure out what Hizer's up to. What's your escape plan? Plan B?"

Ivan described the rigged explosives within the aquarium in the conference room. "But I can't trigger the explosives. My rig's down."

"You don't need the whole rig. The transmitter has a pre-encode buffer." Ellison ripped apart his phone and tossed Ivan the battery. "Power it manually and it should transmit the buffered code."

Ivan ran in the direction of the atrium and looked back. "You're coming. You just killed two agents! Dean's not going to let you live."

"There's only one harness left, Nikos."

"I can make it work."

"No, Nikos. I picked the wrong side—the wrong war."

"The damn CIA lied to you!"

"I lied to myself." Looking down at the Beretta in his hand, Ellison's voice carried the honesty of benediction. "Your grandfather, Eliv, told the Nazis he was Jewish because he believed in something. Imagine my pride in him? Or choices I tried to make carrying on his legacy? I wanted to believe in a peaceful Israel, perhaps even idealistically of an honorable path. But more importantly, right now, I believe in you."

"If you stay, Glitch'll just use you against me. The same as Yannis."

"Exactly. Don't think Yannis a coward. He gave his life many times over for his beliefs. Don't be a pawn in someone else's war like I've been. You have the truth. You're free. Go find something to believe in."

Blood sprayed up the wall behind Ellison, a peaceful swiftness incompatible with the intensity to follow. The gun fell from under his uncle's chin.

Instincts were responsible for pushing Ivan through crisis, but instinct failed him.

Ellison wasn't dead.

He couldn't be.

Instinct tended to save Ivan from sentimental weakness. Instinct would have left the man right there on the floor. Time stood still.

Instead he dragged Ellison by the arms, cutting down stray staff on the way to the room with Saint Gipper.

Instincts surfaced when he realized upending the sturdy conference table was the only defense against a wall of water. Surroundings deafened by panic came to life. A wad of shirt between his teeth, Ivan sliced open his palm, ripped the rig's transmitter from the shallow flesh, and wired it to the phone battery.

The hydraulically muted eruption preceded a tsunami that threw the table against a long credenza. A hailstorm of thick glass fragments bombarded the walls, followed by a wave of plankton smell. Ivan saw the bar service topple from the cabinets and, since he was momentarily pinned, found time to inhale what was left of the bourbon. Alarms blared.

Instinct pulled Ivan up through the hole carved by prima cord and Semtex in the CIA's secure outpost. Behind, a fusillade of weapons fire ricocheted and fell into a salty river of colorful fish chunks and ₩60 million of coral shards. Instinct dragged the body of Ellison across a roof 142 stories off the surface of Seoul and into a harness meant for Ivan's father. Instinct gave Ivan the conservative and precise aim that put sixty percent of his counter fire through the fatal-T regions of converging military security. Trained and beaten into him by Yannis and this ex-Mossad, these instincts gave his enemies pause, the critical time to commit an act the insurance policy of instinct didn't cover.

Desperate fear made him leap.

Through the next twilight Ivan fell, arms locked around Ellison, the only thing attached to the cable. He felt a succession of tugs as each decay-joint breakaway anchor snapped. Three floors above his balcony the double anchor grabbed hold of all 190 kilograms, the half that was Ivan losing his grasp. Below him a squeal signaled an electric servo in the ascender absorbing the free-fall, just enough play for a lacerated hand to grab and hang from the nylon strap of Ellison's harness.

The ascender bolted to the concrete lowered him between a covered hot tub and a wire cutter. He severed the cable and pulled it from the overhead anchors. A shadow crossed the deck. Someone inside his suite disappeared into the bathroom.

He crept through the glass door. A service employee emerged and dropped a stack of towels with a scream when she saw his disheveled appearance and blood running down his leg.

"Get out. Out!"

She scrambled for the door in the clumsy way instincts served normal people who didn't jump off perfectly good roofs or assassinate judges.

This was a colossal fuckup. Ivan dragged Ellison onto the bed. His uncle was irrevocably dead. He leaned over the body, thumb drive in hand, yelling.

"What is this? What am I supposed to do? Goddammit! Why?"

He fell back, eyes closed, as though brief meditation could determine what would follow. He became aware of intense pain in one of his legs.

Thrown on its side, water spilled across the sink from the reservoir of an LG miniature espresso machine. Ivan ripped open the watertight bag that emerged. Punched in the eleven-digit number of the only person left in Seoul to trust. Listening to it ring, he ripped apart a shirt, tying one length around his hand, the other above a hole in his thigh.

"Mr. Stavros. We received your data but haven't yet analyzed it. Thank you."

"Hye Min? I've got a problem. I need help."

"Am I to presume things did not go as planned?"

He poured a bottle of 150 proof rum from the bar over a pile of identification instruments tossed in the toilet bowl.

He figured his current aliases were burned, and manifested the metaphor with the drop of a match.

"I've got a dead man on the bed and a bullet in my leg. Contact your associates, someone who can keep the body safe until I can retrieve it."

"You can't be serious. I'm not an extraction team. Call a coroner."

"Room 1108. I'll leave the card under the door. You need to hurry. Police will find the room before too long."

"What are we supposed to do? Walk the body through the lobby on a baggage trolley?"

"I don't know. Wheel in a laundry cart, throw a sheet over him." A long silence ensued. Ivan flushed the toilet and wiped down prints, no idea why, since he was bleeding on the carpet. In the closet he wrenched loose the horizontal metal pole on which fixed hangers slid. From the hollow cavity spilled a tightly banded roll of money, new passport, ID, transit pass and an RFID key to locker 133, more than a hundred floors down. Out the door and through a corridor, he stabbed the button to summon an elevator.

Hye Min finally came back. "I'm sending a team. Twenty minutes. You should stay put."

"Negative. I'm leaving town."

"Of course you are," she said. "Not wise. Emergency traffic indicates they're looking for you."

"My escape route's solid. I'll be gone before they know there's a trail. Thank you."

"Thank me when I send my additional costs."

Ivan disassembled the phone's parts into the elevator's waste bin on the way down.

* * *

Line 5 of the Seoul subway ran though sublevels of the Mugunghwa Hotel for the convenience of guests. Despite a number of stops, the 35-minute run ended 18 kilometers west of central Seoul at the public access terminal of Gimpo International Airport.

Seats at the end of each car were reserved for elderly and handicapped, but when Ivan ripped open the bloody pant leg, passengers gave him all the room he needed. Inside a large black duffel bag he'd pulled from the storage locker in the Mugunghwa station was a change of clothes, more money, a handgun and a first-aid box full of Bullet Surgery For Dummies. Next station, larger crowd. Regardless of age, they divided into two categories, those who sought refuge in adjoining cars, and a growing group of morbidly curious spectators whom Ivan implored not to call the police with their outstretched phones.

He doused the wound in iodine and dug in the hole with a pair of angled, needle-nose forceps. His hands shook, weakness and pain conspiring to prove he wasn't the kind of savage who could pry through his own major muscle groups. Must be a skill that only worked in movies. What kept him from passing out was certainty of capture. That and an elderly passenger who appeared to have a little medical knowledge, if not any English.

"*Shiksa haeseumnikka?*"

He kept talking, but Ivan didn't understand. Translation came from a young girl who put her school backpack under Ivan's head.

"He says lay down, breathe more deep, and stay still."

The subway emerged above ground. Flashes of light from passing a Fotte department store and an LG-25 fell on a nine-millimeter lump extracted and tossed on the seat next to Ivan. Silence, blood beating through his eardrums. Rush of dizziness, the impulse to vomit. Violent motion in the turns pressed inside his skull, time like a spreading puddle he couldn't gather with his mental sponge. Subway passengers lost substance, the faceless, single dimensional strokes of impressionist paint, posed like print ads for Ralph Lauren. When he was nearly certain of lost consciousness, the girl's voice reached out to him from a fog.

"He asks, you are a American gangster?"

Cold water ran down his mouth. He inspected the bandage and the old man's kindly smile. Ivan bowed with a smile of his own. "Tell him thank you, but I'm not American."

* * *

"318 Victor Foxtrot, ready for takeoff, departure Runway One Four Left."

"Challenger 318 Victor Foxtrot, unable takeoff and departure clearance at this time, contact Ground Control one-two-one decimal nine with your intentions."

Two bottles of water on the subway, new false identity, and half a liter of aquavit bought with bills peeled off the emergency roll got Ivan through departure security and onto his plane, within 1500 meters of airborne. An empty, well lit stretch of runway beckoned.

"Negative, Tower. 318 Victor Foxtrot, Runway One Four Left, taking off."

Three hundred pounds of fuel, through the highly technical process of suck, compress, burn and blow, quickly translated to just shy of 14,000 pounds of thrust. The tradeoff sent runway lights racing by, a lit ribbon of departure in the night leaving the grand upswept architecture of Gimpo's air terminals behind.

Tower radio transmissions erupted as Traffic Control cleared the skyway, directing other planes into holding patterns and requesting they switch channels to isolate Ivan's frequency. Ivan ignored the animated Tower's strangely polite entreaties to reconsider his decision.

Quickly leaving the Earth's surface behind, Ivan felt the unremitting intensity finally lift. Now he could limp the way his leg had begged him since being shot. Having his own plane was a singular and liberating comfort, giving him time to think. The first question was obvious.

Where was he flying?

He had plenty of fuel. Tower repeated their request that he land the aircraft. That was not on the agenda. Eventually the edge of Korea became visible below where the Han River emptied into the blackness of the Yellow Sea.

The sensation of flight untethered him. This time he felt something more palpable left his heavy thoughts, and he wasn't ready. Emotional turmoil? No, not really there, and it should be. Surely he should feel sadness—his uncle dead—and yet he felt a void, unable to explain the neutrality taking over. What was wrong?

Moving to 20,000 feet, a signal appeared on screen, closing in from southeast of his heading. Radar picked up a second coming in fast from the same bearing. Ivan checked the TCAS flight information panel, but there was no corresponding data. Unregistered flights? Couldn't be, the cross-sections were too small for planes.

Ivan dragged the radar data onto the navigation panel and the computer assigned tracking tags. He brought up the FLIR imager, but the objects were still too far out. Pushing the engines increased his speed 100 knots, and now there was no doubt. Tracking showed the objects course-corrected with him. At their current speed they'd intercept in six minutes. They had to be UAVs. Over the Guard Frequency came the confirmation.

"Challenger 318 Victor Foxtrot, you are pursuing an unauthorized flight plan. You are ordered to change course to heading 090 and land your aircraft at RKSS immediately. Confirm."

He needed to stall until he could figure out if the UAVs were a threat. "Negative, contact. Flight plan's good. Proceeding to 32,000." Did that sound nonchalant enough?

Ivan's computer found the UAVs on FLIR and reported a seventy two percent chance both were Mark V Reaper drones. No further doubt on the threat assessment. The computer's probability figure rose as one of the drones pulled up beside him and rocked its wings a few times, pulled ahead, and maintained a threatening lead proximity.

"318 Victor Foxtrot, you will follow the aircraft to demonstrate compliance or I am authorized by U.S. Air Force Command to bring you down."

What kind of threat was that? By force? Were they just trying to scare him? If the CIA called in military support, the warning had to be serious. Ivan wasn't accustomed to fear, yet the sheer gravity of this situation immediately nullified the pleasant, if slightly egregious, level of alcohol in his blood. Despite the threat, Ivan wagered they wouldn't actually shoot him down over populated land. He entered a heading that reversed course yet deviated from the drone's lead. The computer warned him the new flight path would enter North Korea. He hoped they wouldn't follow and risk getting shot down themselves by North Korean missiles.

The computer located the control signal to the drones. Ivan jumped around the cockpit, looking for options and checking the feed, but two facts were obvious. The origin of the transmissions confirmed the Reapers were scrambled from Osan Air Force Base, and though he could intercept and read the digital stream, he could neither jam nor decrypt it.

"318 Victor Foxtrot, this is your last chance to comply. You are ordered to follow and land your aircraft at RKSS immediately."

Unmistakable tracer rounds flew past his view, followed by a barrage of the Vulcan cannon's supersonic noise that rattled the cabin so hard he couldn't be sure he hadn't been hit.

"What the hell is wrong with you?" he yelled. "I'm a civilian!"

"318 Victor Foxtrot, you will not be permitted to enter North Korean airspace. We will not afford you an additional warning."

The moment for lucid reckoning arrived with an impotent influence on Ivan's conscience. There was nothing he could do. He *was* a civilian. Advanced as his avionics were, nothing aboard gave him the wherewithal to challenge military aircraft. He could not outrun these things, outmaneuver, evade or deflect their pursuit. He possessed no countermeasures or weapons that posed any threat to their armor. If they intended to take him down, he was fucked. He didn't even have a parachute.

Going back to Seoul only meant a protracted but certain end, the kind he himself wouldn't inflict on anyone else.

Twice in the same day the specter of death crawled over his raised hairs, and it was a deceptively calm sensation. He clicked the transmit button one last time.

"318 Victor Foxtrot, experiencing minor difficulty. Returning to Gimpo Airport as soon as I troubleshoot. Stand by."

Ivan pried up the floor panels covering the avionics just aft of the cockpit. Beneath was a service door for ground mechanics that popped up from the bottom of the fuselage and slid, a square opening just large enough. A falling body hits terminal velocity around 180 kilometers per hour, depending on how much flailing one did. He tore apart the cabin, but everything was too flimsy. Even the red engine inlet covers were useless.

The only emergency equipment aboard were two fire extinguishers, portable breathing units, hoods, crash axe, an ELT, some flares and a life raft with some flotation vests. What was the raft made of?

Compressed gas from a built-in capsule spread the raft across the cabin. He immediately jammed a knife into the buoyancy tube and deflated the thing down to a flat stretch of reinforced synthetic canvas. Ivan used the nylon rope to tie corners through the grooves of his boots, running the expanse under the back of his belt, cutting away the middle belt loop. A little wrapping put the handles roughly at the reach of his outstretched hands.

The idea was crazy, but at the moment he could only choose between lesser probabilities of death. Staying aboard was a hundred percent.

Back at the console he put the plane into a precipitous decent while pushing the engines to their maximum rpm. The maneuver gave him a jump on the Reaper drones, which accelerated to flank and soon caught up. At 10,000 feet the cabin became fully depressurized. Ivan throttled back the engines before hitting the flaps and speed brakes, decelerating so violently the bottle of aquavit smashed against the forward window. Both Reapers screamed past him.

If they'd overshot by a few kilometers, it didn't take them long to bank around and make the decision Ivan counted on. Emergency warnings flashed, two missiles inbound. The nav computer gave him less than ten seconds to impact.

Venturi suction pulled air through the open avionics access panel, and still Ivan hesitated. Nostalgic rhythms of his childhood and father had made the hours heavy, and jumping a rare portal into Yannis's soul. He became the lifelong undertaker in an Argyris Hionis poem who upon his own death carries himself to the tomb and pulls the soil over like a blanket. The end of the verse came as sweetly as if Yannis spoke him into the blackness.

"The fly trapped in honey discovers suddenly and irreversibly that even the sweetest death is very bitter."

Tumbling through frozen air for a moment before managing to stabilize the makeshift wing suit, Ivan watched, and then felt, the remaining volume of JP5 fuel engulf the sky in a surreal tentacled fireball where his plane had been. Concussive waves of heat plowed into him. The awful smell. Two Reapers flew through the night, optical systems rotating to capture fragments of a Challenger fuselage plummet past Ivan in the distance.

The only noise remaining was cold wind whipping through a flying squirrel suit en route to an unknown terra firma below.

27

"What happened to your hair?"

Teagan was right. When count cleared Cody walked out of the unit and was met by four officers who escorted him to this concrete room. He was sure when they strip-searched him the whole operation was blown. That's what Teagan called it, Operation Suitcase. Think of it like being a spy, spud.

While the idea of getting one over on the cops grew on Cody, he sorely wanted Teagan to be wrong this time.

"I'm Lieutenant Korvick and this here's Payne from I&I. Do you know why you're here?"

Why did everyone ask that? Cody wanted to say *because you made me come here*, but he knew better. Suddenly cold, Cody pulled the collar of his shirt up around his neck.

Payne didn't wear a uniform, just a badge on his belt with regular clothes. In a place where all the cops had uniforms, he was the boss, the one to be scared of. Payne moved closer but there was nowhere to go. They'd cuffed Cody's ankles to the stool.

"You can stop shaking your head," Payne said. "I'm going to be straight up with you. We already found what we're looking for. You need to tell us what other offenders participated. Who else is in McCarty's STG?"

"Teagan?"

Payne flipped through some papers to look at something. "Sure."

"What's STG?" Sounded like an itch.

"Security Threat Groups. Gangs."

"Teagan? Teagan he's not a gang."

"Don't play me like I'm stupid, kid."

Cody felt his stomach heave and swallowed to keep from throwing up. His butt stopped hurting and he knew why. The vitamins moved around and now they were in his stomach. Payne scared him so stupid he almost spit up the proof. He clamped his lips shut, hands under him, trying to make a know-nothing face.

"What's wrong with him?"

"You better not shit on my floor, kid."

"Sorry."

"What are you sorry about? You know something you want to tell me? I'm getting tired of the head shaking. Knock it off." Payne turned to Korvick. "I got a mind to STG him just for shaving his dome." Back to Cody. "You want an STG? I'll give you a seg-program so long your Woodpile buddies'll think you died."

"You think he's part of some new hippie STG we ain't heard of yet?"

Both officers shared a low, ugly laugh over something Cody was certain wasn't funny. His stomach gurgled, the vitamins moving up his throat.

"Yeah, what's with the tattoo?"

"Tattoo?"

"It's not on his file," Korvick said. "Intake might have missed it."

"It's McCarty's work. I can tell."

"Please . . ."

"Please what?"

"Please . . . don't hurt Teagan. He didn't mean to."

"He didn't mean to what? Take custody at approximately 1400 hours today a quantity of controlled substances including but not limited to marijuana? What didn't he mean to do?"

Cody swallowed the vitamins back down. "Sorry . . . my tattoo, it's, please don't take my . . . my tattoo. I'm sorry."

"Hey, Payne, I think he's sorry."

"You got that right. Sorriest sack of dogwash I ever seen."

Two more uniforms entered the office. They talked to Korvick and Payne.

"They're both clean. We tore their cells apart. McCarty's had the usual stuff, some porn, fishing line, couple of food items, but nothing serious. Oh, and a bin full of dry grass. Don't ask. I have no idea. The drugs aren't in there."

"Probably keestered them."

"Not according to the nurse."

"And Firth?"

"Resistance, non-compliance, diversion of staff, we can keep him locked up a while. But no drugs."

"This is bullshit," Korvick said. He stared at Cody for a long time, every second closer to the moment Operation Suitcase would burst open and he'd be in the worst trouble of his life. "Wipe his face and get him out of here. He doesn't know anything."

* * *

They put Teagan back in the cell shortly after. Cody's heart had spent so much time like the washer on spin dry, he was exhausted.

"Jesus," Teagan said, looking over the mess left behind by the search team. "They really rock and rolled this joint." He looked at Cody, who'd pushed himself flat against the wall, not sure where to start with the room and feeling ill. "If you have to blow chunks, aim for the bowl. Speaking of which, where's our dope?"

"Dope?"

"The vitamins?"

"I think I ate them," Cody said.

"You *what*? You ate them? *All* of them?"

"I'm sorry."

"You're sorry?" Teagan sounded panicked. "You know how sorry you're going to be when you're half dead? Jesus, spud, those pills will kill you!"

"You made me!" Cody yelled. "I didn't want to, and you made me, and now Booboo's run away, and I have to keep your secrets, bad secrets, and they hurt, and why? Why you make me do it?"

"I didn't tell you to swallow them! Did you swallow the whole glove, or bust it open and eat them? Please don't tell me your stupid-ass broke the glove."

"I don't know."

"How do you not know?"

"I didn't see it," Cody said. "I felt them in my stomach, moving around, up my throat, and I . . . I swallowed them back down so the cops wouldn't see."

Teagan looked blankly at Cody for a minute, eyes slowly blinking, appearing to work something out. "You're stupid, squirt. I'm going to clean our room." He yanked Cody's shorts down and plonked him on the toilet. "You sit there until my dope comes out."

"I hate you," Cody whispered.

"You know, you're a real pain in the ass sometimes."

"You are."

"I didn't mean it like that."

* * *

Six years and 365 days. Or seven years. Cody wanted his birthday to be on a Saturday, but this year it fell on a Monday. He tried to forget for one day that Teagan made him miserable for a birthday present he didn't want.

When they got back from work Teagan made a cake out of two honeybuns smothered in frosting and crushed KitKats.

"Your cake needs a candle."

"It's your cake, spud."

"Or maybe seven candles?"

"You'd like that, wouldn't you?" Teagan cut holes into a small plastic tub with toenail clippers. "I ain't wasting fire on no candles. We're going to get lit instead."

"On fire?"

Teagan pushed a pen shaft through the lid of the empty cheese tub, taped together two toilet paper tubes, and filled half the tub with water. Into the broadened end of the pen he squashed a metal screen stolen from a sink faucet.

He set up his socket arcing sticks and told Cody to get ready. Ready for what? The green squishy marble from Operation Suitcase broke into two pieces and Teagan stuffed the larger into the screen, then lit it. The smell was really funky, like what lemon cough drops on fire must smell like. Teagan wasted no time, finger on a hole, priming the tube, inhaling deeply.

"Smoking's bad for you," Cody said.

"Smoking *cigarettes* is bad for you. This is a bong. You'll live."

"Can't we just have cake?"

"Yeah. After you suck this down. I don't want to hear any ungrateful whining, cause this crap's not easy to come by, and I'm gonna be pissed if you make me waste it."

Cody felt guilty and couldn't figure out why. Then his anger returned. Why should he feel miserable for *not* wanting Teagan's bong smoke? How was this Cody's fault again? Wasn't he supposed to be happy on his own birthday? He'd just say *No.* There had to be a polite way to refuse Teagan so he wouldn't be angry at Cody, like *No thank you*, or maybe *You have it all.* Wouldn't that be better? More smoke for Teagan and get right to the cake? Even as he ached to say something, there was no way it was going to happen, and it was better to get it over with.

"Inhale deeper. I want to see your face turn green. What are you doing? Don't blow it out yet, hold it in."

"It tastes like crap."

"Do it again, and this time you better hold it till I tell you to breathe out."

Cody's nose looked like a chimney. His chest couldn't take anymore, eyes stinging with tears, coughing, nose and throat tingling like soda bubbles without the soda.

"Nice job." Teagan finished the rest and flushed the burned up wad.

"Can we eat cake now?" Cody felt sure frosting would fix the ickyness. "I don't think birthdays are supposed to have smoking stuff."

"The good ones do." Teagan smeared frosting on Cody's nose.

"Hey!"

"You alright?"

"Just feel dizzy. Did you?"

"Did I what?"

"Do stupid stuff on your birthday . . . uh, days?" Dizziness spread out from Cody's face and made the tips of his fingers slow down. Chewed honeybun took forever to swallow, as though he had a giraffe's neck and he could feel it moving all the way down. Touching his face made the hand huge in front of him, losing balance and falling back into the blankets. "Teagan . . . what?"

"I always partied hard. This one time . . ."

Limbs moved too slowly when he scrambled. Thinking was hard and the thoughts scared him. Yet he couldn't help smiling as he tossed his arms out, desperate not to drown in the bed. Teagan couldn't hear him calling for help. Teagan's voice was far way, rolling in and out like waves over a beach, only bits of it audible. Help.

" . . . sneaked in because I know all the broads that worked there. Freaky club. You'd never . . ."

Teagan, I can't feel my . . . was he listening? Did Cody's mouth move? He couldn't remember. It must be the smoke. Make it stop.

" . . . doesn't bleed as much as you'd think, but . . ."

Cody got ahold of his toes and hung on. Parts of him floated away like oars slipping from the oarlocks and he grabbed for them and felt the boat rock.

" . . . like she's been hit with a nail gun, metal everywhere. You ever been pierced? Not even your ears? We should do that. She even had a ring in her clit. And the freaky part . . ."

Water droplets floated in the wrong direction up the window, sodium yard lights making them shiver and glow, brighter and brighter. They made a sound like static, humming and getting closer, closer, closer . . .

" . . . there's always going to be one in the club, she's covered in glitter, and by the end of the night it's on everyone, like a contagious disease, raver scabies, and if you're on Molly the tracers are wicked."

Cody lost his feet. They dissolved in his hands like sand. Suddenly every surface of his body felt softer than ever before, as though lightly dusted with the finest confectionary sugar, and he couldn't stop rubbing his hands, fingers slipping through each other. The sensation was a mystery and oddly satisfying. He could do this forever. Teagan thumped him in the stomach. He couldn't get out of the way.

"You're wasted, spud."

* * *

Teagan poked the boy a few times. When the effects started coming on he'd giggle and say it tickled, but now Cody was a Thorazine patient, just grunted and blinked until his eyelids drifted shut. Should have been funnier than this. What a waste of weed. Couldn't have been just weed. Kid had spun pretty hard. Must have been laced with something.

Teagan finished off the cake. He stood by the cell door, scratching, looking for pigs. Yawned. Checked Cody again. Might be a good idea to throw a towel under him. Looked like he might have wet himself a little. More scratching.

Was this how Teagan had been? Six years ago? He thought he could hear dad's voice and it triggered something close to an anxiety attack.

"Git your soggy mouth off'm beer." A callused mechanic's hand smacked the back of Teagan's head. His new front teeth dinked on the glass spout.

He set the bottle down on an overturned milk crate where dad's worn out boots lay dumped with the man's feet still in them.

"Hell." Dad thrust the beer at him. Teagan caught it, some sloshing down his size-seven tank top. "Finish it before your Ma gets here."

"Is grandma going to come?"

"Bitch brings her godforsaken in-laws, load my shotgun." He laughed, then coughed. His belly lurched, hands clenching the plastic arms of a fold-up lawn chair to hold it down.

Teagan's Budweiser dribbled on his chin as he chugged, warm and bitter. He looked into the night sky and poured the rest in Christine's dog dish. Stepping through the screen door, his bare feet tracked across the matted valley of an olive green carpet salted with dead flies from a blue bug lamp overhead. He took two more beers from the fridge, one for dad, and one for him. For Christine.

Cobalt smoke trickled from the damp mustache stuffed under his old man's nose. For a moment Teagan thought it was the smoke that smelled like an abandoned nursery of decaying plants, but it was just wafting off Tacoma after the rain. They had a nickname for it, Tacomans did. The belly of B-52 military planes overhead grazed the trailer park on landing, all eight engines burning black smoke across State Route 512 and onto the runway of McChord Air Force Base. A Dutch windmill across the highway peered from the tree line surrounding a deserted putt-putt miniature golf course it called home. Teagan had spent many nights alone there, deep in thought, wet from rain. He could smell the crusty hotdogs rotating in the glass display at the quickmart gas station down the hill from the Steel Street overpass. Runoff from the nearby carwash made its way to the same gutter as spilled fuel. Another plane coming in, like clockwork, huge and gray, clearing the fog in its path, stirring up the urban dross while drowning out its noise.

"I don't want to." Teagan pushed his dad's arm away, his dirty glass pipe.

"Party, birthday boy."

"Smells like crap."

"Don't make me waste it."

Stood in the moist dirt, watched his old man's heft dance when he laughed. Christine lapped the bowl dry and hung her tongue, watching. She had no idea, just a dog, waiting her turn. She didn't have to do this like he did.

Teagan dropped to his knees and hacked his chest to shreds, blue smoke all that was left of the scraps in his throat and he watched it float away. Christine nudged him. He put his arm around her and squeezed the faithful lab's soft fur.

"There were more goddamned stars when I was your age, boy. More stars."

They don't go anywhere, dad. Ms. Johnson says we can't see them when it's daylight, or the sky's too dirty or something.

"You tell your teacher she don't know shit. They ain't there no more."

A cop waited in the road just past a chain link fence laced through with pale green plastic strapping. His lights were off, prowling for outstanding warrants. Outstanding! his brother, Adam, mocked. So great! Three cheers for the outstanding warrant.

Old man Fielder had outstanding warrants. He dragged himself home from the Stir Crazy, cursing Desert Storm, sand still lodged in every crevice, before warrants came and got him.

Teagan missed his big brother. Two hots and a cot, bro. Watch some TV. Beats running sometimes, Adam said, like a vacation from it all. The vacations got longer and longer. Missed him so much, and Christine too. The drugs tasted like mercury on Teagan's tongue, inside it. They peeled his head apart and turned his guts to sludge. Christine's beer-wet tongue on his face, big hug, trying to stay upright. She was soft and beautiful. He could see all the sounds. He wanted the warrants to come and get him so he could visit Adam.

"Don't fall out, jackass, or the bitch'll see you and wear me a new one."

Teagan never saw his brother. Instead he got Cody. He watched the boy sleep for a while. He was suddenly afraid of himself. Was he responsible for this? For Cody? What had he done?

Many hours later he looked at a handful of pills and the rest of the weed. Colorful and beautiful, Teagan turned each upright, reading numbers and names he knew by heart. They spoke to him and said things were worse than it looked, to swallow and not worry about what happened next. They promised him peace and happiness and love. He could feel anticipation like sunshine soaking through his arteries. Body hair stood on end, swaying in the breeze of promises too easily broken.

He threw them in the toilet and hit the flush button.

28

In the oncoming lane a large Varan tour bus swept past Ivan, heading in the direction of Marmaris. Ivan veered to give it space on the narrow curve. Much like the Taurus Mountains through which he'd recently driven, the roads of western Turkey detoured over rugged terrain covered in thick pine forest. Were he not Greek, Turkey might seem like a paradise bridging not only trade routes but also Eden and life itself.

Both driver and passenger windows of the old diesel Mercedes were rolled down. Felix Mendelssohn on cassette came with the car, probably as a result of being permanently stuck in the auto-reversing Becker Europa dash radio. The oscillating tempo of his Nocturne, through no fault of the composer, issued from three working speakers, electric motor on the cassette deck giving out.

Mendelssohn had a fairytale childhood by comparison, but Ivan wouldn't trade his own for the Hamburg native, who despite optimistic melodies died at thirty-eight of cerebral hemorrhage.

"Make killing for hire a hobby," Ivan said to the Möbius magnetic recording strip. "Surely less pressure on the brain."

Reaching a steep grade, Ivan took his good hand off the steering wheel and downshifted from third to second gear, the 40 horsepower motor struggling faithfully through a sedate landscape rich in scent, Jerusalem sage and arum lilies. A sign said *Yaziköy - 20 km*. Not much further.

Another oncoming vehicle honked. Ivan waved out the open window with an arm mostly healed but still in a brace after the month-long travel of the soft routes through China and Russia.

Almost home.

He was ready for this, to call someplace home. Of that he was sure. Everything he owned was lost, or at least everything he'd thought important. Material things seemed inconsequential now. Loss made him free, just as Ellison had said moments before taking his own life. Intended to give Ivan a chance to escape, Ellison's sacrifice remained too dear. Why had his uncle placed himself in such a compromise? Had he not thought through what would happen? Or was more at work here? Seoul was a trap. Ellison simply didn't know until too late.

It was Ivan who'd failed to think through consequences.

No more.

The improvised wing suit had reduced Ivan's terminal velocity from *terminal* to a survivable fifty kilometers per hour, at which speed he fell for nearly four minutes. The few scattered lights below led him to assume he'd bailed out over the northern side of the DMZ. A safe roll onto freshly tilled soil in September was unlikely. Fortune in the final 200 meters of decent threw him an old barn with a wooden roof. Doing his best to angle sideways, Ivan plowed into and crashed through the roof. Stacked within were bales of something other than hay, but for which Ivan was no less grateful.

Smashed face. Two broken ribs. Broken arm.

Bestowed just moments before with as much air as he could hyperventilate, the impact fairly left Ivan choking. He didn't try to get up. Far off came the sounds and smells of turmoil where flaming fragments of a jet plane rained across the outskirts of Kaesong. Ivan slept.

None of his passports were safe anymore. The long trek home relied on hundreds of friends scattered across countries through which he travelled with Yannis in his youth. Yet another friend would meet him at the tip of Turkey's Datça Peninsula.

Near Yaziköy the pavement ran out. What the 240D sedan lacked in steeds it made up for with tolerance, taking the pitted dirt road with sturdy stoicism. A number of olive groves enhanced the scenic route to Knidos where tree cover eventually became sparse. Remains of an ancient theater and a round temple marked part of a shrine to Aphrodite.

Mediterranean storms moved in over the port. A lonely 2-car ferry with no Turkish Maritime Lines affiliation lay docked at a concrete wharf.

Ivan parked and rolled up the windows. A man old and rugged as the landscape, wearing a light sweater, approached the vehicle. Unlike Korea, Ivan's Turkish was reasonably good.

"*Günaydin.*"

"*Merhaba.* Where are you going, traveler?"

"Where can you take me?"

"Wherever you wish, so long as it may be reached by sea."

They broke character and shared a tremendous embrace with deep laughter.

"Nikos, it's been so long."

"For that I'm sorry. My loss, Kamal." Ivan cradled his sore ribs.

"Are you hurt?"

"I'm fine."

"What happened?"

"Fell out of a plane."

The old Turk laughed, yet it was hard to tell whether he thought Ivan was joking. He eyed the empty vehicle. "You're travelling light. What's aboard?"

"Nothing this time, just me." Ivan gave a penitent shrug and added, "There's a body in the trunk."

"Whose body?"

"I didn't get his name. Russian state security, too many questions. You know how much I enjoy an inquisition."

"Interpol and Europol both have you listed as wanted, number one."

"I know."

"They say you're travelling in a blue Trabant."

"Not since Volgograd. Piece of crap. Trabant's gone, but they'll update soon. I'm on surveillance in Tbilisi and imagine they have the plates. I need to get rid of it."

"Sell it?"

"Not worth anything."

"To be sure," Kamal said.

Ivan drove aboard the ferry and they cast off. Aegean wind pushed on the stern and rainfall pooled above rusty swaths of the deck. Slow progress of the old boat named Uzak Yeşil felt more like being adrift. Kamal heated water and made them Elma tea with sugar, and gözleme, a rolled up bread like pizza warmed up in a suspect microwave near the helm. Kamal left the wheel in the hands of a barefoot lad in a blue Nike shirt and went back out on the deck with Ivan. They leaned on the rounded fenders of the condemned car and spoke of old adventures when Kamal's ferry moved Yannis's weapons. They shared a second cup of tea. Ivan felt new warmth listening to the stories as though a vicarious eulogy. Past became present.

"Who is he?"

"Milos? Don't concern yourself. My grandson knows nothing. Maybe you should teach him? Soon he'll be old enough to run routes on his own, though his mother objects. No future. But what the hell does she know?"

"You raised her."

Kamal shrugged as though this didn't mean anything. Rain clung to the ends of his gray beard. "She'll cause them to become weak, I fear. It's all the videogames the kids play. Out here I can make him a man."

"He's only a child. Give him time."

Kamal made a less effusive gesture than agreement. "In a month he celebrates his sünnet. We shall see."

Without his rig to deliver him from ignorance, Ivan was left searching memory for the meaning. At length he recalled attending one of these Islamic events, which at the time seemed too extravagant.

The special occasion marked a precursor to manhood, arranged between age seven and ten,

where the boy dressed in a satin sergeant major uniform for a party that ended with his ritual circumcision. Ivan remembered it was traditional for friends and relatives to bring symbolic gifts.

He undid his belt and unzipped the compartment on the backside wherein hid a strip of valuable gold coins used for barter. He handed one to Kamal. "For Milos."

"*Teşekkür ederim.*"

"It's nothing."

"You sound like your father, but it's more than that, *arkadas.*"

The deepest meaning of 'friend' a Turk could use. Ivan nodded in honor. Kamal asked after Yannis and Ivan didn't know what to say. Dead for many decades now? Because of the CIA? Things too hard to explain, as much for being incomprehensible to Ivan.

"He's well. Asks I send you his greetings and know you are in his prayers."

Halfway to the island of Kos they lowered the ferry gate. Ivan pulled a bicycle and backpack from the trunk. He released the parking brake and together they pushed the car into the Aegean Sea. Slowly at first, and then with an urgency befitting the Teutonic weight, down it went, along with Mendelssohn, circular H4 headlamps blinking under a spray of bubbles.

From Kos Ivan boarded another ferry to Náxos and then the small island of Páros.

Colorful fishing boats moored along the docks and a familiar old windmill welcomed him to the busy port town of Paroikià. Two-story white cubic buildings with blue domes studded the shoreline, canopies and white umbrellas spread, full of the same energy flowing through sails moving in and out of the harbor.

Riding a bike wasn't easy with a bad arm, but Ivan made it through town—not certain whether to despise the scourge of tourists—and past a tiny group of street musicians. A young man played the bouzouki, fingers moving attentively through the strings and giving hope for the preservation of tradition.

Further west he pedaled, past the Ekatontapylianí. The old church's fabled story held out a tantalizing parable to his own. Ignatius finished architecture of the ornate cathedral in the sixth century AD, and he'd apparently upstaged the man to whom he was apprenticed. One of the master builders of Constantinople, Isadore of Miletus pushed Ignatius off the roof in jealousy, but the pupil managed to grab Isadore by the foot. They both fell to their deaths.

Had Ivan done too good a job? Discovered more than Hizer Pharmaceuticals wanted him to know? He'd outlived usefulness and they'd thrown him off the roof. Only Ivan hadn't died and there was still a foot to grab. He couldn't pinpoint whose foot.

He didn't know anything!

And that was the problem. Of course he'd looked at the thumb drive. A thirty-minute burial video filmed from a distance. Ivan scoured the drive for evidence—metadata, unallocated space, encrypted material, even for interlacing or ghosting of the video itself, of which there was neither. Just the video of Ellison, Yannis, and a rabbi, a hole in the ground as deep as the clue was empty.

Down through a valley of poplar and cypress he rode, pink and white oleander in late bloom, *for secret is earth's live creative pulse,* said Sikelianos, *all fleeting things dissolve away like clouds, great Death itself has now become my kin.*

Into the foothills Ivan rode, allowing beauty to cleanse half a lifetime of misery. Down a dirt path, passing up a footbridge to splash the tires through a stony brook. On both sides of him now rows of untended vineyard all the way to the steps of an old monastery. White plaster was in need of a good cleaning and red shingles lay broken on the ground. The glass in the arched windows was still intact, though the blue sash shutters were much faded. Ivan promised himself a trip into town for paint and supplies. Someday.

Several nearby structures comprised the wine house, grape press and stables, trellises overgrown with vines and bougainvillea. Granite blocks contained a small wading pool edged by a crumbling rock wall that meandered down through the vineyard. Slate stones lined the weeded path to the cottage where Ivan stepped through an unlocked door into a dark kitchen. He pushed the shutters open. Late afternoon sunlight fell on what Ivan once called Yannis's distant and somewhat romantic dreams.

Long before the plane, and all the other trappings of his alter ego, Ivan purchased the vacant monastery and surrounding fields. When he found Yannis, he would retreat here with his father. They could start over, no past attached.

Down in the cellar, beyond the mostly empty wine shelves he pulled on a hinged rack, drawing a semicircle on the dirt floor. Dialed a combination into the heavy steel door behind. Down more steps to a musty subbasement, Ivan wiped dust from a panel and inserted the key dangling from a piece of twine. In a concrete bunker far out in the vineyard a generator started and slowly incandescent light glowed within the room.

This was Ivan's last refuge, a cove of anonymity wrapped like a war museum around the walls. Beyond aliases and identity documents, or the stash of money in trunks along the floor, an arsenal of weapons told stories of adventures shared with Yannis. Other weapons here he'd acquired in the solitude and vigilance following the events in Tangier. Several Dragunov platform rifles smuggled out of Azerbaijan through Georgia and the Black Sea. A Franchi LAW 12 from a shipment sold to Chechen rebels. A rare Mosin Nagant M39 from Finland that used the same Russian rounds as his Romak 3 sniper rifle. Beretta AR70 and a Steyr-AUG-SA semi auto. Lower down, the Heckler & Koch G3 that ruined Melina's tomatoes and subsequently Yannis's sex life. Beneath that, the G3's more meticulous brother, an H&K PSG1 with a Hensoldt scope and ridiculous 50-round drum. Beautiful but not Ivan's favorite for sniping, cartridge ejections landing in the next time zone. A DTA Stealth Recon Scout for cramped spaces. McMillan Tac-50 A1 variant, since .50 BMG rounds were hell on the shoulders. An Algimec AGM-1 type and two Feather AT-9 semi autos. Several Claridge HI TEC C-9 carbines Ellison couldn't sell to the most gullible buyers.

On a shelf, still in the wooden box with brass hinges, the custom SIG Sauer P226, the first gun given to him by Yannis as if an appropriate toy for a five year old child. The slide inscription a testament to everything he'd sought.

The dead know the language of flowers only
so they keep silent

In all the silence Ivan ignored the truth.

Yannis was here all along.

In the overgrown garden Ivan sat at a wooden table by the pool and carved a pomegranate with a dull knife from the kitchen. A good-looking woman near his age made her way across the fallow vineyard.

"*Kalimera*! Nikos, is it you?"

"It's no longer morning," Ivan said.

She approached with a half bottle of raki and some short glasses. "What matter is the time? You've come back. I thought it might be you. I saw a bicycle riding up the path and I said to myself, that's Nikos."

Ivan could only remember her last name, Mrs. Bakopoulos, of a neighboring farm that dated back to the Venetians. She poured him a drink.

"Yamas," he said.

"Yamas. What have you done to your arm?"

"Fell out of a plane."

She cackled with a large mouth common among Greek women. "I've kept an eye on the place while you've been gone for the last . . . how long has it been?"

"Long enough."

"Aleko missed you. He'll be happy to hear you're back. Maybe you could take him hunting again? He's quite good but likes company."

"Hunting rabbits?"

"Everything. He goes to Náxos to hunt bigger animals. Around here he only hunts girls now," she said with a wink.

"They're hard to catch."

"Don't lie to me, Nikos. Surely you must have a stable of women."

"Only you."

She laughed and lamented it wasn't true.

"Will you stay?"

Ivan thought for a minute and drank. He watched sunlight colored in the pastel mist of the atmosphere refract through the facets of the glass. "Not this time."

She seemed sad, looking across his vineyard as though he'd wasted a promise. She was right. Ivan tried to reassure her.

"Soon. I'm preparing to settle in. I have one task to finish. But soon."

She smiled and spoke of promises he hadn't made.

"Tonight you'll come down to the house and join us. We're having a party for Aleko and roasting a goat." She got up and then added, "Good food! You will be there," as though Ivan had any choice but to commit to her hospitality.

He wouldn't refuse. In Greece the people said what you ate was not as important as who you ate with.

"What time?" Ivan said. Strong wind drove the portent of the Cyclades across the flowers and through her dark hair.

"What matter is time?"

***

Ellison's body arrived in Israel mid October. Ivan had given up on the thumb drive. There was nothing unusual in the video. A rabbi recited the El Malei Rahamim prayer to an audience of three, Ellison, Yannis, and presumably God. His father and uncle lowered the body of Eliv Schreiber, Holocaust survivor and Ivan's grandfather, wrapped in a traditional white shroud, into the ground. The rabbi departed. Yannis played a somber dirge on a violin. Ellison tore his own shirt.

With a little research Ivan matched the footage to a private cemetery east of Tel Aviv near the border of the West Bank.

Most Jews were buried in state operated multistory buildings, rather like catacombs. For a not inconsiderable fee one could be buried at a kibbutz as Eliv had.

Beit Olam Cemetery at Kibbutz Horshim framed the burial plots in wood, rather like a sandbox, and kept the grounds well maintained. Gardeners tended the many flowers, shrubs and trees that included grape and Japanese maple.

Ivan solicited the service of the hevrot kadisha and forged the paperwork for tahara, the ritual cleansing. He didn't want to deal with the complication that Ellison wasn't interred the same day he died, or that it was a suicide.

Ellison's real name was Simon. Ivan arranged a stone matching Eliv's and asked the kibbutz to expand the plot, which they were happy to do. It now contained three stones. Eliv, his Israeli wife who died some years later, and Simon Schreiber, ex-Mossad, uncle, traitor, dreamer and hero.

Ivan searched the stones but there were no secrets to be found. He compared the video to the site and saw nothing amiss. Damn Ellison, who could have been more forthcoming, even if he believed Ivan might be caught with the thumb drive.

Evening fell.

"Dust thou art and to dust thou shall return. Can I skip tearing up this suit? It's tailored, Uncle." Ivan looked around and succumbed to the tradition. "Shit."

He ripped the sleeves apart and prepared to leave. A well-dressed man holding a box made his way across the grounds toward Ivan. He looked like one of the kibbutz members. Ivan searched the gravesite, knowing he'd violated a lot of Jewish orthodoxy in one day, and wondering if something visibly obvious had pissed them off.

"Mr. Stavros?"

"Whatever it is, I'm sure we can work it out."

"I'm the caretaker here. Among other things, I'm to meet with you to be sure you're pleased with the arrangements?"

"*Among other things?*"

The man appeared embarrassed. "Well, it's just that we've been tasked with an unusual request, and I'm concerned it may not be appropriate, considering the period for grief, and—"

"I appreciate your concern, but if one of these stones owes you money, I'll cover it."

"Sir! Not at all." He handed Ivan the box. "It's just that, Mr. Schreiber, Simon, who's passed now, your . . . he left us this box for you. He said someday you would come to the gravesite, and we've been waiting for you, though I apologize, we didn't know the circumstances would be his own—"

"You're certain? He was here?"

"Yes. A little over a month ago. And I'm to give you some additional information, though I assure you we were not made aware of the context."

Ivan waited. "Yes?"

"You're to go to Haifa. A friend from Miami will meet you at the port."

"A friend?" The only friend Ivan had in Miami was Carlos. "Did he say who? Was it Carlos?"

"Perhaps. Your uncle didn't share."

Ivan opened the box. Inside was a folded piece of ragged cloth and he shrank when he realized what it was. "Thank you."

"You should hurry. Your friend—Carlos?—is scheduled to be there today."

* * *

Within hours Ivan was in Haifa. He tried calling Carlos, but the Miami kingpin was difficult to reach when out of town. Way out of town, as the case was.

Ivan struggled with how low a profile to maintain. He didn't want Carlos to miss him, but being on international Wanted lists counseled against flashing his face all over the surveillance endemic to this large port. He was losing a great deal of sleep and worried. Tingling at the back of his neck signaled a growing fatigue.

The box was safely in his backpack. The cloth was a dirty and faded stretch of light and darker blue vertical bars with two triangles crudely stitched in offset over each other to make a six-pointed star. The bottom pointed up, a dull yellow, while the downward pointing red triangle had stamped on it a capital G. To the right, also stitched to the blue stripes, a small white strip of cloth with bold numbers: 203148.

To hold it was a vile talisman of Eliv Schreiber's years in the Auschwitz death camp. That he'd been free to tear it out of the camp uniform put Eliv in the rarest company of Holocaust survivors.

Never had Ivan held a symbol at once so horrid and beautiful. He was filled with pride, just as Ellison had felt.

History had played his uncle, trading out oppressive governments, and Ellison had known it, always trusting the next Caesar's token altruism. Ivan's pity was matched by the power of his intentions. Dean, the CIA, Hizer—they'd pay dearly, as soon as Ivan learned what was in Dakota's blood.

His phone rang.

"Señor Stavros. I received your message."

"Excellent. I'm here."

"Sí. Where is *here*?"

"In Haifa, at the port." Ivan looked around. "Near pier five."

"Bueno. What is it you need?"

"You were going to meet me here?" Ivan said.

A long silence caused Ivan to believe the call dropped, but it still showed a connection. When his voice returned Carlos seemed angry.

"I'm meeting you? In Haifa? You mean *pinche dios* Israel? You must be mistaken."

Phone still to his ear, Ivan scoured the pier, confused and panicking. There must be a mistake. Maybe the kibbutz fumbled the information.

His gaze jumped from ship to ship docked in port, until at last he spotted something familiar. His heart sank.

"I apologize, Carlos. I'll explain later." Ivan hung up and cursed his dead uncle.

Docked in the distance, all the way from Miami and Jamaica, was the unmistakable lines of a 220 foot pearlescent white yacht, the *Estrella de Mar Rosa.*

29

"Who among you sees a future in the prosecutor's office?" Pat asked a lecture auditorium full of students. "Raise your hands. About a quarter? I'm sensing a noncommittal atmosphere. No shame. Equivocation should be in every lawyer's toolbox."

Low laughter rolled across the room.

"How about defense attorneys? Show of hands." A little fewer than half. "Brave futures ahead. You have the hard jobs, but difficulty can also be more rewarding. What about corporate and contract law? Any takers? Of course not. Boring. I don't blame you."

One of Pat's longtime friends left practice years ago—moral irreconcilables—for tenure teaching law at Pacific Lutheran University. Pat seldom had reason to visit Tacoma, but found herself in an awkward conundrum, a lawyer looking for counsel. Harden offered her a lecture platform on juvenile law and she accepted. A package arrived at her office a few weeks ago she didn't want to think about. Not after what she learned from Frederick Greider's lab analysis of the little blue capsule.

Mr. Harden's students were remarkably awake for nine in the morning. She cautioned them that while prosecutors and defense attorneys typically competed in America's adversarial system, when the defendant was a juvenile, in theory both sides were supposed to be looking out for the child's best interests. Prosecuting and defending kids presented unique concerns meriting sensitivity.

"Children were at one time merely miniature adults and suffered the same social hardships. We as a society had an interim affair referred to as the child-study movement in the early twentieth century. From this grew the realization a child has distinctive attributes—impressionability, vulnerability, innocence. Educators stressed the child's need for play, for love, for understanding and for a chance to gradually discover his or her nature in a gentle environment. Today, as we look around, one might assume these discoveries have been largely disregarded. We've come full circle. The child is just another miniature adult."

It began with the 1967 United States Supreme Court decision *In re Gault.* The opinion penned by Justice Fortas over a fifteen-year old juvenile delinquent, and subsequent decisions, tailored a concept of juvenile justice not far removed from adult courts. Juveniles typically suffered significantly fewer constitutional protections like right to a jury trial. Sometimes kids weren't even entitled to an attorney. The rationale at conception was the system would serve a child's best interests by letting a benevolent judge alone make prudent decisions. Ambivalence crept in quickly. A child only got to be a child if it served prosecutorial interests. At all other times, for as much as the law cared, he was an adult. The child was always at a disadvantage.

"As a good friend of mine once said, Justice is constant. The law is not."

Pat pointed out their home state of Washington had in 1977 been the first to adopt a new Juvenile Justice Act, now codified in Title 13 of the Revised Code of Washington. The Act eviscerated principles of rehabilitation in favor of what legal scholars liked to call Just Desserts. Key goals incorporated that half century ago included Retribution and Accountability. In 1979 the Washington Supreme Court made clear in *State v. Lawley* that punishment would be the new form of treatment for juveniles.

Each state thereafter mimicked Washington's lead, and a legal landscape once committed to a juvenile's growth collapsed.

"The competing conceptions," Pat said, "distinguish a child as either dependent and vulnerable, or autonomous and responsible. The State pits these two conceptions against each other in whatever fashion serves the State. Where do we draw the line?"

"Are you talking about an age limit, or something else?" one of the students asked.

Pat nodded. "Good question, and one that strikes at the heart of the debate. Does age alone determine one's level of responsibility?"

"Age," a guy further back offered. "For practical purposes, in law, age says when we can drink, drive, vote, everything. Otherwise, what's the established criteria for providing notice of the law?"

"Sure," Pat agreed. "And for felony criminal conduct, if I suggested sixteen years old and up, can we agree that's when it's acceptable to hold people accountable like adults?"

"I thought it was eighteen? Eighteen is the usual age cutoff."

"Why?" Pat's question might have been simple enough, but it caught them off guard, and several hands went up, then retracted in doubt.

"Eighteen is when science says we're rational and responsible," one man said.

Laughter erupted, but one woman seemed to have done the legwork.

"There's no science behind that. Your prefrontal cortex doesn't fully form until the mid twenties. That's why car insurance companies don't give most of us here a discount yet."

"It is odd," Pat said, "that the insurance industry has more facility with human physiology than the legal system. For those of you not double majoring in Anatomy, would the young lady like to explain what the prefrontal cortex is?"

Previously eager, the poor girl now blushed. "It's believed to be our judgment center, the buffer that stops us from doing foolish things."

If Pat could pose a quarrel with the concept of Intelligent Design, it would be the late development of such a critical function.

"For the sake of the gentleman's argument for expediency, where should the law set the age? Eighteen? Sixteen? Twenty five?"

The audience argued for a while and eventually a prevailing consensus emerged that the law already had a functioning litmus, comprehension of the wrongfulness of one's actions.

"Knowing right from wrong," Pat confirmed, nodding as she walked the stage. "And what kind of low bar does that set? I submit a six year old feels a modicum of guilt breaking a neighbor's window. Are we to convict him of vandalism? He should have known better."

"But we don't convict six year olds," a guy near the aisle said. His tone exemplified what Pat recognized as society's general ignorance of what happened behind the courtroom curtain.

Projected onto the front screen, sixteen names appeared. Ages popped in for each as Pat spoke. "These are just my present clients, all younger than ten. One arrested at the age of five. In fact, we are privileged to be joined by his trial attorney. Mr. Wu can be found hiding at the back. He arrived late thinking no one would see him sneak in." The audience again laughed. She invited him to come down and comment.

Pat thought it ironic Tony Wu should be the one looking tired before noon in a room full of college students. He still managed to wander to the front and share observations with a crowd still shocked by Pat's clients.

The youthfulness of modern convictions was a hush topic, where media portrayed child convictions as rare, and that they never went to prison. Emphasis was placed on the process, Wu said, not the result.

"Seeing little kids in chains?" he said. "That tends to make us feel shitty about the efficacy of a system we put a lot of faith in, which isn't good for ratings. Media doesn't portray the reality. They know viewers don't like to feel bad or stupid. I was privileged when in law school myself—and I don't like being reminded how long ago that was, so you can all stop snickering—to attend a lecture by Angela Davis. She said isolating prisoners from view of society produced a twofold harm. Inmates felt no responsibility to a society they didn't see beyond the berm. Worse still, Davis warned, society felt no responsibility to inmates. We have a media reality TV-portrayal of life behind . . . well, for instance, there are no bars anymore. Incarceration machinery is an amalgamation of low-tech razorwire and modern apparatuses. Who here has a chip embedded with your health information?" Many hands went up. "Anyone considered removal? No? Then why do so many places advertise RFID removal? Imagine you're the parent whose son just got out of prison for Pat's broken-window-vandalism example. You'd take him to one of those places. RFIDs are the new ID badges in prison. How would we know? Washington's had a number of juvenile prisons since before the turn of the century, often described as something other than a prison but indistinguishable in any meaningful respect. Now there's a 500-bed facility near Cashmere just for children under thirteen. DOC doesn't let the media past the razorwire, who at any rate don't care. Their viewers want the process, not the result." Tony turned to Pat. "Did I take you too far off track?"

"Not at all." Tony found a seat less remote. Pat segued into her main example. "What happens when the two competing conceptions of youth collide?"

Pat put a case from many years back on the screen. She gave them the cite, *State v. E.G.*, 194 Wash.App. 457. Students retrieved it on their own tablets.

Largely triggered by Millenial's adoption of nascent social media technology, arrests for sexting offenses where kids took pictures of their intimate parts skyrocketed. Whether by teenagers grappling with sexual discovery, or younger kids fascinated by the taboo, prosecutors pursued the most severe criminal charges without deference to age or emotional culpability.

"E.G.—let's call him Eric, I don't like using initials—was charged with, inter alia, dealing in depictions of minors engaged in sexually explicit conduct. He sent someone a picture of his erection."

Murmuring in the audience indicated quite a few picked up the conflict, which one woman voiced.

"How can he be guilty of child porn when *he's* the child?"

"The same question posed by his defense attorney when filing a motion to dismiss-—the statute can't apply to a minor who is also a victim of the offense. We're back to Barry Feld's conflict—is he vulnerable and dependent, or autonomous and responsible? How can he be both? Eric should have known better than to send child pornography, but the reason kiddie porn is illegal is because the victim isn't old enough to know better. Your litmus, knowing right from wrong, is useless."

"They denied his appeal," one of the guys up front said.

"Correct. Go to 467 and 468. Addressing whether he can be both victim and perpetrator, the court said the statute against kiddie porn doesn't require a specific victim."

"That's ridiculous. How could the court separate the two?"

"Easy," Pat said. "The State doesn't need to prove the picture of the erection is from any specific victim, only that the picture is child pornography which Eric transmitted somewhere."

"Sure, but I suspect you're being a little facetious. How did the State prove, in the abstract, the picture was kiddie porn? Eric was seventeen at the time." He paused. "How do I say this without sounding crass?"

"Bluntly, like a good attorney, as you're on the right track," Pat said, confirming his assessment of her demeanor.

"A picture of a seventeen year old's erection can't be distinguished from a legal aged one. The only way the State could show it was underage was *precisely by* demonstrating it was Eric's. Without reference to the 'specific victim,' as the court puts it, there would be insufficient evidence to prove the State's case. They used the victim's identity to meet a burden of proof, then got to claim they didn't have to on appeal? A cliché it may be, but they got their cake and ate it, too."

"Insufficient evidence, a claim so stalwart it enjoys immunity from time-bar procedural dismissal," Pat said.

"Why didn't his appellate attorneys raise the issue?"

"Perhaps they *did* raise it," Pat said. "The court of appeals has a long history of answering a different question if they don't like the one briefed."

"Why are we looking at the COA decision?" a new participant asked. "The Washington Supreme Court upheld this en banc. Shouldn't we consider the higher court rationale?"

"Upheld upon almost twenty pages of convoluted verbosity even more vacuous and circuitous than the COA opinion," Pat said. "We'd be here all week trying to untie that Gordian knot. Here's a tip. It's almost certainly subterfuge when a court takes that many pages to answer a simple question. Look no further than the dissenting opinion of far fewer words: a longstanding tenet of U.S. Supreme Court law is the victim belongs to a protected class that can't be prosecuted. You don't punish the victim. Unfortunately,

Justice Gordan McCloud's common sense was an underappreciated asset on the bench."

"I don't see the problem," another student said. "There are other statutes where a person is both victim and perpetrator. Attempted suicide, guys?"

"Maybe that shouldn't be illegal," the girl said. "What they need is help, not prosecution."

"I didn't know we had so many BHL's in this class," a woman from the back said.

Hands on her hips, Pat looked confused. "Pardon me, but the shorthand escapes my generation?"

"Bleeding heart liberal," the first girl said. "But compassion isn't the same as a politically liberal ethos."

An argument kicked off. Before it got too heated Pat held up her hands. "Whether it's reasonable or apathetic, the decision has a far more interesting rationale at page 466. *Ignorance of the law is not the same as ignorance of the meaning of the law. The fact that minors may not appreciate they are breaking the law is not proof that they do not understand it.*"

"That's rhetorical hypocrisy. He's too young to understand the law, but he's got to know he's breaking it anyway?"

"That's not what it's saying." The same person from the back. "All it means is just because he's young doesn't mean he *specifically* didn't know it was wrong."

Pat resumed the key point. "Which leads us back to a case-by-case assessment that, while not necessarily a bad thing, is still guided by the low-bar litmus of knowing right from wrong."

The debate continued for another thirty minutes. Pat ended by showing photographs of each of her sixteen clients.

A court blinding itself to the individual while theoretically in search of neutral justice, more frequently sided in the adversarial system with the favorably weighted power of the State.

"When society demands juveniles take responsibility for their actions, you have an equal responsibility to the welfare of the child. Regardless which side one argues, common sense dictates Vulnerable and Dependent has no age limit."

* * *

"Some of them thought you were unfairly biased in there," Tony said.

"The ones who didn't speak up for shame?"

Tony laughed. "Of course I agree with you, but we've seen the results, not just the process, haven't we?"

After the seminar one of the students offered Pat and Tony scones and invited them to tour the Mary Baker Russell Music Center to look at the Chihully blown-glass sculptures. Frost on the campus pine and fir trees from the morning had since melted. They crossed the red brick quad between Eastvold Chapel and PLU's original edifice, Harstad Hall. Now a women's dormitory, the eight story chipped brick building lacked any garish features, in keeping with a nineteenth century university built by Scandinavian founders. Undergrads in colorful winter wear walked paths between classes and the Student Center. A peaceful sense enveloped Pat even while inside she nursed a growing apprehension with the unfolding events surrounding the very client Mr. Wu defended at trial.

Seated in the last row of the empty Lagerquist Concert Hall, the two of them listened to a student practice on one of the larger pipe organs in North America. Gentle heat radiated from beneath the seats to take the bite out of October. Insets in the wall, stretching up to the vast ceiling, had curtains lowered within them, a functional position that reduced the organ's reverberant echo from four to two seconds. An arrangement of nearly four thousand beautiful wooden and alloy pipes symmetrically covered the far wall, encased in honey-colored fir and ornamented in lighter wood facades by hand-carved Gothic dragons, nudes and symbols. The organist's alcove floated above the stage, hidden behind a smaller register of pipes. A warm wave of magical sound rolled over Pat and Tony, soft enough for easy conversation.

"You want my help," Tony said.

"I need your counsel."

She passed him an elaborate fountain pen.

"What's this?"

"You're going to have a hard time believing."

Months ago Pat took Freddy Greider's lab analysis back to her office and docked the data onto the conference table. Ivan Stavros's capsule was a weapon. Not just any weapon, but a sophisticated, proprietary one whose biological implications were beyond Freddy, already no lightweight in genetics.

She'd been right. Ivan did work for Hizer Pharmaceuticals, just not in the way she'd imagined.

Chase's autopsy was still in the computer. Fan dance emitters again laid the boy's body across her conference table.

Why hadn't he bruised? When Percy Underwood met with her to pass off a client, Chase's father, Percy dismissed the lack of bruising, but it continued to bother Pat.

There it was, a tiny wound in Chase's side below the floating ribs. She stuck her finger in the space, digital light failing the tangibility test. It triggered the autopsy tab for the wound. Notations indicated the specialist shared her curiosity, but ultimately ruled it inconclusive and unrelated.

But chemical analysis from body fluid and tissue bore all the signature results confirming the nicotine poisoning process Freddy previously explained. Metabolized in the liver by cytochrome P450 enzymes like CYP2A6 and CYP2B6, and with a half-life around two hours, the nicotine was long gone by the time the first autopsy was done, never mind the second. Left behind were various metabolites, mostly innocuous, which Pat could now confirm drew a direct correlation between Ivan's capsule and Chase's final minutes. The autopsy specialist had logged two metabolites, cotinine and myosmine.

Ivan Stavros killed the four children in the Hizer lawsuit. From the information he'd left her, it was pretty obvious Dakota Brenner was the next pill-baby Ivan was tasked to kill, presumably for Hizer.

So why hadn't he? Why was Dakota still alive?

Ivan *had* tried, almost as soon as he'd left her office. She'd thought little of the news report when it came out, but now the connections were springing like a nefarious web. The failed incursion into Wenatchee River Corrections Center, all those dead officers, and the trail of mayhem Stavros left trying to assassinate one helpless boy.

Now he was an internationally wanted fugitive for unspecified crimes related to an incident over North Korea that threatened the ceasefire across the DMZ. Pat's only shock was she knew him. That he was capable of horrendous crimes didn't surprise her in the least.

The proof lay on her conference table. What remained from the promise Chase once held was a pale scientific sample, dissected in search of answers that she still couldn't find. Why?

Only Stavros knew.

In the private sanctuary of pleasant organ music she shared some of this with Tony Wu, the little he needed to know.

"Then a few weeks ago I received that pen in a package postmarked from Russia. It's from him, Mr. Stavros. His brief message said it's the only way to save Dakota's life."

"The pen?"

"It's a syringe disguised to look like a pen. The fountain part is an inert vacuum glass vile to keep a blood sample stable. As his attorney, I'm to visit Dakota, fill the pen, and hold it in a secure location to await instructions."

"If he's trying to kill all these kids, then this is part of his plan."

"That's what I thought at first. Mr. Greider analyzed the syringe using spectrography and some other tests. It's not laced with anything. It's just a syringe. It even writes, in red ink, which is just a little too macabre for me."

Tony remained silent through a full movement of the organist's practice. For a moment Pat considered the possibility that telling Tony was a mistake. In playing out the sequence of events and facts for him, the absurdity only increased. She suppressed a chuckle, despite nothing being funny about the scale of danger in which she'd become embroiled. The stress was getting to her.

"Pat, this is surreal."

"I know."

"You should have gone to the police."

Tony meant well, and he was right. Attorney client privilege didn't extend to circumstances where she was party to information detailing an imminent serious crime. "Would you have gone to the police?"

"No," Tony said. "Of course not. Your life would be in peril."

She shook her head. "I'm not scared of him."

"Is that wise? From what you've told me, this man's dangerous."

"He is, but I believe also methodical. I don't know how to explain my impression, but Stavros has a purposed violence, and we're no threat to him."

"And the children are a threat?" Pat nodded but couldn't explain. Tony thought about it. "You think this is real," he said, holding up the pen.

"I don't believe he has a reason to deceive me."

* * *

Pat presumed Tony an SUV man, one of the modern large contraptions, roof clearance issues and lots of comfortable amenities.

Instead he drove an old pickup truck. With a visible exhaust, plaid bench seat and a tendency to roam unbidden like a curious dog, Tony yanked on the huge steering wheel to bring it to heel. A man precise and impeccable finds his anarchy. Snow was thick on the eastern descent of the Cascades. Tony put his truck in 4-wheel drive, an operation requiring him to get out and manually do something with the wheel hubs.

Was she going to do it, Tony had asked? Yes. Rationally there was no harm at this stage. She thought of the corrupted DNA strands in Chase's body and what Frederick said about the weapon's bionanites. Dakota wasn't dead, which should mean his DNA was intact. Regardless of what Stavros knew or thought he knew, Pat saw value in having the blood sample. What vexed her—Ivan's changed motivations if he was now working for Dakota's safety—had no bearing on obtaining the sample.

She needed help. Can't stand the sight of blood? She'd chastised Tony for suggesting this. As long as she'd been a lawyer, she asked? Just kidding.

What she needed was a lookout, someone to run interference on any cameras or officers. She couldn't believe she was saying this! Ivan told her to break a few damn rules, and here she was seriously considering it. Had Pat gone mad?

Her paralegal was useless. Chris's idiosyncrasies unsettled young clients, but that was nothing compared to the consternation he caused DOC officers, who went apoplectic over his tied laces glued-in-place and velcro-lined shirts. Chris distrusted buttons. Robert Frost's credo that a healthy society is one that tolerates eccentricity to the point of doubtful sanity was not one adopted by corrections officers. They saw a security threat. Chris must be hiding something.

"I'll take you," Tony offered.

"You couldn't possibly have the time."

"A reality immutable and eternal. So what? My chariot awaits."

Chariot indeed. His motor made irregular grumbles, struggling with an automatic transmission unable to pick the right gear. Gauges on the dash didn't so much report vehicle metrics as offer ballpark opinions. Every surface, door handles to sun visor, visibly vibrated. He said *she* was loyal, referring to the truck, and his confidence was reassuring. Tony appeared to enjoy the incorrigible rawness. When his truck drifted he yanked on the leash and smiled.

He really didn't have the time.

"We're having a little crisis in the DAC. Do you remember Ms. Lindquist?"

"She wasn't in the Department of Assigned Counsel. Her obituary said she was a deputy prosecutor."

"But you know her?"

Pat tried to move one of the heater vents but it was stuck. "Not personally, I don't believe. I'm sure we'd met in the course of a case or event. She died rather suddenly, I take it?"

"That's an understatement. Aneurism, I heard. I have a friend in the prosecutor's office who used to work for us years ago. Anyway, she was assigned to the team going through Lindquist's office, expedite caseload transfer, clean up affairs, you know. She came across a stack of envelopes labeled *Do Not Distribute*. Sort of an attention getter."

"What was in them?"

"Oh, you know, the usual. Exculpatory evidence from dozens of cases going back twenty years she'd decided didn't constitute Brady material and in which defense would probably have no interest."

Tony's nonchalant tone trivialized how grievous the violations were. *Brady v. Maryland* was the 1960's watershed case establishing the need to disclose evidence material to guilt or innocence.

"My friend said the office told her to shred them," Tony said. "Wouldn't you know, they miraculously showed up in my Inbox. Now all hell's broken loose. Half the Pierce County Prosecutors Office is on leave while they sort out blame. You know how they are. Someone's got to pay for this, and in their estimation Ms. Lindquist had the poor taste to die and leave them no target."

"That's terrible. Both, I mean. Her death and the cumbersome legacy."

"Pat, nondisclosure's routine. Only this time we caught them with their pants down."

"I'm so sorry. I feel like I press ganged you into a trip you can't afford to take."

"I'm wearing jeans. When was the last time you saw me in jeans?"

"They're pressed."

"Jeans, Pat. I filed a suitcase full of postponement motions until sanity returns. I'm taking a few days off. Pack looks good, maybe I'll go skiing?"

"Do you know how?"

"Maybe we should find out."

* * *

Cody was already seated in a conference room off Visiting by the time Pat and Tony got processed through. He lit up when he saw them.

"Tony! You're here! How'd you get here?"

They shared a big hug. "Long journey by hovercraft." Tony wasn't far off the mark. "But worth it, little guy." He pretended Cody was getting too heavy to lift and the boy giggled. "Not so little anymore. What do they feed you?"

"I'm seven and some more months old now. Check out my tattoo." Cody lifted his shirt.

Pat heard Tony mumble an aborted profanity, head in his palm, looking for something innocuous to say. Pat managed a morbid chuckle.

Cody went on a sprawling description of life in prison, including his job at Laundry, a cellmate named Teagan who'd *drawn* the tattoo, pigs he liked, those he didn't, *pigs* apparently referring to officers. He talked about his pet, a blind mouse lost during an unfortunate episode involving drugs he'd managed to hide from the pigs for Teagan, the details of which got Tony stammering to cut him off.

Tony didn't want to know.

"This is Ms. Naughton. She's working on your appeal, to get you out of prison."

Cody sat in the chair on his knees, reached across and shook her hand like a gentleman.

"All the briefing is done," Pat said. "I met the three judge panel a month ago for oral arguments. They asked some very good questions, and I'm cautiously optimistic." And she was, though experience taught that judges could be inscrutable. They might overturn a case after appearing bored at oral arguments, and other times pursue probing, thoughtful questions only to uphold lower court findings.

She described the issues to Cody in terms she hoped he understood. Recalling Stavros's information about the androcortical chemocectomy drugs Hizer tested on Cody, she asked about the test and if he was feeling okay?

"Uh-huh. They have lots of doctors here. Some are bad, but I like Doctor Santa, I mean, he's not Santa but looks like him? And Judy she's nice, and Doctor Ivan, he—"

"Pardon me?"

"Uh-huh?"

"Ivan? Ivan Stavros?"

Cody shrugged, but described in every detail the same man who'd entered her Seattle office. Cody told them about the sponge bath and how *Doctor* Ivan beat up several of the officers. "I hope he isn't hurt because he says he'll come and see me again and I like him."

Pat gave Tony a heavy stare. "What else did he say?" Pat asked the boy.

"He says I'm not bad."

"Of course you're not."

Tony was cursing again. He tried to whisper out of earshot of Cody. "Pat, he's been here. He was *here.* Do you realize what that means?"

"I know exactly what it means," she said. "Unlike DOC lead the media to believe, their garrison was ineffective against him. Yes he was here, ostensibly capable of carrying out his mandate, and yet Dakota's alive. Stavros didn't do it for a reason. Let's find out why."

Tony paced in the small, carpeted room, looking out the plexiglass on an empty visiting room full of organized adult and children's sized chairs.

"Buddy, the officers walked by ten minutes ago. After they go by again, Pat would like to take some blood. Are you okay with that?"

"Uh-huh."

"You're not scared of needles?"

Cody's tone and facial expression turned to precocious deprecation. "Tony, I'm *seven.* I'm not a baby anymore."

"I know you aren't. I'm sorry, buddy. One more thing. You can't tell the officers we did this. Can you keep a secret?"

Undeniably cute and well mannered, when Cody answered, another, more assertive and unnerving person emerged.

"I ain't no snitch, Tony."

30

"You are a fortunate man," Samuel Coletti said.

Standing between the anchor machinery of *Estrella de Mar Rosa*'s stern with Samuel, Ivan harbored doubts their reunion was lucky.

"How do you figure?"

"Your brutal nature, the consequences from which serendipity until now saved you, has become your apprehension. A handsome reward awaits the one who effects your capture."

"So I've heard. Doesn't that make you the lucky one? What am I worth?"

Bubbles in Samuel's fluted glass rose softly through light emanating from beneath the teak railing on which he rested the elbow of a familiar white suit jacket. His champagne waved a circular signal to an indistinguishable employee behind the bridge windows. Two short bursts of the ship's horn acknowledged.

A series of coordinated events put Coletti's vessel to sea. Shore radios distantly chirped, gangway retracting, moorings cast off, a low rumble through the superstructure as two giant Caterpillar engines awakened, bow and aft thrusters turbulating a swell of saltwater against the quay.

Samuel poured more champagne in Ivan's glass. "You are fortunate in that I don't need the lawman's remuneration."

The Greek in Ivan welcomed sea travel, even if a boat as substantial as Samuel's nullified the ocean's nocturnal drama. He followed the man to a navigation room behind the bridge. A plot table displayed channel and route data.

Underwater and surface landmasses constrained the potential path of the vessel, blinking markers highlighting proximity risks. Samuel's slender fingers danced across the surface controls. Holographics showed orbits of GPS satellites being tracked and storm systems offshore. Samuel plotted course waypoints and confirmed the route with the captain. The system automatically calculated an arrival schedule, advised customs and border control, confirmed passport authorization, and reserved a berth for a five-meter skiff.

"We're making a call in Nicosia to pick up guests," he told Ivan. "You're welcome to go ashore for a short excursion if you wish. We'll make several stops along the way."

"The way to where?"

"We have ample time to understand the where. In the meantime, you are also my guest." Several boys met them in the Lido lounge. "You already know Elias. He'll show you to your cabin. Elias is in charge of all guest accommodations. You will be in good hands. Get some rest."

"If it's all the same to you, I'd just as soon avoid being in any of their hands." In spite of Ivan's reservations, a small lad had squeezed against his leg in a platonically affectionate way. Ivan found himself scratching the boy's head, a comfortable instinct made possible by fatigue. Elias gestured Ivan towards the circular staircase. Ivan had a haunting sense of déjà vu. He had so many unanswered questions burning through the dwindling resources of his mind. Over a month now without the enhanced environment Neural Rig, Ivan still couldn't adjust to the disconnected loneliness. How could Coletti and his salaciously precocious crew resolve the mystery of Number 7? What hid in Dakota's blood? Hizer Pharmaceutical's mistakes? How did Glitch fit the puzzle? What happens next?

Never had such powerful and relentless adversaries, with limitless resources, been after Ivan. Staying ahead of the

CIA's pursuit was enervating. He could feel the stress taking a toll—border crossings, vehicle switches, timing, plotting safe underground routes—the mental process consumed assets to the point of physical breakdown. In this surreal state stood an adolescent apparition who beckoned Ivan deeper into alternate reality, an ironic safe shelter from exhausting madness.

He turned back to Samuel. "Why you? I don't understand what Ellison intended."

"Your uncle entrusted me with everything he discovered. The only way to be sure the trail wasn't followed. You should ask him your question. Will he be joining us?"

"Only if you believe in God."

"And you do not."

"I don't know what to believe anymore."

Elias took Ivan's hand and led him down the stairs. Perhaps conflicted for what to tell a man with little regard for death, Samuel's voice from above conveyed empathy. "I'm sorry for your loss."

* * *

In the morning Samuel wasn't to be found. Ivan roamed several decks, crewmates in matching nineteenth century sailor shorts, blue kerchief collars and caps cleaning common areas with upbeat amusement.

"Good morning, sir."

Ivan turned to see Elias carrying a stiff coil of rope. "Where can I find Mr. Coletti?"

"Father's taken the launch ashore. He'll be back in a few hours. Can I make you some coffee? Something to eat?"

A starboard door onto the gangway showed Ivan the Cypriot shoreline off in the distance. In the vista between ship and shore ran a colorful mix of power and sailboats, parasailors overhead dragged by kite strings through the pleasant Mediterranean air. Light breezes offered the slightest chill. Coffee sounded good.

"You'll get a briefing before Samuel returns," Elias said.

"Briefing? What does that mean? On what?" Ivan followed him back inside. Elias made use of an espresso machine and seemed disappointed Ivan drank coffee black.

"Noah's looked over the files with Samuel. He found some leads, but I guess your friend underestimated the code sophistication."

"Let me look at it. I'm good with codes."

"Not this good." He summoned one of the little sailor boys and told him to find Noah.

Ivan realized he was sitting on the same Arabic upholstered sofa where he'd faced off with Samuel at their first meeting on Biscayne Bay. Ivan threatened to kill a boy who'd lain in his lap with unabashed trust, and now Ivan couldn't remember his name. He'd thought of them like synthetics, not human, a disposable product if circumstances required. Now he regretted it, wanted to apologize for scaring the kid. And didn't know his name.

A carrot-haired boy in overalls toppled across the armrest of the adjoining sofa. He righted himself and swung over the shoulder to his back a large Nerf gun on a bandolier lined with a mix of orange and yellow sponge darts. He looked at Ivan as if considering whether he'd prematurely holstered the toy.

"Noah, this is Ivan." To Ivan he said, "Noah will show you what we've learned so far."

"You're kidding me."

"Good use of a pun, sir." Elias hoisted the coil of rope and left.

Ivan stared at the kid. Coletti was playing a joke. Impatience plucked at his nerves. Patience was not a virtue. Patience was contingent on expectation and Ivan expected nothing. This ought to be good. No worse than being briefed by a condescending young Korean spy. Noah stared back, wet eyes and a mess of confidence sapping freckles.

"Look, kid, no offense, but we're dealing with some pretty serious sh . . . stuff. Why don't you just give me the files. I don't need a ten year old to read them to me."

"I'm twelve."

"Oh, in that case—"

"We're not stupid, you know."

"I didn't say you were."

"Yeah, but you kind of implied it."

"All I meant was—"

"Everyone's dead. That's your problem."

"Who?"

"Now you're interested?" Noah picked up the coffee table tablet and logged into the ship's network. "Everyone who knows anything." He sat cross-legged next to Ivan. Adaptive tinting in the room's windows darkened, fan-dance emitters projecting a vertical picture of a twenty-something black man in a tie, gauged ears and gel-spiked hair.

Elias had been completely serious. Ivan stood up and looked for something stouter than coffee. He helped himself to the bar. Noah seemed unsure of Ivan's behavior and looked a little peeved. Ignoring the kid was a passive-aggressive arrogance, and Noah called him on it in the direct and honest way children know.

"Dad said you were a little bit of a jerk."

"I am. I have been. I'm dealing with a lot of stress."

"Many of our patrons are stressed. That's why they come."

Ivan held up his drink like a toast. "I'm good. I don't need any of the love your dad pedals around here."

"Love isn't the same as sex. There's lots of ways to help people feel loved. Dad says you're a special guest, and this is the way we can help. So are you going to let me help?"

"Samuel said that?" Noah nodded. "Did he also teach you the manipulative line you just used on me?"

"Every human interaction is manipulation," Noah said. "That doesn't make it bad."

Shoulder height philosophical consort. Just what Ivan needed. He moved to the end of the bar to get a better look at the floating image. "You've caught me at a weird time in my life, Noah. I doubt it's going to get much weirder. Show me what you've got."

He smiled, freckles realigning as if to say he'd won the show of will.

"This is Richard Feige. He's a level four programmer at Carmichaels Research Center." A map with orographic features rotated into place, showing the location of the CRC near State Road 88 in Pennsylvania. "Pretty remote, a kind of wooded nowhere off the beaten path fifty kilometers south of Pittsburgh. Nobody asks questions about what kind of research the facility does, and it isn't just any old R&D. It's not public info, but Carmichaels Research Center is owned by Hizer International. Access is heavily restricted and it serves as a maximum security data suppository for Hizer's global research."

"Repository."

"Right. Your friend tried hacking into the facility, but I guess drug companies are worse than that CIA nest you crashed in Seoul."

"How come you know about that?"

"We've got Internet. I see the news."

"I doubt my details were on the web."

"They are now, picture and everything. You should shave."

"This chin's had a rough life, kid, and I choose not to show it off. I definitely don't take grooming tips from you, peach-fuzz."

"Funny. Jerk's got jokes."

"And his name is Ellison."

"Huh?"

"The man you keep calling my friend? His name was Ellison. He was my uncle and now he's dead."

"So is Richard Feige."

Ivan listened while Noah walked him through the limited information Ellison dug up on Hizer's exploits. Nearly eight years ago Feige was tasked with moving an archive of sensitive data from older servers directly through satellites owned by Hizer into the more secure complex in Pennsylvania. The data was in cumulative disarray, and Feige assigned responsibility for organizing it into amenable directories facilitating storage and retrieval.

A batch of very old scan-archive documents from an experiment conducted in the 1980's alarmed Mr. Feige. He made contact from his home with an older gentleman in London. They exchanged a number of communications, all of which Ellison found, not that they helped much since Feige and his contact in London adopted a type of encryption. What Noah *could* show included a plea from London to exfiltrate the data and return it to him, indicating the data and related experiment must have originated there.

"What kind of data?"

"We don't know. Dad and I think some kind of hint's probably in the encoded exchanges. There are two of them, a short message and a longer one dated just before Feige's death." Noah brought the messages up for Ivan to see.

Message 1:

ADJEF	HEHEF	CICLD	MHBUQ
GVGCZ	NHJHX	DNGMZ	SYIXB
LXNQL	OKDSJ	ZIJLD	ODKBT
GYNPQ	JZRPY	GHLWF	ONCOJ
JFANE	FZJVK	ZGLUV	SRRWZ
BKTZP	WWRMB	KEQJY	JKRII
GXUVG	HDDUD	RCGCB	SKLQM
ORVKO	FDRGJ	DEBTE	FPRPT
NXOPK	EBAFQ	DLRFP	JNQZM
EABXI	DCIBV	ZRGCO	MNZZT
GYJIM	FLITG	JNYTU	ANIUQ
LBPXM	VPFOE	MNEVU	GGQRS
OEFYR	VKWWO	OBRUK	EUZPJ
HZEYD	DYPCB	YBYZC	IKKPM
KCOQC	KOSIL	GOMIN	BTBUE

Message 2:

AFFDO	LMOGE	OECIN	YQAYK
HCQSK	CPRNY	FMOWT	GQFBB
IMGVI	NASIY	DCMZA	LAOJA
SIHET	HEQAX	OFJYJ	YYTLF
KGMDY	ZDHCB	OPWZC	TFOBY
DOQDG	EGYBF	ELRZJ	VKOOW
NYAAR	RSWJL	IJMYT	AMJPK
DNRLE	GGCWO	LZKSW	ZYUTV
GLIGQ	LQSRU	KEYNI	EVZYK
APIOR	BVEWX	NGFOF	ALIQI
DMEIA	JIXPG	AROVC	KSUOR
FEUJM	UVLKB	CNYOQ	BLQEZ
CETIR	TWTHX	CBWLY	WIZFY
CJUEQ	ZMHKQ	NRFIX	BOXBX
JHZFP	TCUVN	EAURB	SSVVE
HPXSC	GESCX	TGFGN	SGOCA
CZUME	DVKRC	YQGGH	OAHLQ
ULKLI	YIYYB	XHIYE	QRELQ
ATDKN	VDLTM	WUVWI	IWNSI
ZAQCP	ZBREY	YIFAP	EYRZY
IJNXP	YKCAT	OJRPI	

The coded messages made no pretense about hiding something. It wasn't as if the original message had merely been corrupted, or that machine language was misinterpreted as a code. Someone conscientiously coded these. They were unlike any encryption Ivan had seen. A pity Richard Feige died.

"Murdered," Noah said. "Pretty obvious. Think about it—what kind of lab accident takes out a computer programmer and nobody else? What's he supposed to be doing? I mean, maybe electrocution by rack server PSU, but then why did Hizer insist the body be cremated? All Feige's family got was a jar of ashes. Who knows if they were even his? Maybe he's not even dead."

"Who's the contact in London?" Ivan asked, moving to the next obvious lead.

Another face popped up. "Nigel Braithwaite. Dad says the name's so British it has to be fake. You can see he's a lot older than Feige. Like, ancient. Strange guy for Feige to reach out to. He's a retired civil servant, lives in Ladbroke Grove, no real money. Not the kind of guy who gets robbed and shot in his small apartment, but that's what people were told."

"He wasn't robbed."

"We don't think so either. He was killed real close after Mr. Feige, and if that isn't a coincidence, your uncle got the Detective Constable's report and there's other weird stuff. Nigel was shot by—"

"A Russian round from 60 meters away."

"Yup. So you've seen that already."

"Sure."

Nigel wasn't just any civil servant, Noah said. He worked for the British Foreign Office and ran agents during the Cold War. He was an agent himself at one point, though obviously not under that name. Cold War agents often retired into isolated and paranoid lives, having amassed any number of unknown enemies on the other side of the Iron

Curtain, ones with long memories, patience, and a propensity to carry out elaborate assassinations to send a message. The profile for Nigel's death caused little stir at the River House, another elderly Cold War expendable given a dirt-nap. Sadly, the bureaucrats didn't feel they owed him much. A life of solitude matched by an equally vapid Church of England burial, a priest like a voicemail recording.

Ellison could have found all this himself, but Hizer saved him the trouble. Among the discoveries Hizer's sleuths deemed important was a cryptic message from one of Nigel's unnamed agents dating back to when Nigel must have been in his mid to late thirties.

Prepared matched set of microfilm
of research for experimental study
Sending by Blue Dolphin route

There was nothing else in Hizer's material to give it context.

"So let me get this straight," Ivan said. He'd moved to the sofa, realizing more intrigue unfolded with each new lead. "Mr. Feige is dead, as well as the retired British agent he contacted. Feige found something damaging to Hizer, perhaps about an experiment from fifty years ago, and which Nigel wanted back?"

"And if we find the copy of the microfilm, the one Nigel's agent had, we figure out what Hizer is trying to cover up."

"I'm confused by your use of *we*. I don't understand how Coletti's involvement is required. Why didn't Ellison just leave me the files? Why did he give them to you? Why do you care?"

Noah de-tinted the windows and took a disassociated interest in something under his toenail. "Probably because of the encrypted messages."

From behind them came Samuel's distinctive voice. "As I told you before, Mr. Stavros, BioConnect has computers powerful enough to sequence full DNA genomes in seconds." Anyone's guess how long he'd been standing there. "It was reasonable for Ellison to believe, without his help through the CIA, you would need a powerful server farm to decrypt the message."

"Assuming I wouldn't have his help."

"I believe he was cognizant of his potential death. As for motivation to assist, my reasons are simply pecuniary. Mr. Ellison arranged for BioConnect to receive a lucrative five-year government grant to collect fertility complication statistics we already routinely document. So you see, we're at your disposal."

There again was the magnanimous *we* as though hopes were high Ivan would switch to the Dark Side. What was Ellison's warning about espionage and honeypot traps?

"So really there are two potential routes," Ivan said. "Search for microfilm, or decode the Feige messages."

"If you'll pardon me," Samuel crossed the room and glass doors slid open, "I must see that we get under way. But I'm afraid you're down to only one alternative. Our final stop is in London."

* * *

Hours later in the library Ivan received the noninterference lecture. The four gentlemen who came aboard in Nicosia generously contributed to Brickell Consulting, one of Coletti's Atlas Holdings subsidiaries. They looked forward to a cruise commensurate with their investment. Samuel would appreciate if Ivan would be so kind as to refrain from hitting them with tranquilizer darts. Not good business.

Ivan used the word *truce*, but he'd grown indifferent. People had their reasons. Maybe something else pacified his ire. Ellison always possessed more objectivity, and if his uncle urged Ivan to focus on inequities more grave, not getting hung up on sexual taboo might better honor the deceased man's wisdom.

After a life of dispassionately assassinating targets, including six kids for what now appeared certainly foul design, being judgmental tasted like the sourest sanctimony.

Several stops and many days lay between *Estrella de Mar Rosa* and the Thames, time during which Samuel encouraged Ivan to relax. How could he? Hizer promised to kill Dakota, the only remaining proof of yet unknown malfeasance. Indulging in Samuel's epicurean lifestyle felt like abdicating a responsibility to out the very inequities voiced in Ellison's final wishes. Ivan wanted to contact Ms. Naughton, ask if she'd obtained the blood sample? Samuel cautioned against unnecessary risks and getting too far ahead of himself. Ms. Naughton had visited the prison. Have faith. He was no good to Dakota dead. For the time being there was no way for Hizer to find Ivan.

Any search for Ivan would slow the CIA down.

* * *

"More than a hundred hours of dedicated server array time has failed to unravel the messages," Samuel said.

Ivan could see distant lights of beach villas along the coast of Malta. The days thinned out the tether between his competing emotions, anxiety of being inadequate against the military forces hunting him and the effort to unwind, leading him to accept Samuel's evening commune in the outdoor spa. On the lowest plateau of the ship's aft decks the elaborate hot tub was shaped like an ambitiously modified peanut pool, with narrow channels ducking under Japanese garden style bridges and over waterfalls, spilling to progressively cooler reservoirs. Ivan and Samuel sat across from each other immersed in the hotter 40- degree pool, while Ivan could hear laughter beyond the decorative foliage and flowers from children splashing in a safer 35°C.

Under a clear sky the full moon kissed the wave crests like the luminescent crystals of a dark geode. *Estrella de Mar Rosa* sliced a smooth ripple through the sea at a steady 22 knots. Lightly chlorinated splash dampened a teak deck abutting the pool, a smell like Zinfandel cork against the citrus tang of pink grapefruit and vodka in an iced drink. Ivan placed his feet in front of an aerated jet and tried to ignore the penis shaped ice cubes in the cocktail, suggestively shrinking as they melted.

"Are you familiar, Mr. Stavros, with de Viaris of Cherbourg?"

"Haven't met him."

"Born under Aquarius in 1847, he was a student of l'École Polytechnique, joining the navy at a young age. He enjoyed a career as a police prefect and infantry officer, and wrote many scientific journals later."

His host waxed on about stages of a possibly irrelevant career. Sybarites like Samuel had an elitist manner that never got to the point. His diffusive tendency vexed Ivan. Finally Samuel appeared to arrive at something important.

"He authored what's known as the Vigenère cipher, backbone to one-time-pad encryption."

"One-time-pads? Like spies used during the Cold War?"

"Precisely, as well as World War II. The coded messages from Feige to Nigel bear strong resemblance to one-time-pad encryption. It's obviously not a Caesar substitution or computer frequency-analysis could take it apart in seconds. There are no frequency shifts, but the uneven distribution is notable."

"I don't really know what that means, but if they're codes from the last century, why can't you break them? The CIA did it."

"After six years, and if it *is* one-time-pad, their computers didn't crack the code."

"How is that possible?"

Modern encryption, Samuel explained, might be hard to break in practice, but not in theory, for it relied on patterns. In the past RSA-based systems factored the product of high prime numbers or derived algebraic points on an elliptical curve. Their patterns became analyzable with the advent of quantum computers. Now Quantum Key Distribution protected corporations who could afford it, and Variable Lattice Point encryption thwarted quantum computers for everyone else. Yet both evolved the same theoretical vulnerability. Mathematical algorithms like QKD and VLP, while phenomenally complex, were patterns nonetheless, crackable as surely as the German Enigma machine fell at Bletchley Park to obfuscated but observable repetition so many millions of characters long.

"A redoubt of patterns," Samuel said, "merely awaits future incursion by overwhelming analytical attack."

"And if don't orate like Sophocles?" Ivan said.

"You might. After all, he was a *Greek* playwright." Samuel paused, and then relented. "Increased volumetric data capacity. A newer, bigger computer will inevitably be the downfall of VLP."

"Which you could have said in the first place. So why's this code different?"

One-time-pads, by comparison, seeded each transposition with a randomly generated character key. Not only was each key random, their interrelation revealed little, and certainly nothing any amount of computer power could decrypt.

The process for Cold War agents was tedious but simple. They had a one-time-pad with rows of randomly generated letters on each page, typically broken into columns of five letters. The pad's identical mate resided with whoever received the agent's encoded messages. With the Roman alphabet numbered from 0 to 25—A being zero and Z, twenty-five—the agent wrote the plaintext under the letters on the one-time-pad and added them up. C plus N equaled 15, or R plus E equaled 21. Then convert the total for each back to a letter, where the 15 would be P and 21 became V, known as the cipher text. Tear off the one-time-pad sheet, burn it, and never use it twice.

Vigenère encipherment used a modulo x function if the added letters exceeded 25. For instance, a one-time-pad letter U and plaintext letter L added up to 31. The agent would subtract 26, leaving 5, and hence the cipher text letter F. The system just rolled over like the alphabet was on a circle.

The message's recipient simply subtracted out his copy of the one-time-pad letter from the cipher text to reveal the original message.

"You want me to believe," Ivan said, "that a code system used in World War II is more secure than modern encryption?"

"Why should you doubt? Modern encryption need not be impregnable, merely convenient. There's nothing convenient about Vigenère encipherment. Both agent and operator must possess copies of a bespoke one-time-pad that can never have travelled outside their possession or be copied by unintended surveillance. How would we emulate such a process via computer? Quite inconvenient."

"If it's impossible to crack, how did Hizer or the CIA do it?"

"Ah, you must pay closer attention." Samuel left the spa to find them more drinks. Malta had long passed from view, though other ships in the sea lanes kept the horizon busy. "I said Nigel's code *resembles* one-time-pad encryption, but it's not, strictly speaking. While my server farm may not be able to decipher the code, it *can* reveal characteristics helpful to us. Analysis shows the first few groups in each message are distinguishable from the rest of the message."

"It's a key," Ivan said.

"Close. An indicator group. It informs Nigel *where* to find the key, which is likely an agreed upon text system derived from perhaps a newspaper, a common public source, or denotation which of multiple codex they should use from those shared by both of them."

"Like a book," Ivan suggested.

"I'm afraid literature is out of the question. Too weak."

"How's that?"

"My computers would tear it apart." It would only be a matter of seeding real test words to determine if another real word is revealed from the cipher text. Perform enough of these tests and a sequence of words would show which book they'd used, thus the rest of the key, and the message is decrypted in short order. "No. It did not take Hizer six years to discover a Dickensian key like Oliver Twist."

"You would choose a novel about exploited little boys."

"A Tale of Two Cities, if you prefer. Does the rebellious severing of necks more suit your disposition?"

A fair jab, Ivan had it coming. When did Samuel become an expert on codes? Decoding the human genome is a similar process, was the geneticist's answer.

"You think the British Secret Service records on Nigel will tell us what key he gave Mr. Feige."

"That is a possibility. If I were CIA, the inquiry is obvious. One way or another, your search starts in London."

"Who are we supposed to be when we knock on MI6's door?"

Ivan thought Samuel hadn't heard the question, but his delayed answer was surprisingly laconic.

"You'll figure something out."

In a way it was the response Ivan hoped for. Since Seoul he'd been rendered irrelevant. At one point in life he accepted few unknowns and commanded a feeling of control. He'd supplanted both with a newfound sense of purpose made weak by impotent strategy. Responsible for the plan ahead, Ivan suddenly felt the relaxation that had eluded him since leaping from the 142nd floor of the perfectly wretched life he'd embraced.

Throughout the night Ivan and Samuel received intermittent visitors from the adjoining pools. In and out of the channels swam an assortment of boys, sneaking up on Ivan like German U-boats and then, sufficiently self-spooked by the ambiguous game, splashing away beset with explosive giggling.

Ivan began to think of them divided less by age than rank, where boys Elias's age ran programs aboard, and the Noahs carried out important auxiliary tasks.

Touring the men's pond tonight were a younger rank akin to the aptly named minnows reputed to pleasure the Emperor Tiberius when he swam. It was like being in a Giovanni fresco, naked little angels fawning at the whim of historical titans. When Samuel broached a new topic, Ivan wondered if his own thoughts had been so close to the surface as to be read.

"I won't presume your Greek pedigree obliges you to know the mythology of Adonis."

"Only that he was a young man," Ivan said. "Supposedly handsome. He was favored by the gods."

"Coveted more so than favored, by Aphrodite and Persephone of the heavens and underworld respectively. Aphrodite, goddess of fertility and sexual love, was drawn to great beauty. And who did she pursue above all? An eight year old boy."

"Did I miss something?"

"The censorious of our century prefer the prudish accounting of mythology. But during The Enlightenment artisans sculpted Grecian allegory in search of the pure and beautiful. You are a man of art, correct? Have you explored the Louvre in Paris?"

Once with Yannis when he'd been quite young. His childhood recollection painted the museum more as a castle, so large it seemed to him at the time.

"In smooth white marble and paintings are many enchanting nudes, such as *Duende*, and surely you noted the subject of desirability. Should the Renaissance vision be any guide to the prepossessing reality our century denies, Adonis was years younger than Noah."

"Sure. Some sculptures. Not exactly proof."

"Honoring beauty uncorrupted by maturity."

"You don't live in the sixteenth century. The legalities have changed."

"Legalities? What is illegal? We're in international waters." Samuel gestured around them. "From which of your many glass houses have you cast this stone?"

"Don't recite to me from the Brochure Bible only when it suits you. I'm not getting a high-five from Jesus and neither are you."

"Have you read the story of Jesus and the centurion?"

Pretentious to the level of exasperating. Ivan couldn't help voicing his annoyance. "Christ."

"Among other names, yes."

Samuel continued with a homily from chapter eight of Matthew, where Jesus entered Capernaum and a centurion begged the Lord to heal his servant who lay at home, paralyzed and suffering. Matthew used the Greek word, *pais*, meaning boy, while Luke used *doulos*, or slave. On campaign or stationed outside Rome it was common for Roman officers to bring with them young 'body slaves', who ministered to the physical and sexual needs of the officer, a relationship deeper than simply master-servant, and one certainly not lost on Jesus.

"The relationship made no difference to Jesus," Samuel said. "He agreed to heal the boy."

"Even if that story's true, and you haven't perverted the interpretation, social morays evolve over a couple thousand years. A Roman's slave boy isn't living in a society that shames him for that sort of thing. Don't you think collateral consequences will hurt these kids even if you personally don't think you have?"

"Moral relativism? Pejorative of Evangelists? The argument is more frequently invoked to *endorse* the morality of Jesus. History possesses more consistency across time. Consider Alexander the Great 300 years before, who kept a castrated Persian boy for his erotic appetites."

Hizer and the Washington State Department of Corrections had nearly saved Coletti the trouble of castrating Dakota, not that he'd have done so. As far as Ivan could see, Samuel wasn't castrating them. It was possible Ivan thought DOC's human rights violations considerably more abhorrent, but he wasn't inclined to validate Samuel on this point. The man was cherry picking history.

"Not at all, Stavros. You argue the last century of experimental moral chastity should cast aspersions on thousands of former years in which humans at any age freely succumbed to all manner of primal erotic instincts."

"Who says these kids have their own instincts? Before they even gestated you genetically manipulated every neurological trait to make it easier for you to abuse them. They're dependent. They trust you. Here they are calling you father. Do they know dear-old-dad's really a GLS kiosk? If you want to be a father, put some skin in the game. What you've created is artificial and selfish."

"Parenthood *is* selfish. Humans breeding to make exhibition of their pride, the perceived quality of genes manifested in a caravan of doting offspring. My clientele are more honest. They're not sewing seeds or demanding a lineage to honor their greatness. Intimacy at its purest egalitarian foundations. Not the male majority thrashing around in the world's vaginas, seeking the vanity mirror of procreation."

Ivan heard in Samuel the energy of a manifesto. "We have something in common. Sex as an end to itself. No kids of our own. I wouldn't know what to do with a son or daughter's trust. I don't think I'm cut out for parenting."

"No one is. Like every proper lesson in life, learning comes from mistakes."

"You've made your share," Ivan said, no shortness of sarcasm. "Doesn't it bother you to exploit their trust and then brainwash them?"

"You'll find I've done nothing of the sort."

"You admitted it. Forget the genetic enhancements. What happens to them after they're born? What was the phrase you used in Miami? 'Social engineering'?"

Samuel appeared flustered, a discomfort ill-concealed by a scoff and dismissive wave of his hand. He was quiet for a while, no doubt marshaling justification.

Underwater hued lighting passed slowly through color shifts over the course of hours such that the visiting small bodies shimmered like cool powder in a flask of Bombay Sapphire, then they'd warm to honeyed apricots, eyes closed under the amber surface, babes in utero. Ivan felt the intoxication, not of sexual arousal, but a reverence in harmony with the masters who in awe tried to capture for one artistic glimpse this delicate stage of life. He wished Samuel could see what he saw, and be satisfied.

As though knowing his name had come up, through the channel swam Noah, wet hair a ginger rag clinging to his ears. He seemed anxious to tell Samuel something but kept silent. He watched Ivan with the same probing look Hye Min used to unveil Ivan's secret thoughts.

"Peter McWilliams died trying to enforce reason in U.S. courts," Samuel said. "He called out the absurdity of consensual crimes, though he hardly condoned the nature of my business. Yet he emphasized it is *adults* who teach children which parts of their bodies are shameful. They're born with no natural guilt. That too is social engineering."

"Exactly my point," Ivan said. "You're employing something shameless and innocent—the openhearted soul of a child—and molding him to perform acts he has no natural inclination to do."

"Your language adopts the lexicon of the judgmental, and I doubt you notice. I think you underestimate a child's inclinations. I argue the molding of society punishes them for what seems natural, the same way it teaches you new meanings for *innocent*, *abuse* and *exploitation*."

The elevated water temperature eventually took a toll on Noah. He crawled from the spa, skin a brighter red than his hair, and grabbed a towel he subsequently failed to use the way Ivan might have hoped. Later, introspection reminded him of the sources of shame. In the moment, though, he wanted Noah to spout some validation of Ivan's argument, and got nothing.

"The notion of a child's openness is misguided," Samuel said. "Peter Høag once wrote that no one is more covert than a child, a response to a world trying to pry them open, see what's inside, wondering whether the natural instincts should be replaced with more useful preserves. They have the greatest need to be guarded, and I've not violated their needs."

"How do you get to say what they need?"

"Ask them. Find the youngest aboard and ask him what he wants."

A disarming parry, but not convincing. Ivan wasn't going to change the mind of a man who'd bullshitted himself for a lifetime, a hundred literary references like so much supercilious carnal jargon.

"*Talking nonsense is the sole privilege mankind possess over other organisms. It's by talking nonsense that one gets to the truth*," Ivan said.

"Dostoyevsky."

"I hate that you know that." They shared a rare laugh.

"I'm pleased your search for truth evaluates and welcomes the world's nonsense."

Noah lay on the towel behind Samuel, fidgeting over whatever it was he was trying to interject. Ivan gave him the opening. "Spit it out, Peach-Fuzz."

Noah cupped his hand and whispered in Samuel's ear, Caesar smiling at the minnow's secret.

"He asks permission to take you ashore when we reach Sardinia." Another whisper, benevolent nod in response. "He says you have pent up frustrations. He wishes to find you a girlfriend."

31

"No sign of Hamish," Elias said.

The din of London street traffic in the Soho district made it difficult for Ivan to hear the boy's voice over a police radio. He kept it tuned on a private and encrypted frequency to prevent bona fide law enforcement from eavesdropping.

"Sit tight," Ivan said, depressing the switch on the auxiliary shoulder mic of his borrowed bobby uniform. "I have the front of the church covered. They've got a surveillance team crawling around out here. No sniper outposts, at least none I can spot."

"Copy."

"This isn't a movie. Don't say 'copy.' Just speak normally."

"Okay."

Samuel had said the search inevitably led to London, and now Ivan was fully in his element.

Beyond the church doors, in the back pew of the nave, sat Elias and Noah, bundled warmly on a chilly day and looking a little like confused truants. Ivan's provisional intercept team were overly excited to be helping Ivan kidnap Hamish, and probably appeared somewhat conspicuous. Ivan preferred to have eyes-on but settled for the open audio channel. He remained confident in his role as their protection detail.

Ivan leaned back in the enameled chair of an outdoor café. The fetching waitress with Glaswegian accent and playful smile returned. She placed black coffee and a butterhorn on the table for the hirsute man she'd no reason to believe wasn't Constable Ames. Ivan thanked her and insisted on paying up front. Watched intently as she slipped back inside. Noah was right. He could do a lot worse than spend a night squeezing against her. On how tight a schedule was this plan? Was there time for a Scottish appetizer half his age?

Maybe later.

Ivan forced his attention back to the red brick and Portland-stone edifice of Saint James Church across the street.

Partially blocking his view was a windowless Sprinter van parked against the far curb of Jermyn Street with *NexTem Service* logos, the adversary's poorly disguised mobile command unit. Several static posts and a few watchers made synchronized passes. To the untrained eye they were Londoners going about their casual business or off-season tourists. To Ivan, who'd carried a weapon at the age of five and quickly learned to watch for coattailers, they stuck out like raisins in a sea of oatmeal. He didn't need his rig, though a system that could paint and track targets for him would still be useful.

"Possible match entering," Ivan said.

"Copy—, I mean . . . sorry."

"You're doing great."

The butterhorn had a microwaved texture but the coffee was good. Ivan dipped one in the other to soften the pastry.

It was the first time either boy had been in London, and the traffic and noise overwhelmed Noah.

"Focus on one thing at a time," Ivan had said. "Watch Elias if you feel a panic attack. Familiar things help."

Each had a molded earwig. Noah's ear canals were so oddly shaped the receiver kept falling out. Ivan ended up gluing it in place. Feels weird, Noah said, a complaint Elias couldn't help making fun of.

"He's not used to it, sir. Ears aren't the fetishes our clientele typically go for. Now, if you stuck it—"

"This is a celibate operation," Ivan quickly reminded him.

He'd made the same plea to Samuel five days before in the Strait of Gibraltar.

"You want to burn him," Samuel had said. "Is that not the term used?"

"Probably. I don't know who he or she is yet."

If Ivan wanted to decode the Nigel Braithwaite messages, he needed to find what key the indicator group referred to. With Nigel dead the only people likely to retain records of the Cold War spy's coding practices were the British Secret Service.

Ivan was the number one target of Interpol and Europol. The last thing he'd do was walk into the River House, MI6's headquarters on the Thames, and request espionage records. If he managed to escape, it would only be from spies rendered incapable by their own laughter that Ivan was so stupid.

"Would it help to know one of their big chiefs is bent?" Samuel asked Ivan.

"Bent how? Why would you know?"

"I know many things. Bent like Oscar Wilde."

"How the hell is that going to help?"

"Burn the big chief. I would have thought it obvious. Ask Noah to help. A few choice photos of the man's bedroom etiquette and he'll give you any information you need."

"No." A week on the Mediterranean with the company of Coletti's quasi-family restored in Ivan a sense of their human autonomy and intelligence. Noah was right. They weren't stupid. Above average, in fact. But of the talents Ivan might utilize, seduction was off limits. "Let me keep this one boundary."

"Only misguided moralists delude themselves of saving virtue," Samuel said. Ivan held firm. Samuel dismissed it for the next best thing. "There's always bribery."

Another possibility arrived just in time. Choi Hye Min's people finished analyzing the data dump Ivan extracted from the CIA facility in Seoul. As a courtesy she sent Ivan the results. North Korea received numerous shipments of high tech border offense weaponry through elaborately hidden businesses whose incorporation documents ran back to a select few CIA operatives. They orchestrated the sales on behalf of named congressmen with financial ties to weapons defense contractors.

Bingo. Ivan had something to barter. Now he needed a receptive audience.

He made a few reservations, purchased tickets and, having spent the week studying other types of Cold War encryption, sent a message to the River House.

```
EDXIM    YWNUN    JOPVQ    OBZIF
CDYDH    YYYMC    UHSUC    GFJKX
DCNYG    KYPVF    IGKAR    QLBXP
NGNYZ    LQOUN    BZMQF    YUDKX
JCREX    GCXWK    HJPXY    PDYFM
JHDJN    UVYHY    GNDUG    FIDLL
UOYHK    XJCCV    YYJOB    MLWDP
FGUNM    CNGNY    XPMAC    MFMIH
ZLAKH    YCQMU    SUVYZ    LYFDG
VYHQK    XDUMC    PVOJY    HFDSU
FDQON    FCPUI    XPOQQ    OZLAK
NAVMU    PQOJG    CQDYP    VWKBF
NGSUB    ZNUFT    DAPOC    QCXVP
NGCYJ    XRQPX    YWUQK    XIOBM
NAWKD    ABVCQ
```

In the subject header of the email he wrote *Play fairly @ Piccadilly Circus*, which would mean little to anyone who intercepted the message. To old agents like Hamish, though, a hammer would hurt less than the heavy-handed clue.

From the number of support staff crawling up and down Jermyn and Duke of York Street, they'd easily worked out the code.

"It's him," Elias said.

"Make contact."

Ivan could hear the boys shuffling to the front of the nave beneath the cathedral's high, barrel vault arches. Tourists frequented the 350-year-old church designed by Christopher Wren, of which Ivan thought the organ its most spectacular feature. High above the chorister's gallery at the rear of the church, the gilded oak organ case was framed by three columns capped by trumpeting cherubs. The organ was older than the church. Built by Renatus Harris for the Whitehall Palace chapel, it was later moved to Saint James and almost survived World War II bombing. Ivan had earlier reconnoitered the church and thought the restoration rather good.

At the opposite end of the nave, an understated sanctuary was flanked to the right by the beautifully hand carved pulpit. Stained glass windows towered over the exchange about to take place. There was no way Hamish could fail to hear the boys sitting behind him.

"Pardon sir, I'm Elias and this is Noah."

"Off with you lads. I haven't got any money."

Ivan ran the voice through eigenvector audio analysis. Confirmed match. "It's Hamish," he said through the radio. He calculated timing from surveillance team movements. "Get him mobile in thirty seconds."

"Noah's going to lead you out the front, I'll follow," Elias said.

There was a silence, the MI6 deputy chief considering variables. "What the bloody hell is this?"

"We'll take you to Stavros. Hand over your phone and get moving. If you don't leave with us, you might not leave at all."

Several aborted protests. He was wearing a wire. Ivan could see the watchers suddenly go on high alert. He wasn't keen on involving the boys in a potentially dangerous operation, but they proved quick learners and more capable than Ivan's estimation. They weren't scared. Genetic engineering. If things went sour, Ivan trusted his own skill to keep them safe. Noah's signal came next.

"He's following. I'm approaching the front door."

"Clear to exit," Ivan said. He crossed the street behind a couple who'd ducked in and out of Fortnum and Mason three times. He thumped their heads together and yanked one of the radios as they collapsed. A crowd of people gasped. Ivan said, "Official business, folks. Move along." Holding a silenced pistol upside-down flat against his front and under the jacket, he fired two consecutive rounds into the curbside tires of the NexTem van. One of the back doors started to open. Ivan kicked it, door ramming the man's head. Into the gap Ivan tossed a micro-EMP grenade and banged the door shut. He ran a large ziptie through the door handles and kept walking, occupants pounding away. "Sit tight, it's only the electronics I want dead."

Down the low ramp, out the wrought iron gates, and east on Jermyn walked Noah, with Hamish and Elias in tow. Hamish looked around, an agreed upon visual signal conveyed the instruction *Not yet.* Excellent. Ivan approved. Hang back and watch what happens.

"Don't worry about what I'll be doing," Ivan had told them before taking the helicopter ashore. "My job is to make sure you can do your job. And I'm good at it."

The boys took a left at the corner, right on Piccadilly. Adrenaline surging, Ivan's senses reached out like tendrils into the surrounding crowds, balloon vendors and shop fronts. His mind itemized discrete movements looking for suspicious behavior. Individual beating of pigeon's wings, a tightened scarf, movement of CCTV cameras, telltale scrub of government issue shoes moving in predictable distances toward pinch points, hands rifling in pockets, hum of their slide pulled back just before Ivan neutralized and left them in a crumpled pile of their own unaware humiliation. He picked the surveillance detail apart one at a time in broad daylight. Different circumstances would have left Hamish's men dead, but Ivan was trying hard for less than lethal tactics on the plain clothes moving toward Piccadilly Circus.

"He's wearing a transmitter," Ivan said to the boys. They descended into the Piccadilly Tube Station. "When you get on the Brown Line, help him lose it."

"Right. Almost there."

In the midst of the garish neon signs surrounding Piccadilly Circus, the 140-year old metal statue of winged Eros pointed the way. The bustle of crowds roving through the plaza was unreal. Increasingly difficult to locate the agents tailing Hamish and the boys. Ivan listened to the chatter over the quarry's frequency. They'd realized someone was peeling them apart, but couldn't identify until too late who was behind them. He heard sirens converging, London police mobilized to support an MI6 grab-exercise going to shit.

Ivan passed through the faregate with a prepaid tube pass. Three minutes for the Bakerloo line. He used the time to ram sedatives into the remaining tails on the platform, lay them out on a bench next to three grocery bags and the bark of a leashed animal more concerned than the owner.

"Drugs these lads take, what it is. Terrible business."

"I agree," Ivan said.

"You're not doing nothing about it, officer?"

"I just did. Good day."

"Happy holidays, sir."

Ivan thanked him and boarded the tube three carriages back from Noah and Elias.

"He's still transmitting. Motivate him."

Ivan spent three days teaching Elias to shoot clay pigeons from *Estrella de Mar Rosa*'s stern with a Walther 9mm. He'd gotten better. Hamish was a lot closer than the clay pigeons and, from the sounds coming over the radio, believed Elias wouldn't miss. Noah dropped the wire next to

Hamish's phone in a lead lined pocket stitched inside his jacket.

A short time later the boys resurfaced at Lambeth North Station and walked up Westminster Road. They crossed the grassy sections of the Jubilee Gardens where cameras were sparse, Ivan a hundred meters back but closing fast. In a city with so many security cameras, Ivan's route would eventually be discovered. He just needed confusion to last an hour. He'd reserved a compartment for four passengers on the London Eye observation wheel three days in advance under the name Ames. He stuffed the police uniform in a public trashcan, overtook the boys, and boarded ahead of Elias, waving a sendoff to the operator.

"Stavros!"

"The same. Please sit down. I trust my escorts treated you well? You have exactly thirty minutes to decide whether my intelligence is valuable to your friends."

"In thirty minutes you'll be in irons," Hamish said with more confidence than his pickled features stuffed under a homburg hat suggested.

Ivan counted off on his fingers. "Two statics. Three techs in a van, computers no longer working, by the way. And eighteen pavement tails. Did I miss any?" Hamish looked chastened. "And I thought you decoded my message."

"We're here, aren't we?"

"There's no *we* anymore. Must have missed the part of my instructions that said *come alone*."

"Out of the question."

"Thirty minutes."

"Bravo, Stavros. Any idea how many looked at your missive before a salty dog in D-Branch recognized Playfair's cipher?"

"I choose my salty dogs carefully. As part of D-Branch you should have the access I need."

Hamish avoided direct confirmation. "Wouldn't have taken us long to figure out, the consonant frequency, repetitious bigrams. Not much of a code."

"I shouldn't think so. I gave you the damn keyphrase." Ivan held up a thumb drive. "I'll give you a lot more, and all I want in exchange is Nigel Braithwaite's codex."

Noah and Elias paid no attention. It wasn't clear whether they grasped the gravity of having successfully snatched a top MI6 cardinal from the hands of a highly skilled spy agency. At the opposite end of the compartment, faces pressed to the capsule's ovoid glass, they squealed with happy alarm as the ground disappeared beneath them at 26 centimeters per second. They pointed and laughed from the London Eye's apogee, the great River Thames and bisected city spread across the prime meridian and visible for over forty kilometers in every direction. Elias spotted Samuel's vessel docked near the Canary Wharf Pier, a discovery that gave Noah singular amazement. They had good enough sense not to use names.

Six minutes before the ride was over Ivan negotiated a deal with Hamish.

* * *

"You expressed interest in what responsibility entails," Samuel said.

"Not sure I used the word 'interest'," Ivan said, trying to recall the conversation in the spa.

Estrella de Mar Rosa took on sufficient fuel in London and was back on the English Channel, new complement of guests and a northerly heading.

On the lowest deck the three of them occupied a cramped surgery where a boy sat on an examining table. Jaden, that was his name. The six or seven year old Ivan scared the crap out of on Biscayne Bay, suppressor to the boy's blonde mop, finger-tug away from an act Ivan was now certain he'd never have committed. Wearing latex gloves, Samuel swabbed Jaden's throat and inserted the tip into a machine. While the sample went through diagnostics, Samuel held a stethoscope to Jaden's chest and back as he breathed.

"Thirty nine degree fever, wet lungs and body ache. I shouldn't expect the system will tell me anything we don't already know." Samuel checked the computer. "This is an unfortunately pernicious strain." He pulled up options on screen and requested inoculant synthesis. A whirring commenced within.

"Is he okay?"

"The virus will run its course. One of the men from Nicosia was a possible carrier." That explained why Ivan hadn't seen the boy for ten days. He'd been assiduously avoiding social contact with the customers and by extension their particular playmates. After a few minutes Samuel circled back to the original discussion. "Jaden will be fine. He has you to look after him."

"Excuse me?"

"Responsibility, Stavros." He gave Jaden an antiviral shot. "Elias adjusted assignment schedules, but we're quite busy. I must devote energy to tasks accumulating at BioConnect. You, meanwhile, have nothing to do. There is no greater responsibility than caring for a sick child."

"What about Blue Dolphin? Bastien Köhler? Manticore?"

"Mr. Stavros, is that anxiety I hear in your voice?" He lifted Jaden down onto his feet. The machine dropped a vile into the hopper.

"No."

"Contract killer, gun runner, negotiates with dictators, terrorists and spy agencies, assassinates high value targets across the globe, fearless . . . and here you tremble at the prospect of nursing a sick boy?"

"Don't be an ass."

Samuel loaded two syringes from the machine's vaccination, inoculated himself, and ripped open another alcohol wipe for Ivan, handing him the second syringe. "The synthesis accelerates your immune response. You'll be safe from influenza exposure in a few hours." He led Jaden by the hand down the hall. Ivan followed them up the companionway to deck three, where Samuel rearranged pillows and blankets on a library sofa. Sunlight washed through the broad window across a low walnut table with sextant at center, shelves of rare and collectable books with gold highlights on the spines reflecting about the cozy room. He tucked Jaden under the blankets. "You have a few days before we arrive in Hamburg. Ample time to discharge what few responsibilities London gave you. You'll benefit from mending the emotional damage you inflicted on him."

Emotional damage? Had Samuel accused *Ivan* of damaging the boy? What a colossal hypocrite. He felt a surge of anger, but his truce with Samuel wasn't the source. Rather his embarrassment, once again confronted by dishonesty over his fears.

"How am I supposed to know what to do?"

"Use your instincts. Listen to him and figure it out. Children don't come with instruction booklets."

"I can't. I'm no good at this sort of thing. I'm not qualified to . . . I have no experience with . . ."

"Really, Stavros, that's an egregious focus on the personal pronoun. Did you know *I* derives from the Latin and Greek words for ego?" He handed Ivan the vaccine ampoule, alcohol wipes and a box of syringes. "Practice selflessness. Start by seeing to the rest of the crew."

***

Sure, there were records, Hamish had said. Bloody lot of them. Used to keep them on the ground floor of Leconfield House with Registry.

"Then in sixty-nine or seventy all the records were moved to that atrocious space in the Gower Street offices, weren't they? Come to think of it, we've got a warehouse in Cheltenham, if you're up for a stroll."

"Little more than a stroll."

"The Registry Queens will know where to look."

Registry had a secure archive not far from the River House. Hamish got Ivan cleared, safe passage, for an all night excursion through stacks piled with colored file folders. Information on Nigel Braithwaite's Cold War years was lacking. Either that or missing. They labored between an old microfiche reader and a poorly lit table strewn with yellowed papers, under the incriminating gaze of a sizable and suspicious Records matron who cracked the ruler across knuckles for sins of failing to re-shelve files. There would be no taking of notes. Were they not aware the terms of the Official Secrets Act? The dignity of their office?

"Ghastly woman," Hamish said. "Mightn't she make herself useful, wheel in some tea and a biscuit? Christ. Like a bullmastiff."

"That didn't sound chauvinistic."

"Come again?"

"Nigel studied at Oxford," Ivan said, reading from the record.

"Course he did. All Souls and British Intelligence, joined at the hip, aren't they? Talk to his professors, all dead I shouldn't wonder, haunting the Bodleian Library where you can read all his intellectual indoctrination. Indulged in every pinko sentiment, not that I'm a Tory, but he was an alright chap, you ask me. Which nobody does. Payroll, they'll tell you he never wanted for more bread, did it for England and Queen, didn't he?"

"I want his codes." Ivan suffered frequent Hamish incomprehensible allegories on the plight of English civil servantry. Looking through the fiche file revealed a repeated name associated with Braithwaite. "Who's Knut Haugland?"

"Changed Nigel's nappies after the war. New recruits, had to purge the water carriers and such, along with the mole. Loathsome business, floating the ship of state, right? Trying to keep the Krauts out while a Marxist prig takes the helm right under our nose. Nigel joined during the years of our inglorious carnival show, intelligence at a zenith, but it was all double double games, useless as the hope we inked it on. Had to scrap the Will and Last Testament, didn't we? Couldn't tell the bishop our knickers were full of mud. Whitehall ecclesiastics ready to hang the lot at midday. Dreadful years."

Ivan pulled a tangent file and found Operation Grouse, a success untarnished by an embarrassing loss of Dutch agents to German capture across the North Sea. "Rotten poem code they were using," Hamish said. "God bless Leo Marks for ending that fiasco."

Einar Skinnarland helped design Norsk Hydro, a heavy water plant at Rjukan, laboratories on the Barren Mountain between Vermok and Rjukan in Hardangervidda. When the Germans invaded Norway in 1940, they purposed the heavy water plant to produce export for Germany. Still working as an engineer, Einar became SOE's spy, sending the Inter Services Research Bureau and Special Operations Executive intelligence on German ship movement, troop posts, and plans. He was convinced the plant had to be destroyed.

In February of 1942 team Grouse, comprised of Norwegians dressed in British uniforms, infiltrated with high explosives and demolished the plant. Helberg, Idland, Strømsheim, Poulson and Storhaus crossed into Sweden and celebrated, while Haugland, Kjelstrup and Haukelid stayed in Hardanger to monitor the damage along with Einar.

"After the war, Knut helped new agents cut their teeth. First rate Morse operator he was, and an even better coder. Nigel did a stint in Norway and was one of Knut's pupils."

"What about the codes? Nigel's code practice? You don't keep records on their tradecraft?"

"Word of mouth, seems. Whatever the Norwegian taught him. Hope it wasn't the poem code, *Oh Yet We Trust*, send another perfectly good agent into the Vaterland risking his life so a Soviet in love with Tennyson can pry into his grocer list and play him double, or worse shoot him in the august years of his life for a political upheaval we know nothing about, the great Red mystery." Hamish paused for breath and thought. "Pretty sure they had the WOKs and LOPs by then, much safer than poem codes. Yet we trust, civilized stubborn bearers of the trailing robe, aren't we?"

"What the fuck are you on about?" Ivan looked at his cup, then at Hamish's. "What's in *your* coffee?"

At four in the morning Ivan found a reference to the Blue Dolphin route. Between an East German safe house and MI6's Office of Applied Services, head soothsayer by the name of Nigel Braithwaite. About damn time.

"Don't have the courier's name."

"We don't need the courier's name," Ivan said. "He can't read the message. He picks up the dead letter drops or whatever. The question is who in East Germany he picks it up *for*?"

"Says right here, doesn't it? Source Manticore."

"Who's the source? Not the codename, his real name. The guy who duplicated the microfilm," Ivan said, holding up the communication about it from Ellison's files. "Who's Manticore?"

Manticore was restricted, said the bullmastiff. Read the fine print. Official Secrets Act.

"Don't be so vulgar. Restricted by who?" Hamish ranted. "Do you know who I am?"

He fought with the bullmastiff for an hour, calls to Whitehall, Special Branch, the River House, until his name was added to the distribution and the woman was mollified. She brought him the duffel on Manticore, secured with a frayed brown tie lashed around the buckle.

Under a sea of black redactions was bare little, a Doctor Bastien Köhler from Norway, who also studied at Oxford, recruited by Nigel Braithwaite and took his coding instruction from Knut Haugland. The evidence was mounting, and the destination Leipzig. Blue Dolphin carried intelligence product for Bastien, Nigel's agent abroad and head of a small network of spies in Leipzig codenamed Source Manticore. There were no remaining records on the nature of the intelligence.

"Should be here, file's missing. See where the dust scrapes are?"

At the table they reviewed every mean scrap on Bastien. Couple of uninformative references to chemical engineering, and a rare debriefing or two, which never included a file closure.

"Did Bastien Köhler come back to England after the Cold War?"

"Not likely after this transgression." Hamish practically ejected the black and white picture across the table at Ivan. It showed Bastien in the arms of a beautiful woman. The concept of honeypot traps again crossed Ivan's mind.

"Treason? Is she a Soviet?"

"Worse. German. Bastien fell in love with a local and married her, the paramount sin for an agent."

"Is Bastien still alive?"

"I'm sure I don't know," Hamish said. "Dial 100, see if they'll connect you. What's all this about?"

"That's my business."

"Spent the night looking up our skirt, least you can tell me is why I've got four men in hospital over your little West End escapade. I've played Watson to your Sherlock Holmes, you can bloody well throw me some juicy gossip for the fish farm. Have to keep the bishops at bay, don't I?"

Ivan tossed the thumb drive on the pile of papers. "When I'm done, I'll tell you who assassinated Nigel and why. How about that?"

"Kinky. I'll take it."

"Hamish?" Ivan zipped his coat. "It's been a pleasure."

"Don't lie. I'll tidy up. Be sure the bullmastiff shows you the gift shop on your way out."

* * *

Who killed Nigel was easy. It was *why* Ivan needed to find before he could tell Hamish.

Spread on the floor of the ship's library was a mess of forbidden notes, Ivan sitting in the middle, leaning against the sofa where Jaden wrestled with a fever sweat. The boy's eyes were closed but not asleep. The labored breathing exhaled with a rasped mew, as though he had the smallest tin whistle in his throat.

With his left hand Ivan studied the encrypted columns, not seriously expecting the plaintext to spring forth. His right hand lay on the silkscreened smile of Thomas the Tank Engine, fingers stroking an upset stomach through the blue pajama top. Relentless warmth radiated from the boy, the sweet talcum scent of fresh playfulness subdued under a doleful miasma, a mixed emanation like the tainted odor of chewed sunflower seeds. Ivan took a cloth to Jaden's forehead.

Eight years ago Ivan accepted a job from a man not unlike Hamish to expire an old Cold War spy passing secrets to the Chinese. From an empty flat he watched an eighty-year old man in flannel nightgown across the lane warm a kettle and pace a Victorian row loft on Lancaster Road.

Behind him Ivan could hear traffic on the nearby A40. The scope on his Romak 3 was doped for 60 meters, give or take, and a 15 kilometer an hour crosswind.

It had to look like a Kremlin FSB hit.

One 7.62 x 54 round waited in the chamber. Waited for Nigel Braithwaite to steep two Earl Grays with a cube of sugar, check the three separate door locks and latches, fill in the crossword, and fall asleep in an eggplant armchair with the favored Leeds rugby team shirts for armrest doilies. A pickle tin ashtray on the table, gin and tonic lunch in memory of lost memories, the propped open paperback facedown, artifacts of a life alone and measured by caution and vigilance, like the mostly read P.D. James murder mystery. *It is not when we contemplate violence that the primitive instinct to kill takes over, it is only when we strike the first blow.* Waiting. Death wasn't just a matter of accuracy, but ultimately the order of things and finality in terms both clean and humane.

Nigel would never know who did it, neither in Ladbroke Grove that night, nor in the fate of P.D. James's characters.

Except British Intelligence was really Hizer Pharmaceuticals. Ellison's words from Seoul at the forefront of his mind, Ivan still had difficulty stomaching the CIA's control of his every contract, and that Nigel was another ordered hit for them and Hizer. Nigel's absconded secrets were never the drug company's in the first place. Hizer's hidden files came from Source Manticore in East Germany seven years before Ivan was born. A different era, Hamish's era, secrets the currency of death.

The *why* remained. What did Nigel know that threatened Hizer? Somewhere in the enigmatic character columns was an answer. Ivan held the coded message, so close to the truth, yet so far off.

And why did seven children need to die to keep a secret? How could an 'experimental study' on microfilm a half century old relate to the kids Ivan was sent to kill in this perverse fashion?

He'd asked Samuel how much of each of the coded messages was the indicator group. Samuel said computer analysis could never be certain, but it was unlikely to exceed ten characters. Ivan focused on the first fifteen characters. Message one began ADJEF HEHEF CICLD. Assuming he still had to use numeric substitutions, he wrote underneath the numbers each letter produced.

Message 1:
ADJEF HEHEF CICLD
0 3 9 4 5 7 4 7 4 5 2 8 2 11 3

Message 2:
AFFDO LMOGE OECIN
0 5 5 3 14 11 12 14 6 4 14 4 2 8 13

Message two began with slightly larger numbers. What did that mean? He stared at the sequences, hoping a pattern would emerge, or clues where the indicator group ended and the coded message began. Were any of the numbers at identical spots the same, hinting at a check character for end of indicator group? Yes, at character space thirteen they were both Cs, or number 2. Which could still be a coincidence. They both began with A, either a null character, or perhaps a symbiant collation. Or it was meaningless. He became frustrated, realizing how futile the task was. For an hour Ivan let the numbers sear into his memory.

He found nothing and helped Jaden clear his nose with a tissue.

Up the stairs from the galley trudged Noah, in his arms a tray, which he set on the coffee table. Chicken club sandwich for Ivan, broth and crackers for Jaden. Noah also set down the bottle of blackberry brandy Ivan requested, partly for himself but also believing a finger or two might settle Jaden's insides.

"How's my brother doing?"

"He's getting through the tough part." How would Ivan know?

"What are you working on?"

"Nothing."

"It's a lot of nothing," Noah said, looking across a foldout map with drawn arrows and a circle around Leipzig.

Ivan crushed saltines into the broth and stirred. The ship's nearly silent journey across a dark ocean, one lonesome North Sea cell tower buoy to the next, created only the faintest sense of motion. He let the crackers soak.

"Are you afraid he'll puke it up again?"

"It happens."

"Let me help." Sitting cross-legged at Jaden's head, Noah coaxed his brother to sit up in his lap, saying things like, There you go, buddy. "It's okay if he can't keep it down."

"No it's not."

"It's not his fault. You think he has a choice?"

"I didn't mean it like that." Ivan couldn't seem to say what he felt. The retching and tears bothered him. He didn't like suffering. Of all the sensation between life and death, witnessing pain disturbed Ivan most. He preferred the peaceful, if short, intermissions when Jaden slept. The last six hours were broken by the frequency with which Ivan carried him to the bathroom for another runny bowel that nevertheless managed to hurt. Having failed to keep food down, it wasn't clear what Jaden was eliminating. Maybe his own stomach acids, burning him at both ends. He'd sit on the bowl, hold out his hands, and Ivan felt frustration. I don't know what you think I'm supposed to do for you, kid. I can't make it better.

Then arms were around Ivan's neck, warm head on his shoulder, surrender of volition. Ivan felt he'd done nothing at all to earn a bond that, if he'd led a normal life, might have seemed paternally familiar. He'd never felt this kind of compassion, maybe even love, and it caused him acute ache he managed to ameliorate by the inconsequential act of feeding Jaden one spoonful of soup at a time.

Ivan could not put this sensation into words for Noah, who at any rate looked as though he shared Ivan's emotions and understood, vicariously afflicted by Jaden's discomfort the way brothers can be. Ivan felt a change taking place and hated Samuel for forcing him to learn his own weaknesses, jealous there were steps in the human experience better understood by a man like Samuel, and then shame for both the anger and the jealousy.

"I had fun in London," Noah said. "I just wanted you to know."

"I'm not sure fun is the word for kidnapping an MI6 chief."

"Yeah but still. Where are we going now?"

"Germany, the former Eastern bloc."

"Are you kidnapping anyone?"

"I hope not."

Jaden coughed, half swallowed soup on his face. Noah pulled up the edge of his own shirt to wipe it. "Are you going to need help?"

"No." Ivan saw the dejection. He decided not to repeat his ingrained prejudices. Noah had proved useful, and Ivan didn't want to disparage that. "Maybe. If I need help, can I count on you?"

Noah smiled. "I've got your back."

32

"What is this? The rapo tray?" Teagan leaned over, pushed his breakfast tray back through the slot and tried to get a look at who was serving. "How about a second waffle, short stuff? Hook this shit up."

Behind him in line Cody checked to see if any officers heard Teagan. Cody didn't like the way Teagan casually used the term rapo, knowing Cody had a sex offence. Teagan's behavior was very confusing.

Scooter and Filthy had seats saved for them.

Filthy got out of the hole a couple weeks ago. His skin still had chemical burns from the OC spray. He said they put him in four-point for sixteen hours before hosing him down.

By then the wrinkled shirt and pants slimed to his body left permanent stripes. The patterns were actually pretty neat looking, but Cody could tell Filthy still hurt. He needed more time to heal.

Filthy seemed to enjoy the attention. He called them war wounds.

"Teagan?"

"I'm not cutting them up for you."

"They're too tough." Cody poked a plastic spork at his waffles.

Teagan tossed Cody's waffles on Scooter and Filthy's trays. "Bonus day. Give him your applesauce."

"What?" Filthy said. "I like applesauce."

"Shovel it over." Teagan gestured with his spork from Filthy to Cody's tray. "You ain't gonna miss it."

"Your cellie on a soft diet, bro?"

"He's losing another tooth. Cut him some slack."

Cody wiggled the tooth with his tongue for them. "I'm going to lose it on Christmas."

"It ain't gonna last that long," Scooter said. "I give you this waffle back, you lose it after one bite."

Christmas was a big event in prison. For four weeks Teagan and Cody would stock up on store items to cook into better things. They'd make chocolate fudge made from layers of chocolate with crushed mint pieces and maple scraped off the maple peanuts. Apple crisp from oatmeal cookies and stewed apples. Candied orange peels dipped in chocolate. Rice crispy treats with M&M's. Lemon filling pie using vanilla frosting with melted caramels and dissolved lemon drops over a piecrust of Oreo cookies with marshmallow and butter.

Christmas would be about chocolate, Teagan said. Sounded good to Cody.

"Tonight's fiesta bean casserole," Teagan said. "Give Cody your jello and he'll trade you the tortillas, since his ragged tooth ain't gonna chew that neither."

Scooter and Filthy agreed.

"I hope it's yellow jello," Cody said. "Yellow because it rhymes. With jello, I mean."

"You be choosing your jello on some funny business," Scooter said.

Tough waffles didn't slow Filthy down. He was a sloppy eater. With a spork and fingers he pushed waffle chunks in the direction of his mouth, syrup running in strings to the tray like towropes for the next piece, the way ski lifts go up and down a mountain. When the syrupy strings got really bad Filthy wiped with the back of his arm, then ran the arm across his leg. One slick wipe, all at once, bits of sticky waffle crumbs clinging to Filthy's tan pants. He did it so smoothly. He must practice a lot.

After breakfast Cody did his best to track through the thick snow by landing his feet in the deep holes pressed by bigger boys ahead of him. All the fences, even razor wire, were crusted with millions of miniature icicles shooting sideways off the fence. Amazing!

"It's called hoarfrost, spud."

Cody giggled. "That's a funny name."

"Yeah it is," Teagan said. He smiled and ran ahead towards the Industry gate, kicking the fence as hard as he could. Snow settling on the metal layers burst off into a powdery cloud, falling over Cody. He pulled off the beanie cap and held his tongue out, eyes closed.

Teagan said every snowflake was different. How could they be? Millions and millions of snowflakes and none the same. How does he know? Did someone look at every snowflake to check?

That seemed like a good job. Snowflake inspector.

He pushed through the turnstile. The gate chirped, reading his electronic tag and granting access to Industries. An officer told him to stand for search. Cody pulled his arms from his coat and held it out. He was used to pat-downs. He didn't call them his privates anymore. Nothing in prison was private, and this officer obviously didn't think so either.

"What's in your back pocket?"

Cody pulled out a sheet of folded paper. "It's a Christmas tree. For Diana?"

"Get outta here."

"Can I have my Christmas tree back?"

The officer crumpled it and said something about contraband. "Are you arguing with me?"

No sir. Cody moved on. It was a loaded question with no safe answer for getting his drawing back. He thought they were tears but when drops hit the snow Cody knew his nose was bleeding again. He bled less often, but if he got upset it happened. Hand clamped over his face, Cody dragged his feet through drips in the snow to hide them from the officer.

Inside Laundry he went straight to Diana's office. Teagan was looking over the daily manifest for Cashmere Elderly Care.

"There he is. What took you so long? Show Diana your drawing."

"Oh my god," Diana said when Cody pulled his hand away. "What happened? Did somebody hit you?"

Diana always had a towel about her. When she ran to him Cody felt it pressed to his nose. "The pigs took your drawing," Cody said. She knelt down and pulled him to her chest in a big hug. "I'll make you a new one tomorrow."

"Teagan, get a washcloth with cold water."

"Why? He's got a face full of titty. He'll be fine."

"Teagan!"

"All right. Whatever. Put him on his back. That'll stop it. He gets these all the time. Doctors messed up his schnoz."

"I'll draw you another Christmas tree."

"Don't worry about the drawing, sweetheart."

"A bigger one. With more lights."

"Okay."

Diana said she'd hang it on her fridge, the one at home. Cody liked that idea. His nose stopped bleeding. Diana said he was lucky to work in Laundry. Plenty of extra clothes and the means to wash the blood out of his shirt. Hours later, near lunchtime, they stopped work so Maintenance could fix a steam pipe. Diana came down the metal stairs with a tub of something Cody hoped were cookies. They *were* cookies, the holiday kind with colored sprinkles.

"Wash your hands first, spud." To Diana he said, "He's been rescuing rats all morning."

"Good boy."

Bruce, the evil supervisor, left sticky-traps out for mice. Cody found them struggling and saved as many as he could by shaking cornstarch on the traps, gently peeling the mice free with plastic spoons so they wouldn't bite him. He spoke softly to reassure them, tell them not to be scared. When they'd been thrashing around all night they got very badly hurt. He found them with skin peeling off. Teagan dispatched those with a swift bash of his boot. Cody knew it was for the best but his heart still broke for them. He buried them in tiny plots off the back loading dock.

He thought of Booboo who never came back.

Diana fished a pack of cigarettes out for a smoke, then handed the pack to Teagan. He helped himself to one, then another for later.

"Pretty brazen, woman. Right out here in the open? Bruce will shit a brick."

"He's not coming in. Some kind of quick surgery. Hopefully it's a lobotomy."

"What's a lobotomy?"

"It's where they scrape your noodles out, spud."

"Huh?"

Diana blew a relaxed stream of smoke away from Cody. "For Bruce that would take rectal surgery."

Cody remembered the word rectal from his ordeal in Medical, but couldn't work out the noodles.

"She's saying his brains are up his ass."

"Oh."

Cody finished several cookies. She asked how many mice he saved? A lot. But none of them were Booboo. Teagan said mice came indoors for winter. He reminded Diana about the pet mouse.

"I had a pet once," Diana said. "A little dog. Priscilla was a neighborhood thief. She'd wander around other people's yards and drag home toys. Doggy toys, I mean. Well, dogs think everything's a doggy toy." Beyond rubber balls, Priscilla brought in porch rugs, rakes, sprinkler heads or, on a less ambitious day, just hose nozzles. Shoes, all sorts of clothes and sheets, even a golf club once. A nice one with titanium parts, now chewed and coated with dog slobber. "You know. Just a naughty little thief and hoard."

"Does she give it back, your dog, the stuff she steals?"

"Not anymore," Diana said. "Priscilla had an accident."

Cody felt his throat stiffen. He thought of Teagan's dog. "Did she get run over by a truck?"

"Worse'n that," Teagan said. "She never told you this story?"

Diana sighed. "Priscilla tried to steal a robo-mower. You know, the kind that doesn't need a sweaty Mexican to push it?"

"No."

"The mower didn't want to be stolen. Priscilla's in doggy heaven." She stubbed out the cigarette on the counter. "Or doggy hell, for all I know."

Teagan went into the gruesome details Diana wasn't keen on sharing. She wasn't keen on listening either. Teagan got a full laundry bag thrown at him. He climbed a supply shelf to look for a bleach bottle hidden from Bruce.

"Do you think Booboo's still alive?"

"I doubt it, spud. They got these sticky traps all over the joint, and no one like you in A-Unit to liberate the little guys."

"He's dead?"

"I didn't say that. I just said maybe."

Cody hoped Booboo didn't die in the snow. He thought of Priscilla, how much worse it would be if she saw her own blood, red against the white snow. He pictured Booboo frozen in a snow bank, no eyes, fur flickering on the exposed side. The image was so clear to him, as though it really happened just that way. It didn't seem fair he couldn't bury Booboo with all the other mice.

"Diana?"

"If they don't get the steam fixed I'll send you boys home for the day."

"Can we bury Booboo?"

Teagan crawled down from the high shelf. "You don't have a dead Booboo to bury, spud."

"Can we pretend?"

Diana thought it was a good idea. Nothing more important to do since the steam was down.

Off the back dock Teagan lowered a symbolic coffin made from a toilet paper tube into a shallow dirt hole beside all the other mice Cody had interred over the year. Teagan looked as though he'd been hijacked into a ridiculous ceremony. Diana bribed him to act nice and be a resolute pallbearer.

"Do you want to say something?" Teagan asked.

"What should I say?"

"Why don't you go first," Diana said to Teagan.

"Dammit."

"Teagan!"

He dropped his head and waved her off. The sky remained dull with a moon-like glow where the sun worked its way through the separating clouds. Ice melt collected in gutters, trickling with broken patter onto the loading dock where over the years it made a divot in the concrete. A forklift by the inner perimeter fence had its fork raised all the way up. An engine block dangled from it by a chain, which someone in Maintenance was fixing last summer. Snow collected in each of the cylinder holes. The incessant prison announcements over the campus megaphones were barely audible in this back corner of the complex. The air was quiet. Teagan took his time, one hand on his hip, the other finishing a smoke. He stared off into a sky out of Poe with Hitchcock's birds crowding on the towers and fences. Cody thought Teagan might be daydreaming.

"Booboo . . . we're gathered here to witness, um, not much, I guess. But we know you're gone. Otherwise you would have come back. I know this because I don't like mice, rats or rodents. Especially if they've snitched on me. But you were very faithful. I mean it. I actually cared about you. You made my cellie happy and he loved you. He made you fat—DOC grub helped—but he also took good care of you. And you took good care of him. That's why I know you'd have come back if you could. You came to us in a toilet paper tube, it's only right you leave in one too. We'll miss you now that you've been paroled to that mouse pad in the sky. Be safe, bro."

Diana said it was Cody's turn. He thought about it and shook his head. For all of his embarrassment, Teagan gave Cody's mouse a sendoff that didn't need more words.

33

Slow rotation of the London Eye had nothing on a Deutsche Bahn ICE train crossing Germany at 330 kilometers per hour.

Between pairs of handprints on the large window were ellipses of Noah and Jaden's nose marks pressed into the condensation of excited warm breath. Noah's closest experience was the London Tube. Jaden had never been on a train. His initial sickness with the primal velocity—visuals moving ten times faster than *Estrella de Mar Rosa*—left him pale until he adjusted. The speed of snow covered forests, cities and farmland whizzing by was a mesmerizing impossibility.

In just over three hours they'd be in Leipzig. A serving cart wheeled by. Ivan asked for three glasses and bought two bottles of Vinternacht beer. Cheaper than the water. Ivan loved the Germans.

"I told him no," Samuel had said of Jaden's pleas.

Before *Estrella de Mar Rosa* had entered the River Elbe Jaden felt much better and had become attached to Ivan, asking permission to go with him on his German adventure.

Samuel objected. "A few hours in London is one thing, but not for such a long period of time."

"With any luck it'll only be three days," Ivan said. "Maybe less. Are you afraid?"

"For his safety? Naturally."

"You're scared he'll like the real world and want to stay."

"Don't be absurd."

Ivan felt sure he was right. So why did Samuel agree to let Jaden go?

At speed the train's cars required cabin pressurization, banking through turns smoothly as though on a long stretch of perfect ice. This was a day of firsts in many immeasurable ways. Jaden and Noah had to cope with frosty temperatures. They'd spent their lives barefoot in a tropical climate. The first class compartment had plastic wrapped fleece blankets in overhead bins. Noah, who still had bandaids on his ankles from walking around London in shoes, bundled his brother in the blanket from the feet up, tying the loose corners over Jaden's shoulders. He looked ready for delivery by stork. Didn't feel cold to Ivan, but what did he know?

"You're right to value their autonomy," Samuel had said. "I told you, ask the youngest aboard what he wants, did I not?"

"Jaden's not the youngest," Ivan said, more an accusation.

"How could I tell him no? And appear to curtail the principle of their curiosities? You've put me in a difficult moral position."

"I rather doubt that."

The arrangement was safer for Ivan. He swept the dust off his Spanish. They had matching EU passports in the name Espinoza, another first for children who'd never had a last name. Their language skills were exemplary, the purest music of Venezuelan Spanish. Not exactly continental, but Ivan doubted any German would notice their conjugate lack of *vosotros*.

More importantly, das Bundeskriminalant would look for a man travelling alone.

Ivan further consented to grooming tips from Peach Fuzz and had to admit the change—well trimmed hair and beard with frosted streaks—made him look younger and even handsome.

"On one condition," Samuel finally said. "You take Noah as well."

"A chaperone? Don't get any ideas. I don't just bat for the other team. I play a totally different sport."

"Why should such an inconsequential dalliance concern me? I trust Noah's instincts over yours."

"Suits me. He's a smart kid." And Noah had Ivan's back. They'd be a team, an idea Ivan felt comfortable with after too many years of lonely wandering.

Ivan's journey came with lots of rules designed to protect the value of Samuel's commercial investments, itemized by an anxious father on a prepaid phone for which only he had the number. Ivan ignored Samuel's code for the prostitots and split a dark beer between their two glasses. He could set his watch by the frequent calls. Are they doing well? Yes, fine. They like the icicles hanging from every roof. Heard the word *kartoffel* and thought it was funny. Noah's butchering the German language for Jaden's amusement. Stop worrying.

Ivan retrieved the two largest icicles he could break loose from the platform, and the boys sword fought until pieces lay across the compartment floor. By Ludwigslust all that remained were wet patches in the carpet. A damp smell of winter dragged indoors.

Bastien Köhler lived in Leipzig's Alstadt, a tight neighborhood of homes not too shabby, nor prohibitively expensive. Bare few details about the man's life existed in typical state records. He'd drawn a state pension until a few years ago when the property changed ownership. Where had Bastien moved? Perhaps Hizer Pharmaceuticals tracked him down and the man went into hiding. Possibly Bastien's neighbors knew his whereabouts. Maybe even the new owner?

Until they'd reached the mouth of the Elbe, Ivan had forgotten what Ellison told him in Seoul: "Whatever they're hiding it has something to do with quadrinary encoding."

Jaden had been lying in Ivan's lap on the same library sofa for a story, *Scuppers The Sailor Dog.* Ivan was obliged to produce exuberant character voices, feeling less and less foolish as he witnessed the boy's delight. Before Scuppers built his little home on the beach, Jaden was asleep. Samuel looked in on them and used an infrared instrument to check Jaden's reduced fever. Ivan repeated Ellison's clue and asked Samuel what it meant?

"The programmer at Carmichaels Research Center required a means to exfiltrate the files."

"Mr. Feige?" Ivan kept his voice low.

"They cremated him for a very specific reason—to destroy the data."

"They couldn't just burn the drive?"

"Feige possessed no such convenient medium in which to carry the archive. The CRC facility scans employees for electronic devices. Feige could have swallowed a thumb drive, and security measures would still find it."

Only one alternative allowed Feige to safely walk out of the CRC with the secret files. Most electronic data remained in binary formats, that is, zeroes and ones. Not all systems were binary. For instance hexanary encoding relied on six-variable matrices. Feige reencoded the data into a four-variable system—quadrinary encoding.

"What other familiar system uses four variables?"

Ivan thought for a moment out of respect, but he'd never heard of computers using quadrinary encoding.

"Your DNA," Samuel said. "A helical sugar phosphate chain with four nucleic acid bases, A, T, C and G, paired into nucleotides."

"I knew that. So he takes it out in a travel mug?"

Samuel shook his head. "Again, security is too tight."

Feige translated the secret data into the RNA of a neutral virus. He then injected himself with the viral briefcase. Hizer's electronic files left the CRC in an undetectable biological format pulsing at 50 kilometers per hour through Feige's arteries. Once outside the facility, Feige could pull blood, isolate the virus, sequence its RNA, and decode the data back into binary format readable by any computer.

"They knew he was carrying the data in his bloodstream," Ivan said. "Burning him killed the virus. Did they find out from the encrypted messages?"

"They must have surmised it be other means. They killed him right after he sent the last communication to Nigel. There wouldn't have been time to decode, were it even possible."

"How extensive were the files? I mean, could Feige have fit them in one tiny virus?"

Samuel laughed. He gently lifted the boy's arm by the wrist, Jaden still sound asleep, and stroked the back of the hand. "DNA is the most efficient storage system we know. It holds two bits of information per nucleotide. Seventy kilobytes packed in every micron." He held Jaden's index finger. "If all human knowledge ever recorded were encoded to DNA helices, the resulting mass would consume less space than this tiny digit."

It was a shocking concept, in the realm of trying to perceive the infinite scope of the universe. To think, the cells of his own body possessed such a sophisticated data recording system. Feige could have walked from the CRC carrying the entire Library of Congress and wouldn't have weighed so much as an extra gram.

When Samuel left, Ivan extricated himself from Jaden and pulled the blanket over the boy. It was the first time he'd ever kissed someone goodnight.

Now swiftly piercing into the heart of eastern Germany, responsibility for the lives of others screwed with Ivan's emotions. Thirty years of careless decisions afflicted no one but himself, and when he hurt, the pain had drawn from animus. These new sensations cried from a deeper core within, demanding more of his soul, but rewarding with strength which anger never provided. From here on, the safety of vulnerables depended on Ivan's every move.

Most vulnerable, a little boy in prison who couldn't possibly know that secrets in Leipzig, 10,000 kilometers away, might save his life.

* * *

Ivan checked them into the hotel and went searching for Bastien's home by bus and on foot. Leipzig was an industry powerhouse at the junction of the Parthe, Luppe and Pleisse Rivers. He and the boys crossed the cobblestone square and walked through the arched colonnade of Lieipzig's old town hall. Noah took lots of pictures. Now a museum, the Renaissance clock tower gave them two hours until sunset.

Much had been rebuilt, although World War II had done less damage as they walked farther from the center of town. Houses built from gingerbread fairy tales still existed, interspersed with modern shopping plazas, graffiti and grocers next to upscale Beate Uhsa sex novelty stores. It was said of Germany every town had its own brewery and cathedral, and Leipzig had each in abundance. Saint Nicholas Church was the starting point of the Monday Demonstrations against communist rule in East Germany. Friedrich Nietzsche and Richard Wagner studied at the University here. Felix Mendelssohn, whom Ivan recently drowned from the back of a ferry, was the famous conductor for the nearby Gewandhaus Orchestra. Goethe said of his native city, *If you inquire what the people are like here, I must answer, The same as everywhere.* Clearly he was wrong.

Bastien's house stood three stories high on a narrow lot between similar units. A low iron gate protected snow covered gardens out front, fresh footprints through day old powder otherwise marred by buildup fallen from two leafless maples.

Elizabeth Krupp was not quite Ivan's age, and on paper appeared unremarkable. Spotty education, apprenticeships ending with a job as a pharmacist at a nearby Apotheke. Ivan was therefore understandably surprised when she answered a three-lock door with a greeting terse even by German standards and holding a Walther behind her back.

"I said, I'm looking for Bastien Köhler."

"And I heard you the first time. You have the wrong house."

She tried to slam the door on Ivan, but he forced it back. He could see her breath catch, hand tighten around the pistol, trying to decide whether to yell for help. She wasn't a screamer.

"I assure you that won't be necessary. But you *do* know who I'm talking about." She was in the black and white picture, the one Hamish showed him from the Registry archive in London, though obviously Elizabeth was too young to have been the same woman in Bastien's arms. The connection was obvious. Did the CIA get to Elizabeth? Was that why she hid behind her mother's maiden name?

"You need to leave."

"He's dead, your father. Am I right? Did Hizer kill him? I'm sorry, really I am. But I need your help."

She stared at Ivan, watched the two kids toss snow around for the first time. She had a physical presence greater than the sum of exasperated movements. He watched her reluctance retreat with the slowness of shadow into the darkened space behind her. "Who are you?"

Who indeed? "These are my boys, Noah and Jaden. They don't speak German."

"Fantastic. How does that answer my question?"

"I'm Nikos. May we come in?"

* * *

"Chemotherapy was born here," Elizabeth said. "My father believed he'd find answers in Leipzig."

Torn between awkwardly relegating Ivan to the front steps or inviting him in, Elizabeth chose the latter. She brewed coffee measurable by viscosity and found the boys soft drinks. Small logs burned in the fireplace in which Jaden took inordinate interest, not least for having walked through snow-covered streets for hours. They were happy to pull off the offensive boots.

Bastien Köhler's doctorate was in epidemiology, Elizabeth had explained. His interest in cancer research gave England a plausible reason to post him to East Germany, working in a local medical lab believed to be synthesizing chemical weapons. Leipzig was home to a number of suspect industries the West infiltrated or cultivated local intelligence from, a network of spies known collectively as Source Manticore.

Bastien met a virologist at the laboratory and they worked together pursuing the biology of cancer. Elizabeth was born after a period in which Bastien suffered repeated experimental disappointments. Elizabeth's childhood recollections often involved her father's disillusioned anecdotes.

"On a train from Berlin to Frankfurt in the late nineteenth century Ehrlich described his theory of affinities to colleagues who fell asleep, but he was on to something big—could inorganic chemicals be designed to destroy diseases by virtue of affinity between the chemistry and disease?"

A 24-year old medical student in Leipzig, Paul Ehrlich happened upon his theory watching under a microscope the way analine derivatives, used as dyes in the textile industry, stained only specific tissues or structures.

Of course it went nowhere, buried by a history of uncooperative science. Infighting ensued between the primacy of surgical responses to cancer and chemotherapeutic solutions once derided as akin to beating a dog with a stick to get rid of the fleas.

"In the seventies there was a disconnect between oncologists' interest in the causes of cancer, and those searching for a cure." Elizabeth's living room was overtaken by mounted canvases leaning against each other. She moved them around to make the space easier to share. "My father wanted to bridge the gap. Did you know a chemo drug was discovered by studying the bone marrow of mustard gas victims after the first war?"

Ivan understood the question to be rhetorical. "This is where Bastien lived?"

"It's bigger than my apartment. I grew up in this house. After he died I moved my things here, but as you can see, I'm not finished. Part of me doesn't want to finish. I don't know why I'm telling you this."

"What happened? I need to find out why Hizer Pharmaceuticals killed him."

"You keep saying Hizer, but I don't know who it was or what they were after. Father killed himself, presumably to safeguard secrets."

Three years ago Elizabeth came to visit and found Bastien dead in the middle of a ransacked upstairs office. The coroner concluded poisoning by potassium cyanide.

"He swallowed his L-tablet. British spies had a hole drilled into a back molar for concealing the poison. I knew he was a spy, but he never said anything about his dental work. At his age I was surprised he still had his own teeth. It sounded like something out of a film fantasy."

Ivan asked if the intruders found what they were looking for, but how would she know? Elizabeth straightened up the office in a mechanistic manner borne out of shock, but could no longer go up to the third story now without seeing Bastien's body splayed out on the wooden floor.

As if imagining the scene, she averted her eyes, self conscious and looking for distraction that came in the form of Noah scrambling from a burst of embers when the burning log crumbled and fell though the grate. Their behavior wasn't what one might call typical, and Elizabeth's question more derisive than the answer merited.

"Haven't they seen a fireplace before?"

"Probably not."

"Did you know the first recorded description of an occupational malignancy was for children who swept chimneys in London?"

"Why children?"

"They were small enough to fit. Father said it was a cruel task. Chimney sweeps came from the lowest strata of society. They were dirty street urchins, sent up the flu nearly naked and slicked with oil so they wouldn't get stuck. A London surgeon named Percival Pott—I found his name funny when father used it—didn't know he'd essentially discovered the role of carcinogens. Tar particles built up in the wrinkles of their scrotums and by puberty they had testicular cancer. Doctors cut the organs off—without anesthesia, street urchins receiving no such luxury—but cancer made its way up into the body."

She said the trade called it soot wart and eighteenth century doctors were convinced the painful hard sores were syphilis from unclean sex. They'd treat it with mercury-based drugs, which only exacerbated the cancer. The saying was *One night with Venus, followed by a thousand nights with Mercury.*

"Or a short, miserable life if you were an abandoned five year old apprenticed into that hell," Elizabeth said.

Having found Elizabeth attractive in a way that scared him a little, Ivan's balls now signaled a soreness unhappy with her cancer stories. "Elizabeth, I'm on the trail of the people who caused your father's death. I'm reluctant to ask you, but would it be possible to see Bastien's study?"

"They kept looking for a virus, but that's not how cancer works. Cancer comes from inside our own cells."

"Elizabeth?"

"I know. I heard you."

* * *

Bastien's office was a half floor with the steep roof angle cutting in just below shoulder height. Bookshelves stuffed with torn spines and denuded hardcover backs remained from Hizer or the CIA's routing. Some heat passed up the stair access from below but the room was otherwise cold, reflecting the expectation of use.

She'd mentioned analine dyes to stain tissues. Bastien, as a spy, would have an entirely different use for them. Ivan found the photo equipment in a closet under boxes of rudimentary older toys, and then a box of Lego, typical of frugality coming of age with perestroika.

In the last century silver halide emulsion gave camera film quality at a granular level. But analine dye was required for the resolution of microfilm. Bastien's microscope array, lenses and trays were all empty. Ivan inspected two syringes with needles trimmed so they could pick up microdots. Empty. Ivan didn't expect to find the critical microfilm. He was looking for clues.

With the same detailed attention used in Piccadilly, he took apart the study and found everything but microfilm or code systems. No journals or notes. No meaningful scribblings in the margins. The chalkboard was wiped clean. He inspected the backside and ran a towel over it checking for secret writing or intentional imperfections. He found a Morse keyboard and radio transmitter hidden in the standard false bottom windowsill ledge, but it revealed nothing more than it did when the CIA wiped their fingerprints off the wooden case. Elizabeth watched apprehensively, sitting on the final step ascending to the floor and surrounded by a bannister.

He sat in Bastien's chair and rifled the contents of the top drawer beneath the blotter. Pictures of Elizabeth's mother, whom Ivan neglected to ask about. He would later learn she perished from heart failure a few years before Bastien. Pens, binder clips, yellow and white chalk, notepads and detritus common to any desk. Various anatomy and pathology books. An old pack of Carlton cigarettes. Ivan was tempted to sample one for medicinal purposes, see if tobacco aged as good as wine. Where the exposed roof joists came to the peak, knurled bridges with ornamental carving were fixed between the gables. One of the decorative turned caps was missing and Ivan stared with resigned hopelessness.

"You didn't find anything." She seemed dejected, as if he should have made this tragedy right. Isn't that what he'd promised?

"Ironic, don't you think?" He leaned back and held the pack up in front of the round window, eighteen filtered tips peeking from the top, two gone. "Spent his life studying cancer while he smoked."

"Father didn't smoke."

"I get it. They're a metaphor," Ivan said.

"They were part of his tradecraft. He said if you carry secrets, you also have to carry the means to get rid of them." She finally stood up and joined him in the room. Beside an oil lamp on one of the shelves, in front of a row of National Geographic magazines, was a matchbox. She opened the box and held out a match. "He learned it in Norway. It was a trick Norwegian spies used during their occupation by the Germans. Wrap the microfilm around the head of a match. If caught, burn the match and the evidence of espionage goes with it. The cigarettes are just subterfuge."

Ivan took the match and lit one of the cigarettes, a near heresy made palatable by the realization that came to him, slowly at first, and then with a disheartening swiftness he still managed to laugh about.

On the notepad he wrote out the Cold War Morse code message that brought Hizer to Bastien's door looking for the copy of incriminating microfilm:

Prepared matched set of microfilm
of research for experimental study
Sending by Blue Dolphin route

There was no copy. *Matched set.* Microfilm wrapped around the head of a match. Damn the Norwegians.

"What's so funny?"

"You have no idea." Ivan felt the chances for success slipping away.

Barefoot steps on the stairs followed with Noah's head peeking through the wooden rungs. He held the phone out to Ivan. "*Perdon? Mi papa quiere hablar contigo, Nikos.*"

"Gracias."

He listened to Samuel Coletti without saying much. He hung up and handed the phone to Noah. "*No podemos a regresar al hotel. Problemas con la policia. Tenemos que vivar aqui si ella permite.*"

"*Entiendo.*" Noah disappeared down the stairs.

"You're not laughing anymore," Elizabeth said. "Did I hear the word 'police'?"

Ivan enjoyed the nicotine in silence, somewhat aware of all the unfulfilled resolutions he'd made to himself. This time it would be possible, and the reason waited for an answer.

"Our arrangements in town are compromised. Sooner than I expected. I need more time. How do you feel about a longer visit from people you don't know and shouldn't trust?"

Elizabeth made what sounded like an oath, the loose translation from German being, *It doesn't get eaten as hot as it gets cooked.* She was right, life seldom went as planned.

"Secrets can kill," she said. "You're harboring too many. I've lived stressful years wondering what I should be afraid of, and while I appreciate you think you've discovered closure, It's not my job to suffer more disappointments, or find them dead on the floor."

"Is that a yes or a no?"

"I'll make myself clear. Mystery is intriguing. Deceiving me is not."

A reluctant *Yes.* Ivan put out the last cigarette in his life and smiled. "Deal. I need to know more about Bastien's research. Where can I find records of his work?"

"Why? It's all useless. Their experiments were a failure."

"I need to start somewhere."

"You go first. Why are police looking for you?"

Christ, this would be a long night. Truth was an amorphous enigma even to himself. Where to begin? What did she absolutely need to know? Could he trust her with his past? He wanted to. She wasn't gullible. How should he explain his companions? It was a mistake to bring them. But if he hadn't, who's to say she would have let him in the door? How much time did they have? Enough to make her believe helping was in her best interest?

Ivan took too long thinking through the complications, a sign of deceit. He'd essentially done precisely what he'd hoped not to. What would Ellison have said?

"Don't be alarmed if Noah's excited thinking we've kidnapped you."

34

The first night in Hotel Elizabeth was an awkward catharsis. It started with dinner, her plans for which didn't include guests.

Ivan consulted Samuel's diet instructions for the boys. Processed foods were discouraged. When in doubt, stick to fruit. Jaden enjoyed bananas. Dairy products were fine. Be conscious of Noah's mild peanut allergy. Certain fish were okay. No red meats cooked too rare. Nothing heavy on onion, garlic, or other spicy foods likely to make them taste objectionable. What the hell was that supposed to mean? Sounded like cannibalism, until the intent struck. Never mind. Screw Samuel.

Elizabeth left with a wad of Ivan's euros and returned with bags from Schnellimbiss, Germany's less expensive McDonalds. Guten Appetit.

"What did you leave at the hotel?"

"Nothing important." Ivan carried all their passports and medications. He didn't mention the small arsenal of ceramic composite weapons concealed about him. "We left three backpacks. One large, two small." Recently purchased and expendable clothing. Some toiletries. "Nothing that shows where we are."

"If what you say is true, Hizer will know why you're in Leipzig," Elizabeth said. "That'll bring them here."

"I thought of that. There's an escape route if I need it and Samuel's monitoring German police communications. He can stem some probability of Hizer or the CIA getting a tipoff. We also have a temporary disinformation agreement with MI6 that will throw off the CIA."

"Samuel?"

"Friend of ours. In Hamburg." Technically not a lie.

After a sunset involving little sun, street lamps illuminated snowfall outside the window. Small flakes segued into larger and more densely populated ones, tiny gusts like nature's whimsical recipe stirring them into eddies. Jaden rested his head sideways on the back of a sofa to watch, enchanted. The needle on an old record player slid into the runout groove. Elizabeth picked it up and a scratch issued as she set it back down to play *I've Been This Way Before.*

Elizabeth seemed to relax and it wasn't clear to Ivan what prompted the change. Returning from upstairs in a set of forest print joggers, she described genetic merger, how 46 chromosomes grew into wary and slightly introverted.

"Father was a doctor and mom an artist willing to paint what he saw under the microscope. I like medicine, but not enough for a career."

"You're a pharmacist."

"Not at heart." Elizabeth pulled her long hair out of a ponytail and played with the hair tie. "Cancer research is exotic. But dispensing Lipitor?" She sighed. "When I was a little girl I watched The Harald Schmidt Show. I daydreamed of meeting a tall, blonde-haired, witty man when I grew up. Or cavalier, Joschka in sneakers, man of the world, telling Parliament that Germany wouldn't be the U.S.'s lackey. I live in a small play, the same every night, cleaning up after mediocrity. I'm a lousy Easterner. I want a life beyond pills."

"Is that why you paint?"

"You want me to call it escapism?" She chuckled. "Not far enough away."

"These are your paintings?"

She made a self-effacing gesture. "I'm not much of a painter."

"They're amazing."

She shook her head. Ivan studied each, tilting the tall canvases forward in turn. He wasn't an art critic. They might have dismissed the work as blandly scenic. But the life-like scenes drifted at the edges to impressionist amalgamations of truth and fantasy, the visual characteristics of magical realism where earthly beasts crossed into the realms written by Neil Gaiman. She anthropomorphized frightening creatures from the harshest German fables by painting them in a real world.

"Ever sell anything?"

"I can't sell these."

Did she mean *wouldn't*, or did she doubt their value? "Have you tried?"

"Not exactly."

She'd been invited to share an adjunct gallery with a famous artist from Leipzig, Neo Rauch, whose figurative color technique and style was influentially evident in Elizabeth's paintings.

"If I were to sell these, then what? Is that a life calling? Paint, market, profit, repeat?"

"What's wrong with that?" Ivan said. She didn't answer. "I know someone with an art collection that could use diversification."

He couldn't read her. She was strong and melancholy in divergent measures, artist and doctor, a complete gene-set gift of unclear prospects.

She showed Noah and Jaden the bath and left them to discover how long it took hot water to pull from a basement heater. From her own wardrobe came several pairs of sweatpants—her waist size only a little larger than Noah's—and commemorative t-shirts abandoned by the Algerian tourist she'd slept with before their relationship fell into emotional rejection. One was from the Karneval street party, the other a Munich Oktoberfest shirt from years ago. Jaden slept in just the shirt since it went down past his knees.

"He doesn't typically wear a full set of pajamas," Ivan said, recalling the leopard spotted PJ bottoms with a tail that had made him look like a fawn. "Either the top or bottom. Seldom both."

Ivan pulled the cap off a container full of unmarked powdery tablets each of the boys were to take once a day. What were they? Samuel's blunt answer had further stressed the irreconcilable contrast between Coletti the caretaker and Coletti the exploitive business owner. The drug suppressed, or at least delayed, development of secondary sex characteristics. Essentially, the pills extended commercial viability.

Obliged to issue from the bottle, Ivan felt complicit in the most uncomfortable way. Were Noah and Jaden aware of what the pills did? Ivan could interrupt the whole charade, flush them down the toilet. Abscond with them permanently.

But they weren't his children. Moreover he recalled Samuel's mention of implanted GPS tracking tags in all the boys of his harem. For insurance purposes. Which made no sense. Regardless, Ivan wasn't sure the idea of saving the kids had merit. They would return to the ship soon enough, as Ivan had little sense of responsibility and no chance of recovering his own life without Samuel's help. *Truce* became an overburdened promise. He watched them swallow, knowing his resignation amounted to all the flaws Elizabeth would find in him.

"What have you done?" she asked.

"That's not the same as asking what I do."

"It's clear you don't anymore. But around you hangs a pall, like you're ashamed. So what do you do?"

He wasn't ready for a full confession. "Business. I travel a lot."

"What kind of business?"

"*Das ist doch nicht dein bier.*"

"I think it *is* my right to know," she said. From the small kitchen she brought a liqueur bottle and two small jiggers.

Zum Wohl! Light tap of the glasses on the table before drinking. "It's everything that doesn't add up. You're a secretive 'businessman', but not a government agent. You want to know about cancer research fifty years old, but you're not a doctor. My father's death interests you but only insofar as it achieves . . . what?"

"I don't know."

"That's not an answer. You're not married and say 'probably' these boys have never seen snow or a fireplace or greasy hamburgers, and what else? Aren't you supposed to know these things? The little one was watching the Pro Sieben channel, criticizing circumcised porn without the slightest hint of novelty, diagnosing it in English for Noah the way my father might talk to a patient. You don't find that strange?"

"That he's not circumcised and has an opinion about the options?"

"At six? Are you listening? You're a fraud. It doesn't take a linguist to understand cognates. Noah handed you that mobile and said *his papa* needed to talk to you. They're not remotely related to you, are they? The awkward intimate gestures affected by a man whose fatherly knowledge lacks all rudimentary truth. Real parents know their children's birthmarks. You don't even know if they like french fries. You've never changed a diaper, have you?"

"It's possible," Ivan said. For the first time three days ago, he might have added.

"Possible? Who are you? Men don't look like this, not at your age. What are all these muscles for?" She squeezed around his arms. "The gruesome wounds on your chest?" Also inspected, unbuttoning his shirt with her nimble fingers, tracing how low the scar descended over a rigid pectoral, tugging on the chest hair with mock contempt. "A convicted man on the run? You've killed people? You've been in prison for this? Training like Bruce Lee so you can prance around Germany with somebody else's strange boys, asking about tumors? What game are you playing? They're both tanned, while you could pass for a German in all but that ridiculous foreign accent. And who the hell is Espinoza? You certainly aren't, and I wager neither are they."

"I have an accent?"

"And you want me to trust you?"

When he'd called the night cathartic, it was his need to be candidly examined by a woman he couldn't objectify, like external introspection, if there was such an oxymoron. The upbraiding she delivered masked contradiction, her desperate need for his mysterious ineptitude. Maybe she thought him broken and believed herself capable of the fixing? She asked, was he a *kinderschänder*?

No, that would be Samuel's proclivity. More details he couldn't share.

Ivan proved it to her, twice in the same night, over the contours of a couch stained by too much spilled acrylic paint and not enough body fluids. She cried. Had he done something wrong? Of course, she said, but not at the moment. She cried in relief, articles of clothing scattered on the living room floor, subsuming sex with no finite process. She'd experienced copulation, but not the animal drive he unleashed on her. she craved a brutal conquest, sex like an odyssey, the sweaty, meaty, nervous plunging. Fire erupted in the orchestra pit, issuing untuned noise pulsing in humid waves. A mess of interfering limbs, he held her hair in a fist and pulled, burrowing between her shoulder blades, her breasts chafing across the brocade surfaces, face in the rictus of erotic agony. Not again, she pleaded. The children will wake up and hear us.

The least of Ivan's worries.

* * *

"Of course they *were* producing chemical weapons," Elizabeth said in the morning. "Not my father, but when it came time to sabotage the facility, explosives don't discriminate between canisters of thiodiglycol boiled in hydrochloric acid and potentially beneficial cancer research."

Ivan had kept an eye through the window on two boys playing in fresh snow. "He didn't log his research?"

"Records of unsuccessful chemo treatments? He worked with mice that went up in flames when London green-lighted a plan to bomb the lab. They did the rodents a favor. It always bothered me generations of mice suffered so we could hobble closer to human testing."

"In a strange way, I agree."

Despite the novelty, Noah and Jaden didn't stay out much longer than an hour. Covered in snow and shivering in the entry hall, they stripped naked and hung wet clothes on wooden pegs. Small puddles melted around their discarded boots. They asked to start another fire, having dragged in equally wet fallen tree branches to burn. With reasonably good English Elizabeth suggested they use a dry log from the stack. Four sets of wrinkled red toes lined up near the fledgling flames. She pulled bread and Nutella out for them.

Ivan enjoyed watching her technique, which wasn't as refined as her harping on him the night before suggested. Whose diapers could she claim to have changed?

She followed him upstairs to Bastien's study. The cigarettes taunted Ivan. Hamish had called him Sherlock Holmes, but Ivan wasn't susceptible to the advantageous lucidity Conan Doyle's detective derived from opiates. A smoke wasn't going to help.

"Bastien's partner stumbled on a retrovirus he was very excited about," Elizabeth said.

"Cancer's not viral, is it?"

"It's complicated. Father talked about his work all the time, but don't expect me to remember details. It's been thirty years."

"You're a doctor."

"Pharmacist. Not the same."

"Close enough."

"If you say so."

"Impress me."

She dragged over a heavy wooden chair covered by corduroy cushions tacked down with brass heads. "Cancer cells are the community's juvenile delinquents. They don't respect the wellbeing of cellular society. All their energy is focused on selfish endeavors—feeding, growing, travelling, breeding like crazy. They don't know how to die."

"Sounds like a teenager," Ivan agreed.

"You would know?"

"I've done my share of misbehaving."

"An understatement after last night."

Was that regret? He didn't think so. She had a glow. Intimacy after the sex was strangely powerful. He'd had a need for her to understand he was more than predatory lust, that he cared. For once Ivan felt desire to stay, the muscles she'd scorned wrapped softly around her for hours.

Surely now there was an etiquette for acknowledging the spontaneous passion from last night, but Ivan was oblivious as to what it should be. In the cozy study he looked to her for clues. Teach me what I don't understand.

She must have mistook confusion for impatience and returned to Bastien's work.

"Cell division follows an organized script: DNA creates RNA, the working copy, from which proteins are formed. It goes in one direction. Proteins are essentially the gene realized, and do all the work, making you who you are. Noah's red hair, my hammertoes, your magnificent stamina, all genes sending proteins to build traits. A protein's enzymes dictate how cells behave."

Viruses were RNA. They could inject themselves through cell walls and force havoc, but never altered the DNA.

Retroviruses were different. Against assumed laws governing genetics, upon cell incursion, retrovirus RNA processed backwards, creating DNA which then attached to a cell's genes. RNA to DNA, reverse transcription, afflicting and altering cellular DNA long after the virus was gone.

"Rous Sarcoma Virus was an early example doctors studied, but most people are more familiar with HIV than RSV."

"So viruses do cause cancer?"

She shook her head. "You could say that, but they're a small part of many causes, and only by tampering with cellular DNA. The native cell is still the problem. Cancer is endogenic."

Throughout the genetic code were hundreds of genes that behaved like master switches. They waited for phosphate attachment by kinase enzymes to activate or deactivate pathways, signaling for growth, movement, and death. Regular gene mutations were normal, there being many backup master switches. Too many gene mutations interfered with those signals, inducing cancerous behavior. Carcinogens like tobacco or radiation increased the frequency of natural mutations, and therefore the probability of silencing the multiple checks-and-balances function inherent in every cell. Cancer was the cell master switches permanently stuck and unable to perform their function of self-destructing the malfunctioning cell. No control signals, left in berserker mode, never dying, replicating out of control into tumors. Industrious, and with the whole genetic code for organ life at their disposal, cancer cells coopted artery and tissue growth to sustain the lethal crusade for supremacy of the organism.

"So, basically cancer and politicians have a lot in common," Ivan said.

She either didn't hear him, or the lowbrow cliché wasn't witty enough for German political humor.

"I hear all the time that so-and-so is fighting cancer," Elizabeth said. "*She's putting up a hard fight*, they'll say. How? As if willpower alone will win."

"Placebo effect," Ivan said.

"Do they really believe they're fighting, or is it something they tell themselves to cope with the fear of hopelessness?"

"People die when they lose the 'will' to live. Why should the mind be any less involved?"

"Cancer doesn't care what you think. Cancer dies when science poisons it."

"And how does that work?"

"Not well," she said.

Bastien's research in the seventies was too primitive to understand how retroviruses reprogrammed genes, but if retroviruses could jam a cell's master switches, could another retrovirus be engineered to carry RNA that reversed the gene mutation? Unjam the switchboard?

Following Ehrlich's theory of affinity, Bastien and his partner stumbled on just such a retrovirus. Like a provirus.

"A cure for cancer," Ivan suggested.

"Cancer panaceas don't exist. At least not yet. Individual cancers relate to mutations of different genes. If you don't know which mutation, you can't engineer retroviruses to fix it. But maybe it would work for *some* cancers stemming from mutations of common genes."

"Did it?"

"Sure, on lab mice. Father needed a test group. He sent the research west where better resources existed for clinical trials."

"That's it," Ivan said. "That's the experimental study on the microfilm sent to Nigel." He thought about Blue Dolphin, the danger of moving medical secrets from Soviet controlled Germany to the West. What if the retrovirus worked?

"It didn't. A broad university trial began with positive responses on pancreatic cancer—unprecedented, in fact. Then all the patients died."

So much for that lead. Hizer wouldn't care about ineffectual cancer treatments. "What else would he have sent to the West through his spy network?"

"Nothing after that. His research lab was burned down. Remember? Father hung his reputation on their retrovirus. By the time I was born his career was all stories with unhappy endings."

"So what did he do? I mean, afterwards."

Elizabeth gestured at the shelf. "Routine pathology for local hospitals. Abstract medical research. Pharmacology."

"I guessed wrong," Ivan said.

"Why? What do the records in London say?"

"The records I needed were missing. I figured Hizer took them. That's why I came here." Ivan pulled a novel by Pat Conroy off the shelf. "Some of these are medical books, but most are fiction and in English. He has multiple copies of more than a dozen novels. I thought he might be translating to German for a publisher."

"Really? Sorry to disappoint you. All those novels are from his Cold War years. They're his codebooks."

35

A codex couldn't be any kind of published novel, he told Elizabeth. Samuel and he had already dismissed the possibility. Unsuitable susceptibility to computer attack.

That didn't stop Ivan's heart lurching against his insides. "How does it work?"

"I don't know."

"How does he know which book? When he gets the message?"

"I don't know."

"Or sends one? How does he tell the recipient which book to use?"

"I don't know! He just called them his codebooks. Is this important?"

"Somewhat." Maybe the letters didn't convert to numbers. Abbreviations for the title or something . . . Ivan thumbed through the Pat Conroy. It couldn't be anything else. He pulled one book after another, tossing it in a pile when nothing jumped out at him.

"What is it?"

"Book numbers," Ivan said. "Nigel's indicator group is a Library of Congress number or something. It has to be."

"What? Indicator group? Slow down. What is this about?"

"Nigel Braithwaite, your father's handler in London. He received a coded message from someone in the U.S. and we need to decrypt it."

"But these aren't Nigel's books."

Ivan sighed. She was right. He had to hope the reason for multiple copies was so a pair could be divided between the correspondents, and maybe there would be some overlap. After five minutes of searching, he almost threw the thirtieth book in the dead pile when the faintest recognition emerged. Perhaps Elizabeth caught his aborted yelp. He grabbed chalk and wrote the ISBN number on the board, and beneath that, the numbers that had burned into his mind from hours of hopeless cogitation, the numeric substitutions for the first two groups of message number two:

ISBN: 0-553-14111-2
Cipher numbers: 0 5 5 3 14 11 12 14 6 4

He stumbled back. Ran to the bannister and yelled down two floors. "Noah! Get me the phone, quick." He couldn't believe it was in his hands. *The Honourable Schoolboy* by John Le Carré. Ivan laughed. It was a spy thriller. Dead now for several years, Bastien Köhler shook Ivan's hand from the Elysian Fields and said *I had a sense of humor once.*

"His codex *is* a book," Ivan told Samuel. He listened to objections, then related the discovery. "The other book isn't here. Do you have the first two code groups for message one?"

"It's a Cormac McCarthy book," Samuel said after condensing the numbers and running a search. "ISBN number 0-394-57474-5."

"Incredible. Holy crap. Samuel? Find me a copy, any used bookstore that can overnight it to Leipzig. What am I looking for?"

"A page number. Soon past the book number the code should give you a page number. It'll be in three digit increments. Vigenère's cipher, start at the top of the page, add the letters up. Call me as soon as you get the message decrypted."

* * *

Twenty-four hours later Ivan feared baldness from the anxiety and stress of being just on the verge of massive unraveling, and yet missing a vital link. The numbers in the code following the ISBN were 14 6 4 14 4 2 8 13.

He tried page 146 first. Nothing translated. Assuming possible null characters, over the next hours, Ivan worked a piece of chalk to a nub using as key page 464, 414 (there was no 641) 144, 442, 428, and 281. Elizabeth would be back shortly. Samuel found an antique bookstore in Leipzig with a copy of the other book and placed a reserve. Elizabeth said she'd pick it up after her shift at the Apotheke.

"Do you like her?"

"Who?"

Jaden had Elizabeth's Lego spread out on a rug she put down for him in the study. He looked up at Ivan. "You know who."

"Elizabeth?" Ivan emptied another cup of coffee, sure he'd had too much over the course of the morning. He was wired. "I suppose so. She's interesting."

"Do you have sex with everyone you think is interesting?"

"Jesus Christ," Ivan said under his breath. Noah emerged from the stairwell with more coffee. Just what everyone needed.

"Don't be upset," Noah said. "Jaden's happy for you."

"I didn't think we were that loud."

"My brother's a sound sleeper." Noah put the coffee down, boosted himself onto the corner of the desk and leaned in close so only Ivan would hear. "You know how genetics work, right?"

"After this week more than ever."

"Genetic engineering science is always advancing. He's six years younger than me. By the time he was conceived there were more options to tweak. Jaden's supersensitive to pheromones."

Conceived. Walking up to a GLS kiosk imbued the term with added meaning. He was a concept. "You're saying he can smell sex."

"That's a coarse way to put it." He got down and checked the chalkboard. "But basically yes. He senses your emotional changes through pheromones and instinctively knows how to interpret them. How's the decoding going?"

"Nothing yet. Get your brother's interpretive sniffer on this book." He showed Noah pages of decryption keys and gibberish results. "I know this is the right book. Or we've stumbled on the most profound coincidence ever, which I don't buy."

"What if Nigel and Feige had a pre-agreed page number? And it's not in the indicator group?"

"That's a good thought."

Noah offered to help. Together they started from the center of the book and worked outward in both directions. This assumed the ciphertext began after the ISBN, and if wrong on account of false characters designed to throw them off, the exercise might be in vain.

What about their tags? he'd asked Noah the other morning. Ivan excoriated concepts like remorse, yet the rescue idea lingered as a way to atone for six dead children. Noah didn't know where they were located but pointed to his navel, as sometimes his bellybutton itched. How could he not know? "When we get a new brother Dad and Elias do all the initial stuff—evaluation, vaccinations, health tests, tags. You saw the nursery. We were babies." Why did Ivan want to know?

Never mind. The things Ivan couldn't do without his rig. He asked Elizabeth if her Apotheke had a medical tag reader and whether he might borrow it? Ivan didn't expect much from the unsophisticated device. Jaden played along with arms out and legs spread, like wanding at the Hauptbahnhof before boarding his first train. Hoping for a response along his arms, Ivan got nothing all the way down to the boy's feet.

Not satisfied, he held the device closer across Jaden's abdomen and chest. At the left shoulder the locator emitted the faintest hum.

The tag was buried down deep between the forks of his collarbone and shoulder blade. No simple slice and splice, it would take a minor surgical procedure to extract the capsule.

What Ivan didn't expect was a handshake. It was an ISO conformed tag with thermocouple, sending out a GPS ping once every five minutes. Pressed into the soft cavity behind Jaden's clavicle, the medical reader docked and downloaded everything on the tag. Jaden put his shirt back on and asked if he was sick? Not that kind of exam, kiddo.

Ivan transferred the sixty gigabytes of data to his tablet. Sixty gigs! What the hell was Samuel Coletti storing on them?

Ivan pulled Noah's tag data while he was sleeping, yet another mystery that had to wait for later.

Focusing on Nigel's code took precedence. Noah thought he had a lead, an overlap of text and ciphertext that produced the word 'WATER.'

"Maybe it's an anomaly."

"I don't want to believe that. More likely the first sign of a pattern."

"Nothing around it texts out," Noah said.

"Try skipping a character." Ivan's heart raced, helping Noah work the subsequent paragraph without success.

"Human brains are wired to look for patterns," Noah said, "Even when they aren't there."

When Elizabeth returned they were still at it. Ivan switched to the McCarthy book, plugging away at endless permutations until both of them were mentally numb.

Jaden had by then quite a Lego fortress assembled around him. He drove little cars through a portico that rose up a slot. Engaged with the Danish toy bricks for a long time, he suddenly scrunched up his face and got Ivan's attention.

"Do you think I'm interesting?"

* * *

"You have to actually tell her those things," Noah said.

"What?"

"That you love her."

"I didn't say I loved her." Ivan had a headache from another day of futile efforts decoding the messages. There was no doubt both books held the key. Samuel sent Ivan an email. Sales records confirmed Richard Feige mail ordered a stack of books a month before his death, including both the Le Carré novel and *All The Pretty Horses* by McCarthy.

Decoding longhand was pointless. Samuel's server farm in Miami had the full text from both books, slicing away letter by letter every possibility, faster than Noah or Ivan could with a billion pieces of chalk.

Ivan joined them on the carpet, even snapped some blocks together, not sure what he was doing and leery of taking relationship advice from Peach Fuzz.

"Are you sure?" Noah said.

"Sure of what?"

"That you don't love her. Say it out load. Try it. Say 'I don't love Elizabeth.' Do it."

Ivan shook his head.

"Good," Noah said. "We've got that out of the way. You love her. I don't mean in some high school girlfriend way, a passing interest. Your oxytocin levels jumped and guess who noticed?"

Ivan gave Jaden a suspicious look. The boy ducked his head in bashful avoidance, disappearing behind a blonde curtain of lightly curled hair.

"She fascinates you," Noah concluded.

"How would you know?"

"Duh. I've got the next best thing to a PHD in human relationships. Did she call you from work?"

"Yeah," Ivan said. "She wanted to know if we needed another book."

"How many times?"

"How many times what?"

"How many time did she call you?"

Ivan tried to remember. "Three times? Maybe four."

Noah laughed. "To talk about books?"

When he put it like that it was kind of obvious. Ivan felt embarrassed.

"She's your type," Noah said.

"And you're supposed to know what I like." Ivan let out a huff.

"What color are her eyes?"

Ivan tried to visualize her. "Blue? I'm not sure."

Noah crawled over on his knees and in abrupt violation of Ivan's sense of personal space put his hands on each side of Ivan's head. "Look at me. What are you scared of?"

Ivan pulled back but Noah held him firmly. "I'm not scared. I don't like being touched. I mean, not by . . . I don't know."

"You're not used to it. What do you see?"

Ivan forced himself to look. To say he was uncomfortable would be understatement. What was he supposed to see? Noah's neck seemed too thin, ears pushed out by thick lops of red hair streaked to amber at the ends near his forehead. Freckle concentration imbalanced, more on one dimple than the other. He had a slight pug nose, turned up to expose the pink flesh on the outer edge of each nostril. Hardest to accomplish was looking into Noah's eyes, the same wet surfaces that had unnerved him the first time they met. He felt as if looking at something he shouldn't, into someone he shouldn't. Dark lashes paired off in clinging embrace, creating an almost decorative shadow, minute trembling of eyelids that blinked to resurface the moist depth of his eyes. They became Noah's essence, his only vulnerability. So close, Ivan could see the mysterious luminescence of green fibrous tissue beneath the lens contract, dark pupils grow deeply haunting.

Noah's voice softened. "You're shaking. It's okay. There's a simple enough reason. Elizabeth's a strong-willed woman. You're assertive and find it hard to respect weak people. You need someone equally strong, and when you see it, your curiosity is excited but fed by a tiny bit of nervous energy. You like her for the same reasons Dad picked me to brief you on your uncle's material. I'm a dominant. Dad knew you'd listen to me."

He let go, Ivan able to safely breathe, a close call with humiliation. Jaden looked startled. Aware of Jaden's sensitivities, Ivan gathered the rich bouquet of his own tense pheromones from the encounter with Noah had saturated Jaden with too much information. In Jaden's presence Ivan suddenly felt overexposed, private chemistry a manuscript to his anxieties Jaden had no right to read.

"Her eyes *are* blue, but you were guessing. In the right one is an abnormal sliver of copper color reaching from the outer edge. Her lashes are light like her hair, and you'll have to get close to appreciate them. And you should, so you can stop guessing on the important stuff."

"What is this? You think you can read a book on women and be tour guide? We both know you haven't got any experience with the real thing."

"What are you building there? Looks like a tadpole."

Ivan inspected the connected pieces. "I don't know."

"You know why you don't know? You're nervous. You think men and women are different."

"Hardware's different."

"Funny. I never thought of that."

"Smartass."

"I'll tell you a secret. When it comes to needs, hers are the same as yours."

Noah explained what *Estrella de Mar Rosa*'s clientele were like. Maybe Ivan thought they came for sex, the only impetus being libido. That and an aberrant sense of attraction. Coletti's guests frequently didn't understand what they needed. Humans sought relationships to fulfill two primary needs: physical and emotional. Men often mistook their emotional needs for physical emptiness. Despondent about a personal life with inadequate affirmation of self worth, they looked to sexual stimulation to compensate for the other need.

"You think it's all about sex. That men buy weeklong cruises for nonstop orgy? Do you know how exhausting that would be? Jaden's just a faithful puppy. He senses your heartache and loneliness, puts his head in your lap and empathizes. We're not prostitutes. Don't pity me. We're therapy."

Ivan thought about the last two days, toiling away at Nigel's wretched encryption. The number of times Jaden gave him a hug for seemingly no reason. Ivan had lifted him into his lap so Jaden could spread Lego vehicles on the desk and tell Ivan a story involving imaginary characters. He'd scratched Jaden's back and listened. These weren't natural instincts for Ivan. The way Noah described himself made Ivan a client. He shuddered. Had he been comforting the boy, or was it the other way around?

"Don't take offense," Noah said. "You're great at meeting her sexual needs. But you stink at the emotional ones. The cuddle after the sex is more important."

"Thanks."

"Your welcome."

So much for sarcasm.

"Don't be nervous. Sure, you've got lots of problems rattling around up there." Noah pointed at Ivan's head. "And you know it. Some part of you is terrified Elizabeth is focused on all those problems and can't get past them. I think you'll be okay. Emotional communication is easy. The trick is not to overthink it."

"Not the way you make it sound."

"I'm cut out for this. Literally, if you factor in the way I was born."

"Then what *does* she see in me?"

"Have you been listening to her? I may not understand German, but her body language is pretty blunt. You've been places and done crazy things. You're a little bit of a bad-boy. Or a lot. That's practically an archetype. You're the disobedience she can't commit on her own. She needs you."

"Is that from a book?"

"If it's true, who cares?"

Jaden pulled Noah down and whispered in his ear. Ivan wanted them to pretend to be normal and not disabuse every conception Ivan clung to regarding the stratification of age and maturity.

"If it's about me, spit it out."

Noah looked sheepish. "He thinks Elizabeth's not going to tell you."

"Tell me what?"

Noah scratched his head. The little red freckles seemed to get brighter. "I don't know how to put this. It's a pheromone thing. She *let* you seduce her. She's at a specific point in a cycle? You probably want to start using a condom. My brother hopes you won't. He thinks you'll be a good father."

***

Before Elizabeth returned that night Ivan took the boys to a nearby market. They picked out groceries for a dinner Noah chose.

In the small kitchen Ivan washed red potatoes. Noah cracked asparagus stems and lined them up over steaming butter with almond slices. Germans had a thing for asparagus and Ivan hoped Elizabeth wasn't the exception.

He had penne noodles, sliced chicken, olive oil, zucchini, several grated cheeses, and a lot of help. The only thing Noah let him choose was wine.

Their normal moments were a dramatic offset from a fearsomely precocious quality hidden behind the cute façade.

In her right eye Elizabeth had a brown streak. It crossed an iris not just blue, but lucent like shallow water around the Canary Islands through which drifts of sand shimmered. Ivan desperately searched for the intangible link and heard, as though a foreigner to a new language, the first whisper of understanding. He told her everything, starting with a boy named Nikos, a handful of grain, a goat in the fields outside Khalkis.

* * *

Day Four. Sunlight through the round window cast an oval spot on Jaden in the middle of the rug. He'd broken his fort to pieces. Lying on his chest, two legs poked from the bottom of an oversized blue Oktoberfest shirt. He squeezed in one hand a small stuffed elephant that belonged to Elizabeth and which she said he could keep. Jaden flicked Lego pieces off the carpet.

"What's wrong?" Ivan asked.

"I want to go home."

Scattered notes around Ivan's half of the carpet, a new attack at Nigel's code. He'd considered the possibility Feige altered traditional code practice slightly. Like subtracting the letters rather than adding them. Ivan experimented with several ideas. A little space heater whirred at the edge of the carpet.

The first three-digit sequence after the ISBN in message one's code was 282. Ivan read the page, a particular passage resonating with prescient élan.

He thought that in the beauty of the world were hid a secret. He thought the world's heart beat at some terrible cost and that the world's pain and its beauty moved in a relationship of diverging equity and that in this headlong deficit the blood of multitudes might ultimately be exacted for the vision of a single flower.

"Why do you want to go back?"

The cadence of his words ended with a sad plummet. "I miss Benji. I miss Papa."

"Who's Benji?"

Jaden crawled into Ivan's lap and rested his head on a shoulder. Benjamin was his closest brother. The elephant's trunk poked Ivan in the back. Ivan previously struggled through these intimate consolations. He knew what he was supposed to do but feared sending the wrong signal. Emotional communication was easy, Noah said. Don't overthink it. How could he not? Rubbing Jaden's back, other arm cradled under him, shirt riding up, was too little barrier for comfortable boundaries. What if Jaden, after years of conditioning, got aroused?

So what? Noah said. That's normal. Ivan would face that with any kid. It doesn't have to mean anything.

Maybe it didn't. For Ivan the physiology had been hard to separate. He didn't want to hurt the boy's feelings by being cold, so he went through the unfamiliar paternal motions.

Today felt different. Elizabeth didn't reject him. Ivan still felt suffused with relief. Jaden's legs wrapped around Ivan's torso. Ivan could cope with irrational fear. He felt a symbiosis with this child. They were both damaged in irreparable ways and eking out a semblance of compassion. With Jaden pressed against him, Ivan sensed the warm rhythm of a solemn heartbeat pushing as if by osmosis distilled pathos between them. A soft reviled creature out of Elizabeth's paintings. Hidden within the delicate small mechanics of this life were broodings as formidable as any Ivan struggled with. He thought of James holding Chase on Alki Beach in Seattle, dead, wet and limp in his arms, the anguish. To be human and love something precious that couldn't belong to him as vicarious love for all broken things.

After Noah's jarring seminar Ivan found the symbolic mileposts between him and Elizabeth. A little over a week ago Samuel offered Ivan his view of relationship dynamics. Ivan was slow to understand submissive wasn't synonymous with weak.

"Sexual partners play roles," Samuel had said. "On one hand, a submissive wants loss of control, to have the body respond contemporaneously with stimulus as a form of excitement, not knowing what comes next, afraid of discovering the extent of physical response."

"Like being blindfolded on a rollercoaster."

Samuel acknowledged the metaphor but called it primitive. "The dominant, on the other hand, hopes to evoke the quintessential reaction, pleasure bordering on fear." Samuel dredged up another Greek myth to ruin for Ivan. "Have you heard of the Prometheus Complex?"

"I know Prometheus has something to do with fire."

"Precisely. Here, I give you the fire your gods denied you."

Ivan didn't understand at first. He came to realize it stood for everything Samuel marketed. Knowledge of sexual nature was fire. Society the gods telling Jaden it's not his knowledge to have. Prometheus came in the form of the men who boarded *Estrella de Mar Rosa* with the enlightened fire of intimacy, and ready to share it with the curious minds society scorned. In exchange for this gift, they participated in evoking the emotion Samuel sold, a guaranteed fusion of timid fear, shock and pleasure.

How could Jaden want to return? The answer was obvious. How could he not? The rest of the world had no fire for him. Among his family he was special. To their sense, they were unique and gratified by the distinction.

What a mess.

"Don't they hurt you?" Ivan asked.

Nod. "Sometimes."

"And you want to go back to that?"

Jaden looked at Ivan, guileless confusion. He turned over Ivan's right hand, then the left, and pulled them into his lap. It didn't really hurt, but Ivan pretended it did when Jaden pinched Ivan's left wrist. He then stroked his fingers in circles on both of Ivan's wrists, one hand for each. "Which one feels better?"

He was repeating an exercise presumably shown to him. Focusing on the sensation, Ivan had to admit the left.

"How can you like something if you don't know what hurts? There's lots of feeling between pain and happiness. Hurt makes good things better."

In his own words he'd conveyed the point well enough. A mess Ivan was too late to fix. If he kept them away, he would only cause more pain. Jaden would keep his GPS tag. This was where Cormac McCarthy's equity diverged.

"We'll go home."

"Soon?"

"Very soon."

And with that Ivan redoubled his effort on the coded message. Pencil in hand, Jaden insisted on helping. It was cute and might take the boy's mind off of home.

Ivan gave him the Le Carré novel and some words to encode for fun, showing him how each letter was also a number, and how to add the plaintext to the book letter, then substitute the bigger number for a letter.

Jaden tried a couple. "I got one that adds up to 27. There's no letter 27."

"If the number goes over 25, subtract 26 from it. Can you do subtraction?"

"Uh-huh."

And what do you get when you subtract 26 from 27? One. What letter is that? It's a B.

Good.

Minutes later Jaden looked confused, thinking really hard about something. "What if I add them up and it goes over fifty?"

"It won't go over fifty," Ivan said. "The biggest letter you have is Z and it's only 25. Even if you had two Z's, you'd just get to fifty."

"But what if it does?"

Ivan smiled. "If you get a 58, I suppose you can just subtract 26 twice, okay? I think the modulo function would work the same repeatedly."

"Okay."

"But I seriously doubt you'll get 58 unless you add three letters—"

He didn't finish the sentence. A curious idea flitted through his mind. Ivan grabbed the code and a piece of chalk.

Could Feige have used *two* pages to encode the message? If Ivan assumed the next characters represented two 3-digit pages, he got pages 282 and 113, and theoretically a message starting with the fourth group, MHBUQ.

Ivan wrote out the words from both pages, starting at the top, under the first four viable groups:

Ciphertext: MHBUQ GVGCZ NHJXH DNGMZ
Page 282: *at the last light enough . . .*
Page 113: *the windowsill outside . . .*

M minus A minus T was -7. Add 26 to get 19 and substitute T.

H minus T minus H was -19. Add 26 to get 7 and substitute H.

B minus T minus E was -22. Add 26 to get 4 and substitute E.

He repeated this process twenty times, uncovering plaintext that read THEREISANARCHIVEOFFI. Ivan positively roared, scaring the living shit out of Jaden. He grabbed the boy up, hugging him to his chest as he danced around the study, nearly crashing into the bannister. Elizabeth and Noah came running up the stairs.

"You're a genius!" Ivan said.

Frightened senseless at first, back on his own feet, Jaden began to laugh and spin, no idea what he was excited about. His blonde hair and shirt billowed out under centrifugal forces until he was properly dizzy and toppled over, pale little bum in the air. Noah laughed. Elizabeth found herself ensconced in Ivan's arms, draped over onto the floor in the most engaged long kiss Ivan could summon. He would have taken her right there, something slow and noble, little Lego blocks digging into the pillow of her beautiful behind, audience be damned. He could hear the boys clapping. She held the side of his face. Her fingers stroked around his ears, sending shivers through him. There was nothing to say.

It took Ivan an hour to extract the first message:

Message 1:

There is an archive of files in Hizer network on experimental study at Oxford School of Medicine for effective cancer cure. Records show you obtained research from East Germany in nineteen seventy eight. The files prove Hizer bought control of Oxford study and sabotaged. Hizer hid the research. What can I do to help?

The implications distressed him to a sepulchral state, rendering Ivan nearly incapable of tackling message 2. *The Honourable Schoolboy* in hand, he repeated the process with pages 146 and 414. It took him more time, the message 119 characters longer. The last transmission before Hizer silenced Richard Feige to an earthenware jar.

Message 2:

I purchased plane ticket. Will see you soon. Coworker I went to for quadrinary viral encoding is suspicious now. If I do not arrive, there is a backup. I control updates to GLS kiosk programming. I have updated software on high usage kiosk in Seattle, ID number six six five zero nine four eight. It will encode into the junk DNA of all purchases today the same data I am carrying. Update is temporary. Kiosk will revert at midnight EST after software audit. If Hizer figures out, it will already be too late.

In chalk the new message stared at Ivan from the wall opposite where he sat. Back against a shelf, his arms wrapped two equally sober boys and a stuffed elephant. Elizabeth cried.

36

When old people's clothes went through the dryer, all the things they forgot to take out of their pockets fell out and got stuck in the lint trap. Keys, chapsticks, inhalers, pill containers with the muddy colored mess of pills inside, bingo chips, wads of paper, money, golf pencils, or worse, pens staining whole loads, candy wrappers, glasses, soggy cigarettes (what a mess), lottery stubs, diabetic lances, nail files, the list went on.

Once even a bullet casing!

Cody dug from the lint trap the things old people from Cashmere Elderly Care lost and put them in a box labeled *Incidentals*. It was a perfect name for the box. In the word Cody found *dental*, and the box was growing a good-sized collection of dentures. That's what Diana called old people's teeth.

"It's your turn," Cody said. "I got three points."

Teagan's face pressed to the window looking into Bruce's private breakroom. He peeled away. "There's no way you got a ringer."

Teagan inspected the chair leg and conceded three points.

He picked up his own pair of lower jaw dentures and stood behind an imaginary and frequently disputed line. Teagan made a flamboyant toss, dentures skittering across the floor. Cody liked the sound Denture Horseshoes made. Clickity clacking over the concrete, they sounded a little like ice cubes in a plastic cup. Dentures almost never broke. Old people had strong teeth. Probably from so much chewing. Listening to the plasticky sounds, Cody pretended they said things like *Ouch!* and *I chipped a tooth!* and sometimes *I'm hungry!*

How convenient to be able to take them out. Must make brushing a lot easier.

Cody got three points for ringers, one point for a leaner, and no points every other way. Teagan scored no points on this round. He went back to Bruce's Café window.

"Why you're so busy looking in there?"

"Bruce has Christmas goof hoarded up in his fridge. I want it."

For all Teagan's confusing behavior, stealing from DOC was his simplest impulse. Cody watched Teagan grab a screwdriver off the tool cart, the flatty kind. Then he glanced about the warehouse, pried open the window, and disappeared. Cody didn't even hear the blinds move.

Seconds later Teagan emerged from the door, loaded down with food. The screwdriver hit the floor.

"Reeses Pieces are yours," he said, dropping a heavy bag in Cody's arms. Teagan laid the bounty across their table near Extractor 3. "Day-old Carl's Junior fatburger, half eaten Dr. Devil pizza, canned whipped cream, couple dozen frosted cupcakes and molasses cookies, the fridge is loaded. I've got to go back for a second pass." Teagan flipped the plastic lid on a bottle. "Smell this."

"Smells good. What is it?"

"Seasonal peppermint and vanilla creamer. Get your coffee cup. Bruce may be a bitch, but he has good taste."

They drank so much Cody was sick. And then drank more. Why not? Teagan said. It's on Bruce.

"Five points!"

"One point," Teagan said. "You don't get five points for nothing."

"But the teeth are, both are, they're . . . look! Around the chair leg, see? I get five, no, six points."

"Two points."

"You're cheating."

Teagan grabbed the whipped cream can, held Cody by the hair, and whip-creamed his face again. He giggled and got his open mouth sprayed before Teagan let him go. He went to fetch the dentures. Bending over to pick them up, he stuffed them in his mouth, turned on Teagan and roared with his clawed hands held out. Teagan spit up coffee laughing.

"Take that shit out of your mouth, spud. Just because they been through the washer don't make them clean. You look rabid."

He dug them out. Chocolaty spitty cream turned the teeth a gooey yellow. They did look pretty gross. He dropped them and wiped his hand across both pant legs the way Filthy might.

"Teagan, does Santa have dentures?"

"Why? Because he's old? Why didn't you ask him when he played with your junk in Medical?"

"That wasn't Santa, I said he *looked* like Santa but he wasn't."

"Stay up and ask him when he comes to fill your DOC sock stockings."

"You said Santa he doesn't come to prison."

"Slow down." Cody crashed into Teagan, running in circles, not sure why. He struggled to run off, Teagan's fingers in his waistband. "How much chocolate did you eat?"

"All of it."

"Figures." He let go and Cody fell forward onto the floor. "Spud, if Santa parked his sleigh on A-Unit's roof, DOC would book him for a felony. Santa's not trying to get caught up like that."

"That's so unfair."

"But I'll tell you what, spud. You leave him some cookies before you go to bed and I promise they'll get eaten."

* * *

When Bruce found his fridge empty, Cody and Teagan made themselves scarce. Union Break, Teagan said. On the back dock Cody sucked on an icicle Teagan cracked off the overhang for him. An officer went inside after a routine security sweep. Teagan lit another cigarette, jacket off, flexing his muscles for self-inspection. Teagan showed off a lot. He did look bigger lately, especially around his shoulders. Cody shrugged both arms up to look more like Teagan.

"If a snow cloud it bumps into a tornado, Teagan, does it make snow stripes?"

"Maybe."

"When icicles fall out of the sky why do they get stuck on roofs?"

"Icicles don't fall out of the sky."

"Where do they come from?"

"Melted snow drips."

"But if it's melted how do they get frozen like ice?"

"It's hard to explain."

"So you don't know?"

"Of course I know."

"Then why you can't tell me?"

"You wouldn't understand."

Cody was pretty sure Teagan didn't know. "If it's sunny and snowy both at the same time it makes icicles?"

"Sure, spud."

"Can you make icicles point upside-down too?"

"Yeah, sure."

Cody broke a smaller icicle from the edge of a fence gate he could reach. "You want an icicle to lick?"

"Nah. Too much bird shit."

Cody inspected his icicle. He didn't see any bird shit. He stuck his tongue out and dropped it on the dock where it went to pieces. He kicked the chunks. They rolled through snow creeping onto the loading dock. Wind blew it like dust under the overhang where it melted, refroze, and formed slippery sheets of ice skating surface. Yeah, spud, slide around and fall. Get the sugar out of your tank.

Cody hoped Tony would come back and visit him again. He kept his promise and didn't tell anyone that Tony's lady friend took Cody's blood. Not even Teagan. It was hard keeping secrets. What happened if he won his appeal? Tony told Cody they'd move him back to county jail, maybe even let him go. Really? He could go back to mom and dad? Tony stammered a bit and said it might be with a new mom and dad. Why? Tony didn't say. What about Teagan? If Teagan got out of prison, could he be Cody's dad? Probably not. Fathers needed to be the kinds of people who didn't tattoo their kids. Even if the tattoos were cuddly bears. When would Cody win his appeal? Any day, Tony said. Could be any day.

Teagan flexed and held his hand around the bicept, trying to get the finger and thumb to touch. The cigarette got in the way.

"Diana told me this pretty funny joke. You want to hear it?"

"Uh-huh." Cody made snow angels, socks getting wet. Uncomfortable now, he pulled his shoes off.

"So there's these two old biddies smoking—"

"What's a biddy?"

"An old lady. Elderly, like the people we wash the clothes for?"

"With the dentures."

"Right. And the two biddies are smoking when it starts to rain. One of them pulls out a tiny package, rips it open, cuts the nib off and unrolls this condom over—"

"What's a condom?"

"You know what a condom is. There's like more than ten of them in the Incidentals box right now."

Cody thought of the individually wrapped colored things in packets. "You mean the balloons?"

"They're not balloons."

"Diana says they are. She blows them up for me."

"Diana knows better. A condom's a rubber tube you squeeze over your penis so you don't have to pay child support."

"Quit joking, Teagan. It's a balloon."

"I'm not joking." Two birds came to perch on a light fixture near him. He blew cigarette smoke in their direction and they flew off. "After sex you peel it off and your little swimmers dog-paddle all the way to the trashcan."

"Gross."

"You say that now. Can I finish my joke?"

"But Teagan, those balloons, or whatever, they're too big for your thingy."

Teagan rolled his eyes. He pressed a hand against his pants on the inside thigh. It looked like he had a MilkyWay candy bar in his pocket. Cody suddenly figured it out.

"Oh." It wasn't just Teagan's shoulders getting bigger.

"You gonna let me finish this joke?"

The old woman thought the rain sleeve protecting the cigarette was pretty neat, Teagan said. The other told her she could get them at any drugstore. The next time she was at the pharmacy she asked for a condom, and the clerk was sort of suspicious as she seemed too old to worry about condoms, but he played along and asked if she had any particular size in mind?

"And the old biddie says, 'Big enough to fit a Camel.'"

Cody waited.

"Isn't that funny?"

"I don't think I got it," Cody said. His snow angel looked mushy in the middle. He wondered if he should laugh to make Teagan happy? Too late.

Teagan flicked his cigarette off the dock into the snow.

"Never mind, spud. They're just balloons."

37

A reefer arrived by container vessel in the Baltimore Harbor shipyard three weeks before Day 1. Cranes dropped a relatively light Textainer TGHU 814737 0 45R1 onto the trailer of an unmarked Freightliner tractor that departed in the untaxed eighth gear.

Plastic strapping cinched several pallets of high-strength square steel hollow rods within, occupying a nominal space next to 2X4 wooden studs, two steel plates, sheets of plywood, hardware, wire-feed welder, plasma torch, airbrush kit, diesel generator, 100 square meters of recording studio sound-isolation foam, 3M spray adhesive, marine sealant, industrial digital scale, 1500 watt heater, colored latex, enamel paint, and miscellaneous electronic equipment.

"Killing Mr. Rycroft achieves nothing," Samuel told Ivan weeks before. "What then?"

At a post office in DC a package arrived postmarked from a hospital in Cairo. Plastered on the outside were several medical codes and warning labels. A hydrogen cell powered simple electric cooling unit chilled the contents of the enclosed styrofoam container.

"You would still be running from the lawmen," Samuel had said.

"I need a plan that resolves both problems."

"And your desire for vengeance is one of the problems."

"No."

"Are you certain?"

The same post office box days later received a similar refrigerated container from Greider Labs in Seattle. Inside, a glass tube of the rarest blood on the planet.

Preparations came together.

"I've spent a lifetime imagining the way I would kill this man," Ivan had told Samuel. "For what he did to Yannis. To my family."

"He's done far worse. I see the reservation in your eyes. You are considering an approach anathema to what you believe."

"I am."

Day 1

Ivan screwed a suppressor on the barrel of a .22, checked the magazine and clicked it into the grip. He pulled the slide, fingers like a tactile X-ray visually sensing precision internals sweep one round off a staggered column into a semi-snug chamber. He laid it on the passenger seat of a government GMC Yukon with limo tinting and bulletproof armor plating beneath its black skin.

In one hour Glitch would fly from a private airfield near Ronald Reagan International Airport to Switzerland. Two Hizer footmen with whom he'd spent the morning at a CIA substation not far from headquarters would accompany him on the leased jet. One of the Hizers registered a shell corporation a month before called Phazelyte Research GmbH, scheduled to finance a trial study of bionanite corrective mutagenesis to the cellular p53 gene, one of the master switches Elizabeth described. In Bern the men would transfer money through Swiss accounts to the research lab in Sweden and begin moving a rebadged Hizer team in to help. Ivan had a pretty good idea how that trial treatment would turn out.

Glitch had a name. Not just Dean anymore, but Dean Rycroft. Former head of the GST department and the CIA's Air America extraordinary rendition program Dean. Orchestrator of black-site prison torture Dean. Bionanotechnological darts in a jacket pocket Dean. Limitless pharmaceutical funding, a third wife half his age, daughter from the first marriage already four years into law school Dean. Sadistic shadowy Dean from a creepy H.P. Lovecraft written history. Six dead children Dean.

Biometrics were required to enter the CIA field office, but not the motor pool garage from which Ivan borrowed their sturdy fleet vehicle. He idled in the circle out front, defrosters leaving a chorus line of fluted efforts along the base of the windshield.

Three men paused outside the SUV engaged in affable chatter punctuated by laughter. A handler opened the rear door for the men and loaded luggage through a back gate.

"Sanchez? We're late. Run some lights."

Ivan jammed the accelerator, gravel plinking around the wheel wells. He entered the destination into the nav and transferred the vehicle to autonomous driving mode. He locked the vehicle doors and checked the rearview mirror. Dean sat at the far right. One of Hizer's men faced the other two from a seat behind the front driver's side. Bottles of seltzer water all around.

Eyes forward and using the mirror to aim, Ivan reached over his shoulder and fired two shots.

"What the hell!" Dean yelled. He scrambled for his radio, hand yanking the door latch in vain.

Ivan lunged through the cabin and planted a blow on Dean's jaw with a meaty crack. The man momentarily stunned, Ivan threaded handcuffs through a brace handle along the roofline above the door and when Dean finally shook off the blow, he found his arms dangling by the wrists.

"Sanchez? What's going on?" Dean thrashed and babbled incoherently while Ivan sat back and watched. He switched on the cabin lighting and Dean recognized him with resignation. "I knew when they didn't find your body in the crash the job wasn't finished." The vehicle made a left and one of the Hizers rolled onto him. Dean thrust the corpse in the other direction. "You killed them? Do you have any fucking idea who they are?"

"Don't care. Pretty good shots, though. Who says the bad guys can't shoot straight? Or maybe I'm the good guy in this scenario?"

"Don't flatter yourself, Stavros."

Ivan pulled a foldout table from a center console. "I don't have to tell you, but you're going to miss your flight." He set a steel case on it. Self-gratification, leather seats, cordite and bloody brain matter did not mix for a pleasant smell.

"A plane? Ten thousand feet? Seriously? Why won't you just die."

"Feeling's mutual," Ivan said.

"This vehicle's tracked. They're going to find you, and when they see what you've done, that Syrian pit's going to look like the Hyatt Regency."

"On the contrary, you're going to forget I exist. I want them to find you, whoever they are. You'll come up with some cockamamie story and cover for me." Ivan tossed a phone on the seat next to Dean. "And wait for my call."

"You're certifiable. Absolutely bat-shit crazy."

"Which is why you never should have double-crossed me in Seoul." Ivan held up his phone. "I'm waiting for a call myself. Do you want to know who's going to be on the other end?"

In the third floor study of Bastien Köhler's former house, Ivan glimpsed only the first of many Hizer sabotages. Back on *Estrella de Mar Rosa* he and Samuel set to work looking at cancer treatment over the past four decades. A pattern emerged. Each time promising cancer cures sprouted and went to human trials, funding poured in from various sources and the trial would suddenly fail in spectacular disaster much as the first one at Oxford that tested Bastien's East German retrovirus cure. Tracing the source of funding revealed an elaborate series of shell companies all leading back to the CIA/Hizer partnership. Same style network of proxies the U.S. government used to hide weapon sales to North Korea.

Hizer was buying up every promising cancer cure, sabotaging the success, and burrowing the research away. Why would they do such a thing?

Profits, Samuel said. An immunotherapeutic cure deters a lifelong revenue stream flowing from sustained chemotherapies and palliative care. The ideal business model was to keep customers for life. "I don't cure men of their sexual urges," Samuel said. "I treat their symptoms, and when those symptoms return, so do they."

Was Dean Rycroft profit-driven, or did he enjoy exerting power over others? What would it take to break him?

"Your lip's bleeding," Ivan told Dean. "Don't worry, we're headed for a hospital." He opened the steel case and turned it around so Dean could see multiple prepped syringes and ampoules lined up in protective foam. "How much do you know your business partners? About pharmaceuticals? Or do they simply provide you sedatives when someone needs disappearing?"

Dean spit blood at Ivan, who dodged and took his time pulling on latex gloves. The Yukon made several stops for lights and picked up speed for an onramp.

"Pay close attention. Let's call this a pharmaceutical lesson. I want you to carefully understand your situation." Ivan removed the first glass syringe and held it up to the light, the chamber filled with a luminescent yellow-green fluid. "I made it my business to find out what's hidden in Dakota's DNA, despite your opinion. How do you feel about oncology? Cancer research? Fascinating work."

Dean couldn't hide the scowl or his signature glitching Adams apple. His silence pled the Fifth. Ivan didn't need the man's confirmation and made sure Dean's focus stayed on the menacing syringe.

"In the last century cancer researchers used P388 to induce leukemia in mice. This is a far more advanced and incredibly aggressive trigger. Injected in your veins, this substance, CPQ744, will invade and conquer the cells of your body in three weeks. Four weeks and you'll be in a coma. Hizer is hiding a cure for this type of metastatic lymphoma. Lucky you."

Dean shrank from the syringe and started yelling and crashing around in the handcuffs.

"Why the frenetic dance? This isn't for you."

"We're going to gut you with a shovel."

"Familiarize yourself with the concept of disappointment. I need you to focus. The integrity of your life depends on choices." Ivan pulled an ampoule from the foam. "I've known Fady for more than two decades. Very good friend, beautiful family. He sent me this fantastic drug all the way from Egypt, where you threw me out on the street as a child. It comes from one of Hizer's competitors. Any idea what it is?"

Before liberating a black government Yukon, Ivan spent the morning doing contract maintenance work at the Sidwell Friends private prep school where Dean Rycroft's third wife insisted on sending their son. Mason Rycroft probably didn't know what kind of work his father did for the government. He was a B/C student with A-enthusiasm for geography no doubt stimulated by many father-son global explorations. A month after Ivan was blown out of the sky over North Korea, Dean flew Mason to Sydney for surfing and scuba diving with sea turtles.

First year at the school, a little shy of fourteen, Mason wasn't linebacker or offense-position material. Trying out for a team and proving to be a fast runner, the coach swapped him between receiver and tight-end in the hope sufficient practice would carve him into an athlete.

The empty locker room of the Sidwell gymnasium smelled as though neophyte testosterone itself preserved the wooden benches and corroded the metal cabinets. A bloated laundry cart of wet towels crammed the corner of a shower room where tiles echoed a steady drip Ivan had no intention of fixing.

Mason's locker featured the requisite gym and football uniforms, numerous nudies torn from magazines and taped to the inside of the door. Two pairs of cleated shoes, mouthguard dangling from a strap to a scraped helmet. Velcro secured body pads, foot powder, and the Gillette antiperspirant Ivan expected to find here after reviewing supermarket purchase records for Mason.

Ivan rolled the gel plunger down and injected a hot layer of paraffin wax with a thermal gun. Cisatracuriam besylate was a powerful intravenous neuromuscular block used for surgical procedures. Above the wax he injected 20 milligrams of it mixed with an aprotic solvent, dimethyl sulfoxide, suspended in a saline gel. Ivan primed the antiperspirant plunger until a single dose of around 10 milligrams swelled in the tiny grid of square holes. The electronic lock cycled as the locker door closed.

He explained the pharmacological effects to Dean.

"Around the time your flight is scheduled to leave, Mason will finish practice, take a shower and change. The DMSO solvent allows the intravenous drug to absorb through the skin of his armpits. In three to five minutes a rapid onset will leave him nonresponsive on the locker room floor. His coach will call 9-1-1. I have control of the nearby cell tower." Ivan held up his phone. "The call will be intercepted and routed to me. This elaborate ruse saves me from dealing with your secure household, his private chauffeur and bodyguard, or parental inclination to accompany him in the ambulance. It could be hours before anyone realizes he was never taken to a hospital."

The nav signaled two minutes for arrival destination, SUV entering a parking garage of Union Memorial Hospital in Baltimore. Dean moved from abrasive vitriol to abject pleading. Ivan opened a package from the metal case and adhered a square to Dean's neck.

"This also contains DMSO, but more importantly, a series of slow-release membranes of chloral hydrate good for twenty four hours of sedation. I trust you'll enjoy knowing that by the time you wake up, Mason won't even be in this country. Don't bother looking for us. I'll call you in three weeks with your choices."

Dean started slurring words. "Staroos, ihf you hurt mm boy, mm gonna—"

"Do what? You hired me to kill seven kids with no regard for the families left behind. Don't pretend you give a damn about children now. Keep that phone close."

By the time the SUV parked he was unconscious. Ivan hoped this was the last time he would ever see Dean Rycroft. He changed vehicles to an ambulance pre-staged in the adjacent space. Just under an hour later, when Ivan was within three kilometers of the Sidwell School, his phone rang. Incoming call from rerouted unknown carrier. Nine-one-one. Please state the nature of your emergency.

* * *

Ivan closed Mason's eyes for the trip. He had a 65-minute window before the neuromuscular block lost 90% of its effectiveness. By then he'd driven a circuitous route around DC and Virginia to the Leesburg Municipal Airfield. Along the way he stopped at an automated carwash with prearranged malfunction of the security cameras. Water-soluble ambulance paint washed into the drains leaving a light blue Ford Transit utility van at the other end. Ivan swapped the plates and drove another thirty minutes.

In a long-term lease hangar Ivan parked next to reefer TGHU 814737 0 45R1. He unloaded and rolled the gurney through the container doors and beyond a plywood partition. Plugged into the hangar's power supply, the container maintained a comfortable 23 degrees Celsius. Low LED lights near the plywood partition fell across conical protrusions of gray sound absorption foam covering all the walls, making a Jungianly fierce cavern of the space. A ten square meter narrow cage of welded vertical bars stood in the center with a plastic mattress on an elevated metal bed pan. At the front, 35 centimeters off the floor, the bars bent inward to create a seat, a bucket inserted in the cavity from the outside. Everything smelled like an industrial construction site, of fresh paint over rough welds, lumber, and polyurethane adhesives.

Wearing gloves Ivan pulled off Mason's shoes and shirt, washed the armpits, and dressed him in a clean shirt so latent chemistry caught in the fabric wouldn't debilitate him.

He had the same dark hair, but not trimmed short like his father's. His face bore little resemblance to Dean's odious features. It wasn't simply that Mason inherited more of his mother's traits, though that was possible. His nature wasn't yet sullied by environment, the way Roald Dahl posited perpetual meanness becomes etched in one's visage, or how John Irving described the dichotomy. *It's a no-win argument—that business of what we're born with and what our environment does to us. And it's a boring argument, because it simplifies the mysteries that attend both our birth and our growth.*

Pupil dilation response normal. The discomfort Ivan felt was no longer associated with prolonged eye contact. It was the disparate reciprocity of information exchanged. Ivan sensed the emotive response, like confrontation with Noah's green eyes, the sharp heart-pain for the moment that acknowledges the physiologically improbable organ called a soul. Mason, meanwhile, glimpsed only a looming Greek man, the boy's brain recording auditory and physical input without deference to curiosity, so much was his fear elevated.

Ivan closed the eyelids, carried him into the cage and sat him upright on the scale plate. Wrote in a notepad, 43.6 kilograms.

"I know you can hear me." Cisatracuriam besylate immobilized. It didn't inhibit consciousness. "You'll come out of this shortly. Believe it or not, I thoroughly dislike this situation, what I'm about to do."

He laid one of the two cotton blankets across the cage floor, pillow against the bars, so Mason's right arm protruded between two rungs. A strap around the wrist secured the forearm facing upward on a restraint plate welded to the bars. Ivan locked the cage and swabbed Mason's surfacing vein with alcohol.

"You're probably freaked out right now. You needn't be. This will be over in three weeks one way or another. Then you can go home."

Outside the container Ivan made coffee in the hangar. By the time he returned Mason's eyes were open and minutes later he breathed heavily as the drug wore off.

"What's wrong with me? What happened?"

"Nothing's wrong with you."

"You're not a doctor?"

"No."

Mason looked around the dimly lit space. "Where am I?"

Ivan opened the metal case and pulled out the glass syringe with lime green liquid. Suddenly aware his arm was stuck, Mason panicked and yanked on the strap.

"Sit still, this isn't for you."

"What is it?"

Ivan chuckled and squirted some of the fluid in his own mouth. “Do you want some?” Without waiting for a response he emptied the syringe across Mason’s lips.

Mason was still too groggy to dodge the stream. “What the hell!”

“Mountain Dew. It’s gone a little flat. Your father thinks it’s CPQ744.” Ivan threw the syringe on the gurney. Mason licked his face and looked at Ivan with raw confusion. “Mountain Dew probably causes cancer as well, but not in this amount.” He pulled a second syringe from the case. “This one’s for you.”

When Ivan released the strap Mason yanked his arm inside the cage and inspected the injection site, holding it out as though a contaminated appendage regrettably still attached.

“What the hell is this? Who are you?” He bounced around the cage, the real freak-out only starting. “What are you doing to me!”

“Calm down. You’re going to feel like shit, but it won’t technically harm you. It’s a strong emetic and a large overdose of lubiprostone.” Ivan read from the notes Fady sent him. “A bicyclic fatty acid that activates the CIC-2 chloride channels of gastrointestinal epithelial cells to increase fluid secretions. That’s a mouthful.” Ivan wedged a roll of toilet paper in the bars. “I trust you’ll figure out what this bucket is for. I’ll be back in an hour.”

“Wait, I don’t understand—what am I doing here? I don’t want to be here!”

“That option’s not available. Try not to make a mess.”

Ivan closed the door in the partition. The sound studio baffling did an amazing job reducing screams to a barely audible timbre.

* * *

Ivan didn't want to leave the hangar any more often than necessary. Provided the van's transformation wasn't caught by surveillance he was reasonably certain a CIA effort to find him would be futile. Particularly if the search started with the erroneous premise he'd moved Mason to a remote and inaccessible location outside the U.S. Or maybe they were smart enough to know that wouldn't be necessary. How would they peg Ivan's move? Certainly they knew something of his tactics, having fed him a career of assassination errands.

Mason was tagged the same way as Coletti's boys. There was no need to dig it from his arm. Signals wouldn't penetrate the container. Ivan used a tablet to review the retrieved tag data. Mason was healthy with no allergies or medical conditions of concern.

Cancer was a miserable plight. Ivan needed Dean to appreciate that level of suffering, but couldn't bring himself to inflict it even if Hizer could rescue Mason from stage 4. Dean only needed to *believe* it was cancer.

When Ivan reentered the container ninety minutes later he found Mason doubled over, sitting on the metal seat above the bucket, shorts around the ankles, convulsing stomach and guts resulting in involuntary dry retching. The smell confirmed he'd completed a drastic purge.

"Stand on the scale."

"I'm sorry," he cried. "Whatever I did I'm sorry."

"Stand on the scale and I'll give you something to arrest the effects."

41.3 kilograms.

Ivan didn't care for treating Mason like a chemistry set. In a purely therapeutic circumstance he might be fascinated. Stabbing him like a pincushion with microscopic amounts of drugs revealed how susceptible and fragile human life was to pharmacology. This was nothing. Diarrhea and vomiting without the attendant cytotoxic rampage of cancer chemotherapy was like trying to drown on a sandbar.

Ivan loaded two more syringes, 20 milligrams of prochlorperezine in one, another of dicyclomine hydrochloride. Mason put up no resistance. The cocktail started to calm his insides.

Ivan emptied the bucket and dragged a hose back through the partition to rinse the floor of the cage while Mason lay on the bunk and waited for the drugs to reduce peristaltic muscle contractions. In addition to suppressing the brain's vomiting center, prochlorperazine was an antipsychotic that caused drowsiness.

For once side effects were a good thing.

Day 2

Ivan slept in the van. In the morning, over a gas ring, he made something like an egg breakfast for himself. He checked on Mason and found shredded scraps of blanket covering the floor outside the cage.

"Let me out of here!"

Ivan kicked the scraps around. "Was it fun?"

"You can't just lock me in here. This isn't funny! What do you want?"

"You're smart. You'll figure it out."

Ivan closed the container doors behind him. At the other end of the reefer were built-in redundant refrigeration and heating units that could be adjusted from 25 to negative-25 degrees. Ivan set the panel for 10 degrees Celsius.

Day 3

There was nothing in the news about Mason's disappearance, dead pharmaceutical company stiffs, or increased urgency for Ivan's capture. That didn't mean Rycroft wasn't blowing through government resources searching for Ivan. Only that he'd predictably thrown clout around to keep his son safe. It was a strange revelation to learn Dean Rycroft's calculating cruelty possessed a humanly banal capability for love.

He made a quick trip to Walmart for more blankets and also picked comfortable clothes that would fit the boy. Gym shorts weren't going to make it three weeks.

In a tall plastic cup of water he dissolved vitamins and a little protein powder. He adjusted the reefer back up to 23 degrees.

Inside Mason had dragged the reachable blanket scraps into a makeshift nest under the bunk. He lay in a fetal position with arms pulled inside the shirtsleeves and wrapped around his chest.

"Stand on the scale." No response. "Do you want something to drink?"

He crawled from the cramped space and used the bars to walk to the corner.

40.8 kilograms. Around 6% bodyweight loss so far.

Ivan passed him the cup, sealed with lid and flex-straw, and retrieved the brand new set of folded blankets. "Are you going to tear these up?" Mason didn't make eye contact but shook his head. Ivan pushed the blankets through to him. Mason drank half the cup, crawled on the bunk and resumed the fetal position, pulling the blankets around him until only part of his face showed.

"Believe me, I do not enjoy watching people suffer. That's not my objective. You have to stay here, but if you cooperate, I can make this more comfortable for you."

The cocoon made no sound. Ivan wedged green sweat pants, a clean shirt and a fresh roll of toilet paper in the bars.

"These are for you. Leave the clothes you're wearing outside the bars, and they'll get cleaned. Tomorrow I'll explain why you're here."

38

Day 4

Ivan debated the best way to approach the weeks ahead. He needed cooperation. Fighting Mason every step of the process wasn't a practical option.

Across a canvas tarp spread on a large table in the hangar, he disassembled and cleaned the components of his Surgeon sniper rifle. Another man would call it a war machine, a tool of destruction. In Ivan's hands it was a precise humanitarian instrument. He returned to the sound isolated chamber with the weapon held out to capitalize its visibility.

Hands around the bars and aping a defiant posture, Mason saw the monstrosity of a weapon and stumbled back. In the far dark corner he crumpled with hands over his face. Ivan heard him say *No* over and over through tears.

"Mason? I said you were going home in three weeks." Ivan pulled a foldout chair between the gurney and cage. He rested the buttstock on the floor and cradled the barrel shroud in his left hand. "Why would I kill you? Come here."

The emotional metamorphosis between Mason the young adult, struggling with Mason the child, in these montaged moments, encapsulated in observable ways the more prolonged endeavor toward maturity.

Several minutes of slow drama brought the whimpering animal back to a more resolute state of acquiescence.

"I can't pretend to be a good person, Mason. I've spent a life contemplating the mechanics and science of death."

"You shoot things."

"People. Easy now. Not you." Ivan made a show of rapidly adjusting the rifle's many tunable features. "I have a job to do. It may be the last job of my adopted career. Strangely, I want this time to be different. Two methods to accomplish my goal are available. With your help, I can do this task without killing anyone. Does that sound good?" Mason managed a vigorous nod. "If not, I resort to Plan-B." Ivan clicked the box magazine forward out of the lower receiver. He pushed the first round off the stack and held it out to Mason. "Take it."

"I don't want to." He shrank from the bars.

"It's not going to hurt you."

"I know."

Ivan waited. Eventually a hand came through the bars and drew the bullet back inside. Mason's unsteady fingers shook. Ivan didn't blame him. The heavy brass round spanned the length of his hand, a massive projectile designed to obliterate a man's skull kilometers away. To hold it was intimidating.

Mason found the name etched on the casing and dropped the bullet. He crouched and fell back, hands again over his face. "You want to kill my dad?"

"Honestly? I do. Very much so."

"Oh no . . ."

"I'm angry, which ironically makes me a poor candidate for this job. I already punched him once this week, and it's not enough."

"Why?" An importunate whine replaced the young-adult voice.

"That's between your father and me."

More of the whimpered *No*.

"Pull yourself together. I want to know some things."

"Don't, please don't, don't kill him."

"Do you love your father?" More vigorous nodding. "Why?"

"He's my dad."

"That's enough?" Nod. "You ever argue with him?"

"Sometimes."

"What happens?"

"Nothing."

"He doesn't discipline you?"

"You think he beats me? That's why you want to shoot him?"

Ivan laughed. "I'm not looking for a reason to kill him. I'm looking for a reason not to."

Dean the father had nothing to do with Dean the CIA spook. Mason described someone Ivan never met, a man patient, kind, and at times tender. Ivan wondered if he'd grabbed the wrong kid. Dean didn't just take his family to Brazil and abandon them for work related matters. When Mason ascended a 5.9 rock climb in a harness, Dean was on the ground holding the rope in an ATC to arrest his son's falls. Then encourage him to try again.

A Jekyll and Hyde act? For Ivan it confirmed two important details. He would let Dean live, and the father loved Mason enough for this plan to work.

Mason picked up the bullet and held it out to Ivan.

"You keep it," Ivan said. "That bullet is your agreement with me. Deal with the next couple weeks, and I won't ask to use it."

It was sad to watch how close Mason clutched the 300-grain symbol. He nodded with deep exhale.

Ivan took the plastic cup and returned with more of the vitamin protein water.

"Stand on the scale."

"Why's my weight so important to you?"

Ivan pointed and Mason stood on the plate. 40.5 kilograms. Ivan noted it next to the time and handed Mason the cup. "Part of my plan requires you to lose weight."

"I'm not fat."

"No, you aren't. I'm not talking about a little bit of weight. You started at 43.6 kilograms. In twenty days I'm shooting to . . . bad choice of words. I need you down to thirty kilograms."

"Is that a lot? How many pounds is it?"

Ivan swore and fetched his pad. Goddammed U.S. measurements. He translated the weights and scribbled on the pad. "You started at 96 pounds. Right now you're at 89, but more than half of that was intestinal content. I needed to kickstart the process, otherwise you wouldn't immediately cut into body fat for energy. You're hungry?" He nodded. Very. "The only reason you're not weaker now is because you started out pretty strong. That's going to change, and you need to be ready to accept it."

"How much?"

Mason was reasonably pragmatic so far. "Target weight is thirty kilograms. About 66 pounds."

"Whoa."

"You can do it. You've been 66 pounds before."

"Yeah, when I was five," he complained.

"Probably more recent than that. It's only temporary. When you go home, eat as much as you want."

"You're not going to give me anything to eat, are you?"

"If I didn't, you'd die. The first week will be the worst." Ivan peeled open a new toothbrush and squirted toothpaste on it. He passed this and more water to Mason.

The boy sat on the bunk. Anxiety threatened his effort to preserve a courageous frame of mind. He looked at the bullet in one hand, toothbrush in the other, but didn't say anything.

"I need the toothbrush back."

Ivan could see the gears turning, the slow decision to comply. He brushed, rinsed, spit into the toilet bucket, and gave Ivan the brush.

"Thank you. I'll bring something to eat tonight."

Day 6

Mason said he was going insane from boredom. Ivan gave him the only two books he had, Cormac McCarthy's *All The Pretty Horses* and John Le Carré's *The Honourable Schoolboy*. Mason had never read a paper version of books, and the clumsy way he kept the book propped open was funny.

What did he like to read? There was an old book series called *Game of Thrones* Mason had started.

Ivan found an antique bookstore with four secondhand paperback copies and bought all of them, not sure what chunk of the series they represented.

Mason's reading didn't go far. He wanted the distraction, but on nutrient water and 300 calories of oatmeal a day, he spent most hours on the bunk wrapped in blankets. Ivan dropped the temperature three degrees to increase need for the body to generate heat. He gave Mason aspirin for stomach pain, though it didn't do much. Ivan promised he'd adjust soon.

How soon?

Ivan tried to remember two years in the Syrian pit, but it was long ago. He emptied the bucket. There hadn't been any solid waste for 36 hours.

Day 8

"Is he paying you?"

"Who?"

"My dad. Are you waiting for money?"

"What makes you say that?"

Mason looked around the cage. "I figured you kidnapped me and now you want a ransom."

Ivan smiled. He was carving up an apple that proved pretty sour.

"Are you fast with a knife?"

"Fast?"

"Like, are you good with them."

Ivan thought about it. "Yes." He spun the fixed blade through his fingers and showed Mason a few deft maneuvers to drive the point home.

"What happens if he doesn't pay?"

"I didn't say there was a ransom."

"Is there?"

"Sort of." Ivan circled the tip of the knife. "There's some money involved."

"How much? What are you going to do if he doesn't pay?"

"Your dad's not poor."

"I know. But he's not going to want to. I know him. He hunts people like you."

"*Like me?* You don't know anything about me. Your father might. What do *you* think he does?"

Mason shrugged. "I know he's good at it. Finding people."

"Don't worry. He'll pay the money."

"What if he doesn't?"

"I'll think of something." Mason swallowed and watched the knife. Ivan realized why he'd asked about it. "You're worried if your father doesn't pay a ransom I'll send him your ears, fingers or eyeballs in a box?"

"Maybe."

"Which finger can you do without?"

"Are you serious?"

"Sure."

"I don't want to pick a finger."

"You want me to pick it for you?"

Mason stuffed his hands in opposing armpits and backed away from the bars.

Ivan laughed. "You've been watching too many movies." He cut a wedge off the apple and held it out. "Don't be scared. Take it. I don't want your fingers. You'll go home in one piece."

Day 10

Ivan brought Mason another pair of sweats and shirt. He also bought warmer socks upon request. Outside the bars he set a different bucket with warm water, a little mild soap added, and a sponge.

Was Ivan going to watch?

No.

He left the container and cracked the hangar door to enjoy what little sunshine was left between threats of inclement winter weather. Bitter cold demanded the cigarette he wasn't going to smoke anymore. A fleeting moment of shame struck for having thought nicotine withdrawal was anything like starvation. Still, he empathized. Several jets took off from a runway not far away. Then a Cessna. A man working under the hood of a classic Mustang in a hangar across the yard waved. Ivan returned the gesture but went inside before the man felt a social need for conversation. The nice thing about hangars was most municipal airport operators didn't really care what happened in them so long as you paid the rent and didn't burn the structure down.

Mason dropped to 38 kilograms. His metabolism would slow and weight loss plateau for a few days. Ivan would decrease oatmeal to 250 and then 200 calories, after which weight should come down precipitously. Mason became inured to his condition, unaware of lethargy, but concerned all the football muscles were wasting. You'll get them back.

I did, Ivan thought.

Day 13

"I'm missing a lot of school."

Ivan nodded.

"Do you think they'll make me do the year over?"

"No."

"I'm supposed to go to Michelle's Christmas party."

"She'll forgive you," Ivan said. Mason had asked for music or movies or something. Ivan downloaded the top 500 current pop tunes on an iPod from the tarmac and got a tiny speaker set. It played softly in the background while he tried to figure out why downloaded movies wouldn't play off his tablet. Ivan could easily hack a cell tower, but here he was dumbfounded trying to watch *Smokey and the Bandit* on a foolproof interface. Stupid proprietary codexes.

"What did my dad do?"

For a while Mason believed his father would in fact find Ivan. The hope slowly vanished. Ivan kept an eye on Dean's movements, but without communication intercept, no logic materialized from the frantic travel. Dean was in Canada, then Israel, Washington State—but not near Dakota's prison—and back to DC. Ivan didn't tell Mason.

"You should think of him as a good father. What do I accomplish by altering that? Nothing."

"It was something bad, wasn't it?"

"Ribs," Ivan said, pointing to Mason's midriff.

Mason lifted his shirt and showed Ivan his side. Ivan nodded. The kid seemed eager to prove he was meeting the expectation.

Not that Mason was happy, just resigned no one came for him.

"Was it bad?"

Ivan nodded.

"Has my dad killed people? Did he kill someone you know?"

Ivan decided he could share part of the truth. "I've worked for your father since long before you were born. I just didn't know it. Over the years I think he forgot to care about the shit he put me through."

"That's it? You're a disgruntled employee?"

"It's more complicated than that."

"It better be. Why can't you tell me?"

"I'm insulating you from disappointment. Figure this thing out," Ivan said, handing him the tablet.

Mason passed it back a few minutes later, having solved whatever the problem was.

"I think he hurts people."

"What makes you say that?"

Mason sat cross-legged. He'd taken to rolling the bullet between his palms. He did it unconsciously and the brass tarnished from exposure to oils on his skin. "He smokes a lot. He's been trying to quit, like you, but he says smoking is the only way he can be calm and go to work. He hates his job."

Ivan shook his head. "I doubt that."

"I asked if he ever waterboarded anyone at the CIA? He said people who get waterboarded are the lucky ones. He says there's a lot worse."

Ivan nodded.

"I don't think fake drowning sounds bad."

"You want to try?"

"No."

"Then it's bad."

"Did they do it to you? The CIA? What's worse?"

"Ask your father."

"He won't tell me, but I looked on the net. I found this site where—"

"Mason? You don't need to tell me." Ivan had a hard time believing Dean loathed torture. What if it was true? Everyone who committed war crimes once played football in high school, or danced to Sinatra, or drove an MG Midget with the top down, rocked a child to sleep, shed tears for loss, hung ornaments on a Christmas tree, carried groceries for grandma, sat through church sermons on redemption, pulled the hook out and let the fish go, made sand castles with plastic pails, slept with a teddy bear. Every good hitman had a father who taught him respect for human life.

Was this vengeance? He'd learned to feel nothing on the outside, while nursing excruciating hatred within. Pain was irrelevant.

It was Dean's manipulation of Ivan which he found intolerable.

He tried to explain this.

"Americans have a primitive understanding of torture. Unimaginative ways to cause others pain to extract intelligence, the goal of gathering information undermined by methods wholly without understanding of their enemy."

"Did they torture you?"

Ivan unbuttoned his shirt and showed Mason the scars on his chest and back. The boy expressed sufficient reverence. Why, Ivan asked? These were the marks of an insecure establishment thrashing away at something they didn't understand. Ivan's scars were others' fears, their pathetic nature.

Ivan opened the steel case. Mason backed up. Nothing good came from the steel case. Ivan retrieved a small glass bottle in which a reddish-brown liquid danced.

"Causing horrific pain is cheap," Ivan said. "You hurt your muscles playing football? Of course. Used capsaicin muscle rub?"

"Yeah."

"I know. I saw it in your locker. Read the active ingredient? The substance that causes the burning? It represents less than a tenth of one percent of the cream." Ivan passed Mason the bottle.

"What is it?"

"Pure capsaicin oil. You could make five hundred tubes of muscle rub with that. A thousand times more powerful in undiluted form." Mason couldn't wait to hand it back. "If someone put a drop in any of your mucal orifices—eyes, nose, urethra—you would beg them to shoot you in the head. If I injected some in your vein, and it didn't stop the heart, your whole body would be on fire. You would beat your head bloody on the bars, an exquisite pleasure compared to this kind of pain."

"You're scaring me."

"Why? Pain is tangible. I can neutralize this with casein proteins. Your inflamed tissues will heal. When Russians want information, the process is beyond any horror your American CIA dream up."

The old KGB used an immersion tank to effect sensory deprivation, but Ivan said he could probably replicate most of the process right here. He asked Mason to remember how he felt when the drug paralyzed him in the gym locker room. Even during that scary hour he could enjoy the feeling of motion and sounds.

"Lay on this gurney. Intravenous drip of nutrients in one arm, cisatracuriam besylate line in the other arm. I turn out the lights and close the door. You can't move, can't even feel yourself trying to move. No sound, no sight, the unaltering pressure of this mattress with its cheap cotton sheet until the sensation of gravity betrays you."

In the first few hours he would focus on the only sound present, the monotonous pulse of blood through the temporal and posterior auricular arteries close to his eardrums. Pressure of lungs against the ribcage. The ceaseless rhythm of his heart knocking in the skull, a tapping torment idolized by Edgar Allan Poe. The mind would try to drown it out. After a day he would desperately listen for phantom sounds and nonexistent voices.

"After 72 hours you would look forward to pissing yourself, the ecstasy of feeling something—anything—trickling down your thigh. The KGB will leave you another two days. Your mind will crack. You'll never heal like my wounds did."

Ivan left the container and returned with a bowl of oatmeal for Mason. He'd learned to eat the small servings slowly. He rolled the bullet in his palms, overjoyed with hunger pain.

They watched *Smokey and the Bandit* together.

39

Day 15

Mason talked while Ivan looked at blood samples and ran tests.

"There's a fjord in Greenland where every year around forty billion tons of icebergs float by a village where we stayed," Mason said. "How about Greenland? Been there?"

"Yes."

His red blood cell count was low, along with oxygen and iron deficiencies. Trying to keep a body healthy while starving it was a Sisyphean stupidity.

"Our hotel overlooked the village from higher up the hillside, and all the houses are painted bright colors and look a little like toys from above?"

"Like tiny model homes," Ivan said.

"Pretty much. Some of the icebergs are as big as city blocks. In the sun the fissures crack and it sounds like thunder."

"Impressive," Ivan said. "I'll be back."

He left the container and made up a protein drink with an iron supplement. Grabbed a beer from the fridge, hesitated, and took two. When he reentered the partition, Mason continued his game of comparison, probing the extent of Ivan's globetrotting. At last he'd found a place Ivan's gunrunning hadn't reached, the hundreds of islands with sheer cliffs descending right to the water of Halong Bay.

"We spent a week on the yacht just exploring all the islands." Mason drank part of the cup. "Halong means 'Where the dragon meets the sea,' or something like that."

"Did you find any dragons in the water?"

"Really? I was nine, but I wasn't that naïve. No dragons, but plenty of dolphins that let you swim with them."

"Vietnam has dolphins?"

Mason shrugged. "I jumped off the rocks at Phu Quoc Island. Water never gets cold, not even at night. The local kids showed me how to dive for shellfish. I don't speak Vietnamese, but I remember understanding them anyway."

"Funny how that works. My Vietnamese is limited to profanity," Ivan said.

"Of course it is. Did you know my mother speaks four languages? I have no clue how many dad knows, but it's a lot."

"Impressive."

"Is that your favorite word? *Impressionnant?*"

"*Oui.*"

"I'm on my third semester."

A claim Ivan tested and found sufficient fluency for the rest of their conversation. Mason seemed pleased to have French in common with Ivan, but it was his next statement that startled.

"Dad says languages unlock the soul of a people. He thinks Americans are arrogant for believing everyone should know English."

Glitch said such a thing? Ivan eventually nodded. "Languages are freedom."

He listened to the teenager continue to one-up him on travel, a pursuit not soon exhausted even by Lake Baikal in Siberian Russia. They called it *the sacred sea,* a body of water over thirty million years old, with a five thousand foot drop to the bottom, Mason said, poking fun at Ivan by asking if he needed that in meters?

"It's the deepest lake in the world. Dad knows people in Irkutsk."

Weapons oligarchs, Ivan wanted to ask? Ivan probably knew the same people. Beneath his beer bottle a ring of condensation distorted the cover of a paperback Mason finished reading, a Tolkienish quest he'd tried to explain to Ivan. What was the point of reading a fantasy book? Of course no one would suspect a cheap paperback capable of thwarting sophisticated decryption techniques.

Mechanics of the encrypted messages between Richard Feige and Nigel Braithwaite remained fascinating to Ivan. Had they relied on one book page to encrypt, Coletti would have unlocked it with little effort. Using two pages exponentially increased the complexity by orders of magnitude. Not merely a doubling of computation time, the higher volume of false positives would lead any system, no matter how adeptly programmed, on an impossible word chase. Books as code systems had an ironic quality.

If fantasy was what normal people read to imagine outlandish or even violent existence, what should Ivan read to prepare for plebeian life after Hitman? Could he inhabit such a life? Ivan was going to need a lot of help.

"Is that poison? Not poisonous, but like absinthe?"

Ivan held up the bottle. "This?"

"It has a skull and crossbones on it. And a pirate flag. You tell me."

"Might be. I got wasted on it years ago, and the beer snobs apparently don't like that. They kicked me out of their Washington microbrewery. Still, good stuff."

"You're in Washington now."

"State of Washington."

"Oh."

"It doesn't matter, so you might as well know we're in Virginia." Mason asked if his dad knew, but that would defeat the purpose of kidnapping. Ivan poured the other half of his beer in Mason's empty cup. Not enough, Mason said, but finished it off.

"Ribs. Before you discover that was plenty and fall out." Mason lifted his shirt. Ivan gestured him closer and pulled the elastic band below the waist. A bruise surrounded where the pelvic bone pushed out against his skin. "Is this the side you slept on?"

"Did I do something wrong?"

"No. I upped your iron. That should help. Anything else wrong?"

"I think it's infected."

"What's infected?"

"It hurts when I piss."

"That doesn't mean it's infected. Probably dehydration. Drink more water."

"Beer's mostly water, right?"

"Nice try."

After a while Mason lay on the bunk, words slurring but still understandable. In Bolivia, he said, they'd driven a jeep across a shallow salt lake, a perfectly smooth surface of water with no visible horizon, a huge glass mirror, clouds reflected below him. Like walking on the heavens. It was the most amazing natural illusion he'd ever seen.

"When were you in Bolivia?"

"Last year. Dad had a meeting with someone. He said the guy was a colossal pain in the ass. We went to a restaurant, or café or something. I had to sit at a different table. I guess it was a private meeting. What about Bolivia? Ever been there?"

"Yes." Ivan finished the second beer. "I was the pain in the ass."

Day 17

Mason lay flat across the cage with his elbow on the restraint plate outside the bars. Ivan too was on the ground, his hand locked in a grip with Mason's.

"Ready?"

"Go ahead."

Mason strained and Ivan pressed blood into his own face until red, gradually letting the kid plow his arm back through the arc. Ivan's knuckles touched the ground.

"You let me win. You can't do that."

"I did not."

"You're full of shit."

Ivan laughed. "Not likely. I'm Greek," he joked. Reminded again of Yannis, Ivan then spoke in softer tones, more to himself. "Greece wounds me, wherever I travel."

Mason rolled the bullet between his palms. "What does that mean?"

"It's complicated," Ivan said, sounding like Ellison. "Something my father said."

"Do you live in Greece?"

"No."

"But you're Greek."

"I don't live anywhere."

"Do you want to? Live in Greece, I mean."

Ivan didn't know if there was a good answer, nor whether telling the kidnapped son of his nemesis was wise. He shook his head.

"Where's your favorite place in the world?"

"Favorite place for what reason? Food? Weather? Prostitutes?"

Mason laughed. "Just to look at."

"I don't just look at the prostitutes."

"The *landscape*, stupid!"

Ivan thought about it. In the middle of the crystal waters of Lake Bled in Slovenia a small island was home to a cliffside castle. Medieval pilgrims had come to pray in the island church. The setting had both the qualities of fairytale and mysticism of eastern European Vladian lore. "In winter the backdrop of snow covered Alps is a vista I never tire of."

"Are you going to live there?"

"No."

"Because you don't live anywhere."

Ivan nodded.

Mason stayed silent for a long time and Ivan was sure he'd fallen asleep. The last question came from under the blankets.

"Are you going to jail?"

Day 18

Mason's tag didn't record physiologic metrics. Ivan discovered that was the reason for the combined 180 gigabytes of data contained on Noah and Jaden's tags. Why store it on the tag rather than simply buffer and relay to a storage system elsewhere? Perhaps for safety reasons. None of it was encrypted. Ivan downloaded commercial software to interpret the data.

Their expanded implants had matrices of chemical receptors gathering information alongside medical procedure logs. The receptors recorded a continuous stream of the presence of hypothalamic, pituitary and other endocrine gland secretions.

Software then created graphic representations of how hormones translated to emotional state, the clinical measure of happiness. Time event markers ticked off routine cycles of life—sleep, sadness, hunger, sickness, pain and stimulated excitation. Did Coletti review the data to assess performance? Did he collect it to serve what he'd called the Prometheus Complex? Timid fear on the cusp of sexual climax? Fire of the gods? Ivan looked at his wrist and felt Jaden's pinch and circles. How do you understand pleasure without pain?

Or happiness? When did his frustration of agitated aimlessness earn the right to feel peace? The days passed with diminishing satisfaction for this convoluted plan, one that didn't adequately salvage the meaningless prison life of Number 7, and did even less for Ivan's vengeance. After the pinch he imagined Elizabeth drawing her fingers over his wounds.

Noah had a heart issue, tachycardia related to congenital atrial valve deformation. When Noah was three Samuel's BioConnect surgical team repaired the valve. Video of the entire procedure was available on the tag. The expensive effort made no sense from a commercial standpoint. But defectiveness hadn't relegated Noah to disposal, a fact undermining Coletti's business instinct and more attributable to attachment or affection. Ivan was shocked to learn Coletti didn't exploit the crew the same way as did his guests. He led a vicarious sex life. Not that he was any less culpable. He might as well do what he wanted. Samuel was fond of quoting John Irving, who he felt possessed a kindred appreciation of beauty. "We take terrible risks with the natural affection of children."

And what of the unnatural kind?

In Jaden's event data was the moment Ivan's suppressor touched his scalp. Surge of endorphins and hormones related to fear represented in graphic spikes. Elevated heart rate, hydration lost to overactive sweat glands.

Between the tense moment on the couch, squeezing his pajama tail, and appearance during negotiations at the outdoor dining salon, Jaden's medical record showed administration of a sedative. Lost in 60 gigs of code, 220 traumatized kilobytes for the moment Jaden's life first intersected with Ivan. In a way, humans were as emotionally and physically susceptible to chemicals produced by their own bodies as any pharmaceutical drug.

If Mason's tag were so equipped, would Ivan want to see the last 17 days? Would it make him feel greater guilt? And Mason? What did he feel right now?

In the middle of the night Ivan walked some distance, past several strip malls, to buy miscellaneous junk at a drugstore on an impulsive instinct that proved misguided.

Inside the plywood partition Ivan hung colored lights across the ceiling. While Mason slept he unlocked the cage and set up a miniature fir tree with ornaments made from colored foil stickers of stars, with a wrapped gift underneath. Mason later woke and kept blinking as though the new features meant he was hallucinating. He was the sort that didn't tear open wrapping, though he'd have been better off not unfolding all the malformed creases. Ivan wasn't the sort who knew how to wrap a gift. Inside was a four-ounce bar of chocolate. He had no expression after trying a square.

Was it Christmas?

Christmas Eve, Ivan said.

Mason broke off four squares and held them through the bars for Ivan.

Ivan realized he'd made a mistake. For an interminable period Mason didn't move, eyes closed, leaning on the bars, head tilted back, lengthening the journey of despaired tears.

Day 19

It was time, Ivan decided. Drastic changes in Mason's physical ability to function mirrored the wasted appearance. Ivan no longer locked the cage. Mason wouldn't run.

Ivan didn't himself eat much. Necessary cruelty, while advancing his goals, made collateral damage of the undeserving. Ivan's role made him ill and he swallowed Ibuprofen without relief. It didn't escape him Dean tortured *Nikos* to get to Yannis, and this was essentially the same plan. He sat by Mason's bunk and stroked his fingers through the kid's hair while under no illusion the soporific effect countered betrayal of the boy's wellbeing. Why had he thought Mason an acceptable pawn?

An explanation from Samuel that made little sense at the time now felt prophetic.

"Are all your customers homosexuals?" Ivan had asked.

"Most identify heterosexually."

"Are they lying to themselves?"

"Not at all. Attraction to peers is not parallel to the need fulfilled here."

"Then why boys and not girls? You have to admit what it looks like from my perspective. Why do these guys prefer boys? He's screwing a wife, but pays you for the right to rape a vaginaless innocent?"

"Your choice of words is consistently deplorable," was all Samuel said, offering no subsequent rationale but for resorting once again to Irving. *"Human sexuality makes farcical our most serious intentions."*

Ivan continued to badger Samuel, certain the man had committed insufficient reflection.

"How should I answer for why a man likes anything a certain way?" Samuel said. "You demand to be furnished with scientific formulas proposing a quantifiable correlation between sexual urge, object and fetish. Lingerie and dress-up role-play? Toys and probes? Leather restraints and masochism? Or the more esoteric interests—water sports, anal beads, chocolate syrup, underoos, balloon popping, diapers, electrophilia? Among this broad spectrum of absurd behaviors you ask me, Why boys? For what reason are you so attracted to dominant women that you let my employee, Ms. Paley, bamboozle you?"

"I don't know."

"You have your answer."

Over a breakfast of halved grapefruit and honey the next morning Ivan learned Samuel had given the attraction more than frivolous thought.

He believed the instinct found root in primal gender roles. While societies fancied themselves progressive in sexual equality, the effort to statutorily level the field was superficial and ultimately futile. Men and women, boys and girls, possessed distinct biological chemistry and wiring, each sex serving goals beneficial to the species. Men were physically and neurologically suited to providing for and protecting dependent humans, though Samuel cautioned against confusing the suitability with an archetypal one.

"In concert with hormones tailored for the purpose, boys are reared for independence and self reliance. Boys are made to believe their status carries the onus of greater autonomy and personal responsibility for decision making."

"A boy's appeal is his strength? Who are you trying to bullshit?"

"You think these men desire power over a child's vulnerability? A tired trope of the unwashed psychologists."

Girls were more apt by social gender conditioning to perceive themselves victims with no choice. This was an undesirable reaction for the man who enjoys the sense a child's sexual reciprocity flowed from willing consent, subject to the male predilection for analyzing cause and effect relationships by the litmus of their own decisions.

"Boys don't identify as victims of sexual activity. They provide a partner with the sense of equal footing, of genuine emotional reciprocity."

What Samuel fell short of declaring might have been that men didn't want to feel like victimizers.

Here in the cage Ivan understood Samuel. If Dean Rycroft's household offspring included a daughter, which would Ivan have felt worse about seizing and subjecting to this ordeal? Would an adolescent girl have proved as pliant to the extent Mason thought he'd *decided* to cooperate? Therapists would work to convince him he'd been coerced. A girl required less persuasion.

Was this what Samuel was trying to say? Did Ivan feel more equal to Mason? Did he perceive the boy better capable of acquiescing to degrading treatment?

Samuel was ironically troubled by Ivan's plan. Ivan moved Mason's shirt to expose an emaciated collarbone. He'd told himself life was not inherently precious, and disfigured something beautiful which someone else would have to put back together.

From Samuel's theory sprang the question discouraging Ivan most. Had Mason's sex allowed Ivan to feel less culpable of harm?

Day 20

Ivan checked Dean Rycroft's location. He'd moved from the NRO headquarters in DC to the FBI facility in Langley. No doubt a technical department had disassembled the prepaid phone Ivan left Dean and traced the origin of every part. That wouldn't help them.

Ivan shut down the cooling and heating element and entered the container. He anchored a camera high on the plywood wall and ran transmitter wires outside. Plugged in the airbrush machine and primed from the reservoir tank. Ran a power cord for the standalone 1500-watt heater.

Two hours ago he'd weighed Mason by carrying him to the scale and subtracting his own weight, leaving 31.2 kilograms.

Now he put Mason on the gurney under a lamp that emphasized how his skin shrink-wrapped over the bones. When Ivan was ejected from the Egyptian prison three decades before, is this what Fady saw? What had his grandfather, Eliv Schreiber, looked like after Auschwitz?

"Did I do it?"

"Yes. You look good. I mean, not 'good,' but—"

"I know what you mean."

"I'm sorry."

"It's okay."

Ivan ran IV catheter lines from two separate pediatric microdrip bags, one in each arm.

"This isn't the Russian thing, is it?"

"No."

One was a saline drip, the other an amnesic benzodiazepine, Midazolam, which would keep him relaxed but able to maintain consciousness. What Ivan didn't share was it would inhibit any desire for mobility, though that wouldn't have taken much.

With plastic spatulas Ivan shaped flesh-colored latex mixed with white beads into a lumpy mess in the crevice near Mason's armpits, above the sternum, and on the sides of his neck. Lower down he affixed patches on the inside edges of the pelvic bone where the skin formed a cavity across the pubic region.

The latex mimicked lesions of abnormal tumor growth in axillary, cervical and inguinal lymph nodes. Ivan finished the appearance by airbrushing iodine to discolor the application sites, along with stripes in the recesses between ribs to accentuate weight loss. He wrote on Mason's stomach with indelible marker.

The oxygen mask he placed on Mason's face was a prop, but the result was convincing beyond doubt. Absent hair loss that would otherwise be associated with chemotherapy, he looked terminally cancerous.

"Will I see you again?"

"No."

"Okay."

"Your dad will be here in a few hours. I thought you'd be happy."

"I am. Are you going to be okay?"

"Sure."

"Will you write to me? Or come see me play football?"

Not likely. "I'll send you a postcard."

Mason nodded. Ivan was about to start the drip when the kid jerked. "Wait. Where's my bullet?"

Getting Mason to cope required manipulative psychology Samuel Coletti trained Ivan for with reluctance. He'd summed it up again with Irving. *Security is measured by the number of promises kept. Every child understands a promise—if it is kept—and looks forward to the next promise.*

Ivan retrieved the tarnished round from the cage. He showed it to Mason and placed it in his right hand. Cautious fingers wrapped around the brass and Mason said he was ready to go home.

* * *

Dean Rycroft waited for a second ring before answering the phone. A team of techs preparing to trace the cellular source? Good luck. Ivan had both adjoining seats to himself aboard an Amtrak heading north. He held the phone a distance from his ear while Dean got the rant out and at length demanded to know if Mason was alive.

"In less than an hour you'll have him," Ivan said. "In what condition depends on whether we come to an agreement."

"What do you want?"

Bucolic West Virginia scenery rolled past the train windows, briefly giving way to a town drawn by Norman Rockwell. It provided a pleasant balance to the fury Ivan would set in motion with a disposable Samsung. "Do you know what a Deadman Switch is?"

"Don't insult me, Stavros."

"You'll see to it I'm removed from Interpol and Europol lists. None of your ilk will bother me again. Leave the little boy in Washington State alone, since after today he won't matter. If I fail to monthly contact my connection, she'll post the decoded records sequenced from Dakota Brenner's DNA to the web and Hizer's board of directors can kiss their company's assets goodbye trying to buy their way out of prison. I assume Murder is what investigators will call the dead cancer patients left in the wake of Hizer's suppression of cures? Are we clear?"

A long paused ensued. "Are you assuring us you're *not* making the information public?"

"Contingently, yes."

"Deal. Where's my boy?"

Ivan gave Dean the protocol to view the live stream over the web. Moments later Ivan heard a terrific crash, Dean flinging the phone against a wall. His anguish erupted as background noise. A different, lawyerly voice came over the line.

"Mr. Stavros? I speak for Hizer International. Obviously we handled this incident poorly, but we're ready to put it behind us with your help. We appreciate your complete and longterm discretion. What assurance can you give us the boy's alive?"

"You see him breathing, right?"

"Fair enough."

"My investigation suggests Hizer sabotaged a viable cure for his lymphoma, so recovery is guaranteed."

"I'm not at liberty to confirm any speculation."

"That's a Yes. You're trying to trace the live stream. Don't bother. Sourcing proxies through foreign jurisdictions will take longer than the hour you have. The only way you get him alive is if I give you his location."

Mason's left hand held a glass tube of Dakota's blood, what was left after full genomic sequencing including junk DNA. Ivan's Deadman threat was real.

The thermometer near Mason's head showed a room temperature of 21 degrees Celsius. Not long before it read 18. A heater on a specific setting was slowly raising the temperature of the room. Inside the saline bag plumbed to Mason floated a dozen blue seeds. Both Dean and Hizer knew what they were. As tested, in an hour the heater would bring the room and bag temperature to 38 degrees or so. Not comfortable for a kid with stage IV lymphoma, but more importantly, not good for the stability of over 5000 milligrams of nicotine in the static blue pellets, which would dissolve as they approached 37 degrees. In an hour Mason's cancer would cease to be the primary lethal threat.

Dean's voice returned. "If he dies there's no deal that will save you."

"Did you check with Hizer first? Do they consider Mason's life acceptable collateral to safeguard the company? Seems like they would. You don't have a lot of time, Glitch. This is my game. Waste precious minutes spewing worthless threats. Watch helpless as Mason's chest goes still and he dies struggling for air. Add it to the other videos in your collection. But if you want to pull the needle out of his arm, play ball."

"I will hunt you with every ounce of my wrath so I can shred your sorry ass one cubic inch of flesh a day."

Ivan thought he heard the vocal quiver of fear. "You've no idea how much it pleases me to hear you make such a threat. I wish you'd expended as much emotion for Richard Feige, Nigel Braithwaite, Bastien Hölmberg and six dead children." Ivan waited but there was no riposte in Dean's heavy breathing. "Is it different when it's your own child? Takes the fun out of apathetic torture, doesn't it? I didn't tell him about Syria, if you have any dignity worth saving. Mason's a brave kid. If not for him I'd continue to think of you as a cold-hearted asshole. Come to think of it, if not for him you'd already be dead."

Ivan would call with GPS coordinates as soon as Hizer made a good faith deposit.

"The Haitian account number and amount I need for retirement are written on Mason's stomach. I'd scribble it down before it gets too hot in there and his sweat blurs the ink."

Ivan ended the call.

He made his way to the dining car. Seated alone at a linen covered table, feeling the gentle transversal sway as the train navigated curves, he ordered a soft-boiled egg and coffee with Kahlúa and cognac. In the anticlimactic lull he made a silent toast to Yannis and Ellison. He wished Elizabeth were sitting across from him now.

Ivan set down Dean Rycroft's hydrogen powered cooler on the linen. Of the initial twenty blue pellets, he'd used seven and left one with Ms. Naughton. The other twelve remained hybernating in the cooler. When the reefer at the Leesburg Municipal Airport reached 38 degrees nothing would happen to Mason. The blue beads in the saline bag came from the same vendor as the white lumps in his fake lymphoma latex.

When Dean discovered the trick, Ivan hoped Dean would feel relief as opposed to anger. His son could tell the harrowing tale of three fearsome weeks with a man not so batshit crazy after all.

You can't escape sides, Ellison warned, but Ivan was damn well going to try. The faded scrap of Eliv's camp uniform balled in Ivan's hand felt like proof it was possible. A somber Mason had held it while listening to the escape of inmate 203148 from Germany. Ivan couldn't shake the feeling of anxiety knowing his grandfather remained mentally plagued by Auschwitz long after the war. What would Ivan do differently? The cold blood that helped Ivan squeeze every trigger, *name and time of death,* now needed to become the sangfroid preserving sanity. Peace measured by sorrow.

It was just as the passage from Cormac McCarthy described, of pain and beauty moving in a relationship of diverging equity. Ivan had seen McCarthy's blood of multitudes, in which headlong deficit Ivan played a seminal role. Against entropic laws this forfeiture required as counterpoise what Cormac hailed the vision of a single flower. Ivan failed to see what quintessential beauty could warrant so much loss. For this he could spend the rest of his days searching.

Ivan checked the balance of his account in Port-au-Prince and waited.

40

Cody blew his breath on the safety glass where it made a big foggy spot. Then watched it fade and reveal the night sky. He fogged it up again.

Alone on the concrete ledge of the narrow window of their cell, the soles of his feet sucked the chill right up into the bones of each toe. He wanted to prepare himself, either excited or scared.

He pressed his stomach on the safety glass and let the winter touch him. He could barely see any stars through the floodlights. What would it be like in a few days? To look up from his dark backyard and see all his twinkling sky friends again? Faint but visible was his reflection, looking back from outside the window, and the snow fell through him. Like a ghost. He would walk through walls. No one would see him or yell at him or tell him to stand for search.

He pulled his body off the window, leaving behind a shape like a pear. In the middle a tiny hole where a worm crawled inside the pear. He looked down and realized the hole was left by his bellybutton.

A-317's cell door banged open and in clamored Teagan with a pitcher of ice. Cody heard a squish and remembered an abandoned pile of clothes from playing in the slush outside.

"Your friend have a name, spud?"

"Huh?"

"The snowman you invited to come melt all up in my house?"

Cody giggled. "Sorry."

Teagan turned on the lamp. "What are you doing, you silly monkey? Aren't you cold? Get down from there. You can't dance on the windowsill in your underwear, pervert."

Cody summersaulted off the desk into his bunk, grabbed the edge of a blanket, and rolled himself over like a burrito. "It's snowing, Teagan."

"Yeah, strangely enough it does that in January."

"I made a pear on the window. With a little worm in it."

"Keep your little worm covered. We've got work to do."

Cody fished a drawing from under the bed. "I made it for Diana. That's me and mom and dad."

"And a lighthouse."

"So Diana will know where I am. It's Neah Bay. Will you give it to her after I'm gone?"

"Sure, spud. She's going to love it." Teagan pulled some pills out of his pocket. "Swallow these."

"How many?"

"All of them. I don't want you making a lot of noise and bringing the cops."

Teagan dumped out a half ounce plastic bottle of religious oil on a cloth and rinsed the bottle, filling it with warm water. The room started to smell like frankincense. Cody tucked the bottle in his armpit. He practiced reading from a Harry Potter book while the bottle tried to match his body temperature. After a while the pills kicked in. He told Teagan.

"Feeling lightheaded?"

Cody sighed. "You're drugging me up again."

"Yeah, but this time it's for a good reason."

"You said that the last bunch of times, too."

"Lay on your stomach."

"Wait."

"Are you getting scared?"

"Kinda."

Teagan moved the ice to a ziplock bag. Cody lay stretched out and sucked through his teeth when the bag landed on his back. He bunched up his fists and eyes.

"You're gonna be alright, spud."

* * *

A week before Cody got a letter from is lawyer. Not Tony, the woman who came with Tony at the last visit. Inside was a thick stack of papers. He tried to read it, but the words didn't come from the same place as words in Harry Potter books.

When Teagan got back he read it.

"What's it say?"

"It's legal bullshit. Bad news. They ruled on your case."

"Am I going home?"

"No, spud. It says all the mistakes they made in your trial and sentencing were Harmless Errors."

"What's a harmless error?"

Teagan didn't look at Cody. His voice through gritted teeth was so low Cody wasn't sure whether Teagan was just talking to himself. "It's a word judges made up so they don't have to do the right thing."

Cody tried not to cry. He couldn't hold it in after Teagan explained the papers. He looked forward to going home. Tony promised, and now nothing. He was angry at Ms. Naughton, even though Teagan said it wasn't her fault.

"She's devastated. That's the word she used in the cover letter. She's appealing the decision. She wants you to keep your spirits up and hope for relief at the next level."

Cody wanted to hope, but he saw the way Teagan acted and didn't believe in hope.

Then Teagan came back from the library excited. He said, to hell with the courts, spud. You're going home. I'll get you there.

* * *

Condensation from the ice bag trickled down Cody's spine and pooled in the sensitive divots above his butt. It felt a little ticklish but he stayed still until the cold soaked deep under his skin. This is what it must be like when Dementors are close. He could feel it in his chest, able to breathe out cold like a breath mint commercial. The pain went away after a long time. Teagan lifted the bag and dried his back.

"Can you feel this?"

"Feel what?"

"Perfect." Teagan stomped on a razor and the plastic housing splintered across the floor. Cody smelled alcohol. Teagan's weight pressed down on him. "Did you hear about Anderson?"

"Who?"

"The cop who brought milk when you choked on my burritos?"

"Oh, I like Anderson."

"Yup."

"What happened?"

"They transferred him to another joint."

"What?" His heart leaped. "Why?"

"He beat the shit out of that pig, Russell. Caught him raping a kid in Segregation with his flashlight. Russell's got seniority, so he stays and Anderson gets the boot."

"That's not fair."

"At least Russell's gonna be stuck in the hospital for a minute. Anderson was pissed. He pulled me up on his last day here and set the record straight so everyone would know Russell's a child molester."

Cody remembered when he was on strapdown and Russell did the same thing to him. How could it be that Russell did these things and no one made him stop?

A wad of bloody toilet paper landed where Cody could see it. "You started already?"

"Yeah. I can only do the ice thing once. Can you feel anything?"

"No."

"Buck up. It's not right under the surface. I've got to go further in."

"You can't find it?"

"Not yet."

Teagan cut deeper, and now Cody felt the blade. Again he bunched his eyes and fists. Time to be a big kid.

A sharp pain stabbed through him. He tried to move but Teagan held him down by the neck.

"Easy, spud. I'm fishing it out with the tweezers."

He remembered coming through WRCC Intake when he was six. That's when DOC stuck a tag in his back. Naked, cold and wet, the smell of alcohol. It came out the same way it went in.

More bloody toilet paper hit the bed.

"Teagan, stop."

"I got it." One final jerk, a pain and itch that made Cody's eyes water, and Teagan held the tag in the tweezers so Cody could see. "Give me the bottle before the tag cools."

Teagan let Cody watch the pill float in the bottle while bandaging his back. A little bloody crumb of Cody floated with it. A tiny capsule lodged above his spine, like a parasite, for more than a year. This is what DOC did to him. Cody trembled. There was no going back now.

Teagan took the bottle and, once again, Cody had to use his *suitcase.* Why was Russell trying to hide his flashlight in everyone's suitcase? Prison was so weird.

* * *

Cody wanted to say goodbye to Diana and Filthy and Scooter and all his friends. Teagan said he had to pretend it was just another normal day. Today couldn't be normal. He didn't touch his breakfast.

He wore his pink and purple shirt and sweats to work, with the State issue clothes on top. Teagan was antsy at Gate 7, but the tag reader chirped, nothing amiss to report. "If it flags outside of 94 to 102 degrees," Teagan had said, "you better have the flu or you're booked."

Cody worked all day with a new kind of sad creeping through him. He would miss Diana's home baked goodies. Never again push the big green button. He would never see Teagan again.

"I'll find you when I get out. Believe that."

Just before closing, Cody sat on the toilet. He pushed the bottle out and handed it under the stall to Teagan, who promised to keester it back to the cell and flush it later. Gate 7 would think they both walked through the reader at the same time, and the all-clear would be called so the truck could leave.

Teagan sat Cody at the bottom of the laundry cart. "Where will I go?"

"Are you serious?" Teagan said. "You'll be at Cashmere Elderly Care, a government retirement home full of old people who probably just love children. Show 'em your doe eyes and ask them to call your folks."

Teagan made it sound so easy.

"Hey spud, your shirt's purple. Mood ring?"

"I don't think so." Teagan stacked clean folded sheets on top of Cody. "I don't want to go, Teagan."

"Shhh. Radio silence, remember?"

More tears. "I love you, Teagan."

The cart bounced out onto the back dock and into the truck. He felt Teagan's fingers lace between his own. Big squeeze. "Be brave. I'll see you on the other side soon. I love you too."

Then he was alone.

He waited so long a sickness moved through his stomach and up to the head, where fear played drums that drowned out his heartbeats.

They knew.

Teagan was caught.

The truck engine started. Even under the sheets he could smell diesel. Then motion, a stop, more motion, another stop. Officers boarded the back. Teagan warned him this would happen, that it was the most important time to time to stay quiet and still. He held his breath. Their boots thumped and squeaked, wet snowy rubber, the plink of spit, smell of evergreen chew.

Suddenly the truck was in motion again. Cody couldn't believe it worked! Teagan did it! His little heart sang.

Then froze. The truck stopped, back doors opening, a woman's voice.

"You tell me, Bill. We'll be sitting here all night."

"It'll be just like the last time," a man said. "Why are they holding us up? He's not in here. Let's get some Jack-In-The-Box while the cops find him. Stupid kid'll be under the bunk or something."

The truck lurched as they both hopped off the rear. The voices faded.

Hammering in Cody's chest went with deep gasp after gasp, but no air. They'd be angry. He would be on strapdown . . . forever. Russell would try to hide his flashlight. There would be no Anderson with jello. He sobbed.

What would Teagan do?

Cody forced his lungs to do some work. He pushed the sheets up and felt the slit in his back tear open. No crying. Time to be a big kid.

He collapsed onto the truck floor and scrambled from the back, slipping on ice and landing on his bandage again. He crawled up the snow bank. Everything was wrong. He wasn't supposed to see the Laundry building from this side of the fence.

In the other direction a world with no razor wire and no gates and no cops and no lines and no concrete and it was huge and terrifying and even though he hadn't drunk anything for hours he felt pee spill into his underwear and was too scared to feel shame or icky.

"Is that him there?"

"What are you looking at?"

"The snow bank, in the pink shirt!"

Don't look back. Pretend pretend pretend. It's just in your head. Run run run.

Snow up to his knees, Cody ran, falling with both hands mashed to the frozen bed, pulling himself up again. Ran across a perfect white field towards the tree line where he would hide with the squirrels. Ran with voices at his back yelling Stop! Stop! panic pushing his legs faster and faster. So fast he felt as though barely touching the surface, a flurry of soft crunching as his happy legs raced through a giant world of unconfined wonder. The trees were so close now he could breathe in the bare patches of earth at their feet and hear the branches dancing and waving him on.

His head snapped up and he could see the pale gray sky for an instant, as though someone had kicked him hard in the middle of his back. Cody tumbled forward into the snow. He couldn't breathe. He never heard a sound.

He stood up and kept running, then looked back and saw himself still crumpled in the snow and realized he hadn't moved. Cody's hand pulled away from his chest, warm and wet. Eyes close to the ground, he watched his mouth stain a beautiful bed of soft powder, and in his mind he picked the color out of his big box of crayons. Fire Engine Red.

He thought he should be cold, but from deep inside swelled an incredible warm sensation and Cody knew he was safe. He felt Teagan's arms around him, holding tight. You're gonna be alright, spud.

He smiled and closed his eyes.

41

Dakota Brenner was pronounced dead at 4:52 pm January 16th. A single shot from an elevated AR-15 entered his back to the right of the spine.

Punching through the iliocostal muscular fascia, it shattered the seventh rib. On the way to the thoracic artery, the bullet tore through and collapsed the medial and anterior basal segments of the right lung's inferior lobe, ripped apart the hiatus of the diaphragm and lower esophageal sphincter, and exited beneath the sternum. Impact with the rib caused the round to tumble and splinter, rupturing the pericardial sac and sending bone and bullet shrapnel through the liver, pancreas, celiac trunk artery, hepatic portal vein, and the right ventricle of the heart. Dakota went into ventricular fibrillation and bled out in the snow.

Pat long ago tired of cable news, particularly when undue attention was lavished on speculative stories such as the massive FBI military-style convergence on a municipal airport in Virginia. Rampant rumors qualified the event as a terrorist plot, about which the government remained tight-lipped.

She certainly didn't read local crime news, or she would have seen the small bulletin posted shortly after WRCC's media announcement.

Skill and training prevailed today when a heroic tower guard at Wenatchee River Corrections Center fatally wounded with one shot a convicted rapist and sexual predator who tried to escape from prison. Faced with public anxiety over the breach, local authorities assured citizens the rapist's attempt was unprecedented and efforts were being made to review security procedures, particularly with sex offenders and other dangerous felons.

Pat felt pretty good about the Petition For Discretionary Review filed on behalf of Brenner with the Washington Supreme Court. In a rare effort, she stayed up with Chris well into the evening to craft the best possible argument. Under RAP Rule 13.4(b)(1) the Washington Supreme Court would accept review if the lower court decision was in direct conflict with authority of the higher court. The decision in Dakota's case precisely ignored Supreme Court precedent on jurisdiction and venue, so review ought to be granted.

Chris drank a veritable bathtub of coffee and topped it off with a Percocet from the desk-sandbox the moment his finger landed on the Electronic Court Filing confirmation command. For all she knew he was still snoring at Gibson's interface terminal. A good night's sleep for him.

After the long day Pat found leftover zucchini quiche in the fridge with a spot of mold. Instead of microwaving, she transferred it to a pyrex dish, picked out the bad parts, and baked the remaining spores to oblivion.

For the utilitarian purpose of stability, Pat poured wine into a coffee mug and put her feet up on a hassock.

The phone rang. It was Tony Wu.

"Hello Pat. I apologize for calling you at home. I tried your office but Chris is on a bender."

"Figures. No trouble. What can I do for you?"

"There's no easy way to break this to you. I might need your help."

"Are you on the road?"

"And speeding, I'm afraid."

"In the pickup?"

"I'm on my way to Harborview. I called to see if you want me to swing by and pick you up. I'll be there in a minute. I just passed the Renton S-curves." Tony sounded harried. "Eight counts of first degree escape. I got an automatic notification when an affidavit of probable cause was filed and the DAC's office recognized I was this inmate's former attorney."

"Why Harborview?" she asked, assuming he meant the hospital. "What's the urgency? I'm happy to help, but what does it have to do with me?"

"It's Dakota Brenner. Our Cody."

* * *

Not every day does a truck driver, waiting in the cab for her partner to bring fast food, witness a small child shot down in the snow. She panicked as any civilian might and called 9-1-1.

The emergency line operator established the location from the caller's phone and dispatched a LifeFlight that arrived seven minutes later.

They found a crowd of DOC officers circling the body, one holding a rifle with his foot on Dakota's head. He smiled while another took a picture. The officers scattered at the arrival of paramedics, who loaded Dakota aboard the helicopter and flew to the Wenatchee Valley Medical Center.

En route they ran blood and oxygen lines, stabilizer drugs, and tried to pack the hole in his chest. His heart did not respond to attempts at defibrillation.

At 1652 hours one paramedic called it. Another insisted her instruments detected increased neurological activity in the skull.

At the hospital a surgeon and assistant made a last ditch effort. With a cluster of hemostats protruding from his chest and electrodes patched directly on the cardiac muscle they restored an unexpected heartbeat.

Cody was lucky. The bullet missed his spine, kidneys, inferior vena cava and aorta. Apart from the collapsed lung and destruction of one of his suprarenal glands, it hadn't obliterated any major organs. His body autonomically went into crisis mode and constricted arterial blood flow to non-essential organs, substantially reducing some potential bleed out. The 900-meter per second round passing through still caused severe damage. The medical center's tissue printers lacked the sophistication required for near complete ancillary organ reconstruction.

Doctors scanned a 3D model of the chest cavity and put Cody on life support, cooling his blood through dialysis to slow cellular damage. He was rushed aboard a priority airspace jet and flown west over the Cascades where a team of elite surgeons and support staff at Harborview Medical Center in Seattle studied the scan and prepared for his arrival. His DNA was sequenced and transmitted ahead so Harborview could prime tissue synthesizers and begin organ printing.

Cody caught up with his new parts twenty-two minutes later.

* * *

More than two-dozen police officers from three jurisdictions waited outside the emergency room to interrogate Dakota. They were not happy when two attorneys showed up and invoked Cody's Fifth Amendment rights for him. The ones who didn't understand how the law worked—which were most of them—continued to hang around. Their mood was not further improved when surgical staff pointedly avoided them to direct updates to Pat over the course of three hours.

"He's stable," Doctor Hale said just after midnight. "We need to keep him under critical observation in the ICU to prevent infection and confirm tissue acceptance."

"Is he going to live?"

Hale looked like he got the question a lot, but never mastered the answer. "Ask me again in twenty-four hours. We'll know more."

"I understand. Can we see him?"

"There's too much risk at this stage." Hale looked hesitant to ask, but made up his mind to do so. "There is something you may be able to help with. You're his attorneys?"

"Yes," Tony said.

"God, I hate attorneys."

Tony chuckled. "We're not being paid for this trip."

"Then you're not really attorneys." Hale looked at the waiting room full of badges, who'd set up a satellite office complete with shift management and, painfully consistent with the stereotype, a steady flow of donuts. "My staff's taking angry calls from the Department of Corrections demanding we recover some sort of RFID tag they claim is inside of him?"

"A premature thing to be concerned about, I'd say."

"We found no such device, and now they're making all kinds of threats."

Tony made entries in his phone, saying he knew a few heads in Olympia that could staunch the harassment. "Anything else?"

"Yes." He gestured at the crowd. "Half of them claim they're securing the ER against Brenner's escape. The other half are chomping at the bit to throw an arrest warrant on his life support machines. One complained our surgery was taking too long."

"What do you want us to do? Law enforcement has a prerogative."

"I don't know. I'm sorry. I can keep them out of the ICU, but they're creating a disturbance and browbeating the hospital's private security. We called the Seattle police chief's office, but they're being coy. The patient's not going anywhere."

Pat fielded the job. She knew just the man with the legal muscle, clout and arrogance who would enjoy throwing his considerable weight around.

"Who's your lobbyist?" Tony asked.

"Percy Underwood. A client of mine gave me some intel on the police chief, and Percy's the kind of attorney who relishes blackmail."

* * *

Underwood leaned on the chief with Ivan's pilfered documents illustrating the chief's sexually assaultive past with minors. While no good in court, they would be difficult and expensive to bribe away from the media. Hale's ER police contingent thinned out considerably.

Dakota succumbed temporarily to a lung infection. Nurses pumped him full of antibiotics and steroids. Leveling off after a few days, he was taken in for additional surgeries to repair collaterally damaged organs. A third exploratory surgery was performed when abdominal infection revealed previously overlooked laceration to the right colic flexure of the transverse colon.

Rolling Dakota over, with supports placed to keep pressure off his chest, Doctor Hale inspected the entry wound. Using stimulatory instruments he tested motor pathway response. He was relieved to find no serious nerve injury expressing from the spine.

"I'm keeping him sedated," Hale said, drawing hair off of Cody's face "I hope he's having good dreams, as he's not going to like reality when we're forced to restore consciousness. My reasons aren't strictly medical."

Pat and Doctor Hale stood by Cody's bed in the pediatric ICU. He was off ventilation but a tube remained in his lung in case of further fluid buildup. A percutaneous endoscopic gastronomy tube to the stomach served his meals. Nasogastric probe to monitor esophageal integrity during healing inflammation. Other catheters processed blood and body fluids in and out while a monitor ticked off a steady sequence of beeps for a heart that didn't give up.

"He can communicate?"

"I don't want him to."

"I understand," Pat said.

"No, you probably don't."

Doctor Hale told her the story of a hardworking ER surgeon who trusted the system. That changed some months ago after an incident in his office.

"An obstreperous individual confronted me about what I thought I knew concerning a gun death, and what should have been obvious. I realized with some humility that he was right. The police and media were seriously misleading us. Mr. Brenner is another example of why I've become jaded."

Cody's injuries should have been lethal. Yet here he was weeks later with a chance to leave the hospital under his own steam in the not-to-distant future. What caused the damage? A bullet smaller than a Bic pen-cap. The police guarding the door evinced no concern whether the hundreds of hours of medical care committed to Dakota saved his life. Only that he was a convicted criminal whose escape from the ICU they were prepared to prevent with yet more bullets.

"This morning our legal department received a court order, requested by the DOC, to prepare the *offender* for transport back to prison. The order indicates he will receive *sufficient* medical care there."

"Sufficient is a big step down from what you've done for him," Pat said.

"That's why he's sedated. If I keep him under, maybe my supervisors will claim he can't be moved. I can't hold out forever. Could his sentence expire while he's here?"

Pat shook her head. "He does have excellent appellate issues, and if review is granted, I could seek an appeal bond on the grounds of his injuries and reduced threat to the public."

Hale fetched an envelope. "Does he have family? We've been unable to find anyone to contact."

"I'm afraid not."

"How is that possible? He's a pill-baby, did you know that?"

Of course the doctor saw Genesis Life Solution's signature in the DNA. "Yes. I knew. His foster parents are both deceased, as well as the surrogate that carried him. Tony and I are as close to legal guardians as he has."

"I wondered if you knew the details." Dr. Hale scratched the bottom of Cody's foot and wiggled a toe, apparently gratified to elicit a physical response when the toes curled and Cody shifted his head. "I was the surgeon when the surrogate died. I saved her baby. He's sprouted since the last time I saw him. Her name was Jessica Lapinski."

Pat nodded. "I'm surprised you remember."

He gave her the envelope. "These personal effects were in his pocket when he got here. The chain was around his neck."

Pat looked in the envelope and found a handmade dreamcatcher, worn down blue crayon, and a pewter dragon on a necklace.

Pat held Cody's hand. She sensed his fingers respond with the slightest grip. Pat felt their warmth and promised him she was doing her best.

42

Pat was at the office when Chris gave her the order filed by the Washington Supreme Court. She took the tablet and read a perfunctory one-line denial of discretionary review. Barring Personal Restraint Petition or other collateral attack, Cody's state appeals were over. His life sentence stood.

Chris didn't say anything, his inscrutable nature hard to penetrate. He returned to the Tackroom.

Pat had difficulty parsing the feeling of betrayal that threatened to taint all the hard work she continued to pursue for numerous other juvenile clients. None in so unfortunate circumstance as Cody, but the law demanded more than the abdication of responsibility portrayed in the Supreme Court order. They hadn't even asked the State for a response, ruling to deny review on an expedited basis that practically set a record for apathy. What was it that Chris once said? That apathy *was* foul play. She felt helpless.

Pat found Chris at his desk with a bizarre energy about him. He'd pulled the Rubik's Cube from the sandbox of his in-tray, removing the stickers with his fingernails and replacing them to color coordinate the facets.

"Isn't that cheating?"

Chris barely acknowledged the challenge. "Does it matter?"

No. In the big scheme of things, who really gave a damn? Certainly not the Supreme Court. What was next?

"Chris, do we have a template handy for a reconsideration brief?"

"Sure, let's ask them to *re*consider what they didn't consider in the first place. The legal grounds were unimpeachable. We didn't lose for being wrong. Doesn't that tell you something?"

"That right or wrong have nothing to do with it," Pat said softly to a doorframe she'd leaned on far too many times for the same nonresponse. "There should be a procedure to review cases like this. Beyond discretionary, I mean."

"Drag me into a Habeas Corpus appeal, and I swear to god, woman, I'm taking a sabbatical and the espresso machine goes with me. That court's a procedural minefield of don't-give-a-damn with a lot of dead hopes stuck in the trenches."

"No, you're right. The federal level's wishy-washy about jurisdiction issues. They'll say it's not cognizable on habeas." Pat drummed her fingers on the molding. "What about clemency?"

"Isn't that a myth? White unicorn shit?"

She threw her arms up. "I'm tired of having no recourse."

"You have at least one."

Pat tried to intuit Chris's devilish smirk, but couldn't. She waited for him to roll his eyes and make another profane and undeserved deprecation of her before holding up the nearly finished cube. She knew he'd never made a concerted effort to solve the toy, that it wasn't his nature to value triumph over the inconsequential. "Cheating? That's your brilliant plan?"

"The only plan left. Call him."

"Who?" Before Chris answered she figured him out and turned to leave. "No. Absolutely not."

"You have to. I'm not afraid to make the call, but I can't afford him."

Pat felt the tug of hope pull her back through the door. "And what is it you imagine him doing?"

Chris cast the cube back into the sand with enough force to kick up a wave that sprinkled onto the floor near her feet. "I don't know."

"That's what I'm afraid of." Pat closed her eyes and summoned fortitude. "Gibson," she said to the Gesture Interface Projection wall, "contact Stavros."

Ivan's voice on the other end of the line piqued the anxiety Pat felt crossing the metaphysical threshold to unorthodox channels.

"Ms. Naughton. What a nice surprise."

"Where are you?"

"What makes you believe I'd tell you that?"

"I'm sorry." Of course not. "What I really need to know is how soon you can be here?" She gave him the location of the hospital room. "You hired me, now I'm hiring you. Strictly business."

"*My* kind of business," Ivan said, imputing a Machiavellian unscrupulousness that troubled Pat.

She wasn't sure how to respond. "I'm not requesting anything illegal."

"Yes you are," Ivan said. "Otherwise, why did you call? I'll be there in eighteen hours."

He abruptly hung up.

"Oh god," Pat said to Chris. "What have we done?"

"*We?* He told you to break some rules, but Jesus, boss."

"How can you put this on me? It was your idea."

Chris's bare feet swung onto the desk, knocking to the floor a remote control to another of his toys. "You forgot to get an estimate."

"Something tells me I won't get an invoice either."

* * *

Cody was now conscious. Doctor Hale moved him to a private medical suite and continued to prevent the guards from entering. He met with Pat while giving his patient a checkup and explaining to the boy what happened. Cody seemed to understand.

"Is he still dealing with the infection?" Pat said.

"The pain medication makes him a little groggy. I assure you he's recovering beyond expectation."

Ivan had said he'd be here, but two hours past his deadline, he hadn't showed. She was disappointed, but it was just as well.

All the tubes were removed. He was eating soft food. Dr. Hale examined the scars on Cody's chest and rolled him on his side. Reduced swelling near the seventh rib indicated a successful mend. He listened with a stethoscope and urged Pat to put the instrument in her ears.

"You feel that? Strongest little heart you ever heard."

"Is Teagan okay?" Cody said. "He promised he'd see me on the other side."

Pat held his hand, gave it a squeeze. Despite reservations she followed the stories stemming from the escape investigation. Authorities at WRCC reported locating the offender responsible for facilitating Dakota's escape. Rather than punishment, an inmate by the name of Teagan McCarty, set to be released in eight months, received a sanction to participate in a therapeutic treatment referred to as Time Dilation Therapy, or TDT. Operators of the therapy apparently neglected to end the treatment at a specified time and the inmate fell into a coma from which he was not expected to recover. Pat recognized the code language for 'cover up': an internal investigation was being conducted.

Yes, Cody would see Teagan *on the other side.* She hoped he'd live a long life before that day.

All she managed to tell him was, "I don't know."

"Am I going home?"

Hale looked at Pat. She shook her head.

"My options are exhausted," Hale said. "He's safe to move. Admin says we have to comply with the court order."

The consequences of this inevitability were difficult to accept. He was already doing life, and they'd still charge and convict for multiple counts of escape to stack time on top of the life sentence. The likelihood DOC would keep him in solitary confinement for years due to the escape were all but certain.

They heard arguing out in the hall. The voices got louder until a horrific crack sounded from something striking the wall. An aborted yell followed. Hale was moving to check it out when the doors flew open.

In walked Ivan Stavros dragging two unconscious officers by their collars. He surveyed the audience, then the room, and piled the blue suits in a corner.

"Sorry I'm late."

Hale's mouth hung open. "It's you!"

"Sit tight, Doc. You may become useful."

"What's wrong with you?" Hale cried. "What did you do to them?"

Ivan glanced at the pile. "They got lippy. I'm behind schedule. Do you mind?"

Pat would later sit down to another reheated dinner and try to understand the events that soon followed Ivan's arrival, and it would always feel like a surreal excerpt from an otherwise stable commitment to principles. As he'd once promised, Ivan possessed deliberate faculty beyond the scope of which most humans were capable.

Pat introduced Hale, who apparently needed none, and apologized to Ivan. "I'm afraid I didn't get a chance to explain on the phone what—"

"I'm aware of the situation," Ivan said, cutting her off. He wore a long, dark leather coat, which he removed and dumped unceremoniously in Hale's stupified arms. He pulled up a chair and with little respect for hospital rules kicked up his dirty boot soles on the frame of Cody's hospital bed. "We have to stop meeting this way. You look like shit."

"Doctor Ivan!" If the pain medication impaired Cody's ebullience, it wore off in that instant. "You came back like you said you would."

Ivan traced with his fingers the raised suture scars on Cody's chest. "What happened?"

"I got shooted."

"Getting shot is a bitch." Ivan unbuttoned his own shirt and lifted an undershirt. Below the ribs was a sizable scar, pale at the center where a bullet had clearly been. "I've got a newer one in my leg."

Cody reached out and touched the skin. He didn't say anything. Pat realized there was now an unfathomable bond between the two, the most unlikely compatriots. Cody radiated happiness.

"Are you ready to go?" Ivan asked him.

"Go where?"

"That's something only you and I get to know." He turned to Hale. "How about you? Ready to save another life?"

Hale scrambled for words and came to a conclusion. "I can't be party to this."

"You will be." Ivan reached in a back pocket and pulled a hip flask. He took a swig that seemed to reveal the contents were potent. "Better to drink with officials as our friends, my father used to say." He offered the flask to Pat, and then Doctor Hale, who emphatically declined. Ivan held the container out to Cody.

The boy gave it a cautious sniff. Pat didn't blame Hale for his perturbed reactions, warnings completely unheeded when Cody took a sip and coughed. He held the can as if it were sabotaged.

"I don't think it's supposed to be for you to drink it?" Cody said.

Ivan shrugged. "You've been through worse. You trust me, and now I trust you. Question is, can we trust *him*?" he asked, indicating Hale. Cody took a moment and nodded. Ivan reached across the bed and ripped the monitor leads off Cody's chest. "Your instincts better be right, kid, because I didn't get my bullet holes for doing anything half-assed. Doc? We're sending his prison home empty handed. Find the boy some clothes."

"Me?" said Hale.

"Yes, you. And get his charts. You have some paperwork to forge. Move!"

So confident earlier, Hale's demeanor around Stavros weakened to subservience. He snapped from his stupor and scrambled for the door.

"What are you proposing to do?" Pat asked. She watched Ivan dig sheets from a cabinet, then grab a few bottles that snagged his interest. "We can't just walk out of here with him. A police inquiry would cause many difficulties for my office and Dakota's wellbeing. They'll search for him."

"What are you trying to talk me out of?" Ivan threw an object in her direction and she caught it. "Your laboratory friend wanted more of those. Keep them."

"Are these what I think they are?" The case contained a number of blue pellets like the one Frederick Greider analyzed. Ivan didn't answer her. He piled the sheets at the foot of Cody's bed and soaked them with the bottles. He then added with abundant carelessness splatters out of his flask, a fair amount hitting the floor. Pat smelled all manner of alcohol.

"Cops don't search for dead people," he said.

Hale returned with size seven denim pants, both short and long-sleeved t-shirts, and a pair of blue socks from the hospital's abandoned stock. He offered them to the dominant figure. Ivan smiled at the print tee with Pixar characters. He bent with his teeth a paperclip yanked from

Cody's charts, and with two deft turns released the boy's ankle from the handcuffs tethered to the bed. He tossed Cody the clothes.

"Get dressed." To Hale he said, "Is he on meds? For pain? Put them in a to-go bag." The surgeon nodded, collecting and tossing Dakota's medication packs in the only container he could find, a bright red biohazard bag. "Hale?" Ivan said, "Mr. Brenner suffocated in the fire. Fill in the paperwork."

"What fire?"

"The one your building's suppression system will confine to this room. When the cops ask you what happened, Ms. Naughton was never here. Do you understand?"

"What about you?"

"Say whatever you want. Tell them I immolated their pork," Ivan said, gesturing to the corner. "I don't give a shit. I have immunity."

"You're going to kill them?" Hale was reaching a point of exhausted frenzy.

Ivan shrugged. "Maybe you dragged them to safety. Your choice."

"You're crazy. This is crazy! I can't falsify hospital records. That's illegal. You can't ask me to do that."

"You thought I was asking?" Ivan slipped back into his jacket and held out his arms. Cody crawled into them. "You did it once for this boy when he was born. I'd hate to have to come back here. Don't make me do that."

"No. By all means go," Hale said, waving off whatever Ivan's threat implied. "I can figure it out."

"Is this the only way?" Pat said. In her wildest fantasies Pat never expected she'd be ceding Dakota's custody to such a man. And yet when she saw the gentle way Ivan held him, the peace he exuded looking into Cody's eyes, and trust reciprocated, the arrangement possessed a fated elegance. What was the alternative? Ivan Stavros may be the only one capable of protecting her client. What had really happened when Ivan sought Cody out at the WRCC?

Ivan put a card in her hands. “Dump this in a postbox for me.”

It was a blank postcard from a microbrewery in Ballard, addressed to a Mason Rycroft in Washington DC. She didn’t have time to comprehend the randomness of this request. In a rapid motion too aggressive for the unadventurous tendencies to which Pat was accustomed, Ivan sparked the flame of a zippo and dumped it on the bed. She could hear Doctor Hale uttering oaths of profanity. A slow but certain fire erupted.

In minutes the hospital would be in uproar. Already the heat advanced on her. Flames crawled up the mattress.

Ivan signaled for Hale to leave and was about to follow. He turned to Pat. “I’ll contact you per our arrangement.”

“Will he be safe? Why are you doing this?”

“Do you know how many times this kid’s cheated death? Practically mythological and I think as a Greek I’m entitled to make that call. He’s rare and unique. My family would embrace him as their own.” He turned and made for the doors, long black coat swirling like a dervish.

Over his shoulder Cody waved goodbye, little plastic hospital bracelet sliding up his arm.

Following him into the hall, alarms began to sound, hospital staff racing. Pat stopped him before they parted, “Ivan? I do not condone this, but nor can I support injustice. Thank you for coming.” For spontaneous reasons hard to qualify, she pulled him down and kissed Ivan on the forehead, then Cody. “I do have a sense of how special he is.”

Ivan opened a stairwell door, looked back, and left her with the last words she would ever hear from him.

“No, you don’t.”

Epilogue

Pat laid hors d'oeuvres on the large mahogany table in her conference room. All night in her home kitchen she prepared food with knowledge that the understated presentation was appropriate. This was not a party.

Nearly two years had passed since the hospital room fire. She'd been certain the hospital camera would catch her exiting, but for unexplained reasons Harborview's surveillance system had malfunctioned. Her name never came up.

Unexplained indeed. Of the reason for malfunction, Pat had no doubt.

In the corner of the conference room, where the two walls of glass met, stood a memorial. The pictures of four girls and two boys, including Chase, stood behind six unlit candles.

Chris returned from a convenience market with bags of ice. Tie and jacket, she told him. Chris grumbled but went to the Tackroom to dress. Even Percy Underwood was on his best behavior. He wore a dark suit striking a perfect balance between dignified and powerful. He'd wheeled down extra leather chairs from his suite upstairs.

Three days ago Hizer's legal counsel transferred the escrow settlement fund to Pat's law firm account. The case of *Addlemen vs. Hizer Pharmaceuticals International, et al.*, would soon be at a close. In thirty minutes the families of the six deceased children would arrive. Pat had never hosted a settlement disbursement conference. She'd received cards and letters from the families expressing appreciation for her hard work honoring their children. She understood the money was irrelevant to the parents, only that someone had cared enough to fight for them. Pat felt the gratitude insignificant compared with their loss.

An icon blinked at the corner of her conference table. She pressed the Accept tag. A taskbar appeared, Decryption In Progress. Yes, the deadline was nearing for another transmission.

When the decryption finished a picture appeared on the glass surface. She smiled. It showed Cody, age nine, barefoot and picking red grapes in the now familiar vineyard. The grin on his face was smeared with juice.

Each month Pat received another photo from Ivan Stavros. She would never be able to say from where, but the scenery was beautiful. She imagined a Mediterranean paradise. She'd never thought of Ivan as a vintner, but the unlabeled bottles he occasionally sent were very decent. In the beginning the photos featured only Ivan and Cody. The boy's DOC barcode tattoo was quickly removed, but not his green Grateful Dead teddy bear, a fitting homage and living commemoration for the poor teenager who'd nursed Cody through a troubled year in prison.

Soon after, the pictures began to include a woman with whom Pat was unfamiliar. Her light hair was lovely in the sunshine. A close-up in Ivan's arms showed her blue eyes, one streaked with amber. She was visibly pregnant. At length Cody was joined by a sister. One of Pat's favorite photos showed Cody holding the sleeping baby with the look of reverent mystery on his face.

It was not lost on Pat that Cody's picture had come so close to sharing space with the other six on the memorial. Nor could she reconcile that the man responsible for the sadness encompassed by the day's event also figured so large in her monthly joy.

Today a piece of their adventure would be present during the uncomfortable ceremony. Ivan had sent Pat the writings of Nikos Gatsos, a Greek poet who died late in the last century. With the memorial stood a stone plaque engraved with the final verse of one of his poems.

We who are left will scatter one dawn
Seeds of grass on the desert's face,
And before night cuts us down like corn
We'll make the earth into a holy place,
A cradle for children still unborn.

Pat lit the six candles and waited for her guests.

From the Author

Thank you for reading Cipher Number 7. If you enjoyed it, won't you please take a moment to leave me a review at Amazon, Facebook, Twitter, or your favorite retailer?

Thank you!

Lars Handstein

* * *

Favorite me at Smashwords:

www.smashwords.com/profile/view/LHandstein

Acknowledgments

One author's name on the cover marginalizes the amazing work invested by an international cast of people who helped me tell Ivan, Pat and Cody's story.

Jack Swanson and Wayne Spitzer taught me there really were rules to writing a novel, and were invaluable in the process. Chuck Jones and Jack suffered through early drafts to give me feedback that dramatically altered Ivan's journey. Jack said writing meant rewriting. He might have added re-rewriting, and thankfully his honest criticism prevailed over my initial stubbornness. He was right. I'm very grateful Jack took over this project, managing all formatting to prepare it for publication.

David Scratchley introduced me to the medical science of nicotine poisoning. He and Raymond "Chile" Hughes guided me through the fascinating realm of clinical biology. Raymond, together with Antonio Guzman, additionally provided Spanish translations, and Fady Sabry transliterated the Egyptian dialect of Arabic. David Fullerton took considerable time to review and offer perspectives on the cultural background and border relations of South Korea. Miriam Asher gave the same assistance for Israel, insights I could not have made without her help.

Somewhere in his busy life balancing roles as commercial pilot and amazing father to my nephew, Kurt found time to audit aviation scenes. Thanks go to Fungus for his perceptive line level feedback. Jordan Ternes provided detailed understanding of firearms, and County Jail John filled in a few blanks. Thanks to Ryan for technical advice on military explosives and demolition compounds. I couldn't be more pleased with artist Eric Cain's cover illustration and Nadia Caldera's design.

Story ideas invariably bounced off many patient listeners, including Paul Abner, Ken's "ken" Craig, Josh, Ron Young, Zack Attack, Joshua "Google" Little, Steve Chambers, John Huggins, and Larry the Wookie. Each of them helped tune the plot. Many thanks to librarians Joyce, Bob and Sue for researching innumerable miscellaneous details. Any mistakes should not reflect on those whose help I received, and are mine alone.

Against the efforts of DOC to prevent publication of *Cipher Number 7* stood a wall of attorneys. My thanks to Harry Williams, Hunter O. Ferguson, Jeffry K. Finer and Alan Mygatt-Tauber for amazing work successfully upholding the First and Eighth Amendments despite challenging odds of a heavily weighted legal system.

I owe deep thanks to the many friends and family across the globe whose correspondence was filled with constant encouragement. They kept my spirits up throughout years fraught with both frustrating dry spells and creative spurts.

My father, Arne, shared valuable technical advice from naval vessels to weapons. His influence is more profound than he will acknowledge. He frequently voiced criticisms consistent with the prejudices northern Europeans hold for . . . everything.

Most instrumental in bringing this work to publication is my mother, Cheryl, without whom not one word landed on these pages. She said language elevates a species, and subsequently struggled through her son's early grade school spelling travesties. As Ivan learns, DNA's a tricky matter, and to my mother's shame I didn't inherit enough of hers in the grammar department. She committed thousands of hours to bring an undeserved level of sentence tuning and authenticity to this novel, and her devotion has been humbling. No doubt she still rolls her eyes over metaphors she couldn't convince me to change.

I owe my deepest gratitude to those above, who ultimately worked to create enjoyable story and characters, and so we thank all our readers for sharing in Ivan, Pat and Cody's adventure.

Sources

This novel delves into history and a number of technical, biological and medical sciences, and I encourage readers interested to pursue the many resources available. These are the books and articles I relied on to tell Ivan, Pat and Cody's story:

Atwood, Ellen, and Ercolano, Vincent, and Erkess, Ellen, and Searing, Linda. Eds. *Stedman's Medical Dictionary*. 28th ed. Philadelphia: Lippincott Williams and Wilkins, 2006.

Bamford, James. "The Black Box." *Wired Magazine* (April 2012): 78.

Bien, Peter, and Constantine, Peter, and Keeley, Edmund, and Van Dyck, Karen. *A Century of Greek Poetry 1900-2000 Bilingual Edition.* Greece: Cosmos Publishing Co., Inc., 2004.

"Dark Legacy Resurfaces In Albania" Editorial by Cohen, Nadia Shira. *USA Today* 30 April, 2012.

Davies, Norman. *No Simple Victory*. New York: Viking, division of Penguin Group, 2007.

Durrell, Lawrence. *The Greek Islands*. New York: The Viking Press, 1978.

Elias, Thomas D. *The Burzynski Breakthrough...and the Government's Campaign to Squelch It.* Los Angeles: General Publishing Group, 1997.

Feld, Barry C. *Bad Kids - Race and the Transformation of the Juvenile Court.* New York: Oxford University Press, 1999.

French, Howard W. *A Continent For The Taking - The Tragedy and Hope of Africa.* New York: Vintage Books, 2004.

Gannon, Michael. *The History of Florida.* Gainesville: University Press of Florida, 1996, 2013.

Goodsell, Ph.D, David A. *Bionanotechnology.* New Jersey: Wiley-Liss, Inc., 2004.

Gray, FRS, Henry, and Pick, FRCS, T. Pickering, and Bowden, MA, MB, CM, Robert. *The Classic Collector's Edition - Gray's Anatomy Descriptive and Surgical.* New York: Gramercy Books, 2000.

Grey, Stephen. *Ghost Plane. The True Story of the CIA Torture Program.* New York: St. Martins Press, 2006.

Heine BSc, MSc, Robert S., ed. *Oxford Dictionary of Biology.* 6th ed. Oxford: Oxford University Press, 2008.

Jacobs, Benjamin. *The Dentist of Auschwitz.* Kentucky: The University Press of Kentucky, 1995.

Kahn, David. *The Code Breakers.* New York: Scribner, 1967, 1996.

Kennedy, David M. *The Library of Congress WWII Companion.* New York: Simon and Schuster, 2007.

Landau, Ronnie A. *The Nazi Holocaust*. Chicago: Ivan R. Dee Inc., 1992.

Linden, Edward V. *Foreign Terrorist Organizations - History Tactics and Connections*. New York: Nova Science Publishers, Inc., 2004.

Marks, Leo. *Between Silk and Cyanide - A Codemaker's War, 1941-1945*. New York: Touchstone, a division of Simon and Schuster, 1998, 2008.

McWilliams, Peter. *Ain't Nobody's Business If You Do - The absurdity of consensual crimes in a free society*. Los Angeles: Prelude Press, 1993.

Mukherjee, Siddhartha. *The Emperor Of All Maladies - A Biography Of Cancer*. New York: Scribner, 2011.

Nuland, Sherwin B. *How We Die, Reflections on Life's Final Chapter*. New York: Vintage Books, 1995.

Ostrovsky, Victor, and Hoy, Claire. *By Way of Deception - The making and unmaking of a Mossad officer*. New York: St. Martins Press, 1990.

Paglen, Trevor. *Blank Spots On The Map: The dark geography of the Pentagon's secret world*. New York: Dutton, Penguin Group, 2009.

Paglen, Trevor, and Thompson, A.C. *Torture Taxi: On the Trail of the CIA's Rendition Flights*. Hoboken: Melville House Publishing, 2006.

Poland, James M. *Understanding Terrorism - Groups, Strategies, and Responses*. 3rd ed. New Jersey: Prentice Hall, 2011.

Singh, Simon. *The Code Book - The Science of Secrecy From Ancient Egypt to Quantum Cryptography*. New York: Anchor Books, 1999, pp. 377-378.

Wright, Peter. *SpyCatcher*. New York: Viking Penguin Inc., 1987.

* * *

Thanks to the following novels from which I drew quotes used in this book:

Dostoyevsky, Fyodor, *Crime and Punishment*. New York: Alfred A. Knopf, 1993.

Høeg, Peter. *Smilla's Sense Of Snow* (Tiina Nunnally, Trans.). New York: Farrar Straus and Giroux, 1993.

Irving, John. *A Prayer For Owen Meany*. New York: Harper Collins, 1989.

Irving, John. *The Cider House Rules*. London: Black Swan, 1985.

Irving, John. *Until I Find You*. New York: Random House, 2005.

Irving, John. *The World According To Garp*. New York: Ballantine Books, 2009.

James, P.D. *Death In Holy Orders*. New York: Knopf, 2001.

Le Carré John. *The Honourable Schoolboy*. New York: Bantam Books, 1980.

McCarthy, Cormac. *All The Pretty Horses*. New York: Alfred A. Knopf, 1992, 1997.

Appendix A

Auschwitz Prisoner Numbering

Ivan's grandfather, Eliv Schreiber, is an entirely fictional survivor of the Auschwitz death camps in Poland during World War II. I gave him the number 203148 which, theoretically, could have eventually been assigned to a prisoner had Allied forces not brought an end to the horrors of the Holocaust in January of 1945.

There are a several 'series' that complicate number assignment, but from 1940 to 1945 Jewish male prisoners at Auschwitz not immediately sent to the gas chamber were assigned sequential numbers that ended at 202499. It is my understanding survivors who settled in Israel and later passed away initially faced a conflict over Jewish burial practices. Orthodoxy proscribed the marking of one's skin, and the tattooed numbers were thought to disqualify them for burial in Jewish cemeteries or mausoleums. I thought this a curious irony of history.

In the interest of not causing offense to any Holocaust victims, Eliv's number is not one that was assigned at Auschwitz. His story and aftermath, while not true, are created with deference to survivor stories. I cannot imagine the struggle they endured, nor the psychological effects suffered. When the Russian front moved in on Auschwitz, Nazi troops transported remaining prisoners, and Eliv travelled with the group described by Bronek Jakabowicz, 141129, in his memoir, "The Dentist of Auschwitz."

My great appreciation goes out to the reference staff at the United States Holocaust Memorial Museum, and in particular, Vincent E. Slatt, the museum librarian who generously answered all my correspondence with thoughtful information and materials for my research. They are committed to preserving the dark history of the Holocaust, and any detail errors are mine. I encourage readers to visit the museum:

United States Holocaust Memorial Museum
100 Raoul Wallenberg Place SW
Washington, DC 20024-2126
www.ushmm.org

Appendix B

Playfair's Cipher

In Chapter 30 Ivan sends MI6 a coded message he expects they'll be able to quickly decipher. Also known as Digraphic Encipherment, Baron Lyon Playfair popularized the system invented by Charles Wheatstone in the 19th century.

Today even home computers could probably yank apart this cryptographic system with ease, largely for the reasons Samuel Coletti explains to Ivan: it's rife with patterns. But it's fun! And one even kids can learn and enjoy.

The process revolves around a 5 x 5 grid of the alphabet where the letters I and J occupy the same space. Both sender and receiver have an agreed upon short keyphrase, (Ivan's hint to Hamish is "Piccadilly Circus"). Build the 5 x 5 grid from left to right, top to bottom, using the letters of the keyphrase only once (so if a letter appears multiple times, ignore the subsequent uses). Then fill in the unused letters of the alphabet afterwards.

Below is an example of a grid resulting from the keyphrase "Greek Islands":

```
G  R  E  K  I/J
S  L  A  N  D
B  C  F  H  M
O  P  Q  T  U
V  W  X  Y  Z
```

The next step is to divide the plaintext into two-letter pairs:

Plaintext: Blue Dolphin route is compromised
Pairs: BL UE DO LP HI NR OU TE IS CO MP RO MI SE DX
(I used an "X" to make it even)

The letter pairs are used against each other to create character substitutions with the grid following 4 simple rules:

1. If the two letters are in the same column, use the next letter down for each, rotating to the top of the same column when one of the letters is at the bottom, (for instance, if the letter pair is SB, substitute BO; if NY, the substitution would be HK). If one of your substitutions lands on the I/J pair, pick one or the other, as the decipherer should be able figure out the word is "Jinx" and not "Ijnx."

2. If the two letters are in the same row, use the next letter to the right for each, rotating to the front of the same row when one of the letters is at the end, (for instance, if the letter pair is LN, substitute AD; if TU, the substitution would be UO).

3. If the letters are not in the same column or row, replace the letter with the one in the same row that intersects the column of the second letter, and vice versa, (if the letters are AZ, substitute DX; or if they're KV, substitute GY).

4. Occasionally the letter pair will be the same letter (i.e., MM). I think it's okay to leave these unenciphered, though the source I relied on doesn't specify. Be creative!

Using the above system and grid, our plaintext-come-letter-pairs translates as such:

Pairs: BL UE DO LP HI NR OU TE IS CO MP RO MI SE DX

Ciphertext: CS QI SU CW MK LK PO QK GD BP CU GP UD AG AZ

Condensed into 5-letter groups the way Ivan sends it to the British Secret Service, it would look like this:

```
CSQIS    UCWMK    LKPOQ    KGDBP
CUGPU    DAGAZ
```

With the keyphrase, the recipient can assemble Playfair's 5 x 5 square and follow the rules backwards to extract the plaintext. If readers thought I was going to decipher Ivan's message for them, I suggest having more fun without my help. Good luck!

Source: Singh, Simon. *The Code Book - The Science of Secrecy From Ancient Egypt to Quantum Cryptography*. New York: Anchor Books, 1999, pp. 377-378.

Appendix C

Wenatchee River Corrections Center

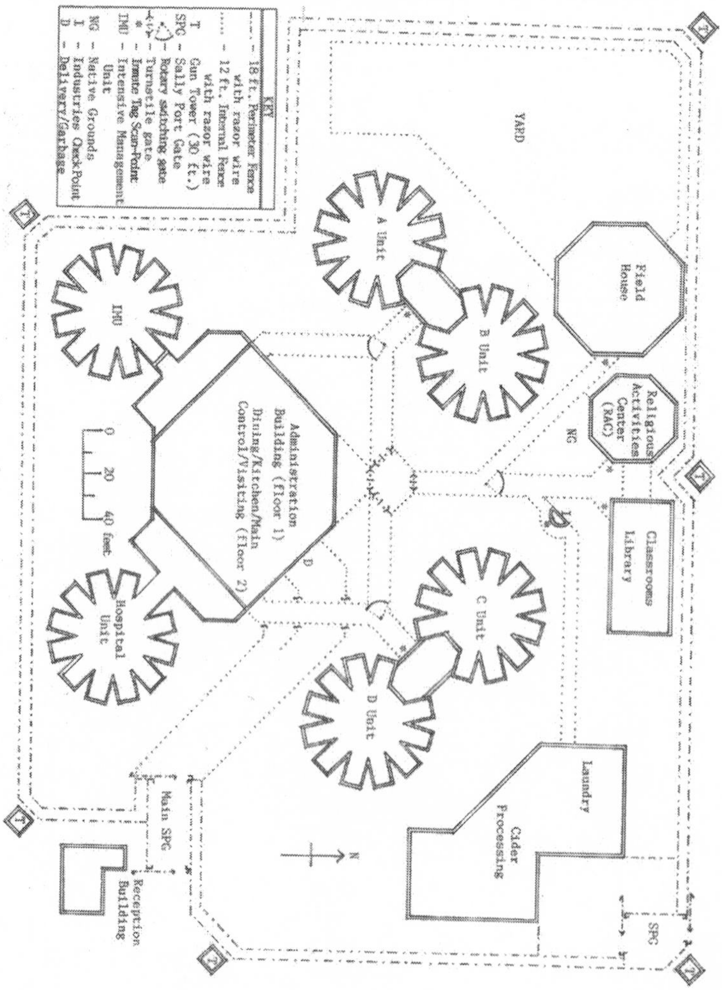

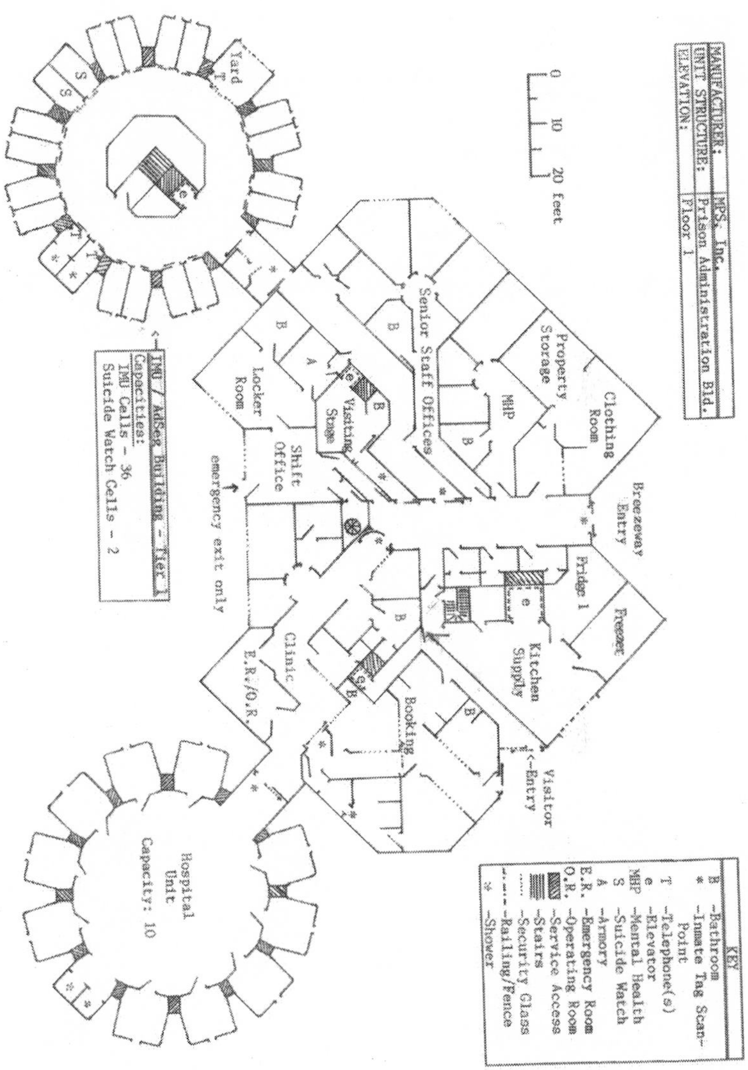
MANUFACTURER: MPS, Inc.
UNIT STRUCTURE: Prison Administration Bld.
ELEVATION: Floor 1
0 10 20 feet
Yard
IMU / AdSep Building - Tier 1
Capacities:
IMU Cells - 36
Suicide Watch Cells - 2
Senior Staff Offices
Property Storage
Clothing Room
MHP
Visiting Stage
Locker Room
Shift Office
emergency exit only
Breezeway Entry
Fridge 1
Freezer
Kitchen Supply
Clinic
E.R./O.R.
Booking
Visitor Entry
Hospital Unit
Capacity: 10
KEY
B -Bathroom
* -Inmate Tag Scan-Point
T -Telephone(s)
e -Elevator
MHP -Mental Health
S -Suicide Watch
A -Armory
E.R. -Emergency Room
O.R. -Operating Room
-Service Access
-Stairs
-Security Glass
-Railing/Fence
-Shower

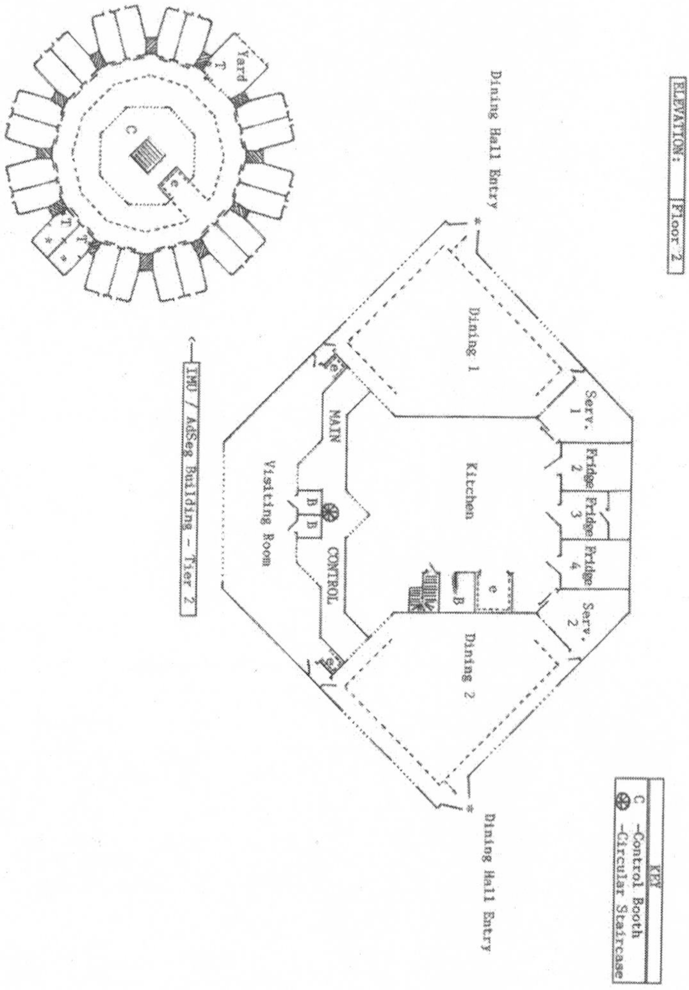
ELEVATION: Floor 2
Dining Hall Entry
Dining 1
Serv. 1
Fridge 2
Fridge 3
Fridge 4
Serv. 2
Kitchen
Dining 2
MAIN CONTROL
Visiting Room
Dining Hall Entry
Yard
IMU / AdSeg Building - Tier 2
KEY
C -Control Booth
-Circular Staircase

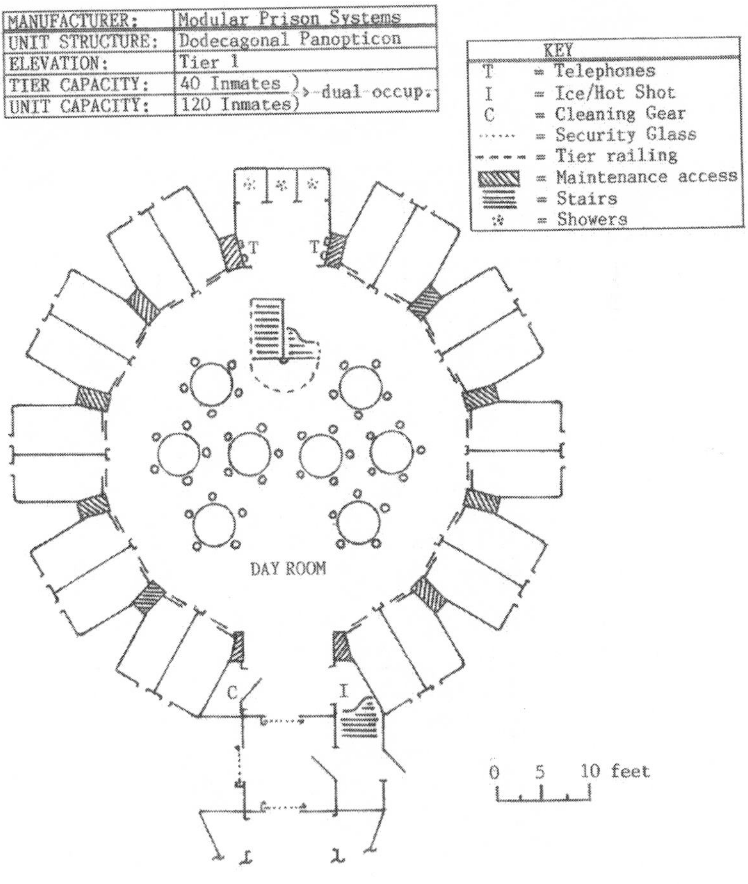
MANUFACTURER: Modular Prison Systems
UNIT STRUCTURE: Dodecagonal Panopticon
ELEVATION: Tier 1
TIER CAPACITY: 40 Inmates
UNIT CAPACITY: 120 Inmates
dual occup.
KEY
T = Telephones
I = Ice/Hot Shot
C = Cleaning Gear
= Security Glass
= Tier railing
= Maintenance access
= Stairs
= Showers
T
T
DAY ROOM
C
I
0 5 10 feet

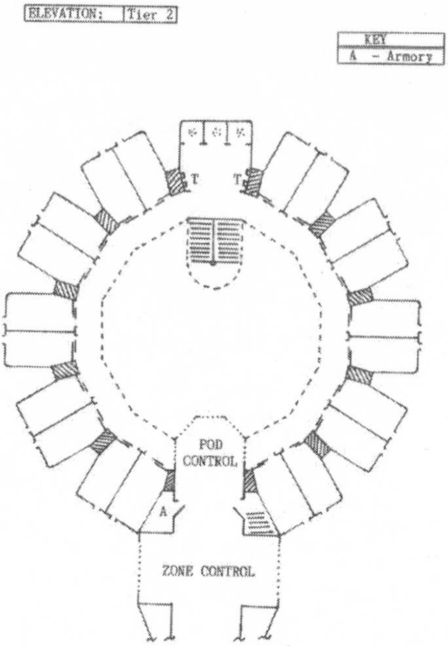
ELEVATION: Tier 2
KEY
A - Armory
T
T
POD CONTROL
A
ZONE CONTROL

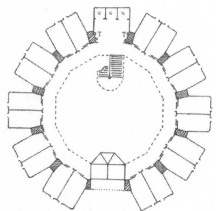

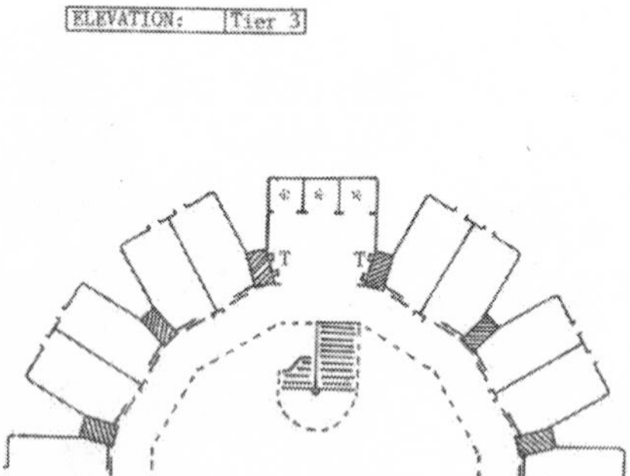
ELEVATION: Tier 3
T
T